Praise for *Finlay Donovan Rolls the Dice*

"Cosimano's fourth Finlay Donovan novel is brilliantly plotted, bringing the witty humor and thrilling, nail-biting action the series is known for while also tackling emotional family dynamics. Cosimano knocks this one out of the park. Highly recommended for all fans of the series."
—*Booklist* (starred review)

"Cosimano nails the tone—breezy but not too fluffy—and maintains a breakneck pace throughout. Readers who prefer their mysteries to lean madcap will eat this up."
—*Publishers Weekly*

"Another rollicking round of high-speed felonies for mystery author Finlay Donovan and those unwary enough to get pulled into her orbit . . . Perfect escapist fare."
—*Kirkus Reviews*

"The story that unfolds is a hysterical runaway train of impossible situations careening off the tracks as the twists and turns keep coming page after page. Plan on reading straight through as there's no more chance of you pausing reading than there is a prayer of stopping the train wreck happening on the page."
—*Mystery & Suspense*

"Fast action and clever wit course through *Finlay Donovan Rolls the Dice,* the fourth installment in a wildly fun mystery series by Elle Cosimano. . . . [Cosimano] ups the ante, once again keeping readers laughing all the way through a maze of well-plotted danger."
—*Shelf Awareness*

T0275365

Praise for the Finlay Donovan Series

"Refreshing, funny, and bright, these are wonderfully escapist novels."
—Charlaine Harris

"I love Finlay Donovan so much I would 100% hide a dead body for her."
—Jesse Q. Sutanto

"Fact: If you're going to bury a body, you definitely want Finlay Donovan by your side."
—Julie Clark

"Finlay Donovan remains the heroine of my heart. Elle Cosimano writes fresh, funny mysteries that are an absolute blast to read."
—Chandler Baker

"I've never laughed so much reading books about murder. Elle Cosimano's accidental hitwoman Finlay Donovan is a darkly hilarious, quick-witted, and surprisingly relatable woman."
—Jennifer Hillier

"The Finlay Donovan series is an unpredictable, fun, funny, page-turning delight."
—Gwenda Bond

"A fun, refreshing series."
—Kaira Rouda

"Finlay Donovan is the perfect twenty-first century heroine—I adore her."
—Sophie Cousens

"A funny and smart, twisty and surprising series."
—Megan Miranda

TITLES BY ELLE COSIMANO

Finlay Donovan Is Killing It
Finlay Donovan Knocks 'Em Dead
Finlay Donovan Jumps the Gun
Finlay Donovan Rolls the Dice
"Veronica Ruiz Breaks the Bank" (e-short story)

YOUNG ADULT NOVELS

Nearly Gone
Nearly Found
Holding Smoke
The Suffering Tree
Seasons of the Storm
Seasons of Chaos

FINLAY DONOVAN
ROLLS THE DICE

ELLE COSIMANO

MINOTAUR
BOOKS
NEW YORK

Published in the United States by Minotaur Books, an imprint of St. Martin's Publishing Group

FINLAY DONOVAN ROLLS THE DICE. Copyright © 2024 by Elle Cosimano. All rights reserved. Printed in the United States of America. For information, address St. Martin's Publishing Group, 120 Broadway, New York, NY 10271.

www.minotaurbooks.com

The Library of Congress has cataloged the hardcover edition as follows:

Names: Cosimano, Elle, author.
Title: Finlay Donovan rolls the dice / Elle Cosimano.
Description: First edition. | New York : Minotaur Books, 2024. | Series:
   The Finlay Donovan series ; 4
Identifiers: LCCN 2023046334 | ISBN 9781250846006 (hardcover) |
   ISBN 9781250846013 (ebook) | ISBN 9781250341303 (international,
   sold outside the U.S., subject to rights availability)
Subjects: LCSH: Donovan, Finlay (Fictitious character)—Fiction. | LCGFT:
   Thrillers (Fiction) | Humorous fiction. | Novels.
Classification: LCC PS3603.O84 F59 2024 | DDC 813/.6—dc23/
   eng/20231005
LC record available at https://lccn.loc.gov/2023046334

ISBN 978-1-250-84604-4 (trade paperback)

Our books may be purchased in bulk for promotional, educational, or business use. Please contact your local bookseller or the Macmillan Corporate and Premium Sales Department at 1-800-221-7945, extension 5442, or by email at MacmillanSpecialMarkets@macmillan.com.

First Minotaur Books Trade Paperback Edition: 2025

1 3 5 7 9 10 8 6 4 2

For Team Finlay

PROLOGUE

"I can't look," I said, clapping a hand over my eyes. I had sworn to myself there would be no more dead bodies. Not that any of the other four had been my fault (at least, not entirely), but I already had enough blood on my hands to last a lifetime—or possibly four lifetimes in a state penitentiary—and I didn't think I could stomach one more corpse. Especially not this one.

"Tell me when it's over." I clutched Vero's arm with my other hand as we stood on the shoulder of a six-lane highway. A tractor trailer whipped past us, throwing a thick wave of exhaust at our faces. When my children's nanny didn't answer, I peeked at her sideways between my fingers. Her long, dark ponytail blew across her eyes and she scraped it away, her attention rapt on the traffic in front of us, her neatly plucked eyebrows pinched in concentration.

"What do you think?" my mother asked, leaning toward her while both of them stared intently at my ex-husband's back. He toed the gravel beside the white line at the edge of the highway, knees loose, shoulders hunched, hands shaking out the last of his nerves as he prepared to make what was arguably the most stupid decision of his life. And believe me, that was saying something.

"I give him twenty to one," Vero said.

My mother's eyes went wide. "You think?"

"It's really more like nineteen to one," Vero said over the whine of a crotch rocket, "but I rounded up because I'm an optimist."

My mother nodded, too, as if this all made sense to her.

"You two are betting on Steven's life!" I shouted over the roar of a moving truck.

"We're not *betting*," Vero said. "We're just calculating his odds of actually making it across—"

"And back," my mother pointed out helpfully.

Vero smirked. "I've got to tell you, Finn. It doesn't look good."

"You two are not helping!"

"You're right," my mother said, touching the cross at her throat.

Vero nodded. "We should probably push him."

"Have you both lost your minds? The children are watching!"

My mother held up a finger. "That's an excellent point. I'll go sit with the children and cover their eyes."

"*Both* of you wait in the car with the children. *I* will handle this." I turned Vero around by the shoulders, back toward my mother's SUV. My daughter's face was pressed against the back window. Her little brother wriggled against the straps of his car seat to see where we had gone.

I had tried to convince Steven to keep driving. I'd insisted we could buy our son a new nap blanket at the next shopping mall we passed, but when Zach had pushed his threadbare blanket out the narrow gap in the open window of my mother's Buick, wailing as it flew across on-coming windshields and under speeding tires until it finally came to rest, caught on a piece of rebar in the concrete barrier in the median like a battle-worn white flag, Steven had been behind the wheel and there'd been no stopping him.

He'd set his jaw and put his foot down on the gas. I'd pleaded with him from the third-row seat not to do it as he'd merged onto the next exit ramp and retraced our path to Zach's blanket, but my arguments had been drowned out by Zach's hiccuping wails as Steven had pulled over onto the shoulder of the highway and put the SUV in park.

I shooed Vero and my mother back to the Buick to sit with the children. Steven hardly noticed when I tapped on his shoulder and repeated his name. His gaze remained fixed on Zach's woobie as he stood beside the white line and hiked up his pants. He leaped back as a mud-spattered pickup on monster tires screamed past him, a pair of steel truck nuts swinging from its hitch. Delia shouted out the window of the van, "You can do it, Daddy!"

Vero called out, "May the odds be ever in your favor."

My mother gave him two thumbs up through the glass, and Zach cheered.

I grabbed Steven by the back of his puffy vest as he rolled up his sleeves. "This is insane! There's a Walmart at the next exit. We can get Zach another blanket. I'll rub some apple juice and car grime on it. He'll never know the difference."

"He doesn't want another blanket. He wants that one," Steven said, pointing across the highway. "And I'm going to get it for him."

"What are you trying to prove?"

He whirled on me, hot breath steaming from his lips. "What am I trying to prove?" He gaped at me as if the answer should have been obvious. "I'll tell you what I'm trying to prove! I'm . . ." Steven's blue eyes grew suddenly wide, focused on something behind me. I turned, my spine going ramrod straight as a state trooper eased onto the shoulder of the highway behind us, rolling to stop a few yards away. I stole a backward glance at my mother's SUV. Vero sank lower in her seat. Steven frowned at the officer as he got out of his car and strode toward us.

"Car trouble?" the trooper asked, removing his sunglasses and tucking them into his coat.

Steven crossed his arms over his chest, his lips thinning as he was forced to meet the trooper's gaze. "No trouble."

The officer glanced at the Virginia license plate on the back of my mother's vehicle. "Where are you folks headed?"

"Pennsylvania," I supplied helpfully as Steven grunted, "New Jersey." The officer's brows knitted, and I rushed to add, "We're taking the scenic route through West Virginia. A road trip . . . you know, sort of a family vacation." I took Steven's arm in mine, pinching him through his sleeve before he could utter a word about why we'd circumnavigated the entire state of Maryland to get here. "See, our son accidentally lost his blanket out of the window as we were driving. He's two," I explained, gesturing to the shredded fabric snapping in the wind at the edge of the median.

The trooper planted his hands on his belt, the sides of his jacket spreading around it, revealing his holster and his handcuffs as he squinted across the highway to see Zach's woobie. "I sure hope your husband wasn't planning on trying to retrieve it."

"He's not my husband," I corrected.

Steven turned to me with a look of disgust. "Is it really necessary to point that out?"

"And of course he wouldn't attempt to retrieve it," I added with a stern look at him, "because that would be a completely idiotic thing to do."

"Not to mention illegal," the trooper said.

"Exactly! I was just telling him the same thing, but my ex—"

"Husband," Steven interjected.

"—can be a little bullheaded when it comes to listening to me. I told him we should just buy another blanket."

"You can't just replace something like that!" Steven snapped. "Zach doesn't want a new blanket! That one is comfortable. It's familiar. It has history! But apparently, history doesn't mean anything to you."

"The blanket isn't worth saving, Steven."

"Our children believe it's worth saving, and so do I!"

The trooper stepped in front of him as Steven pivoted toward the highway. "Put one foot over that line, sir, and we're going to have a problem. I understand wanting to look like a hero for your kids, but they don't want to see their father splattered all over the highway, and I'd sure hate to have to arrest you in front of them. Your family is better off if you just let it go."

"Would it be such a crime to let him try?" Vero called through the open window. My mother clapped a hand over Vero's mouth.

Steven's jaw clenched. I tugged him toward my mother's SUV before he could give the trooper one more reason to arrest him. "Thank you for stopping to check on us, Officer. It was very kind of you. We'll just be going." We had a woobie to replace. Oh, and a stolen car to find, a boyfriend to rescue, a mob boss to avoid, and a painfully long road to Atlantic City still ahead of us.

CHAPTER 1

NINE HOURS EARLIER

Vero hadn't so much as glanced up from the ransom note in her hand since we'd left her cousin's garage, when she'd handed me the keys to one of Ramón's loaner cars and slumped down in the passenger seat, reading and rereading the single sentence on the sheet of paper like it was a puzzle that might solve itself if she stared at it long enough. I turned down the long gravel drive, checking the number on the rusted mailbox against the address printed on the custody agreement my ex's attorney had sent me before the holidays. As I rounded the last bend, I breathed a sigh of relief when Steven's F-150 came into view.

I pulled the loaner car beside it and cut off the engine, ducking in my seat to get a better look at the two-story farmhouse as I took a moment to collect myself. It was eight thirty A.M. on a Friday in late January, but it felt like an entire year had passed since I'd seen my children yesterday.

"We should figure out exactly what we're going to tell him before we go in," I said, raking my soot-stained hair from my face, "to make sure we're on the same page so he doesn't suspect anything." I checked my reflection in the rearview mirror. A pair of raccoon eyes stared back at me, and I wiped them with my smoke-blackened fingers. "Vero?" When she didn't answer, I snatched the ransom note from her hand, folded it up, and stuffed it in the glove box. "Dwelling on that note isn't helping."

"They're going to kill him, Finn," she said in a small voice. A voice that should not, under any circumstances, come out of a mouth as big as Vero's. An hour ago, she'd been cussing up a bilingual storm of expletives, threatening murder in two languages, ready to roll up to Atlantic City in body armor on the back of a white horse, rescue her childhood crush, and kick someone's ass.

But then we'd found the ransom note tucked under the windshield wiper of Javi's van:

You have seventy-two hours to pay back what you owe.

There had been no phone number on the note. No name. Vero hadn't needed one.

She'd paled upon reading it, as if Javi were already dead. But she was moving through the five stages of grief way too fast, and she was skipping the most important one: bargaining.

"They're not going to kill him. It's not a condolence card, Vero. It's a ransom note, which means Javi is alive and they want to negotiate."

"We don't have anything to negotiate with! If it was just about the two hundred grand, we could borrow it. Or steal it. Or come up with some kind of an installment plan using my inessential body parts for payment. But that's not what Marco wants."

"He's a loan shark and you're in debt to him. Of course that's what he wants."

"Marco got every penny I owed him and more when his goons stole the Aston Martin from us."

The Aston Martin Superleggera that had been "gifted" to me by a Russian mob boss felt more like a stone around our necks. If it hadn't been purchased by the mobster and registered in my name, I probably would have let Marco keep the damn thing. But since our names were on the title and Vero's boyfriend was in the trunk, we had two very compelling reasons to find it.

"This isn't about money, Finlay. This is about an eye for an eye. Marco obviously took Javi because he thinks we have Ike. And since what's left of Ike could probably fit in a ketchup bottle, I don't think those negotiations are going to go very well." I grimaced at the memory of Ike—or rather, Ike's shoes—sticking out from under a pile of cars in Vero's cousin's salvage yard. It hadn't been our fault he'd tried to kill us and accidentally ended up squishing himself. What I *did* regret, however, was asking the Russian mob to dispose of his body for us. In our defense, at the time, we hadn't had much of a choice.

Vero turned to the window, drumming the passenger door with her soot-blackened fingernails as she gathered a breath. "This is all my fault. If I hadn't asked Javi to fence the car, he never would have been there when Marco's people came to steal it."

"All that matters now is that Javi is alive," I reminded her.

"What are we going to tell Marco when he asks about Ike?"

"I don't know. I'll make something up." As a romantic suspense novelist, I got paid to make up stories. I'd come up with something. "The police only found Ike's car burned in that field. They didn't say anything about finding any remains inside it. For all Marco knows, Ike is alive. All we have to do is convince him we had nothing to do with his disappearance."

"How are we going to do that?"

"We'll figure it out once we get to Atlantic City."

"You really think bringing the kids along is a good idea?"

"You really think we should leave them with Steven?" Steven had recently been the target of a contract killer called *EasyClean*. And *EasyClean* had seemed pretty convinced that Steven deserved it. "We have no idea what kind of shady business Steven was involved in. Delia and Zach will be safer with us. Besides, we're not going to Atlantic City to start a war with Marco. We're going to handle this using our words, like civilized adults."

"I'm voting for a more violent approach. Maybe we should take the children to your mom's."

"My mother has enough on her plate." My father had just passed a kidney stone that Bruce Willis and Ben Affleck could have blown up with less drama, and my mother had spent the last two days in the hospital enduring it with him. I hadn't wanted to burden her, so I hadn't bothered to call.

"What are you going to tell Steven?"

"The truth. That we're exhausted, stressed out, and in desperate need of a vacation, and we're taking the kids with us." I opened my door, fighting my damp, stiff jeans as I climbed out of the loaner car. Vero followed, slamming her door a little too hard.

A curtain parted in one of the first-floor windows as I hauled our single piece of surviving luggage from the trunk. The front door swung open before I reached the porch. My ex-husband, Steven, stood in the frame, wearing his favorite threadbare plaid pajama bottoms with mismatched socks and a sleep-wrinkled undershirt. His eyes raked over my soot-smeared clothes, down the singed sleeve of my coat to the suitcase in my hand. Water seeped from my shoes as I dragged it up the porch steps.

"Jesus, Finn! I've been worried sick." He ignored Vero's snort of disgust as he grabbed me around the shoulders and pulled me into a suffocating hug. "I've been trying to call you since I woke up and saw the news. That citizen's police academy was all over the TV this morning." He held me at arm's length, wrinkling his nose. "You smell like a chimney. What the hell happened to you?" I could only imagine what Vero and I must have looked like. Neither one of us had slept more than a wink the last two nights, and we'd narrowly avoided being burned alive less than four hours ago.

"I'll explain everything after coffee." Or at least, almost everything. Now was not the time to tell him that the local head of the Russian mob had tried to barbecue us because I had pissed him off. And it definitely wasn't the time to tell him that Vero and I were heading to Atlantic City on a rescue mission because of a gambling debt to a loan shark she couldn't pay back. Steven disliked my children's nanny enough already. I saw no reason to add fuel to his fire.

I looked past him into the house as I came inside and set down my suitcase. Toy trucks and Barbie clothes and crayons littered the floor. My children sat amidst the mess, fighting over a Fruit Roll-Up.

"Give it to me!" Delia snapped. "I had it first!"

"No! It mine!" Zach grabbed a fistful of her short hair and pulled. Delia shrieked and started crying.

Vero reached for Delia and I reached for Zach, prying his grape-jelly fingers from his sister's bangs and pulling the two children several feet apart. I commenced with my usual lecture, about how we use our manners and our words to get what we want. That violence isn't the answer and it isn't kind to hit. But the children had stopped listening, their attention turned to the TV.

"Look, Mommy," Delia said through a sniffle, wiping her eyes. "It's Nick."

Vero angled for a better look at the flat-screen on Steven's wall. "I didn't think it was possible, Finn, but your boyfriend's even hotter in high definition."

Delia looked up sharply, the Cupid's bow of her mouth turning down when Steven stormed into the living room and turned off the TV.

It had been the same clip of the same news broadcast we'd heard three times on three different news channels on the drive here: Detective Nicholas Anthony of the Fairfax County Police Department fielding rapid-fire questions from a gaggle of reporters about the shooting at the citizen's police academy yesterday. About the wounded officer's condition. About the mysterious fire at the academy earlier that morning. About Feliks Zhirov's escape from jail two nights ago, and if Nick suspected the Russian mobster had anything to do with any of it. Nick had danced around their questions like a pro, distracting them with an

Oscar-worthy smile and throwing out the occasional "no comment" when misdirection hadn't worked.

I touched my lips as his face disappeared from the TV screen. They were still chapped and swollen from our tryst in his room last night and our handful of hurried kisses as I'd departed the academy grounds that morning. I hated that I missed him already. That we were less than twenty-four hours into a relationship and I was already regretting the lies I would have to tell him when he finally managed to break free of the media circus to call me.

Vero smirked at Steven. "That particular shade of jealousy really suits you. It complements your pajamas and the bloodshot color of your eyes."

Steven flipped her the bird behind the children's backs.

Delia wrinkled her nose at Vero. "You and Mommy need a bath."

Vero planted a sooty kiss on her cheek. "We most certainly do."

"But first, caffeine," I said, setting Zach down and kicking off my damp shoes.

"You heard the woman," Vero said, snapping her free fingers at Steven. "She wants coffee, and I don't smell any brewing in here, so why don't you go make yourself useful while I get the kids dressed and pack up their things?"

A vein bulged in his temple as Vero took the children upstairs. He dragged me into the kitchen while she herded them into their rooms. "You mind telling me what the hell is going on? And what's *she* doing here?"

"The police academy shut down a day early, so we came straight here to pick up the kids."

"I know that, Finn. It's been all over the news. Does this have anything to do with Zhirov?"

"Yes," I said frankly, removing his hand from my arm and searching his cabinets for coffee filters. "Feliks showed up at the training center last night looking for someone. He shot Nick's partner and started a fire. Don't worry," I said before Steven could ask, "he wasn't there looking for me." That was only partly true.

Steven slunk to the window and peered between the curtains as if he expected to see Feliks lurking in his shrubbery. "Whose car is that?"

I poured a carafe of water into the pot and switched it on. "It's a loaner. Vero borrowed it from her cousin's garage. I'll take the kids' car seats from your truck. What?" I asked at his indignant look. "You're not going to need them."

"Where's the minivan?"

"At my place."

"Why didn't you bring it?"

"Because the garage was closer to your house and it made more sense to come straight here," I said, pulling two mugs down from a cabinet.

"Or because Zhirov's loose and you didn't want to go home?" Steven pushed the cabinet shut when I didn't answer. He leaned in to my space. "You're scared of him, aren't you?" he asked, hovering over my shoulder as I turned to the fridge. "That's what all this is about? You're scared Zhirov will come after you."

"I have no reason to think that." I hid my face from him as I rummaged for the milk. "Feliks isn't even in the country anymore. The FBI says he was spotted in Brazil. We have nothing to worry about." I weaved around him, carrying the carton back to the coffeepot. "As soon as the kids are dressed and ready, Vero and I will take them and go."

"The hell you will! You're not going anywhere as long as that psycho is out there! You and the kids can stay here with me. And *she*," he said, stabbing a finger at the ceiling, presumably toward the children's bedrooms, where Vero was hopefully packing their bags, "can drive that car back to her cousin's garage and stay with him."

"I'm not staying here," I said, pouring two cups of coffee and splashing a heavy pour of milk into both. "And Vero's not staying at her cousin's." I dumped a spoonful of sugar into the second mug as Steven reached for it.

"What are you doing?" he asked, pulling a face. "You know I don't take sugar in my coffee."

"It's Vero's," I said, snatching it away from him. "And we're not staying at home. It's been a stressful week and we both need a getaway."

"Getaway where?"

"I don't know. I was thinking the Jersey Shore. Maybe Atlantic City."

"In the middle of the winter? Isn't it a little cold for the beach?"

I shrugged.

"Fine," he said, reaching over my shoulder and pulling a travel mug from the cabinet, "then I'm coming with you."

"You can't come with us. It's a girls' trip."

"And you can't take our kids out of state without my permission."

"Says who?"

"Says my attorney."

"When did he say that?"

"In the fine print of our custody agreement. Which you signed, by the way, so don't get any ideas about sneaking off to New Jersey without me."

We glared at each other over the rims of our mugs. His lip curled in triumph around a long, slow sip.

"Fine," I said, calling his bluff. "We're leaving as soon as Vero and the kids are ready. If you're not packed by then, don't expect me to wait for you."

He guffawed. "You're not going anywhere looking like that."

I followed him down the hall, arguing in vain as he opened a closet, took two towels from the shelf, and dropped them in my arms, nearly spilling my coffee.

"You can use my shower to clean yourself up before we go." He turned back for the kitchen before I could protest. But there was nothing I could say. I couldn't take the kids out of state without his consent. And there was already a warrant for Vero's arrest in the state of Maryland, after she'd been accused by her former sorority sisters of stealing a large sum of money from their treasury account and fleeing the state. The last thing we needed was an arrest warrant in Virginia for me. We would just have to find a way to meet up with Marco without Steven knowing what we were up to. That, and keep Vero and my ex-husband from murdering each other on the way.

I slung the towels over my shoulder and carried Vero's coffee up the stairs, following the sounds of the children's voices. She had stripped Zach out of his pajamas and was fastening him into a pair of overalls over a long-sleeved onesie in his bedroom while Delia got herself dressed in the bedroom across the hall. It was the first time I'd seen the home Steven had moved into after he and his ex-fiancée, Theresa, had broken up last fall.

I had to admit, the old farmhouse was quaint, nothing like Theresa's luxury townhome a few blocks from my house. This place was cozy, old enough to feel both lived in and solid, the soft creaks in the wood floors and fine settlement cracks in the walls giving it a sense of permanence and character. I peeked my head inside both children's rooms. They'd been sparsely furnished—a bed and a chest of drawers for Delia, with pink gauzy curtains around the window overlooking the neighboring farm, the Barbie DreamHouse Steven had bought her for Christmas set up below it. A race car–shaped toddler bed filled most of Zach's room, with the exception of a dresser that doubled as a changing table, and the land mines of toys that had been dumped across the floor.

Vero fastened Zach's last buckle and set him loose. He tore off into his sister's room, making Delia howl in protest as he made a beeline for her dolls.

Vero rose to her feet and dusted her hands on her pants, though given the filthy state of her clothes, I doubted her fingers were any cleaner now. "Ready to roll?" she asked when she saw me standing in the hallway.

"There's been a small change in plans."

The color drained from her cheeks. "What do you mean?"

"We're going to shower and change first," I said, holding out her coffee. "You can use the kids' bathroom, and you still have some clean clothes in my suitcase." We'd transferred most of Vero's clothes into my luggage before we'd left the citizen's police academy in order to make room for a boatload of cash in hers, all of which had been paid to us and then subsequently taken from us by a very angry Feliks Zhirov—or more accurately, one of his very scary associates.

"We don't have time to clean up, Finn! We have to get to Atlantic City right now! Javi's—"

"Alive," I reminded her, dropping a towel in the crook of her arm and setting the coffee mug in her hand. "One more hour won't kill him, but we can't show up to Marco's hotel looking like this. They'll never let us in." I nudged her into the bathroom and closed the door behind her. "Give me your clothes," I called through it. "I'll run them through a quick wash in Steven's machine." The door cracked open and Vero shoved a smelly, soot-stained bundle at me. I took it, lingering in the hall until I heard her turn on the faucet and step under the spray. "Oh, and there's one more tiny change in our plans. Steven's coming with us."

That's when Vero screamed.

CHAPTER 2

It took an act of will to drag myself out of Steven's shower. I'd scrubbed until the last of the smoke-gray water swirled down the drain, wrapped myself in a towel, and opened the bathroom door to his room. Vero was already there, wearing a pair of yoga pants and my last clean T-shirt, her damp hair perched in a towel on her head as she dumped out the remaining contents of our suitcase onto Steven's bed, searching for a pair of socks.

I found a fresh set of underwear and a pair of clean sweatpants in the pile, and I eagerly dragged them on. "You couldn't have left me a shirt?" I asked, my hair still dripping as I held the towel around my chest. All the mud-caked, sweat-soured clothes Vero and I had worn through our week of citizen's police academy were still tumbling in Steven's dryer down the hall.

Vero waved a sock toward Steven's open closet. "Why don't you borrow one from Captain Buzzkill."

I took one of Steven's flannel shirts off its hanger and shrugged it on. As I pushed up the sleeves and fastened the buttons, I paused, my gaze sliding to the row of moving boxes on the shelf.

Two days ago, Steven had admitted to me that he'd been snooping in my house, in Vero's closet, all too eager to uncover her secrets. But since then, I'd learned Steven was keeping a few of his own.

I reached above my head, turning the boxes sideways to read the moving labels.

"What are you doing?" Vero asked, peeking in the closet.

"Looking for evidence."

"Of what?"

"Whatever *EasyClean* uncovered." *EasyClean* had vetted my ex-husband before taking the job. And right before the contract killer had been whisked away in handcuffs, he'd told me that Steven was hiding some skeletons in his closet. What better place to look than right here?

"We don't have time for this," Vero said. "As soon as that dryer's done, we need to hit the road and start looking for Javi."

"Steven's coming with us," I reminded her. "And so are the kids."

Vero sighed and squeezed into the closet with me, stretching up onto her toes to study the labels on the boxes. "This is all the same stuff he had in the basement when he lived with you. None of these look like they've been opened since."

I thought back to my conversation with Steven two days ago. Vero's closet wasn't the only place he'd gone snooping. Apparently, he'd also checked the nightstand beside my bed, which I only knew because he'd opined about the Costco-sized stash of batteries and the vibrator he'd found hidden in it.

I crossed the room to Steven's nightstand and opened the single drawer. Vero leaned over my shoulder as I rifled through the contents.

"Oh, isn't that cute?" she cooed, holding up an unopened box of condoms. "He's an optimist."

I took them from her and dropped them back into the drawer, shoving aside stacks of random gas station, grocery store, and post office receipts that littered the bottom to reach deep into the back. My fingers closed around a small leather binder. It was worn soft with age, the edges bent as if they'd conformed to the shape of a back pocket. A leather tie held it closed, and I pried it loose. A small pencil rolled out. The unlined pages inside were full of letters and numbers, strings of them scribbled beside dates and dollar amounts.

Vero peeked over my shoulder. "Looks like some kind of ledger," she said, her sharp accountant eyes narrowing as she studied the columns inside it. "It looks like he's had it awhile. Have you seen it before?"

I shook my head. This had definitely not been in his nightstand while we'd been living together, and yet the first entry had been written almost five years ago, not long after Delia was born. I flipped the pages, but there were no clear notes or clues I could make sense of.

Vero and I jumped at a knock on the bedroom door.

"Finn?" Steven's voice was muffled on the other side. He rattled the knob. "Why's the door locked?"

"Because I'm getting dressed!" I called back, rushing to tie the leather strap around the ledger.

"What are you doing?" Vero whispered. "That might be a clue to whatever Steven was involved in!"

"We can't take it. He'll notice it's gone." We argued over it in short, whispered expletives until she tore a single sheet from the middle of the book and threw the ledger back at me. She folded the page and tucked it into her bra.

"Everything okay in there?" Steven called.

"Everything's fine!" I sang back as I buried it back in the drawer. I checked Steven's room, making sure everything was exactly the way we'd found it before unlocking the door.

He thrust my cell phone at me when I opened it. "You left this in the kitchen and the damn thing wouldn't stop buzzing. If you ask me, three texts in ten minutes makes your cop friend look a little desperate."

"So does a pack of unopened condoms and the fact that nobody asked you," Vero muttered.

Steven's eyes darted to his nightstand as she made a show of checking her nails.

I positioned myself between them. "Were you reading my text messages?"

"I wasn't *reading* them," he said, having the gall to look offended, "but it was kind of hard not to notice all the damn notifications popping up. And what the hell did he mean when he said he had a *great time* the other night?"

The doorbell rang downstairs. The children squealed and sprinted toward the foyer. Steven rushed after them, hollering at them not to open the door. Vero and I followed, holding the children a safe distance away as he peered through the front window to see who it was. He shut the blind and swore to himself as he opened the door.

"Susan, what a surprise," he said in a saccharine voice as my mother shouldered her way past him into the house, holding a tin of cookies. He shook his head, grumbling to himself as he retreated upstairs to his bedroom.

"What are you doing here?" I asked as my mother dragged me into a suffocating hug.

"Georgia told me about the fire. I've been so worried." She held me by the shoulders, inspecting every inch of me. Her eyes grew wide as they landed on the misaligned buttons of Steven's shirt. "Oh, god, it's worse than I thought," she whispered, reaching down to cover Delia's ears. "You spent the night here?"

Vero snorted as she took the tin of cookies from my mother and ushered the children into the family room.

"I didn't spend the night here," I said defensively. "Vero and I just got here. Our clothes were a mess, and I needed something to wear until our laundry is done."

She crossed herself. "Thank you, Jesus. I was afraid you'd ruined things with Nicholas."

"I didn't ruin things with *Nicholas*." She was the only person I knew who called him that. "And what do you mean by *things*? What *things*?"

"Your sister told me you and Nicholas are seeing each other. She said you two have been intimate." A dresser drawer slammed in Steven's bedroom upstairs.

"Ma!"

"What? I'm not judging! Nicholas is a wonderful young man," she said as she unbuttoned her coat. "He's very attractive and he's great with the children. I think it's fine that you two are enjoying each other's company." Her eyes twinkled as she lowered her voice. "Just remember to go to confession."

I shook my head as she handed me her coat. "You still haven't told me what you're doing here."

"I saw Nicholas on the news this morning, and I was worried when I heard all those terrible things had happened at the police school, so I called your cell phone. When I couldn't get through, I called your sister. She told me the children were with Steven and that you had gone home. I went to your house first but no one was there, so I came to check on Delia and Zach." She cupped my face in her hands and kissed my cheek. "I'm just glad you and Vero are okay. When she told me you had been trapped in that fire . . ." She clutched her heart, the fretful lines around her mouth forming a hash mark for every year the worry had probably taken from her life.

The dryer buzzed as it tumbled to a stop. "Why don't you go change out of that awful shirt and get your things?" she suggested. "We'll take the children back to your house and I'll make you all a nice, hot brunch."

"We weren't planning to go home," I admitted. She paled, her eyes dipping once more to Steven's shirt. "Vero and I were thinking it might be nice to get away for a while. You know, a girls' weekend. We're taking the children with us."

She perked up. "Where?"

Steven lumbered down the stairs with a suitcase in his hand. "I'm ready when you are, Finn. If we leave now, we can probably get to Atlantic City before dark."

My mother gasped. "You can't go with them. This is a girls' trip!"

"Not anymore. I'm chaperoning."

"They're perfectly capable adults!" she cried. "Why would they need a chaperone to enjoy a relaxing weekend away?"

"Because your daughter isn't allowed to take my kids out of state without my permission, and as long as Feliks Zhirov is loose, I'm not letting the children *or* Finlay out of my sight."

"Then we'll all go," my mother said, reaching for her coat. A stream of coffee shot out of Vero's nose. "What?" my mother asked as my mouth fell open. "You said it was a girls' weekend. I can watch the children while you and Vero go out for a nice dinner. Or maybe the spa. It'll be perfect."

"You can't go," I sputtered. "What about Dad?"

"Your sister can stay with him."

"She doesn't know how to cook!"

"She knows how to use a phone. They can order takeout."

"But we're leaving in a few minutes, and you don't have any clothes."

"I have a credit card. And my Buick has third-row seating, by the way, which means my vehicle is the only one large enough to hold both children's safety seats, four adults, and all of your luggage."

"If it was only *three* adults, we could fit in my sedan," I pointed out.

My mother sighed and drew me into the kitchen. "I don't think it's a good idea for you to go out of town with Steven. What will Nicholas think when he finds out?" She gestured wildly to the flannel shirt I was wearing.

I bit my cheek. Just last night, Nick had voiced his unfounded fears that I might want to rekindle things with Steven, if only to put our family back together. I'd told him he was wrong, that I would never get back together with the man who had cheated on me and left me for another woman. But here I was, wearing Steven's shirt and showering in his bathroom, making plans to take him with me on a road trip to Atlantic City that Nick didn't even know about.

"If I come with you, it will look better," my mother insisted. I pinched the bridge of my nose and drew in a deep, slow breath. I turned and left the kitchen with my mother in tow, only to find Steven and Vero facing off against each other across the foyer. "We're all going," I declared.

Vero and Steven both swore.

"But I have three conditions," I continued. "One, Vero chooses the route." Because Vero was wanted on a bogus theft charge in the state of Maryland, and if we took the direct route, she could end up in jail. "Two, Steven does not drive." Because he would love nothing more than to see Vero behind bars. "And three, nobody fights. The first person to pitch a tantrum or shed blood in that Buick will get out and walk the rest of the way." Because my nerves were shot and I was not going to put up with it.

My mother, Steven, and Vero all raised their eyebrows at my mom-voice, but none of them objected as I glared at them all.

"I'll go pack our clothes," Vero said.

My mother reached for her cell phone. "I'll call your sister and tell her I'll be gone for a few days."

"I'll put the kids' car seats in the Buick," Steven added.

I headed for the kitchen to prepare a cooler of snacks for the road. At the last minute, I threw in a bottle of antacids and a fifth of Steven's gin from the pantry, certain this was going to be the longest road trip any of us had ever been on.

CHAPTER 3

Three hours later, after a circuitous route through West Virginia (and the narrowest, most rural sliver of Maryland on the map), two potty breaks (one for me and my mother and the other for Delia), and a diaper change on the side of the highway for Zach, we crossed the state line into Pennsylvania and headed east toward New Jersey. My mother had taken the first shift driving while Vero navigated from the passenger seat. The children's car seats took up the middle row, and Steven and I sat crammed together in the back since I was the only adult in the car I could trust not to murder him.

I sat with my legs propped on the seat back in front of me, my laptop on my knees, my manuscript opened to the climax of my romantic suspense novel, to a scene my editor had insisted I rewrite because it wasn't sexy enough to warrant my final advance payment.

Every ten miles or so, Vero would lower her visor, open the mirror, and narrow her eyes at me over the children's heads, checking to make sure I was working. The revision was due to my agent by Monday, and I had no choice but to finish it if I wanted to get paid.

Somehow, Vero had managed to stay awake for the first leg of the trip, but once we were safely past the Maryland state line, she had set-tled back into her seat with a vigorous yawn. After a few minutes, her head had tilted against her window and she'd fallen asleep. My own eyes burned. The Styrofoam container of bitter, watered-down gas station coffee contained nothing but cold dregs. Between the slow blink of my cursor on the screen, the quiet that had fallen over the car as the chil-dren napped, and the rhythmic flash of the white-painted lines on the road, the edges of my own consciousness were growing fuzzy.

"What are you working on?" Steven asked, scooting closer.

"My next book," I said without looking up. There was no sense an-gling my screen away as he peeked over my shoulder. He'd eventually read the whole thing anyway, and if my last book was any indication, he'd probably post a review.

If I was being honest, the manuscript wasn't so bad. The story finally felt like it was coming together. Vero had been right when she'd said all I needed was some real-life inspiration, that the story would be stronger if my heroine gave herself over to her desires and let herself be swept away by the one man she'd been too afraid to get involved with. The new scenes I'd written between my sexy assassin and her forbidden cop were some of the hottest I'd ever put on paper, and I was pretty sure my agent, Sylvia, was going to love it.

Steven frowned at my laptop as I typed. "Huh."

"Are you preparing your next great literary critique?" He had the audacity to look surprised.

"So I left you a review. What's wrong with that? You're always com-plaining you don't have enough of them."

"You said the sex in my books was unrealistic!" I whispered, trying not to wake the children.

"I gave you five stars! It brought your average up by a whole quarter of a percent."

I didn't even dignify that with a response.

He pointed at my laptop and I slapped his hand away. "That bit right there. That's exactly what I was talking about. That stuff never happens in real life. No guy has the upper-body strength to pull off a maneuver like that," he said, gesturing to the passage on the screen where the hot cop hoists the heroine up by her thighs, wraps her legs around his waist, and takes her against the wall. "And definitely not the stamina to hold out that long once they actually get down to it. I mean, come on. She climaxed three times."

I slowly turned to face him. He paled as I raised an eyebrow, daring him to ask me about my exceptionally thorough research.

My phone buzzed in the cupholder beside me. DET. NICK ANTHONY flashed on the screen. Steven harrumphed.

I chewed my lip, debating whether or not to answer it. If I didn't pick up, Nick might assume I was just sleeping.

Or he might start wondering why he couldn't reach me. The last thing I needed was a very persistent detective worrying about me.

"Don't let me stop you," Steven muttered, scooting back to his side of the SUV.

He crossed his arms over his chest as I answered Nick's call. "Hey," I said in a low voice, angling my face toward the window for some privacy. "You're still awake? I thought you'd be home in bed sleeping by now."

"I could say the same about you," he said. My stomach knotted. "I came to your place after the debriefing to make sure you, Vero, and the kids were okay. When you didn't answer your door, I tried your phone a few times. You didn't pick up, so I called your sister." *Damnit, Georgia.* Did she have to tell him everything? "If you were feeling unsafe at your place, you could have called me. I would have found somewhere else for you to stay. You didn't have to leave town."

"I know, and I'm sorry. I should've said something. But you were busy dealing with everything that happened last night, and I didn't want to interrupt your meeting with your commander—"

"One, I'm never too busy for you, ever. Your family's safety is my number-one priority, so let's clear up that misconception right now. You feel unsafe, you call me. No one else is more important than you. And two . . ." His voice softened. "I haven't been able to stop thinking about you all damn day, and I'm a little miffed that we'll be missing our date." He was supposed to cook dinner for me tomorrow night. But I wouldn't have minded skipping the chili and biscuits and diving right into dessert.

"I was looking forward to that, too."

His voice got deep and husky. "You know what else I was looking forward to?"

"What?" I asked coyly.

Steven cleared his throat with a grating sound that made me want to stuff a sock in it.

"Not alone?" Nick asked.

"Not even close."

He laughed. "Tell your mom I said hello. And as for you . . ." His voice dropped to an alluring rumble. "We'll continue this conversation later." His provocative tone suggested there wouldn't be much talking involved, but given my present circumstances, that was probably for the better.

"Can't wait."

Steven made a disgusted noise as I disconnected. He glared over our children's heads toward the front of the car. My mother stifled a yawn behind the wheel, her blinks growing longer in the rearview mirror.

Steven called up to the front seat, "Take the next exit, Susan. I'm driving."

"You're not driving," I reminded him.

"Your mom's been at the wheel for hours, and you and Vero haven't had a decent night's sleep in days. You're both too tired. It's not safe." He cut off my argument before I could open my mouth. "We're nowhere near Maryland, Finn. Your fugitive babysitter has nothing to worry about. We need to stop for gas anyway," he pointed out.

"Fine, you can drive for a few hours while Vero naps. But I'll be watching you, so don't try anything stupid."

Vero lifted her head as we turned in to the parking lot of a convenience store shortly after three.

Delia rubbed her eyes. "Are we there yet?" she asked in a sleepy voice. Zach began to whine and wriggled in his car seat.

"Not yet. We're just stopping to use the potty and stretch our legs a bit."

My mother parked beside a gas pump. Vero helped the children out of the car, and Steven and I maneuvered clumsily out of the third row.

He pulled his wallet from his back pocket and took the fuel nozzle from my mother. "I've got this. Why don't you all take the kids inside and get them something to eat."

I didn't have the energy or the money in my account to argue. I slung the diaper bag over my shoulder and hoisted Zach into my arms. Vero bumped into Steven's elbow, nearly knocking the nozzle out of his grip as she took Delia's hand and followed the rest of us to the store. When we were all out of earshot of the gas pumps, my mother leaned close and whispered, "Three times? See! I knew Nicholas would be good for you."

"Mom! Were you eavesdropping?"

"I couldn't help it," she whispered. "Steven's a loudmouth and I was bored. And don't look so embarrassed. You think I've never had decent relations before?"

"I try not to think about you having *relations* at all."

Vero shook her head. "Never would have guessed Paul had it in him."

"That Viagra works wonders," my mother said. "Like a gift from god. The man can go for hours."

Vero choked on a laugh.

It was probably a good thing Steven had offered to drive, because I was suddenly ready to open that bottle of gin.

"I'm just saying, a man who can satisfy you in the kitchen *and* in the bed isn't one you should take for granted, Finlay. Don't let Steven screw it up for you."

She held the door open as I carried Zach through it. Vero disappeared into the snack aisle while my mother and I herded the children into the women's restroom. I changed Zach's diaper, then held Delia suspended over the grimy toilet while she peed before using the bathroom myself. We washed everyone's hands and bought each of the kids a snack before I realized in my sleep-deprived fog that Vero wasn't in the store anymore.

My mother and I hurried the children out to the gas pumps. The Buick's hood was open. Steven and Vero were leaning over the engine. I could hear them arguing from across the parking lot.

"I know what I'm doing," Vero snapped. "I don't need you to mansplain to me how to check the damn fluids."

Steven wiped the dipstick and jammed it back in its hole. "If you knew what you were doing, you would have . . . *ouch*! Goddamnit!" he shouted as the hood came crashing down on his skull. Vero grinned smugly as she watched him fight his way out from under it. "You did that on purpose," he bellowed, massaging the back of his head.

"Did I? I could have sworn you just said I didn't know what I was doing."

"Everybody back in the car!" I dragged Vero into the SUV before anyone could start throwing punches. We climbed into the third row. Steven and my mother loaded the children into their car seats before buckling themselves in. My mother reclined, spreading her coat over herself like a blanket. It wasn't long before she'd fallen asleep.

Zach grew unusually quiet.

Vero pulled a face as she sniffed.

I leaned between the children's heads and called up to the front seat, careful not to wake my mother. "Steven, open Zach's window."

His eyes darted to mine in the rearview mirror. "It's thirty degrees outside."

"Just until we hit the next rest stop so I can change him."

"Change him? We just stopped. You were in the bathroom for twenty minutes."

"What would you like me to do, Steven?"

He grumbled as he lowered Zach's window a few inches. I shivered, pulling my coat tighter around myself.

"Zach's putting his blanket out the window," Delia tattled.

"Nobody likes a snitch," Vero scolded her. "And Zach, don't do that. You might lose your woobie." Zach giggled and continued taunting his sister. Vero rolled her head toward me and lowered her voice. "We'll be there in a few hours," she said, masking our conversation under the children's arguing. "What's the plan?"

"We'll get some rooms for the night, order room service for the kids, and leave them with my mother."

"What about Commander Killjoy?"

"We'll tell Steven we're going to the casino. It shouldn't be hard to shake him if he follows us. Do you know how to get in touch with Marco?"

Vero nodded. "Leave that part to me."

CHAPTER 4

It was well after dark when the bright lights of Atlantic City finally appeared on the horizon. Vero had insisted on driving the last leg of the trip, her foot heavy on the accelerator, eager to get to Javi. My mother sat up in her seat, craning her neck to read the glowing neon lights of Caesars, the Tropicana, and the Hard Rock as we reached the intersection at Atlantic Avenue.

My mother pointed north, toward the sleek glass silhouette of the Ocean Casino Resort in the distance. "I've heard that one's very nice."

Vero turned south instead, sailing through several yellow lights before slowing in front of a run-down mid-rise that seemed to hunch under the shadow of the Tropicana next door. A neon sign flashed THE ROYAL FLUSH CASINO HOTEL. A few bulbs flickered in the gaudy marquee out front, touting cable TV and cheap rooms.

"We should try here," she said, jerking the SUV to a stop in the check-in lane. "I heard the food is good." Vero left the engine running as she leaped out of the driver's seat. "Stay here," she insisted. "I'll go find us some rooms."

Steven frowned out the rear window. "This place is a dump."

"This is Vero and Finlay's trip," my mother said. "If they want to stay here, then we're staying here. You," she said, pinning him with a look in her visor mirror, "are free to stay someplace else."

Steven folded himself back into his seat.

Vero returned a few minutes later and scrambled into the SUV. She handed two small envelopes to my mother. "I got their last set of adjoining rooms. You and the kids can sleep in one and Finlay and I will take the other."

"What about me?" Steven asked.

Vero shrugged. "Try over there," she said, pointing at the Tropicana.

"I'm not staying in a different hotel! *I* can share a room with Finlay and the kids. You and Susan can take the other one."

"Absolutely not!" my mother said, turning in her seat. "Steven and the children will take one room and the three of us girls will share the other, and that's the end of it." Vero caught my eye in her rearview mirror as she put the car in gear and drove into the parking garage. My mother took a deep breath and beamed. "A girls' weekend away, just like we talked about! Won't this be fun?"

Steven rolled his suitcase with one hand and carried a sleepy Delia into the Royal Flush with the other. I carried the diaper bag and Zach, who woke up just long enough to take in the gaudy, bright lights of the hotel lobby before curling up with his new blanket against my chest. My mother gathered up the bags of clothes, pajamas, and basic sundries she had purchased at Walmart when we'd stopped to replace Zach's woobie on the way here. We all followed Vero, who dragged the children's Dora the Explorer rollaboard and our shared suitcase behind her, leading the way to the elevator and, finally, our rooms.

I had never been so happy to see a bed.

Vero dropped facedown on one of them while I unlocked the door connecting our room to Steven's. We left all the lights off with the exception of one dim lamp. Careful not to wake the kids, we slipped off their shoes and settled them into one of the queen beds, tucking them in for the night.

I set the diaper bag on the floor beside their luggage.

"Everything you need for the night is in here," I whispered to Steven. "Diapers and wipes. Delia's vitamins and Zach's allergy medicine if he gets stuffy. Cheerios, peanut butter crackers, and juice boxes if they get hungry, and changes of clothes for the morning." Whatever trouble Steven was into, it probably hadn't followed him here.

"Wait," he said, catching me by the arm as I turned to go. His eyes searched mine. "Would it really have been so bad to share a room with me . . . with us," he corrected, "as a family?"

"Do you really want me to answer that?" Steven and I would always be linked by the connective tissue of our children. But we would never be the kind of family he wanted now. Not the kind that shared beds or vacations together. Not the kind that swept our differences and heartbreaks under a rug so we'd never have to tread over them. "Nick and I are seeing each other." He needed to hear it plainly said, not hinted at between the lines of a manuscript or an overheard conversation. He needed to hear it from my own mouth, before he got any more ideas about marriage counseling and trying to fix what he'd ruined. "I'm going to bed. I'll see you in the morning."

I shut the adjoining door between our rooms. Vero had fallen asleep, facedown on the mattress, still wearing her coat and sneakers, her bedside lamp still on. She'd slept fitfully during the drive, waking frequently to check our progress and the time, as if that might get us here faster, and I was grateful for the short nap I'd taken during the final hours of the trip.

I unpacked my laptop and connected to the hotel Wi-Fi. I drafted a quick email to Sylvia, attached my revised manuscript, and clicked *Send*. At least that deadline was off my plate. As I slid my laptop back into its case, I spotted the page Vero had torn from Steven's ledger that morning.

I unfolded it, studying it under the lamplight. The notes in the margins were difficult to read, written in some kind of shorthand—lots of abbreviations and initials, combinations of numbers that might have been dates. I didn't recognize any of the names listed, but it was the dollar amounts that drew my attention—large round figures, all of them listed in the column for deposits.

I hastily folded it and tucked it away, no closer to understanding any of it, as the bathroom door opened. My mother came out, her face freshly scrubbed, wearing a pair of fleece pajamas that still had a store label stuck to them. "It's all yours," she said, gesturing to the bathroom. "I'm going to call your sister before it gets too late." She settled into the other bed and pulled the blankets over her lap, squinting at her phone.

I grabbed my toiletries and locked myself in the bathroom, listening to her phone call through the door, filling in the gaps between her responses. Yes, Dad had remembered to take his medications. Yes, Georgia had found the meat loaf in the freezer. Yes, she was going to drive him to his doctor's appointment in the morning. No, we wouldn't be gone long, my mother assured her. Only a few days. Just long enough for me to relax and recover from what had happened at the police academy. No, Dad definitely shouldn't take any of the blue pills while she was gone.

I tuned out the conversation that followed as I sat down on the toilet lid and finally scrolled through the missed text messages Nick had left for me earlier that morning. My fingers hovered over his number on the screen, but it was late and we should both be asleep.

I set my phone aside and splashed cold water on my face. As I toweled off, I pressed an ear to the door before slipping out of the bathroom and tiptoeing around the foot of my mother's bed. The eye mask she'd insisted on buying was on, along with a pair of bright orange disposable earplugs. I nudged Vero awake. She sat up and rubbed her eyes.

With a sigh, she rolled out of the bed and scraped a hotel key off the dresser, tucking it into her back pocket as I reached for the complimentary stationery and pen on the desk and scribbled a note for my mother.

Couldn't sleep. Gone to the casino with Vero. Back soon.

Hopefully with all of our fingers and toes. And hopefully with Javi.

* * *

"How exactly does this work?" I asked Vero as the elevator doors opened to the lobby.

"Probably the same way it did the last time I was here. One of the pit bosses at the Tropicana saw I was on a hot streak and pulled me aside. He told me if I wanted to borrow some cash to play the higher-stakes tables, I should go to the Royal Flush and ask for a valet named Ricky. If Marco's interested in a meeting, Ricky sets it up."

"We can't just go to Marco's office?"

"We'd never find it," she said, leading us past the front desk toward the revolving doors. "Marco rotates his meetings between all the big hotels. Even Ricky doesn't know where Marco will be until he sets the appointment."

Vero slammed her hand down on the silver bell atop the concierge desk. A valet materialized beside her and silenced it with his palm. He glanced furtively around the lobby as he tucked it under a shelf.

"You've got some nerve coming back here," he said in a low voice. "You can't just borrow two hundred Gs and ghost a guy like Marco Toscano. You got me in a lot of trouble. I vouched for you."

Vero flicked the name badge on his jacket. "Then it's your lucky day, Ricky, because here I am. Go on, call him."

"Hell no! You cost me a perfectly good gig. Why should I stick my neck out for you?"

"Why? I'll tell you why," she said, jamming a hand into her pocket. "Because I've got a Glock twelve eighty-four in here and I'm not afraid to use it."

"Twelve eighty-four?" Ricky's face screwed up at the finger-shaped bulge in her coat. "Is that even a thing?"

That's not a thing, I mouthed at her.

"It's totally a thing," she said, jabbing it into the side of his ribs and making him jump. "Now get on the damn phone." I pressed my mouth shut.

Ricky looked around us, but none of the members of the drunken bachelorette party stumbling out of the elevator seemed to notice that his hands were up. "Look," he said, "even if I wanted to get you a meeting with Marco, there's no way I could. That disappearing act you pulled over Thanksgiving cost me my side hustle. Marco cut me off. He said I was a bad judge of character because I was the one who referred you to him in the first place. He quit taking my calls after you lost his money and skipped town." Ricky waved his phone at us. "Rolls straight to a recording."

Vero pulled her hand from her pocket and held it out. "Let me see that."

Ricky smirked. "See? I knew you weren't really packing—"

She spread two fingers and poked them in his eyes. He yelped, blinking back tears as she snatched his phone. She scrolled to Marco's name, tapped the screen, and put the phone on speaker. Just like Ricky said, the call rolled to a recording. Vero left a message for Marco after the tone.

"You want me, you got me. I'm here, asshole. You have something of mine, and I demand a parley. You know where to find me." She disconnected, shoving the phone back at Ricky.

"A parley?" he said, rubbing his watering eyes. "Who do you think you are, Jack Sparrow? This isn't *Pirates of the Caribbean*."

She waited a beat as she studied her nails. "Answer that."

"Answer what? It's not even . . ." His phone vibrated. His eyes widened as he glanced down at the text message on his screen.

"Well?" Vero snapped a finger in front of him. "What did he say?"

Ricky tucked a finger in his collar and dragged it away from his Adam's apple, gesturing for us to follow him through the revolving doors of the hotel. He stepped to the curb and raised a hand, letting out an ear-piercing whistle. A taxi squealed to a stop in front of us. Ricky leaned in the window and gave the driver an address.

"Where are we going?" Vero asked as Ricky opened the back door for us.

"You wanted a parley? You got one. Get in."

CHAPTER 5

The taxi rolled to a stop on a dimly lit corner. I craned my neck to see the leaning signpost beside us, but the street name had been worn away, the letters obscured by a layer of filth and rust. Ramshackle houses cast shadows over the pitted, neglected sidewalk.

"Meter's running," the cabbie pressed when neither Vero nor I opened our door to get out. I glanced at the meter in question. It wasn't even on. Marco Toscano seemed to have friends in every shady corner of this town.

"We are not getting out here," I said firmly. "Take us back to the Royal Flush." Anywhere was preferable to the splintered windows and sagging porch of the weary three-story foursquare standing watch over this corner. The lower level was half-sunk into the ground, one foot of the century-old house already in the grave.

The cabbie shifted into park. "Mr. Toscano doesn't like to be kept waiting. Use the side door," he said, pointing down a narrow passage between two houses.

"Have you never watched a slasher film? Or cable news?" Vero asked him.

The cabbie's arm swung over the seat back. There was a soft click as he pulled back the hammer of a handgun and pointed it at us. "Get out."

"Okay, okay. Keep your panties on!" Vero threw open her door and we both scrambled out.

I waved exhaust from my face, my eyes burning from the fumes as the cab peeled off, leaving us alone god only knew where. "Great. What now?" I asked.

Vero pushed up her coat sleeves. "We're going to go in there like the badasses we are and demand they give us Javi back."

"We're not badasses. I'm a mom. You're a nanny."

"We just spent a week at the police academy."

"That does not qualify us to negotiate with terrorists!" I chased after her into the alley, my protests echoing off the brick-and-clapboard siding rising up on either side of us. I threw an arm in front of her before she could reach for the small brass knob on the short cellar door and lowered my voice to a stern whisper. "We can't go in there, Vero! Do you know what happens to women who go into creepy basements? Murder! Murder happens to women who go into creepy basements. And I did not survive being shot at by Feliks Zhirov's thugs just to be tied up and strangled by a loan shark in a creepy basement in Atlantic City!"

"Javi could be in there!"

"This is not a good idea!"

"Neither is leaving! Do you know why?" she whispered back. "Because when I was six years old, I wandered off during a school field trip and got lost at Six Flags, and do you know who found me? Javi," she said, her dark eyes blazing. "And when I was eight, I ran away from home because my mother wouldn't let me see a PG-13 movie during a birthday party sleepover. I decided I was going to live in the woods behind my neighborhood, only it got really dark and I was too afraid to walk back to my house alone, and do you know who came looking for me? Javi," she said, the memories spilling out of her as if a dam had broken. "And in ninth grade, a guy from the wrestling team offered me a ride home from school, only he decided to stop at a park and get handsy instead, and do you know who followed the guy on his ten-speed, yanked the asshole out of his car, and made him regret all of his life choices? Javi. So if you don't want to go into that creepy cellar, I get it, Finlay, and I won't make you. But if there's a chance Javi's in there, then I'm going in."

"Okay," I said past the lump in my throat. It wasn't lost on me that this was more than she had ever shared with me about him, and her feelings for him obviously ran deeper than she'd let on. "Fine, we'll go. But if I see any duct tape or torture devices down there, I'm calling the cops."

She nodded.

We turned back toward the cellar door, shoulder to shoulder, steeling our nerves as Vero reached for the knob.

She counted to three and cracked the door open. We both peered inside.

A wedge of buttery light spilled across our feet. The low hum of conversations and the clink of wineglasses and silverware drifted up the stairs, carried on a breath of garlic-scented air.

Vero's nostrils flared. "Death by scampi?"

I sniffed, too. My mouth watered and my stomach growled. "Fine. We'll go into the creepy cellar—for Javi," I clarified.

Cell phone in hand, I followed Vero as she tiptoed inside, ducking to avoid hitting her head on the frame. The stairs were narrow, the bloodred carpet turning at a small landing so we couldn't see what waited for us on the other side. Frank Sinatra crooned softly beneath the chatter of voices and the occasional burst of laughter. A tapestry of framed photographs covered the wood-paneled walls, most of them signed. I was pretty sure one of them was Beyoncé.

A man in a dress shirt waited indulgently at the bottom of the stairs as we gawked. "Mr. Toscano is waiting," he said, gesturing for us to come inside.

I looked past him into a low-ceilinged room. Tables dressed in linen were scattered throughout, the rich, heavenly scent of Italian food heavy all around us as well-dressed men and carefully coiffed women twirled mounds of fresh pasta into their mouths.

A large man in a bursting suit jacket snapped his fingers to get our attention. The maître d' ushered us to the man's table, pulled out the two chairs across from him, and urged us to sit. A younger man dined alone at a tiny table nearby, his eyes raking over us as we sat down, the muscles in his jaw working slowly around a piece of garlic bread as he studied us. He looked disturbingly familiar for reasons I couldn't quite place, until he turned back to his meal and I saw him in profile . . . the aquiline nose, the thick, dark stubble on his jaw, the contours of his hairline that receded sharply from a widow's peak. This was the sneaky photographer Vero and I had spotted taking photos of Ramón's garage a few weeks ago, the one we'd pursued as he'd raced away in his Audi. He'd shot a gun at us and run us off the road before we'd ever figured out who he was, but we'd seen his license plate. The car had been from New Jersey. It was the same Audi we'd seen in the security footage of the men who'd kidnapped Javi.

I nudged Vero. She spotted him, too. Her fists clenched at her sides, like she'd like to rip the garlic bread from his hands and ram it up his nose.

The maître d' refilled Marco's wineglass from an open bottle on the table. "Will your guests be joining you for dinner, Mr. Toscano?"

"That depends." Marco glanced up at us through a fringe of shocking dark hair that didn't at all match his bushy gray eyebrows or the streaks of silver he'd neglected to trim from the rims of his ears. His eyes made an inscrutable pass over Vero as he sliced into a pork chop, dragging a forkful of meat through a pool of thick red sauce on his plate. "Do they have my money?" he asked. When Vero didn't answer, he gestured loosely toward us with the tip of his knife in some semblance of a response the maître d' appeared to understand. The man excused himself without offering us a menu.

Vero slapped my hand as I reached for the bread basket on the table.

"You have something of mine, and I want it back," she said to Marco.

"Are you referring to the car or the man who was attempting to sell it for you?"

"Both."

"The car is an installment payment against your considerable debt, Ms. Ramirez." Vero stiffened at his use of her legal name—the one she'd shed when she left Maryland. "Don't look so surprised. I know about your unfortunate situation. That's why you were here in November, wasn't it? Desperate to win back the money you owe those girls you went to school with, so you can get their families off your back? Everything there is to know about my clients is here in my book. Especially the ones who fail to pay me back." He tapped his breast pocket. A small leather folio peeked out of his open jacket, not unlike the one I'd found in Steven's nightstand that morning. Only this one hadn't been warped and worn from being concealed in a back pocket. Marco displayed his shiny black ledger right up front like a holstered gun.

I clasped my hands on the table in what I hoped was a diplomatic pose. "That car is worth a lot more than she borrowed from you."

"Not to mention the man you kidnapped and stuffed in the trunk!" Vero snapped.

Marco's sauce-reddened lips curled in amusement. "When you return my man, I'll return yours. You met my courier, Ike, right?"

Vero fell silent. I fought a nervous tic in my cheek.

Marco glanced up from his plate when neither of us answered. "Ike's car turned up in Virginia two weeks ago, burned to a crisp, right after I sent him there looking for you. Odd coincidence, huh?"

I cleared my throat. "Wow, that's . . . a terrible coincidence."

"Between us, I couldn't care less what happened to that schmuck. Poor kid took too many hits to the head in the ring. Dumber than a box of rocks, that one. No better than his shithead cousin. But he's my sister's kid, and that makes him family. Right?" Marco shook his head as he sawed his meat. "My sister's been hounding me all week. Now Ike's wife's started calling, and I don't have a clue what to tell her." Marco gestured absently to his camera-toting, gun-slinging spy at the next table. "My associate here has a theory that the two of you were involved, so why don't you tell me what you know so we can wrap up this nasty business."

Vero slammed her fists on the table. "If you don't tell me where Javi is right now, I will give you some nasty—"

I clapped a hand on Vero's knee before she could leap from her chair and strangle the man in front of god and a restaurant full of people. "We have no idea what happened to your nephew," I insisted. And that was the truth. We hadn't stuck around the salvage yard long enough to know what Feliks's disposal team had done with Ike's body once we'd agreed to swap a favor for a favor.

"Then I guess your friend will be staying with me until you're ready to settle your debt."

"You already have the damn car," Vero said.

Marco sat back and wiped his face with the napkin perched on his belly. "The car's damaged goods. It can't be sold in its present condition, which makes it a liability. Your friend stays with me until your debt's paid in full. Once I get my two hundred thousand, I'll consider letting you have him."

"But that's how much I owed you *before* you stole my car!"

He shrugged. "What can I say? I'm feeling generous. Two hundred grand or my nephew. Take your pick."

Vero shot to her feet, prompting Marco's associate to do the same. He tugged his napkin free of his collar and tossed it onto his plate, one hand slipping into his jacket as she pointed at Marco. "I will kill you if you harm one hair on Javi's head," she said through her teeth.

The rest of the room fell quiet, every eye turned toward us. Marco continued eating, the scrape of his knife against his plate shrill in the tense silence. "I think it's time to go," I whispered to Vero, prying her from the table.

"Have Ricky call me when you're ready to discuss the whereabouts of my nephew, Ms. Ramirez." Vero glared down at him as he mopped up the last of the sauce from his plate with a chunk of bread. "And don't take too long. I already have enough mouths to feed, and your friend hasn't been very grateful for my hospitality. I'd hate to have to teach him some manners." Vero shook free of me, ready to launch herself at him. She paused when Marco's associate stepped in front of her. Reaching around him, she snatched the bread basket off Marco's table, never once breaking the spy's stare as she tucked it under her arm and turned on her heels for the door. I rushed up the stairs after her.

"We're screwed," she said once we were safely outside. She leaned against the side of the house and handed me the basket. "We have no idea where Ike is. If we tell Marco what happened to Ike in the salvage yard, he'll probably kill us. And there's no way we can come up with two hundred thousand dollars to buy our way out of this."

"Maybe it's time we go to the police," I suggested. The thought of it made my stomach turn. There was no way to explain what had happened to Javi—or Ike—without incriminating ourselves. Ike's missing persons investigation would become a murder investigation, and Vero and I would be the prime suspects. But we were running out of options.

Vero stared down the empty street, toward the glittering lights of Atlantic Avenue. "No police," she said. "There's only one way out of this that doesn't involve us being murdered or arrested. You and I are going to find Javi on our own. And then we'll steal him back."

CHAPTER 6

I followed Vero a few blocks to the next major cross street. She whistled between her fingers as a yellow taxi approached. "Where to?" the cabbie asked as we both climbed in.

"Caesars," Vero answered. We braced our hands against the seat back as the taxi rocketed away from the curb.

"Why Caesars?" I asked as we whipped down Atlantic Avenue.

"That's where I met Marco when he gave me the marker over Thanksgiving. We'll start looking for Javi there."

"But these hotels are huge," I said in a low voice so the taxi driver wouldn't hear us. "What are we going to do? Stake out the lobby?"

"No," she said as she rummaged in her purse, "just the parking garage. Marco wouldn't have driven a stolen Aston Martin out to dinner. Especially not one with two bullet holes in it. The Aston has to be parked somewhere in this town, and he's probably keeping it close, where he can keep an eye on it. Where better than the parking garage of whatever hotel he's doing his shady business in?"

I was still trying to make sense of that as she uncapped a tube of burgundy gloss and slathered a thick coat on her lips. When the cab pulled up in front of Caesars, I dug inside my wallet for my credit card to pay the driver, but Vero beat me to it, feeding a couple of bills through the hole in the plexiglass shield as we both climbed out.

"Where'd you get the cash?" I asked. Both of our bank accounts were teetering on empty, and she hadn't been quick to part with what little she had left.

"Took it from Steven's wallet while he was checking the engine at the gas station. But don't worry. There's plenty more where that came from." She waved a piece of plastic. "I got his credit card, too."

"Give me that," I said, too late, as Vero stuffed it back inside her pocket. Steven was already suspicious enough about Vero. We didn't need to give him one more reason to report her to the cops.

She hoisted up her boobs and unzipped her hoodie to reveal her cleavage. Shaking her hair free of its ponytail, she fluffed out the waves as she strode to the valet lane.

One of the young men working there held out his hand for her keys. "What are you ladies driving tonight?"

"That all depends." Vero held a folded twenty-dollar bill between two fingers, teasing him with a smile. She tipped her head toward the parking garage. "We have very specific tastes. If a girl wanted to get a ride in . . . say . . . an Aston Martin Superleggera, could she do something like that here?"

The valet arched a brow as she played with a lock of her hair. He checked around him to make sure no one was looking before pulling a key fob from his pocket. "Not tonight," he said, waving the Porsche logo at her. "But there's a smokin' hot Carrera here for a few more hours if you ladies want to put some miles on it."

The glint dimmed in his eyes when Vero started walking away.

"Wait!" he called after her. "I've got a 'Vette back there, too. Or how about a Jag. Or a Benz! That Benz is freakin' gorgeous, and it's got a back seat!" Vero kept walking. The valet groaned as she whistled for another taxi. "Seriously? Do you know how hard it is to find an Aston Martin in this town? Damnit," he muttered as I started to follow her, "those assholes at the Villagio always get the hot ones."

* * *

An hour later, Vero and I were in the parking garage of the Villagio, less than a thousand feet away from the Royal Flush. We crouched between two parked cars as an attractive valet strolled past us, twirling a set of keys on his finger. Vero's hair was once again tied back in a messy ponytail, her sweatshirt zipped to her chin against the cold.

"We've searched the entire garage and my feet are killing me," I said once the valet was out of earshot. "Why don't you just sweet-talk the valet and ask him where the Aston is?"

"Because if the Aston *is* in this garage, then Marco probably has a reservation here. And if Marco has a reservation here, then Javi must be here, too. By now, Marco could be finished with his dinner and be back in his room, and I don't want him to get wind of the fact that we're here looking for him."

Vero and I waited for the valet to leave before creeping through the next row of parked cars. The brash yellow garage lights reflected off a line of BMWs, Mercedes, and Volvos. "Hey," I said, pausing behind a blue Audi. "Isn't this the same car that Marco's snoop was driving?" It was the same model and color as the one we'd chased away from Ramón's shop.

Vero's eyes went wide as she peered into the tinted windows. "Check your phone. You took a picture of the guy's license plate that night."

I opened my camera app. The last photo I'd taken had been during our high-speed chase, right before Marco's spy had fired his gun at us and we'd careened into a ditch. I held the blurry image between us, squinting at the letters and numbers.

"It's him! This has to be where they're keeping Javi." Vero's hands balled into fists as she started toward the hotel.

"Where are you going?" I asked, scrambling to keep up. "The front desk isn't just going to tell us which room a guest is staying in. They have rules about that kind of thing."

Vero's laugh was dark. "I hate to break it to you, Finn, but you and I stopped worrying about the rules the night we buried Harris Mickler."

Vero looked like vengeance personified as she stormed toward the front desk. I held her back by the shoulders and lowered my voice. "I think this will go better if we take a deep breath and remember to use our words."

"I'd rather use my fists." She darted looks around me at the faces in the lobby, searching for Marco's. There was murder in her eyes. She was in no state for diplomacy.

"Just . . . stay here and let me handle this." I deposited her into a wingback chair with firm instructions to wait for me. I strolled slowly to the counter. The woman behind it greeted me with a smile.

"May I help you?" she asked.

"I hope so," I said sweetly. "I was backing out of my space in the parking garage, and I accidentally bumped into the car parked behind me. I'm so embarrassed. I was going to leave a note, but I thought it might be easier to call the vehicle's owner and exchange insurance information. If I give you the license plate number, would you mind looking it up for me to see who it belongs to?"

"Sure," the woman said, taking down the number. She typed it into her computer and studied the screen. "The owner of the vehicle is visiting a guest in one of our suites. Would you like me to call the room for you?"

"That would be lovely." I rested my elbows on the counter, my gaze drifting down to the clerk's hand as she dialed the suite number. After a prolonged pause, she frowned. "I'm sorry, no one's answering. If you'd like to leave a note, I'd be happy to have it delivered to his room."

"That won't be necessary," I said, backing away from the desk. "I'll just leave one on his windshield. Thank you for your help."

Vero leaped up from her chair as soon as I returned. "What did she say?"

"I think I found Marco's suite, but no one's answering in his room."

"That's good! He probably hasn't come back from dinner yet. We should go up and take a look."

I pulled her up short. "This isn't like hot-wiring a car, Vero. These places all use electronic keys, and there are probably cameras on every floor."

Vero bit her lip, looking past me toward the elevators. "Come on. I have an idea," she said, pulling me through the lobby to an emergency exit map mounted on the wall. She traced the diagram of the main floor with a finger.

"What are you looking for?"

"The stairs to the basement. This hotel is huge, which means they must have hundreds of employees. They probably hire new housekeeping staff every day. We'll go to the housekeeping supply room and pick up some uniforms. No one will notice us snooping around if we're dressed like we belong here." She towed me into a stairwell. Against my better judgment, I followed her to the lower level, to a door marked HOUSEKEEPING. Inside, the place was bustling with staff, their conversations muffled by the rumble of laundry machines as crew members folded towels and sheets in one room and stocked cleaning carts in another. We moved quickly, keeping our heads down as we passed several groups of workers dressed in gray aprons and smocks. Vero snagged two uniforms from an open cabinet. She urged me into a small locker room and handed me one. "Put this on," she said, shrugging out of her clothes and balling them under her arm.

"I can't believe we're doing this," I said as I stripped off my clothes, too. "This is never going to work."

"You only think that because the last time you put on a costume, you got caught."

"Exactly!" I whispered as I tugged the smock over my head.

"We won't get caught." Vero turned me around and tied my apron behind my back, then handed me her clothes. "We're just going to sneak into Marco's suite and see if Javi's there. If he's not, we'll look for clues and figure out where they're hiding him. We'll be in and out before any-one realizes we were there. Here," she said, handing me a pair of dispos-able gloves and a hairnet, "put these on."

I donned my gloves and disposable cap and followed Vero out of the locker room. Freshly stocked cleaning carts lined the hallway outside. Vero walked with her head down, accidentally bumping into a member of another cleaning crew as we passed. Vero mumbled an apology, tuck-ing something in her pocket as she grabbed the handle of the closest cart. "Help me with this," she said in a low voice, pushing it toward the elevator. I stuffed our clothes inside it and took the opposite handle, backing it through the open service doors as Vero pushed. She smacked the button for the seventeenth floor, closing the doors on another clean-ing crew before they could squeeze inside the elevator with us.

"Did you steal that woman's key card?" I hissed once the elevator started moving.

"I did not *steal* it. I *borrowed* it. We'll return everything when we're done. Just keep your head down and don't look at any cameras."

My stomach lurched as we hurtled upward and coasted to a stop. A bell chimed and the doors parted. Vero peeked both ways before steer-ing the cart through the opening. I pushed it behind her, eyes glued to the floor as we rolled past a mirrored dome on the ceiling directly in front of the elevator. I peeped up through my lashes as we rounded the corner, but didn't see any other cameras in the hall.

"I thought there would be more cameras up here."

Vero raised an eyebrow but didn't look surprised. "There are prob-ably two hundred of them in the casino downstairs. These hotels don't care what guests do in their rooms, as long as their casinos are safe."

I glanced up as Vero stopped the cart beside Marco's suite.

She knocked sharply on the door. "Housekeeping," she called out.

"It's eleven o'clock at night," I whispered. "What if they're sleeping?"

She looked at me like *I* was the one who'd lost my mind. "We're in a *casino*. On a *Friday night*. In *Atlantic City*. Nobody goes to bed at eleven o'clock."

"Nobody gets their room vacuumed at eleven o'clock either!"

"Maybe they need towels!" She knocked again, louder this time. When no one answered, Vero drew in a steadying breath and held her stolen key card over the sensor.

The lock opened with a soft click.

Vero cracked the door. "Hello?" Her voice echoed back to us as we slipped inside. An expanse of windows on the far wall reflected our skulking shapes as we tiptoed through the foyer, the outline of our uniforms silhouetted against the night sky. The door clicked shut behind us.

I slumped with relief when we rounded the corner into the suite and found it empty. It was huge, with a full-sized kitchen, a dining room, and a circular sectional sofa in the center of its massive living room.

"Let's look for Javi and get out of here," Vero said, moving quickly through the rooms. She opened the first door on the right side of the hall, revealing an empty bedroom. I checked the coat closet, then the kitchen, before following Vero into the master suite at the end of the corridor.

She jolted to a stop in front of an open door. A strange croaking sound escaped her. "Maybe we should come back later," she said, stumbling backward into me.

"Why? What's wrong?" I peered around her into a lavish bathroom. A pair of men's loafers was visible on the floor beside the vanity. A pair of feet were inside them. The man's legs were splayed wide. His cheeks were slack and waxy, his face turned away, his head resting at an odd angle, revealing a section of blood-matted hair on his crown.

"Finlay," Vero asked in a small voice, "are you seeing this?"

"The dead guy on the floor? He's kind of hard to miss."

"No," Vero said with a panicky lilt, "the naked one sitting in the bathtub."

CHAPTER 7

"No! No, no, no, no," I said, covering my eyes. "There are not supposed to be any more dead guys! No more dead guys! It's only been ten days since the last one! Why does this keep happening?" I dropped my hands and blinked. It did nothing to change the fact that Marco's associate was sprawled at my feet and there was a large, hairy, naked man turning purple in the Jacuzzi. The man's toupee had fallen forward, covering his face like a furry window shade. "Is that who I think it is?"

Vero tiptoed closer to the bathtub, grimacing at his exposed groin through the dissipating bath bubbles. "If it is, I'm guessing his list of admirers wasn't very long." She took a washcloth off the shelf beside the tub and shook it open, dropping it over his crotch. The tiny square of fabric bobbed precariously on the surface, and she made a gagging sound as she reached into the water, plucking out his bamboo back scrubber with the tips of her gloved fingers.

Using the end of its long handle, she lifted the dangling hairpiece from the man's face. Two bulging, bloodshot eyes stared back at us. We both jumped back as Marco's head lolled sideways. Bruises ringed the thick folds of his neck.

"Yep. Definitely him." Vero dropped the scrubber into the water and backed away from the tub, nearly tripping over a sopping wet bathrobe sash on the floor. "We need to get out of here."

"There are two dead men in this room, Vero! We can't just leave!"

"There are two dead men in this room, and that is exactly why we should be leaving!"

Vero and I froze at a scratching sound.

"What was that?" she whispered.

"I don't know," I whispered back. "I think it came from out there," I said, pointing toward the hall.

"We checked the kitchen, the closets, and both bedrooms!" Vero whispered. "There was no one else here!"

"Did you check the other bathroom?"

"What other bathroom?"

We stared at each other as the scratching stopped.

Vero moved silently back through the master suite. I followed her down the hall, back to the second bedroom. Sure enough, there was another door inside. It was closed. Probably another bathroom.

I held Vero by the ties of her apron before she could test the knob. "We should get out of here. The killer might be in there."

"What if it's Javi?"

"What if it's not?"

The door rattled as something shuffled behind it. "Find a weapon," I whispered.

Vero began searching the bedroom while I crept to the kitchen. I returned with a frying pan and found Vero wielding an iron with a retractable cord.

"Don't look at me like that!" she whispered. "At least it's not a hair dryer." She yanked the frying pan away from me and tossed it on the bed. "There's no way you're taking him out with Farberware, Finn. You need Le Creuset for that." She unplugged the brass lamp on the nightstand and thrust it in my hand.

Weapons poised, we tiptoed toward the bathroom. Vero stood

behind me, her fingers digging into my shoulder as I pressed my ear against the door.

The shuffling inside quieted as I reached for the handle.

On the count of three, I flung it open and Vero lunged inside. Someone snarled. Vero shrieked, knocking me backward as she scrambled out of the room and quickly slammed the door.

"What was that?" I asked as she bent over her knees, the iron cord dragging on the floor between her feet.

"I think we found our ferocious killer," she panted.

Cautiously, I cracked open the door.

A small, hairy wiener dog bared his tiny teeth at me through the gap. Mangled bath towels littered the floor beside an overturned water bowl. A roll of toilet paper had been ripped from its holder on the wall, and bits of shredded paper clung to the dog's fur like wet confetti. "The dog must belong to Marco."

Vero extended a tentative hand inside and reached for the dog's collar. He laid back his ears and began barking at us.

"Don't do that! You're making it mad!"

"What do you want me to do?"

"Make it stop!"

"How?" Vero asked, covering her ears.

"I don't know." I'd never owned a pet besides Delia's goldfish, and at least Christopher had been quiet.

I knelt and tried talking to the dog in a calming voice, the one my sister referred to as my hostage negotiator voice. "What's your name?" My brow furrowed as I squinted at the tag on his collar. "Kevin?" The dog went silent. His ears cocked.

"Seriously?" I asked.

He lunged at me.

I quickly shut the door, raising my voice over his shrill barks. "Maybe he's hungry. Check the kitchen and see if you can find him something to eat."

Vero scurried out, returning a moment later with a box of dog biscuits. The barking stopped as she tore it open. There was a snuffling sound. The shadow of his nose darkened the gap under the door.

Vero turned the knob and we peeped inside. The dog's ears shot up as she wedged a treat through the opening. Kevin took a tentative step toward it, reaching out with his teeth to snatch it from her.

She tossed in a few more treats, shut the door, and shook the crumbs off her gloves. We sagged against the wall, relishing the silence as the dog ate.

"You think Javi could have killed them?" I asked after a thoughtful pause.

Vero shook her head. "There are no signs of a fight. No broken glass. No toppled furniture or duct tape. If Javi managed to free himself, I doubt he would have left the place so neat."

My laugh was dark. "There are two dead men in the other room. You call this neat?"

"Fine, maybe not neat. But Marco was obviously strangled, and the other guy looks like he got pushed and hit his head. The Javier I know would have come out swinging." She smiled to herself as she stared up at the ceiling. "Did I ever tell you about my teeth?" she asked, turning toward me. I shook my head, intrigued. "They're not real," she said, tapping her bright white incisors with her fingernail. "I broke my real ones when I was nine. Mikey Bouchard pushed me off the jungle gym at school. I hit my face on the way down and split my two front teeth clean in half," she said, running her tongue over them. "I didn't tell my teacher. Instead, I locked myself in a bathroom stall until dismissal, too embarrassed to let anybody see me. It was awful," she said with a shudder. "I got on the school bus that afternoon and Javi knew something was wrong. He snuck up to the front seat and scooted in beside me. I turned my face away and crossed my arms over my chest, pretending to be mad at him, hoping maybe he'd go away so he wouldn't see my mouth. Instead, he told me knock-knock jokes the whole way home, trying to get me to smile."

"Did it work?"

She laughed softly, revealing her perfect veneers. "Not until he tried whispering a dirty one in my ear. My jaw dropped. I was so shocked, I forgot all about my teeth. Javi took one look at my mouth and asked me who did it. He promised me that no one at school was going to make fun of the way I looked. He swore it. The next day, I bumped into Mikey Bouchard at the dentist's office. He had two black eyes, a broken nose, and *his* smile looked a whole lot worse than mine. I know Javi," she said, sniffling and swatting at her eyes. "If he was here and he managed to escape, he wouldn't have left this suite without cracking some skulls. And I didn't see a black eye or a broken tooth on either of those guys."

I pulled her head to my shoulder as a tear slid down her cheek. "He's going to be okay," I promised, hoping I was right. "We'll search every inch of this suite for clues, and we won't leave Atlantic City until we find him."

With the exception of Kevin's bathroom, we'd searched Marco's entire suite, including the pants pockets of the dead man on the floor, which had contained nothing but a pack of breath mints. Our best bet for finding Javi was to locate the car that had brought him here. All we needed was a bread crumb—a valet ticket or a parking receipt. Some clue to where they were hiding the Aston Martin.

"Nothing here," Vero said, slamming a kitchen drawer shut.

"Hey, I think I found something." Vero hurried to look over my shoulder as I rummaged through the pockets of a suit jacket hanging in the foyer closet. I handed her a key fob for an Audi. "And here's his wallet," I said, flipping it open to show her the driver's license inside. According to his ID, the name of Marco's associate was Louis Delvecchio. "His home address is in Trenton."

"That's almost two hours from here."

I slapped her fingers away as she reached for the stack of hundreds in the bifold. "His business card says he's a private investigator." I passed her the card.

"That would explain his fancy camera and all those photos he was taking of us last week."

"And how Marco knew so much about you and the rest of his clients. Marco probably had this guy on retainer." I searched the rest of the pockets. "The key to the Aston Martin isn't here."

"Whoever killed them probably stole it."

"But left the key to his Audi? And his wallet?" I asked doubtfully. The wallet had been full of cards and cash.

"Any sign of his phone?" she asked.

"It's not in his coat. Check the sofa. Maybe it fell out of his pocket." We started at opposite ends of the sectional, lifting pillows and feeling under the cushions. My fingers closed around a slender cord that snaked over the arm of the couch and plugged into an outlet on the wall. I followed the length of it to a slim silver tablet hidden under a throw pillow. "What about this?" I asked, handing it to Vero.

She tapped the screen. "It's locked." She thought for a moment. Then her eyes skated toward the master suite. She launched herself down the hall with the tablet before I could stop her.

"What are you doing?" Panic set in as I chased her into the bathroom. She stepped over Louis and knelt beside the tub. "Vero, this is not a good idea."

"No, it's a brilliant idea."

"Can't you just hold the screen in front of his face?"

"It's an old device," she said, passing me the tablet and using both hands to lift one of Marco's arms out of the water. "It has a fingerprint reader. Dry his hand for me."

"What?! No!"

"Don't be such a baby! You've touched a dead guy's appendages before. At least this one's still attached."

"I'm not being a baby. You're disturbing a body in a crime scene!"

"I promise, he won't feel a thing. See?" she said, waving said appendage up and down.

"Now you're just being crass."

"*Crass* is a boomer word. You sound like your mother."

"I do not!"

"Fine, I'll do it." She snapped open a hand towel and set it on the side of the tub. I cringed as she hefted Marco's arm, grunting with exertion as she bobbed it up and down, smacking the blue tips of his fingers over and over against the fabric. His toupee flopped, peeling farther away from his forehead. Vero muttered to herself between labored breaths. "You'd think you'd never done something like this before. I mean, seriously, Finn. First Harris, then Andrei, and don't even get me started about Carl. Give me his tablet," she said, sweat blooming under her hairnet. I held the tablet out to her, resisting the urge to gag as she pressed Marco's index finger against the scanner. When nothing happened, she tried his thumb.

"It's not working. His fingers are too pruny! Plug in the hair dryer."

"You can't use a hair dryer! The man's in a bathtub!"

"He's already dead, Finn! It's not like it's gonna kill him!" Marco's armpit squeaked against the porcelain as Vero straddled his arm and stretched it out toward me.

I plugged in the hair dryer. "I can't believe we're doing this."

Vero grunted and tugged. I reconsidered my mother's suggestion about confession as I tried to pass Vero the hair dryer. "The cord isn't long enough. It won't reach."

"Then you hold it. Point it this way."

"Vero—"

"Just do it!"

I turned the dryer on high, extending the cord as far as it would go. She squinted against the blast of hot air.

"Is it working?" I asked.

"I don't know yet," she said over the whine of the motor. "Turn down the power. We don't want to cook him."

Warming Marco's corpse was the last thing I wanted to do. There was a good reason killers kept bodies in chest freezers. I adjusted the dryer to its lowest setting. Something vibrated in my pocket.

"What's wrong?" Vero asked as I switched hands to check my phone.

"It's Nick," I said, stuffing it back in my apron. I couldn't think about him now. Not while I was giving a naked dead man a blowout with a cheap Conair in a hotel bathroom above a casino.

"I think he's done," Vero called out. "Hand me his tablet." I shut off the dryer and passed her the device. She pressed Marco's index finger against the scanner, jabbing it a few times before giving up with a swear. "It's not working."

"Give me that." I took the tablet and knelt beside Louis, pressing his index finger to the scanner instead. The home screen opened. Vero rolled her eyes as she dropped Marco's arm.

"You're buzzing again," she said, taking the tablet from me.

"No, I'm not."

We both paused, ears tipped toward the sound of a vibrating phone. It was coming from the vanity. A pair of folded silk boxers had been left on the counter. I lifted the corner of the underwear, revealing the brightly lit cell phone hidden underneath them. "It must be Marco's." I picked it up, squinting at the number on the screen. "The call is coming from a Northern Virginia area code."

"What do we do?"

The phone dimmed as the call rolled to voice mail. Breaths held, we waited for a new voice mail notification to appear, but nothing happened. I tapped to illuminate the screen once more, but all I found was a string of unanswered calls from two different Northern Virginia numbers and someone named *G.G.*

We both jumped when the phone started vibrating again. A stack of text messages began piling up on the screen. "*G.G.*'s texting him."

I'm back in town. Why aren't you answering your phone?
I can pick him up tonight. Call me when you get this.

Vero read over my shoulder. "Should we reply?"

"We can't reply to them!"

The phone buzzed with another text.

If you don't answer, I'm coming to you.

I thrust the phone at Vero. "Quick! Type something."

"You're the writer!"

I tapped the screen. "It's not letting me in!"

Vero took the phone.

"What are you doing?" I asked as she lifted a strand of Marco's toupee and held the phone up to his face.

"His eyes need to be wider. Get over here and hold them open for me."

"Absolutely not!"

"Would you rather hold back his hair?"

"I can't believe you're making me do this," I said, leaning over Vero's shoulder. I put a thumb on each side of Marco's forehead and drew his eyebrows toward the ceiling.

"You can't do it that way! He looks like Mickey Rourke!"

"What do you want me to do?"

"Hold them open like he's posing for a selfie." I adjusted my grip. Vero waved the phone in front of Marco's face. "We're in!" she said, dropping his toupee. The hair fell over my fingers. I dropped Marco's head and shook out my hands, my skin crawling as Vero skimmed through Marco's messages. "Marco texted *G.G.* after dinner, complaining of indigestion. He said he wasn't feeling up to driving to *G.G.*'s place to make the handoff tonight."

"What handoff?"

"I don't know. But whatever it is, we don't want *G.G.* showing up here." Vero's thumbs flew over the screen.

"What are you telling them?"

"*Don't come,*" Vero read aloud as she typed. "*Been in the bathroom all night. Too sick to meet. It's late. Will text tomorrow.* What?" she asked, narrowing her eyes at me. "He *has* been in the bathroom all night, and he's definitely not answering the door. Let me handle *G.G.* You check in with your boyfriend and see what he wants."

I fished my phone from my apron, wincing as I listened to the voicemail Nick had left while I'd been blow-drying a corpse.

"Hey, Finn. I hope you're having fun with Vero and you're both being safe. Listen, I . . ." In his pause, I could just make out the familiar squawk of radios and loud voices. One of them definitely belonged to my sister. Were they at the police station? It was the middle of the night. Did the man ever sleep? "I know I'm probably worrying for nothing, but I wanted to hear your voice. I'm . . . Christ," he muttered to himself. "I'm sorry. I know you're probably asleep. I'm just . . . I can't stop thinking about you and I wanted to make sure you're okay. That's all." The weight of the sigh he heaved into the phone suggested he definitely had not rested since we last spoke. "I know it's early, but call me when you get this, okay?" I disconnected, confused.

Early, Nick had said. Not late.

"What's wrong?" Vero asked.

I felt the blood drain from my face as I checked the clock on the home screen. "Is that the time?"

Vero glanced down at Marco's phone. "Shit!" She sprang to her feet. "*Shit,* Finlay! What do we do?"

"We're not going to panic," I said, pacing the bathroom. Of course we were going to panic! The sun would be up in less than two hours, and Vero and I were in another hotel, using dead men's body parts to raid their electronic devices. "We have to get back before the kids wake up."

"What are we supposed to do with Marco and Louis?"

"I don't know!" I sputtered as I looked around the bathroom. We were wearing hair caps and gloves, and we hadn't left any fingerprints in the suite. We could still leave and take our chances that the local police would never know we'd been here, but that felt like a risky gamble.

"What would the heroine in your books do if she accidentally stumbled into a crime scene? How would she cover her tracks?"

"She'd probably burn the place down."

"I'll get the matches."

"Vero! We are not fictional characters and this is not a book! We can't burn down a building to cover our tracks! Ricky knows we were looking for Marco, the valet at Caesars knows we were on our way to the Villagio, and the woman at the front desk downstairs will be able to identify us in a lineup. Not to mention the fact that an entire restaurant full of people heard you threaten to kill Marco."

"So we'll scrub down the crime scene and make it look like an accident."

"There are handprints around the man's neck!"

"Then we'll just have to keep anyone from figuring out Marco's dead."

"What are you doing?" I asked as she tapped open Marco's phone.

"I'm going to call the front desk and extend Marco's reservation. I'll say I'm Marco's personal assistant, that he's sick and he doesn't want to be disturbed. Then we'll put up the DND sign so no one comes looking for him while we find Javi and get the hell out of town."

A frantic laugh slipped out of me, probably so I wouldn't cry. There was no running from this. Our only hope for saving ourselves was to figure out who really did this and turn the evidence over to the cops before anyone realized these guys were missing and the police could open an investigation of their own. But solving a double homicide would take time we didn't have. By tomorrow, Marco and his friend would start to decompose, and the smell would draw more than flies. Unless we could come up with some way to . . . "Keep them cold," I whispered.

Vero looked up as I typed a question into the search bar of my phone. *What are the stages of decomposition of a corpse?* I clicked *Enter* and skimmed the results.

Three days. We had three days before putrefaction set in.

I shot to my feet, my mind leaping ten chapters ahead of us as I hurried to the cleaning cart we'd left in the foyer. I rummaged through the compartments for a roll of plastic bags. What if we didn't need to solve the mystery and catch the killer? What if we only needed time to write ourselves out of the scene? I ran back to the bathroom and tore several trash bags off the roll. "Quick, drain the bathwater," I said, handing them to Vero.

"Why?"

"There's an ice machine on every floor. Fill the bags. The longer we can keep the bodies cold, the more time we'll buy ourselves."

"To do what?" she asked as I unlocked the door.

"To come up with an alibi."

Ten minutes later, the bathroom looked like a Halloween edition of *The Hangover*. We'd managed to lift Louis into the jacuzzi with Marco, then we'd filled the remaining space in the tub with ice cubes from the machine down the hall. The men's eyes were half-open, their heads resting at odd angles. Marco's toupee was hanging lopsided on his head, and Louis's tie was slung over one of his shoulders. But they were cold, and for now, that was the best we could do.

Vero called down to the front desk to check on Marco's reservation while I dragged the cleaning cart into the suite and used every tool in it to scrub the vanity and the floor.

"Okay," she said as I finished and closed the bathroom door behind me. "We have the suite for three more days. That ought to be enough time for us to find Javi and get the hell out of town."

"Good. I'm going to head back to the Royal Flush. Steven and my mother are probably worried sick."

"What am I going to do?"

"You're going to use Marco's phone and Louis's tablet to make it look like they're both still alive."

"Great idea," she said, putting Marco's phone in her pocket. "I'll go all over town. Hit a couple of restaurants, some stores, maybe a few casinos. You know, just to keep up the illusion—"

"The only place you're going is the ice machine," I said firmly. "Keep the dog quiet and make sure no one comes in. Dead bolt the door behind me when I go."

"You're leaving me here?" she cried.

"You can use the time to snoop through their devices and figure out where they're keeping Javi. I'll only be gone a few hours." Vero flung herself in front of the door, blocking my exit. "Would you rather I stay here and you can deal with Steven, the children, and my mother?" Vero hesitated as she considered that. "You can order room service," I pointed out. "Anything you want."

She narrowed her eyes at me. "Anything?"

"Anything. Just remember to feed Kevin, too. And don't let anybody in."

I listened for the snap of the dead bolt behind me before darting down the stairwell at the end of the hall. My clothes were rolled into a ball under my arm, and I ducked into an empty bathroom in the casino to change before heading back to the Royal Flush.

It was still dark outside when I finally crept into my mother's room just after five A.M. Her eye mask was firmly in place, her earplugs just visible between the sleep-matted strands of her hair. She hardly stirred when I stubbed my toe on my suitcase, swore viciously, and climbed into the bed beside hers, still wearing my clothes. I rolled onto my back and stared at the ceiling, my mind racing as I listened to her snore. Marco and Louis were dead, and the Aston was gone, both of which should have solved two of our more pressing problems. Instead, these two developments only managed to introduce more frightening ones.

And we still had no idea where to find Javi.

All Vero and I could do was stall the discovery of the bodies until we could piece together a viable alibi while we continued to search for him. Easy, right? We would just have to convince everyone we'd been here at the Royal Flush, having a good time. I rubbed my temples, trying to picture that scene in a book.

Just a relaxing girls' weekend away. In a crappy casino hotel. In Atlantic City. With two small children, my mother, my ex-husband, and two dead guys. I threw an arm over my eyes, trying not to think about how unbelievably ridiculous that all sounded as I drifted toward sleep.

I awoke with a start when a hand grabbed my wrist. I gasped, disoriented and groggy, unsure how long I'd been sleeping as I was dragged out of bed. Steven didn't say a word as I tried to shake him off. I hissed out protests as he pulled me through the open door between our rooms. He walked me briskly past the bed where our children were sleeping, their faces barely visible in the dim dawn light seeping through the crack between the drapes. He towed me around their scattered toys and out the other door, until we were standing in the garish lighting of the hall.

He glared down at me, fully dressed in the same pair of jeans and flannel shirt he'd been wearing when I last saw him yesterday. "Where the hell have you been?"

I jerked my hand from his. "Vero and I were downstairs in the bar."

"No, you weren't. I was down there for the last four hours, and I didn't see you or your little criminal friend anywhere."

"It's a big hotel, Steven! We met up with one of Vero's friends. He invited us out to a restaurant and we stopped at a few casinos after that." It wasn't entirely a lie. "And stop calling her that. She's no more a criminal than you are." I held his gaze, daring him to come clean.

"Where's Miss Sticky Fingers now?"

"With her friend. She's spending the night at his hotel."

His grin was derisive. "Some babysitter."

"Not all of us can be as good at it as you are."

He choked out a laugh. "We're back to that? You really want to do this now?"

"You're the one who was in the casino for four hours while you were supposed to be watching our children."

"Your mom was asleep in the next room," he argued. "I left the door between our rooms open all night. It wasn't a big deal."

"Like it wasn't a big deal when you dumped them on her while I was at the police academy? You haven't changed at all, Steven. You know what? You're right. I don't want to do this right now. I'm going to bed." I turned toward my own door before I realized I didn't have my key. I pivoted back to Steven, palm out for his. His snide grin collapsed as he reached for his pocket. I closed my eyes, certain this night could not get any worse. "Don't tell me we're locked out."

"We're locked out," he said, dragging a hand down his face. "Go knock on your mother's door."

"She sleeps with earplugs."

"Earplugs?"

"She's been sleeping with my father for forty years. The man snores like a John Deere. If I knock, we'll only wake Delia and Zach, and once they're up, we'll never get them back to sleep."

I leaned back against the wall between our rooms, sliding down it until I was sitting on the carpet. It was tacky and smelled like cigarettes and despair. Head tipped against the peeling wallpaper, I closed my eyes, surrendering to my fate. My brief snooze in the car yesterday and the nap Steven had just awoken me from, for now, would have to do. The kids would be awake in an hour or two anyway. Better to sacrifice a comfortable bed than face the wrath of an overtired toddler.

"What are you doing?"

"Going to sleep."

"Out here?"

"You have a better idea?"

Steven patted his pockets once more. Apparently, neither one of us had our phones either.

"Come on," he said, reaching for my hand.

"Can't we just wait here?" I whined as he hauled me to my throbbing feet. "The kids will be up in a few hours anyway. It will probably take the front desk that long just to get someone up here." Without any form of ID, I doubted they'd send someone to unlock it anyway.

"We're not going to the front desk."

"Where are we going?"

"To eat."

* * *

Steven and I walked to the first open restaurant we could find, a few blocks from the hotel. As much as I hated the idea of giving in to him, my stomach didn't have the same willpower, and the promise of greasy diner food was far too tempting to pass up. It had been so long since my last hot meal.

Steven smiled brightly at the hostess as she guided us toward a table. He stopped me as my screaming feet dove for the booth. He pointed to a dimly lit table at the back of the dining room. "Would you mind if we take that one?" he asked her. She glanced at the empty section of the restaurant, a regret already forming on her lips. Steven put an arm around my shoulder and winked at her, and her frown softened.

"Sure," she said. "I don't see why not."

Apparently, I wasn't the only one who was up to something, but I was too exhausted and too hungry to care as I sat down and the woman slid a carafe of coffee and an empty mug in front of me. I poured myself a cup, dumped in a few creamers and some sugar packets, and took a long, slow, glorious sip, hardly listening as Steven ordered for both of us. The server returned a few minutes later with two heaping plates of waffles, bacon, and eggs. I tore into the batter-encrusted goodness like it was the Last Supper as Steven stared at me over his mug, one corner of his lip curled up in amusement. I was halfway through my second waffle and my third cup of coffee when the fog started to lift.

"So where were you tonight, really?" he asked, elbows on the table as he watched me Hoover my last slice of bacon.

"Already told you," I said around it.

"This doesn't have anything to do with Feliks Zhirov, does it?"

"No," I said. At least, not directly. I glanced up from my breakfast. "Why would you ask that?"

"No reason." His eyes slid away from me. They darted around the restaurant as if he was ready for the check. "You finished?" he asked as I used my last bite of waffle to soak up a puddle of syrup and shoved it in my mouth. It stuck in my throat as I thought of Vero, alone, back in that hotel suite. I hoped she'd ordered food and was getting a few hours of sleep, though I was guessing if she had the choice between room service with two dead guys or a waffle breakfast with Steven, she'd probably agree she was getting the better end of the bargain. I swiped my syrupy fingers against my paper napkin. "I can't eat another bite."

"I saw a sign for the bathrooms by the door. Why don't you go wash up. I'll handle the bill."

I meandered back through the diner, smiling at the hostess as I passed her station on the way to the ladies' room. A young woman in a server's apron stood in front of the sink, applying her makeup and fixing her hair, probably getting ready for her shift. Her purse sat on the countertop, her cell phone sticking out of the open zipper. "Would you mind if I used your phone?" I asked her. "I seem to have lost mine. I just need to call my roommate and make sure she doesn't worry."

She gave me a quick once-over in the mirror before passing me her phone.

"Thanks." I carried it a few feet away and googled the number for the Villagio. When the front desk answered, I asked to be connected to Marco's suite. The phone rang several times before the call connected. The woman who answered had a thick, nasal New Jersey accent that sounded suspiciously like my literary agent, Sylvia. "Mr. Toscano's room. This is his assistant speaking. How may I help you?"

"It's me," I said in a low voice, cupping a hand around the phone.

"Oh, thank god," Vero said as she released a held breath. "Where've you been? I've been texting you."

"I got locked out of my room and I don't have my phone. I had to borrow one from a woman in a restaurant bathroom. Don't ask . . . it's a long story," I said, glancing back at the mirror as the waitress swiped on her mascara. "Everything okay?"

"The two dead dudes put a damper on the whole room service experience, but the eggs Benedict was pretty damn good."

"Did you find anything in Marco's phone?" The waitress had begun packing up her cosmetics, suggesting my conversation with Vero was about to be cut short.

"Not yet. I'm still going through all of his contacts, trying to figure out who all these people are. He uses a lot of nicknames, probably so he doesn't get caught doing business with shady people. He texted someone named *S.H.* right after we left the restaurant last night. Marco gave *S.H.* his suite number at the Villagio with instructions to meet him here. Said he had something he needed to move."

"Think it was the Aston Martin?"

"It had to be. But I can't find anything about who this *S.H.* is or where they might have taken Javi and the car."

"What about that *G.G.* person who texted Marco last night? They said something about making an exchange. You think they might have had something to do with it?"

"Good thinking. I'll keep looking and see what else I can dig up on Marco's phone."

"I'm heading back to the Royal Flush in a few minutes. Text me if you find anything. I'll call you from our room."

I disconnected and deleted the number from the woman's call log before passing the phone back to her with a polite "thanks." As I left the bathroom, I spotted Steven crossing the diner toward me. There was something suspicious about his brisk pace and the intense way he was staring right at me. His eyes darted to the server's station as he hurried toward me and turned me around.

"What are you doing—*Ow*, Steven! What's wrong with you?"

"Come on. We've got to get out of here," he said, tucking me close to his side as he wedged open the glass door and pushed me toward the street.

"Hey, wait!" a woman called behind us. "You didn't pay your bill!"

Steven grabbed me by my sleeve and broke into a run. He bolted down a side street as the waitress shouted after us. My lungs were burning, my breath too fast to manage any words as he cut hard to the right and onto the boardwalk. We zigzagged down a wooden ramp, our feet kicking up sand as he pulled me down the beach. He turned to look over his shoulder, making sure no one was following us before slowing to a walk.

He bent over his knees, panting hard, a shit-eating grin on his stupid face when he finally looked up at me.

"You didn't pay the check?" I snapped, kicking sand at him.

"I didn't have my wallet."

"When you suggested we go out for breakfast, I assumed you had some cash! Why would you offer to take me to breakfast if you didn't have any money?"

"Because I wanted to! How's that for honesty?" He paced away from me as we both caught our breath. He turned toward the surf, wiping sweat from his brow as he dropped down onto the sand.

"What are you doing?" I asked, as he rested his elbows on his knees. "We should go inside. It's freezing out here. And someone from the restaurant probably called the police."

"It was a thirty-dollar breakfast, Finn. Nobody's gonna come looking for us." He tugged me down onto the cold sand beside him. "If you leave now, you'll miss the best part." He gestured with his chin toward the ocean, his expression hard to read in the dusky predawn light. "Remember when we first started dating," he asked wistfully, "when we used to stay up all night and watch the sun come up?"

"You mean the nights you made me play designated driver, chauffeuring you and your friends to parties until you got too drunk to stay awake anymore?" I nodded, a deep, exaggerated dip of my head. "Yeah, I remember those sunrises a little differently."

I waited for him to argue. To play back the memories as he had reshaped them in his own mind, but for once he was quiet. So quiet I peeped at him sideways to make sure he hadn't died. Maybe it was hyperbolic to think it, but it had been a very long night, and I wasn't exactly batting a thousand.

"I was a real son of a bitch, wasn't I?" he said thoughtfully, and maybe a little contrite. "Is it so crazy to think things could be different if we gave it a second chance?"

"It's crazy that you think I haven't already."

He winced. "So you and Nick . . . you two are serious?"

I sighed as I considered that. "I'd like it to be." Whether or not it *could* be depended heavily on the next three days, and I hated how much of that felt out of my control.

"Did you . . . you know"—Steven gestured around us and rolled his eyes—"do it on the beach? Like in your book?"

I laughed. "What is this? Twenty questions?"

"I'm game if you are."

"I'm not playing twenty questions with you."

"Why not? Afraid of what you might confess?" The gleam in his eyes felt like a dare. The same one he used to pin me with when we were in college, when he'd slide a red plastic cup of some unidentifiable concoction across the table toward me, his eyelids already heavy with booze, waiting for me to hesitate, like I always did, before tossing me his truck keys and drinking it himself, making some wisecrack about me being a Goody Two-shoes. But those games revealed more about him than they ever had about me. And I had a few questions about Steven I still needed answers to.

"No," I said curtly. "We didn't do it on the beach." He smirked as if he'd expected as much. "We did it in his bed, on his desk, and against the wall in his dorm room. But the rest of the details you read in my book were all true. My turn," I declared as his smug grin faltered. "How many women did you sleep with while you were married to me?" I wasn't sure why I asked, or if I even wanted to know the answer. Mostly, I just wanted to see if he'd be honest with me.

"You really want me to answer that?" I waited as his gaze slid back to the shoreline. "Too many," he admitted. "I could try to count them . . . pull some number out of my ass, but I'd probably forget a few." His answer stung more than I'd thought it would. Maybe because it felt like the first honest one he'd ever given me and suddenly I wished he hadn't. "We don't have to play anymore. You're right, it was a stupid idea," he said, kicking at the sand.

"Are you quitting?"

He turned to look at me, staring at me with that same curiosity he'd worn after I'd saved him from *EasyClean* and whisked him away in the

Aston Martin, like he should have known the woman who was behind the wheel but he wasn't sure he recognized me. "Do you ever miss what we had together? You know . . . our family?"

"We still have our family," I said. "We don't have to live under the same roof for that."

"You know what I mean. Do you ever miss *me*?"

The answer to that was complicated, but Steven had never been one for nuance. "I'm happy, for the first time in a long time. I'd like to hold on to that."

He nodded at my answer, which wasn't really an answer at all, but seemed to satisfy his need for one. "Your turn," he said quietly.

"Have you ever done something really horrible you never told me about?"

"What I just confessed to you wasn't horrible enough?"

"I mean, have you ever . . ." I wasn't sure how to frame the question. *Have you ever hurt someone* seemed too subjective, easy to slip around and avoid answering directly. *Have you ever broken a law* was too broad. Speeding on the interstate, rolling through a STOP sign, misrepresenting your taxable income to the IRS, dine and ditch . . . he'd done all of those things, but those weren't the kinds of crimes I was concerned about. "Have you ever committed a major felony?"

He barked out a laugh. "Other than the one I committed with you? No, Finlay," he deadpanned, "besides burying my murdered business partner on my farm for you, I've never committed a major felony."

"You swear?"

"I swear. *Jesus*." Something about the way he shook his head made me believe him. "Why do you always do this? Try to make me out to be a bad guy? What's this really about?"

"Nothing," I said, feeling foolish for asking. Steven had always been a petty, womanizing, lying opportunist, but I had a hard time believing he'd ever been a cold-blooded, remorseless villain, and I hated that *EasyClean*'s parting words to me had given me a reason to doubt that. "You're the one who wanted to play. Whose turn is it anyway?"

"I lost count," he said irritably. We sat in silence, both of us squinting at the sun as it breached the horizon. Steven's sigh was heavy when he finally spoke. "If you're in trouble, you know you can come to me, Finn. Whatever you need, you can ask me. It doesn't have to be a game."

What I needed was an alibi. Someone who could say I had been with them last night. All night. But with Steven, trust had always been a game. I knew if I asked him to lie for me—to tell my mother and the police we'd spent the night together—he would. But that was one sip too many from a cup I should never have drunk from in the first place. I got up and dusted the sand from my pants. "I'm not in trouble," I said. At least, I wasn't yet.

Sand shed itself from my clothes as Steven and I boarded the elevator. I caught my ruddy-cheeked reflection in the mirrored wall and smoothed down my hair, scratching loose the tiny grains still clinging to my scalp. I was pretty sure I was carrying half the beach inside my sneakers.

The doors opened on our floor. Steven held out an arm, gesturing for me to go first. I took a step out and froze at the unmistakable sound of my sister's cop voice, booming down the hall.

Steven stiffened as he registered it, too. "What the hell is your sister doing here?" he whispered, cowering in the elevator.

"Shit," I whispered. I had no idea. We hadn't been gone more than ninety minutes. Not nearly long enough for my mother to have organized a search party. I peered around the corner and nearly lost my waffles. My sister wasn't alone.

I reached back into the elevator and pressed the button for the lobby. Then I smacked the button to shut the elevator doors before Steven could get out.

"What the hell, Finn—?" His protests faded as the doors slid closed between us and the elevator began its descent.

The scene in the hallway in front of me was pure chaos. The occupants of the two rooms directly across the hall from ours were being escorted from their accommodations, luggage in hand, confusion on their faces. A hotel manager helped carry their bags, guiding them past me toward the elevators while murmuring profuse apologies. My sister watched, hands on her hips, a badge clipped to her belt.

A man wearing an FBI windbreaker stood beside her, arms crossed over his chest. Luggage and computer bags lined the length of the wall. Housekeeping staff scurried between the two empty rooms, carrying fresh linens and towels and stripping the beds.

I tapped my sister on the shoulder. "What's going on here?" A small voice in the back of my mind reminded me that I might not want to know the answer to that question.

Georgia's face broke into a wide smile as she clapped me on the back. "Hey, Finn! Check it out, we're going to be neighbors."

"Neighbors?"

Another familiar face popped out of the room that had just been cleared by the hotel manager. "Hey, Finlay. It's good to see you." Detective Samara Becker, IT specialist and my sister's shiny new crush, leaned out the door to wave at me. A long curtain of dark hair fell over the shoulder of her cashmere sweater as she batted her eyelashes at my sister. "What are the room arrangements, Georgia? I figured girls in one room and the guys could take the other. That is, if you're okay with that?"

Blood rushed to my sister's face. She cleared her throat with a tight nod, answering in her serious cop voice. "Yep. Men in one room and women in the other seems . . . logical."

"Great," Sam said, revealing a full set of pearly whites that rivaled any toothpaste ad. "I'm just setting up our Wi-Fi while housekeeping finishes. I'll be done in a sec. And don't touch our bags," she said, shaking a finger at the bandages on Georgia's hand. "Doctor's orders, remember? I'll carry them in."

"Your bags?"

My sister held up a gauze-wrapped arm. "I'm on leave until the doc gives me the green light to go back to work. Figured I'd come along and see what everyone was up to." Georgia shrugged. "Didn't have anything better to do."

"So you brought the FBI?"

Georgia's FBI friend extended his hand, ignoring my brusque tone. "Garrett Stokes," he said by way of introduction. "Good to meet you. I've heard a lot about you."

A desperate laugh bubbled out of me.

"Agent Stokes works on the joint task force with Nick," Georgia explained, stepping aside to let the housekeeping crew by. She lowered her voice and leaned close to my ear. "He offered to help us get rooms on your floor since we're a little out of our jurisdiction here."

"Out of your jurisdiction for what?"

Sam returned to collect an armful of bags. "Don't mind me," she said at my slack-jawed expression. "I just came along to keep your sister company. I had a few days of leave I needed to burn, and your sister isn't supposed to be lifting anything with that hand."

The door to my room flew open behind me. "What kind of nonsense is going on out here? It's too early for all this ruckus. If you all don't quiet down, I'll report you to . . ." Georgia and I turned around to find my mother gaping at us, her sleep mask pushed up on her forehead, making her hair stand up. She held the door open with one hand and her robe closed with the other. Behind her, Delia and Zach were jumping on my empty, unmade bed. Cartoons played on the TV, Cheerios and toys strewn like a trail of bread crumbs between the open doors of their connected rooms. "Georgia?" my mother said with a gasp. "Why aren't you at home with your father?"

"Don't worry. I left Dad a note and took one of the casseroles out of the freezer for him. He'll probably be on the couch watching football all weekend. He won't even know I'm gone."

"What's all this?" our mother asked, frowning at the piles of luggage.

"I was just asking her the same thing. Will someone please tell me what's going on?" I begged.

Sam beamed as she extended a hand to my mother. "You must be Susan! It's wonderful to meet you."

"And you are?" my mother asked her, casting dubious glances at the bright white letters on Agent Stokes's jacket.

"Samara Becker. But please, call me Sam. I'm Georgia's—"

"Friend from work," my sister rushed to finish for her. Agent Stokes coughed into his hand. My mother's gaze leaped from his smirk to my sister's bright red cheeks. Our mother's eyes widened as they returned to Sam. I was pretty sure she was fitting my sister's new girlfriend for a wedding dress.

"Oh," my mother breathed, keeping one foot wedged in the door as she reached eagerly for Sam's hand. "Oh, Georgina, she's gorgeous! And so put together." My mother smoothed her bed-matted hair, then her robe, one hand holding stubbornly to Sam's as if Sam might disappear if she let go. "Look at me, I'm a mess! I'm so embarrassed."

"You look lovely," Sam assured her. "We didn't mean to sneak up on you like this."

I glared at my sister. She raised her hands in mock surrender. "Sorry, Finn. We left the station in the middle of the night, and Nick didn't think we should call and wake you."

I nearly choked. "Nick's here?"

Everyone turned as a door opened across the hall. I'm pretty sure I stopped breathing as Nick emerged from the room directly across from Steven's. His eyes found mine, his pace quickening as he maneuvered past the stacks of luggage to get to me. He paused beside my mother, his leather jacket stretching open to reveal his holster and his badge as he bent to plant a quick kiss on her cheek.

"Hi, Susan. It's good to see you," he said in a rush. "Sorry, but I need to steal Finlay for a few minutes. Official police business," he explained as he reached for my elbow.

"What's going on?" I asked as he steered me past FCPD duffel bags and laptop totes, into his room.

"Can we have the room, please?" Nick took a stack of linens from the remaining housekeeping staff, ushering them quickly to the hall, leaving the beds unfinished. He closed the door behind them and slid the dead bolt in place.

"Nick, what are you all doing—?"

He took my face in his hands, his mouth hungry on mine as he walked me backward toward the bed. He smelled like coffee and pep-permint. "Jesus, I missed you."

"It's only been two days."

"Way too long."

"Why didn't you tell me you were coming?"

"Tried to reach you last night." His five o'clock shadow trailed down my neck, leaving goose bumps in its wake. "Texted you again when we got here."

His fingers slid under the hem of my sweatshirt and my thoughts scrambled. "I went out for breakfast and forgot my phone."

He captured my lower lip between his. "Mmm . . . Pancakes?"

"And bacon."

A moan rumbled through his chest as his hand dipped into the back pocket of my jeans, drawing me closer. His brow furrowed as he broke our kiss. "Is that sand?"

I put a palm to the front of his Henley, holding him back as I reined in my hormones, which had apparently already slapped on a set of hand-cuffs and surrendered to him. His cheeks were flushed, the dark waves of his hair mussed, his pupils wide and his eyes a little manic, like he'd been using truck-stop coffee to keep them open all night.

"What's going on?" I asked, putting distance between us so I wouldn't be tempted to shove my tongue back down his throat. "And why is your entire department here?"

Nick sank onto the bed. He clasped his hands between his knees as he looked me in the eyes. "Just . . . promise me you won't panic."

"Panic about what?" I asked, already starting to panic.

"An anonymous tip came into the station last night. Someone called in, claiming to be a member of Feliks Zhirov's inner circle. He said that Feliks is on his way back to the United States."

"But he just got to Brazil."

Nick nodded. "I know. And it may be nothing. The tip line gets doz-ens of calls every day, and most of them are just kids with nothing better to do, or people wanting attention, but . . ."

"But what?" I pressed.

His hand tightened around my hip, like he was bracing me for something. "Remember the news story that broke last week, about the car that was found burned in a cornfield in Culpeper County?" My skin rippled with goose bumps. He was talking about Ike Grindley's car. As far as I knew, no one had found Ike's body, but his car had been set ablaze on a remote stretch of farm. One of his gold teeth had been delivered to me at the academy that same night, letting me know Feliks had made good on his promise, and reminding me that it could just as easily be undone. "The registered owner of the car is a man named Ignacious Grindley. He's from Pleasantville, New Jersey, about twenty minutes from here. His wife reported him missing two weeks ago. She said he went to Virginia on a business trip and never made it home. According to the detective working the case, Grindley had a pretty long rap sheet, and his wife was a little cagey about the kind of business her husband was involved in."

"What does this have to do with Feliks?"

"We're not sure yet. But Culpeper County PD got a call from a gas station a few miles from where Ike's vehicle was discovered. Grindley's car was spotted there the night he disappeared, only Grindley wasn't driving it. The driver filled a gas can, paid cash, and took off. Investigators identified him from camera footage taken inside the store. He's a known member of the Russian mob, one of Feliks's thugs. Which means somehow, Feliks and Grindley are connected."

My mouth went dry. I was the one who'd struck a deal with Feliks's cleanup crew to dispose of Ike's body. "I still don't understand what any of this has to do with why you're here."

"Agent Stokes checked into that lead that came through the tip line last night. Turns out a flight plan was registered yesterday morning, by a private charter plane flying out of São Paulo, Brazil. It's set to arrive at an airstrip in Newark. One of the names on the passenger manifest is a loose variation of an alias Zhirov has used before. Stokes thinks there's a chance that tip was legit."

"Newark? But that's—"

"Less than two hours from here," Nick finished.

I stood up. "You think Feliks is coming here?"

"We don't know. He could be meeting someone in New York or catching a connecting flight overseas. For all we know, this could have nothing to do with you. Feliks might not even be on that flight. But you witnessed him try to murder a police officer and Vero can place him at the scene, which makes both of you a threat to him. And given what we know about Grindley's boss, we have a very compelling reason to believe Zhirov has connections in Atlantic City."

"Who's Grindley's boss?" I asked cautiously.

"According to our contacts in the local PD, Grindley works for a loan shark named Marco Toscano. I don't know how Feliks and Toscano are connected, but I'd sure like to ask him a few questions and find out."

My throat closed around the thought. It was me. *I* was the connection. Marco Toscano had probably never even heard the name Feliks Zhirov. They were a Venn diagram of criminal organizations that never should have crossed, but they did, in the thin sliver of a single night, when Marco sent Ike to find us and collect Vero's debt. I had been the one to link the rings when I'd agreed to let Feliks dispose of Ike's body for me. Nick just couldn't see all the pieces to know how the two circles connected yet, but if he went looking for Marco, he was certain to figure it out.

I swallowed. "Aren't you a little outside of your jurisdiction here?"

"That's why Agent Stokes agreed to come along. Hopefully he can grease a few wheels for me while I'm in town. That flight isn't scheduled to land in New Jersey until Sunday afternoon. That gives me plenty of time to talk to Grindley's wife and track down his boss. If I can figure out why Feliks is coming, maybe I can predict his next move before he gets here. Meanwhile, I don't plan to let you or Vero out of my sight. Not until I know for a fact he's not on that plane or the FBI has him in custody." Nick's eyes drifted toward the door. "Where is Vero, by the way?"

I groped for an answer. "She . . . met up with an old friend last night and spent the night at his place."

Some of the tension left Nick's shoulders. "Good. Neither of you should be alone for a while. Agent Stokes and I will be at Newark when that charter plane lands. If everything goes according to plan, we'll arrest Zhirov and haul his ass back to Virginia for trial. Until then, you're sticking close to me."

"So you got an anonymous call and some circumstantial evidence about a burned-up car, and you just decided to pack up the entire FCPD and bring them here to babysit me?"

"I'm not here to babysit you," he said, holding up his hands and lowering his voice. "I'm here because something doesn't smell right with Grindley's disappearance, and because I don't trust Zhirov as far as I can throw him. I know perfectly well you can take care of yourself." Nick gave the front of my sweatshirt a gentle tug. He pulled me closer, until I was standing between his legs. "But I also know what Feliks is capable of, and I wouldn't be able to live with myself if I didn't follow my gut on this and something happened to you." He kissed me, a slow, testing brush of his lips, but I was too distracted to relax into him. How were Vero and I supposed to find Javi and the Aston with Nick clinging to me like a big, sexy shadow?

"What's wrong?" He cupped my chin, capturing my distracted gaze. "We're okay, right?"

"Yeah, we're okay. It's just . . ." I cleared my throat, willing myself to just spit it out. "I have something I need to tell you, too." Nick frowned as he studied my face. I took a deep breath and blurted, "Steven is here. He's staying with the kids, in the adjoining room. I'm sleeping with my mom. And Vero. Or at least, I would be, if Vero was here." I shook my head, my confession devolving into babble. "See, it was supposed to be a girls' trip, but Steven refused to let me take the kids out of the state without him, and he insisted on—"

"I know." He brushed my hair back from my face.

"You do?" He raised an eyebrow, waiting for me to catch on. I

slapped a hand to my forehead. "Georgia told you." His smirk told me
I was right. "I'm sorry," I said, genuinely remorseful. "I know it should
have come from me. I just didn't want you to get the wrong idea. Steven and I aren't even staying in the same room, and if Vero and my
mother had their way, we'd have left him on the side of the highway
in Pennsylvan—"

Nick shut me up with a kiss. A deep, lingering one that made my
heart melt and my toes curl.

Steven's voice boomed down the hall, followed by the unmistakable
squeals of my children. I pressed my forehead to Nick's, lightheaded and
breathy. "If we stay in here much longer, they're going to wonder what
we're doing."

"All the more reason to stay," he murmured, leaning in again.

There was a knock on the adjoining door to Georgia and Sam's
room before it cracked open. I stiffened at the familiar scarred face that
peeked into Nick's room.

"I hate to break up this little reunion, roomie, but if you two dally in
here much longer, there might be a crime scene in the hallway." Charlie
Cox, Nick's former partner and closest friend, greeted me with a casual
nod, as if he hadn't stolen a suitcase full of money from me, threatened
my life, and dumped me out of his car with a warning to leave town
less than forty-eight hours ago. Charlie was a dirty cop—albeit a retired
one—and he'd been making a comfortable living since as a "fixer" for
Feliks Zhirov. Nick had no idea his former partner was passing information to the Russian mob and recruiting cops to handle Feliks's dirty
work. And Charlie had made it clear that if Vero and I didn't want to
end up dead or in prison, we wouldn't breathe a word of it to anyone.
"Good to see you, Finlay." Charlie winked at me with his good eye as he
pulled the door closed again.

"You okay?"

I dragged my gaze back to Nick at the sound of his voice. "Just surprised. What's Charlie doing here?"

"He offered to come. Guess he figured I could use the help. He's going to stay and keep an eye on you and Vero while Garrett and I poke around town and look for Toscano." Was it time to panic yet? Because I was definitely panicking. Nick grinned as he tucked a lock of hair behind my ear. "You and Charlie were thick as thieves at the academy last week, I figured you wouldn't mind." I tried not to wince at his choice of words. I *had* liked Charlie, quite a bit. Right up until he'd shown me who he truly was.

I had no grand delusions that Charlie was here out of concern for me *or* Nick. If Charlie offered to come, it was because Nick was about to step on Feliks's toes, and it was Charlie's job to run interference. Deep down, Charlie liked Nick, maybe even loved him, but money had a way of making people careless, and I had no doubt Charlie would throw every one of us to the wolves if it meant preserving his seat at Zhirov's table.

"What about Joey? He's your partner. Shouldn't he be here instead?" Even Joey Balafonte would be preferable to Charlie.

Nick shook his head. "I needed someone I can trust. And Joe . . ." Nick's mouth thinned. Joey and Nick had been partners for months before he'd learned that Joey was a mole for Internal Affairs, investigating their department. Overnight, Joey had become a pariah to everyone he worked with, which was a shame because Joey was actually one of the good guys. He was also the only person in the department who suspected Charlie wasn't. But while Joey and I were technically still on the same team, he was also growing a little too suspicious of me.

Nick sighed deeply and rubbed his bloodshot eyes. "Joey's got a concussion. He should be home getting some rest."

"Maybe you should be, too. Haven't you earned a little time off?"

"I am off. Commander's orders," he explained. "Mandatory leave pending an internal investigation into the incident on the fire tower the other night. Joey and Wade, too." He gave my hand a reassuring squeeze. "Nothing to worry about. It's all standard procedure. And since I'm not on the clock," he said, placing a soft kiss on my collarbone, then another on my neck. "And I've got no statements to take . . ."

Another a bit higher. "And no reports to write . . ." Another below my jaw. ". . . you have my undivided attention . . ." I arched into him and shivered. "So how about you let me take you out to dinner tonight? And after that . . ." His lips grazed the shell of my ear. ". . . what do you say we come back here?"

"What about Charlie and Agent Stokes?"

His breath fanned my face, his mouth grazing mine. "Garrett's here on the FBI's dime. He's got a single down the hall. Charlie can crash with him for a few hours." He took me gently behind my knee, easing me onto his lap as he kissed me thoroughly, throwing both of our libidos into overdrive.

Voices carried down the hall. First Steven's, then my sister's, their argument growing louder. Nick dropped his head against my shoulder with a frustrated sigh.

"We should probably go break that up before he gives my sister a defensible reason to shoot him." The last thing I needed was one more crime scene to clean up. I rolled off Nick's lap and towed him to his feet, forgetting the healing gunshot wound in his thigh.

"Sorry," I said, mirroring his wince. He favored his injured leg as he followed me to the door. The ruckus outside grew louder as I opened it. Zach and Delia squealed, assaulting Nick with tackle hugs the moment they spotted him and plowing into his thigh. Nick held back a wince as he scooped them up, one in each arm. Steven's jaw tensed as he looked on.

"We saw you on TV!" Delia exclaimed. "Where's Officer Roddy? And Officer Ty?" she asked, lisping through her missing front teeth.

"They couldn't come this time, kiddo. They had to work."

Delia pouted. "Will *you* watch cartoons with us?"

"Absolutely," he said. "But only if I get to pick the show."

"You can watch TV after you both have something to eat," my mother interjected. "Delia and Zach haven't had breakfast yet, and if we don't feed them soon, we'll have a mutiny on our hands. I'm sure there must be an open restaurant nearby."

"One of us should go with you," Nick said, directing a meaningful look at my sister.

"I'll go," Georgia offered, reaching for Zach.

"Why don't we all go?" my mother suggested. "You all must be hungry after driving all night."

"I'm starving," Sam agreed. "I'll get my coat."

"I could eat," Nick said. "You coming, Charlie?"

Charlie's eyes caught mine and held. "I was thinking I might stay here and catch a little shut-eye. You all go on without me."

"What about Vero?" my mother asked.

"I'll call her." I spun for the door my mother had left propped open. Nick stopped me before I could disappear inside. "Vero shouldn't walk to the restaurant alone," he said in a low voice. "Find out where she is. One of us will pick her up." His eyes dropped to my mouth as if he were thinking about kissing it. He pressed a chaste kiss to my temple instead, probably because Steven was watching. I slipped into my room and closed the door.

The cartoons were blaring on the TV inside. I found the remote control and shut it off. I dropped onto the bed and buried my head in my hands, listening to the muffled conversations in the hall as they all dispersed to gather their coats. The children burst into Steven's adjoining room, their cheers loud enough to permeate the walls as they squealed about pancakes. My mother hollered over the din, ordering them to take off their pajamas and put on their clothes.

Steven banged on the door between our rooms. I ignored him as he called my name through it. How was I going to hide two dead bodies, come up with an alibi for last night, and get Vero back here before Nick started putting the pieces together?

Steven pounded louder, rattling the door. I shot to my feet and unbolted it. He yanked it open, falling back slightly.

He recovered and pointed toward the hall. "Did you know your detective friend was coming?"

"Does it look like I knew? I'm just as surprised as you are."

"He doesn't need to be here, Finn. I can take care of my own damn family."

"He was just worried about us. He only wanted to help."

"I want to help, but you never let me!"

"You really want to help me?"

The question knocked him back on his heels. "Of course I do."

I pulled him into my room and closed the connecting door, muting the children's excited chatter as my mother rummaged under the beds for their shoes. I glanced behind me at the door separating us from the detectives in the hall. I lowered my voice, wondering if I could trust Steven with this one small thing. His eyes were alert, his posture eager, as if his whole body were leaning in to hear. "This is how you can help. If anyone asks, I was here in my room, asleep, all last night—"

"But you said—"

"I know what I said, Steven."

His brow creased. "Are you in some kind of trouble?"

"Not if you help me." It was a risk, leveraging his desire to prove himself, but I was running out of options. "I was here all night," I repeated. "Vero was out with a friend. I left the door open between your room and mine, and you checked on me before you went downstairs to the casino. Then you checked on me again when you came back to bed. As far as you know, I never left this room and I was asleep the whole time." Steven's frown deepened. He nodded tightly.

"Okay," he said.

I released a breath. "Are you coming to breakfast?"

His jaw worked as he wrestled with that. "I think I'll stay here and catch a nap," he said as he retreated to his room. He started to close the door.

"Keep it open," I said. If the door to Steven's room was open, maybe Charlie wouldn't be tempted to snoop. Steven threw me a questioning look as he left the door cracked.

I sent a quick text message to Vero and tucked my phone in my coat pocket, my eyes making a quick pass over the room, looking for anything incriminating that Charlie—or even Steven—might find if either one of them decided to poke around while I was gone. I clutched my laptop bag to my chest, looking for a safe place to stash it. If I were Charlie or Steven, that's the first place I'd snoop, but my computer was password protected and I'd been careful to clear my search history. The only questionable file on the desktop was my manuscript, and the only incriminating details in that had more to do with my sex life than with Marco or Ike.

Georgia's voice boomed through the door as she knocked. "You coming, Finn?"

"I'll be out in a minute," I hollered back. I squashed my computer bag flat under a pile of dirty towels. Something small and shiny slipped free of the open zipper. I swore as Ike's gold-capped tooth bounced over the carpet.

In all the chaos of the last two days, I'd forgotten all about it.

Feliks had slipped it into my computer bag while I'd been chin-deep at the police academy, along with a note, reminding me not to step out of line. God (and Feliks) only knew where the rest of Ike was. I hoped Vero and I (and the police) never had to find out.

I stuffed the tooth into the pocket of my coat.

"Everything okay in there?" Nick asked through the door.

"Everything's fine!" I called. I shredded Feliks's note and dropped the pieces into the toilet. "I'll be right there!" I thought about throwing the tooth in with it as I pushed the lever to flush it, but I couldn't be sure the toilet wouldn't cough it up after I was gone.

I wasn't taking any chances this time.

I wiped my hands on my jeans, giving the room one last check as I reached for the door. Nick's hand was poised to knock as I drew it open. His eyes narrowed on my face.

"You okay?" he asked as I smoothed back my hair and discreetly wiped my brow. "You look a little pale."

"Just hungry," I said, pasting on a smile.

"I thought you said you just ate."

I blinked at him, backpedaling. "I did . . . earlier. Before my walk. Must be all that fresh ocean air. Guess I worked up an appetite."

"Great. Where's Vero staying? We'll pick her up on our way."

"She's not coming," I said. Nick frowned, worry lines etching deep around his eyes. "She and her friend are ordering room service, and they don't plan to go out. I told her to call me when she's ready to come back to the hotel." His hand tightened a little around mine, as if he were wrestling against his instinct to keep us both safe. "Let's go. I'm starving," I said, plying him with a kiss as I led him out the door.

CHAPTER 8

I spent the next torturous hour pretending to be hungry as I took nibbles from a stack of pancakes while my mom battered Sam and Nick with cringeworthy questions about their families, their thoughts on marriage, and their experiences with small children. Delia chimed in to ask where babies came from and Zach erupted into a full-blown tantrum, demanding to be let down from his booster seat. Georgia and I took turns redirecting the conversation to safer ground between attempts to keep Zach from eating the complimentary crayons and Delia from using a straw to drink the river of syrup on her plate. By the end of the meal, my kids were so strung out on high-fructose corn syrup and red dye number forty, I was sure they would implode if we didn't let them run it off.

We took the longer route back to the hotel, by way of the boardwalk, where we could safely let them down to chase a few seagulls. Georgia ran ahead of them, surveilling the sand for discarded syringes, used condoms, and broken glass. I took up the rear like a frantic sheepdog, keeping Delia from poking at washed-up jellyfish and half-buried trash bags and herding Zach away from the water's edge so his shoes wouldn't get wet. Nick and Sam looked exhausted just watching us. Our mother walked contentedly between them, lobbing questions like grenades between barrages of commentary on what makes a marriage work. By the time we finally made it back to our floor, I wouldn't have blamed either one of them if they'd decided to pack up and go home.

After what seemed like an eternity, we returned to our room. I held the door open for the kids as they tumbled inside, leaving a path of sandy footprints on the carpet and sticky fingerprints on the walls. My mom wrangled them directly into the bathroom, ordering them to take off their clothes, their excited chatter muted by the loud rush of the faucet in the tub.

Nick stood in the doorway of my room, holding it open with his shoulder. "I had fun this morning," he said softly, his lips turning up with a wry smile as if he knew what I was thinking. "I'm serious. Your mom is great."

"She's . . . a lot," I said with a weary laugh. "I'm surprised Sam isn't running for the hills. For that matter, why aren't you?"

"It'll take a lot more than a tantrum and a few minutes in the hot seat to scare me off. I'm trained in de-escalation and interrogation. Face it, you're stuck with me." He put an arm around my waist, drawing me closer. A persistent vibration in my pocket reminded me that this, indeed, was the problem; Nick wasn't going to be distracted easily. "You should probably answer that," he said. "It might be Vero. Find out where she is and I'll have Sam pick her up." He checked his phone, too. "Charlie's gone out for a few hours. Probably hitting a few casinos." Nick slipped his phone back into his pocket and rubbed his eyes. "I'm going to grab a hot shower and a nap while he's gone. I could use a rest before Garrett and I head to the station to meet with the local PD. Text me if you need anything. I'll be right across the hall." He cast a glance over my shoulder toward the adjoining room as he kissed me goodbye.

I locked the door behind him and took a quick look around. With the exception of the sand the kids had tracked in, everything appeared the same as I'd left it but slightly off, like looking at one of those side-by-side photos and trying to pick out the tiny differences. I peeked into Steven's open door. He was sprawled on his back on his bed. A ball cap covered his eyes and his mouth parted around a snore.

I shut the door between our rooms as quietly as I could, listening for any sign that the sound had woken him. Contented splashing sounds came from the bathroom. Zach babbled as my mother deflected Delia's relentless questions about how babies are made.

"But how does God put them in there?"

"With nagging and wine."

"He turns wine into a baby?"

"Something like that," my mother muttered as the faucet cut off.

My phone vibrated again and I whipped it out. There were no new messages from Vero. Just a string of missed calls and a text from an unknown phone number. The area code was from Virginia.

Call me as soon as you get this.—C

C? I ran through a mental list of every person I knew whose name started with the letter C. The only one who came to mind was Cam, the seventeen-year-old computer whiz I'd hired last fall while trying to sleuth out *EasyClean*'s identity. I'd only recently learned that Cam was also Joey's nephew and a confidential informant for the FCPD, which made Cam a double agent of sorts, since he'd also taken a job working as a hacker for Feliks Zhirov.

With a muttered swear, I tapped the number on my screen.

Cam answered on the first ring. "It's about damn time. What took you so long?" The chatter of his teeth was muffled by the howl of wind against his phone.

I lowered my voice in case anyone was lingering in the hall. "Where have you been? Your Uncle Joey and I have been worried sick about you." The last time anyone had seen Cam, he'd been roped into doing some pretty horrible things for Feliks, and he was now wanted for questioning by the cops.

"I ran into a little problem. I need to see you."

"You can't see me. I'm in New Jersey."

"I know. So am I."

"You're *what*?!"

"Look out your window." I rushed to the window and pulled back the curtain, searching the boardwalk below. "To your left," he clarified. I craned my neck, but the boardwalk appeared empty except for a jogger, a street sweeper, and a homeless man sleeping on a bench. Beyond them, a massive Ferris wheel loomed through the fog. "Meet me at the Wheel on Steel Pier at noon."

"I can't do that. The entire FCPD just showed up at my hotel."

"Is my uncle there?"

"No, he's in Virginia." Cam released a breath. "Cam, what's going on?"

"Just get to the pier. And come alone. You owe me," he reminded me as he disconnected.

I pressed my fingers to my eyes, already cursing myself for what I knew I was going to do, because Cam was right. I did owe him. He'd saved my life twice in one night, betraying the Russian mob to protect me. And now he was here, a wanted minor, alone in a strange city, looking for me.

I checked the time. I had almost two hours before my meeting with Cam at Steel Pier. Nick was sleeping, Charlie was out somewhere, and my children were in the bathtub, fed and happy. I set the alarm on my phone to wake me at eleven forty-five, then crawled under the comforter and closed my eyes, surrendering to a deep sleep.

I woke slowly, roused by the rattle of my phone against the nightstand. I groped for it, jabbing the screen to shut off my alarm. I rolled over and rubbed my eyes, blinking in the semidarkness, struggling to orient myself in space and time. With a gasp, I bolted out of bed and checked the clock, relieved to find only ninety minutes had passed. My mother must have closed the blinds while I'd been sleeping. She'd left a note on a piece of hotel stationery on my nightstand before she'd gone.

I put the children down for a nap with Steven.

Shopping with Georgia. Back in a few hours. Get some rest.

Love, Mom

I hurried to the bathroom and washed my face, unsure how long my window of opportunity might last. If Steven woke up, he would probably suspect I was with Nick in his room. My mother would likely assume the same, and if Sam and Georgia assumed that, too, they weren't likely to bother him.

I put on my shoes and coat and peered through the peephole to the hallway. Sam and Georgia's door was propped open wide, presumably so they could keep a closer eye on mine. Sam was inside, her back to the hall as she hovered over her laptop with the hotel phone pressed to her ear.

I cracked open my door, listening.

"I understand that you can't give me that password without permission from your manager," she said as if she were speaking to a toddler. "What I'm telling you is that I can't access your security feeds without it. I need it as soon as possible . . ."

I hurried toward the elevator as quietly as I could, wedging myself between the doors just as they started to close. I made it out of the hotel to the boardwalk, checking to make sure no one had followed me before flagging down a tram. I pulled back the plastic wind cover and folded myself into the bench seat. "Where to?" the driver asked me.

"Steel Pier," I said, recalling Cam's instructions.

The driver put the tram in gear. I held on tightly as we whipped past the boardwalk shops—candy stores, tarot card readers, and hanging racks filled with bawdy T-shirts. A woman with windbeaten hair pushed a rusty shopping cart full of trash bags, and a man wearing a sandwich board shouted about sin, waving a Bible at us as we passed. A group of teenagers paused their choreographed dance, moving their collection bucket out of the way of the tram as we hurtled toward the pier.

The massive Ferris wheel grew clearer through the gray winter haze. A familiar figure in a hooded sweatshirt paced alongside the railing below it.

"Here is good," I called up to the driver. I handed him a few dollars before slipping out of the plastic cocoon. Seagulls scattered as I ascended the ramp to the pier. The place looked abandoned, the ticket booths closed and the rides shut down. I found Cam hunched by the teacup ride. He checked to make sure I hadn't been followed before steering me behind an empty vending booth.

"I need the car," he said, fidgety and anxious.

"What car?"

Cam rolled his eyes. "What do you mean, *what car*? The Aston Martin. Where is it? I traced it to Atlantic City two days ago, but the signal in the tracker died before I made it here. Tell me you have it."

"You're tracking my car? Is this some new job you're doing for Feliks?"

Cam pulled a face. "I'm not doing this for Feliks. I left something in the car the night I helped get rid of that dude you squashed—"

"I didn't squash anyone! It was an accident. He was chasing me and I . . . oh, god . . ." I felt the blood drain from my cheeks. "Please tell me Ike Grindley's body isn't in the trunk."

"Fuck no! Do you have any idea how much that car is worth? What kind of idiot would put a body in a car like that?"

I refrained from answering that. Or from pointing out that the few times I *had* transported a body in a high-end vehicle, I had at least made sure it was frozen and tied inside several heavy-duty lawn-and-garden bags. "Then what *did* you leave in the car?"

"Something I found on Feliks's computer." Cam wiped his nose on his sleeve and jammed his hands into his pockets.

My stomach bottomed out when he refused to meet my gaze. "What did you take from him, Cameron?"

"The key to his crypto."

"Crypto? Like ... currency?" He nodded. "How much?"

"Fourteen million."

I put a hand to my head. "Jesus, Cameron!"

"And a file."

"What file?"

"A spreadsheet of everyone who's ever done a job for him, including how much they were paid. Cops included."

This was so much worse than a body in a trunk. "Why on earth would you do something like that? You might as well have painted a target on your back!"

"That's exactly why I did it, Mrs. D! The Russian mob doesn't fuck around! One wrong move and Feliks doesn't just fire you, he makes you disappear! He was pissed when he found out Joey was still alive, and he knows I had something to do with it. I needed insurance that Feliks wouldn't kill me, so as soon as he boarded that plane to Brazil, I found what I needed on his server and I took it. I wiped every last trace of those files from his system and walked away with the only copy. If his people shoot me, he'll lose the key to his crypto. Only two other people in Feliks's circle have access to his wallet—Kat, because she manages his entire fucking estate, and Charlie."

Ekaterina "Kat" Rybakov was Feliks's star attorney, but more than that, she was his secret right hand, the "Boss Bitch," as Vero liked to call her. It made sense to me that Kat would have access to such sensitive information. But as far as I could tell, Charlie was little more than a glorified lapdog to Feliks. And since Charlie was also a retired cop, it seemed a stretch that Feliks would trust Charlie so completely. "Why would Charlie have access to Feliks's money?"

"Because Charlie was the one who made me hack Feliks's private server in the first place. He made me give him a back door in so he could snoop around. That's how I found the spreadsheet and the crypto wallet in the first place—but no one can open that wallet without the key."

"And you thought you could use it as leverage against the Russian mob? Do you have any idea how crazy that sounds?"

"Not just the mob. If your boyfriend decides to arrest me for starting that fire at the academy, the list of dirty cops on that flash drive is the only thing that might get me off the hook. I needed a safe place to hide it, and you were the only person I thought I could trust, so I put the files on a thumb drive and I stashed it in your car." He swatted his eyes and his voice cracked. "I need that drive back, Mrs. D."

I wasn't sure what was worse, that Cam had no other adults in his life he trusted to protect him, or that he believed I was the only one who could.

Or did he?

"Wait," I said as another thought occurred to me. "You knew Nick was here?" Cam hadn't seemed surprised at all when I'd told him the Fairfax police were at my hotel. "*You* were the one who reported the anonymous tip to the police?"

"I needed a way to slow down Feliks's people. I knew they'd come looking for the key to his crypto. I've got spyware on Kat's phone. She called Charlie yesterday morning and told him to get his ass up here and find those files, and your boyfriend was the biggest roadblock I could throw in Charlie's way. So I picked some random charter jet with a flight plan from Brazil into New Jersey, added one of Feliks's aliases to the manifest, and fed it to the cops."

That would explain why Charlie had been so quick to offer to drive Nick and the others here—he was already planning to come.

I stared down the boardwalk, watching two seagulls fighting over scraps of a pretzel as I struggled to make sense of it all. "I don't understand. How did Kat know the key to Feliks's crypto was in Atlantic City?"

Cam shrugged, his back hunched against the biting wind. "I don't know. She must have seen me sneak into the Aston that night at the salvage yard. She probably went back looking for it as soon as she realized those files were missing. By then, I was gone and so was the car. And she would have already known you were here. She must have put it all together and figured it out."

"How would she know *I* was here?" Cam rolled his eyes, clearly annoyed that he should have to explain. I made a mental note to check my phone for spyware, too. "Aren't you in enough trouble? Wiretapping is a felony charge!"

"For the love of fake tits, Mrs. D, just tell me you know where the goddamn car is!"

"I don't."

Cam swore. He turned a slow circle, hands on his hips, staring at the sky as if he were praying for a miracle.

"We'll find it. Vero and I have a few leads," I assured him, hoping Vero had managed to figure out who *S.H.* or *G.G.* were since we'd last spoken. "But you should probably stay out of sight until we figure out where the Aston is. Do you have anywhere safe you can go?"

Frost clung to his wet lashes as he shook his head.

"You'll freeze to death out here. You can't sleep in your car."

"I don't have one," he reminded me.

"How'd you get here?"

"Hitched a ride with a trucker." He jutted his chin toward my purse. "You got anything to eat in there?"

I blew out a ribbon of steam as I searched the depths of my purse for a bag of Zach's Cheerios. Cam took it with greedy hands, shoveling the contents into his mouth by the handful.

"Come on," I said, taking him by his sleeve. He didn't try to stop me as I led him past the empty teacup ride, back down the ice-slicked ramp to the boardwalk.

"Where are we going?" he asked through a mouthful of cereal.

"To find that thumb drive before Charlie does."

CHAPTER 9

"What the hell, Mrs. D?" Cam grumbled to himself as we rolled the housekeeping cart down the hall. "Is all this cloak-and-dagger shit really necessary?" The cart slowed as he paused to scratch an itch under the pillowcase I'd tied around the short spikes of his hair like a head-scarf. The housekeeping smock just covered his knobby knees, and he adjusted his apron to conceal the laptop bag slung across his chest. His Doc Martens clomped reluctantly behind the cart as I urged him to hurry up.

"Keep your head down," I reminded him when we reached Marco's suite. I rapped on the door. There was a faint shuffling sound on the other side of the peephole. "Open up. It's me," I whispered.

"Who's that with you?" Vero asked.

"Just open the door." The dead bolt flipped and the door swung open.

Vero frowned at me. Then at Cam as his cheeks flamed. Recognition sparked white-hot in her eyes. "Oh, hell no!"

I shoved a mop in the door before she could slam it. Thrusting it into her hands, I grabbed the cart's handle and dragged it inside, pulling

Cam over the threshold with it into the suite. "He had nowhere else to go and it's freezing out there."

"Too bad," Vero said, blocking his way to the living room, "because there's no way I'm letting that conniving little thief in here."

Cam laughed. "That's rich coming from you. *I'm* not the one wanted for stealing."

Vero held up her cell phone. "I can think of a quick way to fix that."

"Enough!" I said, breaking out my mom-voice. "Nobody is reporting anybody. We have more important things to do. Like rescuing Javi." That got Vero's attention, and she pressed her mouth shut.

I untied my housekeeping apron and tossed it onto the cart. I handed Cam his hoodie and jeans from one of the compartments underneath it. "There's a bedroom down the hall on the right. You can change in there." He snatched his clothes from me, flipping Vero off.

"Whoa," he said in an awed voice as he stepped around her into the living room. "Now *this* is a hotel." Vero glared at his back as he clomped to the coffee table and lifted a silver lid off a room service platter. He stole one of Vero's uneaten french fries and licked the salt from his fingers as he chewed. "So much better than that last dump you took me to."

Vero's hands balled into fists. She gritted her teeth as Cam sauntered down the hall in his housekeeping smock and disappeared into the smaller bedroom.

There was a loud yelp and a door slammed as Kevin started barking. I rubbed my temple, feeling a headache coming on.

Vero rounded on me and stomped her foot. "I can't believe you brought him here after he tried to cook us all alive! We're supposed to be rescuing Javi, not babysitting a juvenile delinquent with mafia problems!"

"I couldn't just leave him out there. I didn't know what else to do."

Cam screamed, his horrified shriek carrying down the hall. From the left. Not the right.

"Oh, god," I breathed.

Vero's eyes went wide. "You didn't tell him?"

Cam burst into the living room wearing a pair of plaid boxers and an undershirt. His boots were unlaced, his eyes glassy with panic. A sheen of perspiration had bloomed between the acne on his brow, and he looked like he might be sick. He gesticulated in sweeping motions behind him, breathing fast. "There are two dead dudes in the bathtub! Why are there two dead dudes in the bathtub, Mrs. D?" His hands shook as he bent to step into his pant legs before remembering he still had his boots on. The thick soles caught on the denim, and he nearly fell on his face in his rush to get out of them.

"I can explain," I said as he shook a foot free.

"Forget it. I don't want to know." He wrangled his jeans on and tugged on one boot as he stumbled toward the door. "I mean, I saw what you did to that guy in the salvage yard, and I thought that was pretty badass, but this—"

I stepped in his path before he could make it past the housekeeping cart. "I swear to you, Cameron, we did not kill those men. You have to believe me. They were like that when we got here."

"Together? In the bathtub?" he cried. "With the"—he gestured to his hair in a frantic pantomime—"thing?"

"Not exactly," I said, taking him by the arm and steering him gently toward the sofa. "Sit down before you hyperventilate." Cam stumbled to the sectional, one boot unlaced, holding the other in a death grip. "Take deep breaths and put your head between your knees." I couldn't remember if that was how you treated panic or a nosebleed, but the last thing I needed was for Cam to lose my son's Cheerios on the floor.

Vero smirked. "Not so badass now, are you?"

"Get him a bucket," I said, waving her out of the room.

Cam took deep, shuddering breaths, his head tucked between his legs as I rubbed small circles on his back, the way I did when my children were sick.

"I gotta tell you, Mrs. D," he said when he'd finally calmed. "That whole sitch in the bathroom traumatized me. I'll probably need therapy. Who's the naked guy?"

Given what Cam had already seen, there wasn't much point in holding back. "The one with the hairpiece is Marco Toscano. He's a loan shark," I explained. "Vero took a marker from him in a casino a few months ago. When she didn't pay him back, Marco hired some muscle to scare her. One of the men he sent after her was the unfortunate victim of gravity you witnessed in the salvage yard. The one in the tie is Louis Delvecchio. He's one of the men who stole the Aston Martin."

Cam's head snapped up. "The Aston's here?"

"Why do you care?" Vero thrust an empty ice bucket at him. He glared at her as he took it, looking like he'd love nothing more than to hit her over the head with it.

I took the ice bucket before we had one more murder to cover up. "Cam hid a very important flash drive in the car."

"What's on it? Your porn?"

"Yeah, pictures of your mom."

"Knock it off, both of you!" I pointed a finger at each of them and then at the couch. "We all want the same thing—to find that car. So let's set aside our differences and get to work."

"Doing what?" Cam asked.

"I don't know. Play to your strengths. You're a computer whiz and she's good with money."

"Bet the naked guy in the tub didn't think so when he sent someone to repo her car."

Vero shot him a look.

I handed Louis's tablet to Cam. "Start with this. Look for anything that might tell us where they took the Aston. I have to get back to our room before Nick knocks on the door and realizes I snuck out."

Vero stiffened. "Nick's here? In Atlantic City?"

I nodded. "Georgia, Sam, and Charlie are here, too. They're staying in the rooms right across the hall from ours."

Vero's jaw dropped. "How are we supposed to rescue Javi with Charlie and the cops watching our every move?"

"I don't know. But the two of you are going to stay here and figure out where he is while I go back to the Royal Flush and make sure Nick doesn't suspect us of anything."

"Who's Javi?" Cam asked.

"None of your business," Vero snapped.

I didn't bother to point out that Cam and Javi had met each other before. It hadn't gone well, and I didn't imagine Cam would be eager for a reunion.

"Fine," Cam said, taking a reluctant seat on the farthest side of the sectional. He kicked off his boot and propped his sweaty sock feet on the coffee table. "But I insist on ordering room service. My brain doesn't work when I'm hungry."

Vero raised an eyebrow at his lanky frame, a snarky comeback already forming on her lips. I scooped up the room service menu and thrust it at Vero. "Great. You get to work. Vero will order food." I dragged Vero aside as Cam swiped open Louis's tablet. "I promise we'll find Javi. As soon as Nick leaves for his meeting, I'll shake Charlie and come back."

"What am I supposed to do with him?" Vero asked, hooking her thumb at Cam.

I tucked the ice bucket under my arm and turned for the door. "Keep him fed and try not to kill him. He might be our best shot at finding that car."

CHAPTER 10

I raced down the stairwell of the Villagio after leaving Marco's suite. I'd been gone from the Royal Flush nearly two hours...way too long. My phone buzzed like an angry bee in the pocket of my apron. I tucked the ice bucket under my arm and slowed to check the caller's name, hoping it wasn't Nick. My throat closed as I read the initials on the screen. Vero had programmed the number into my contact list a few weeks ago, masking the user's identity with a moniker—*B.B.,* the *Boss Bitch*.

There was only one reason Ekatarina Rybakov would be calling me.

I contemplated letting it ring to voice mail. But there was no point putting this off. Kat was an attorney, a highly intelligent professional who resolved her problems with words. She could probably be reasoned with, woman to woman. And given the choice between a phone call and a face-to-face meeting, option number one seemed far preferable.

I connected the call.

"Ms. Donovan," she said in a familiar voice. It was somehow razor sharp and honey smooth in equal measure, like she could cut me from throat to groin and leave my insides on the floor without either of us feeling a thing. "I'm sure you already know why I'm calling, so let's do each other the courtesy of not wasting anyone's time. Where is he?"

"You mean Charlie? Last I checked, your watchdog was taking a nap."

"I'm in no mood for games."

"Is that why you sent him to handle your little scavenger hunt? How convenient for you. You don't even have to play."

"Where is Cameron?" she demanded.

"What makes you think I know?"

"You're both searching for a valuable car in a very small town. I have no doubt you've run into each other. Tell me where he is."

"Why? What's Cameron to you?"

"A problem."

A feral protective instinct flared inside me. "No, Kat! He's a child, and what you're doing is shameful."

"Cameron's age is of no consequence."

"The law says otherwise. But I forgot, you don't really care about the law, do you?"

She paused, as if I'd finally landed a blow. "I answer to a very powerful man," she said in a low, measured voice. "If you don't tell me where Cameron is hiding, mark my words, my watchdog will find him. And he will not be as gentle with his quarry as I will."

"You think Charlie's working for you?" I laughed at how foolish she must be to believe that. "Charlie's only out for himself."

"All the more reason you would do well to let me handle this."

"Aren't you tired of handling problems for powerful men?" The line went silent. I'd poked a viper with a short, sharp stick, and I could practically hear the rattle of her tail through her pause. "Apparently, you're not much of a boss bitch after all. I always thought you were smarter than them. I guess I was wrong." I didn't bother to wait for an answer before disconnecting the call.

I held the phone to my chest and sagged back against the handrail, my heart hammering against the ice bucket as the full weight of that conversation settled upon me. I had just drawn a line in the sand. Picked sides in a turf war against Feliks's most trusted accomplice—a woman who had the Russian mob behind her, a legal degree on her side, and all the resources and power to crush me.

I was screwed.

And worse, Kat probably knew exactly where I was.

I opened the menu of apps on my phone, scrolling through screens of social media icons, search engines, and weather and news sites, until I found an icon for an app I didn't recognize, conveniently hidden on a page of others I rarely used. It appeared to have been downloaded to my phone last week—probably by Cam—and was more than likely tracking my phone for Kat. I deleted the suspicious app from my device, hoping that was the only spyware on it.

My phone buzzed again. I peeked at it, expecting to see the initials *B.B.* flashing hot on my screen. But it was only Steven.

Where are you?

Shit! I hustled down the remaining flights, changed my clothes in the bathroom, and sprinted down the boardwalk, sneaking back into the Royal Flush through the entrance to the casino. I took the elevator to the floor just below mine, following signs for the ice machine. If Marco's ice bucket was going to be my alibi, it would need to look convincing. I filled it and carried it up the last set of stairs, walking briskly toward my room.

Nick's door opened as soon as I rounded the corner. He reached out, catching me by the shoulders in the middle of the hall.

"I was looking for you," he said, raising an eyebrow at my bucket. "What are you doing out of your room?" His hair was damp from the shower, his face freshly shaven. He couldn't have been searching long.

"I was just getting some ice," I said, displaying the evidence.

He held fast to my puffy sleeve as I tried to step around him. "Wearing your coat?"

"I was cold." I slithered under his arm to my door.

His hands appeared beside me on the frame, caging me between them as I fumbled in my pocket for my key. He leaned close to my ear, his body heat all around me when he asked, "Do I want to know where you've really been?" The low timbre of his voice made the skin pebble on parts of my body I probably shouldn't have been thinking about after the morning I'd had.

"Is that a rhetorical question?"

He turned me slowly to face him and plucked the key from my hand, tucking it into the breast pocket of his dress shirt as he waited for an answer. When I didn't offer one, he bent low to meet my eyes. "I know you came here for some time away, and I get that you don't want the FCPD or the FBI or even *me* breathing down your neck. And I know that you can take care of yourself," he said, holding up a finger as I opened my mouth to argue, "but I wouldn't be here if I didn't think there was a genuine risk to your life, Finn, and I really, *really* need you to trust me on this." He took the ice bucket gently from my arm and held it over my head, pointing out the stamp on the bottom that read PROPERTY OF THE VILLAGIO.

I snatched it back from him. Was there anything this man wasn't good at? "Fine. If you must know, I went to find Vero. She wasn't answering her phone, and I wanted to make sure she knew what was going on with all this," I said, gesticulating around the hall. I reached inside his pocket for my key and turned to unlock my door. He followed me inside, leaning back against it when it closed.

"Where are my mom and the kids?" I asked, ignoring his cocky grin.

"Sam and your mom went out for coffee, and the kids are watching TV with Georgia in her room. Where's Vero?" he asked, his cop-bright eyes trailing me as I set the ice bucket on the dresser and stripped off my coat.

"With a young man at a fancy hotel with a very large bathtub. They're ordering room service. She promised me she would keep the door locked and wouldn't leave the room." That was all true. Every word of it.

"Yeah? What's her friend's name?" His eyes went glassy as I peeled off my sweatshirt.

"I'm not telling you."

He pushed off the door and came up behind me as I kicked off my shoes. He took my waist gently in his hands, his breath warm on the back of my neck, making the hair stand on end when he whispered, "I have ways of extracting information from reluctant informants."

"Is this an official interrogation?"

His hands moved down my hips. "Just a conversation."

"Not sure this qualifies as conversation." My breath hitched as he drew me against him. The man was clearly created for this, and I repressed the urge to climb him like a police academy training rope as I turned slowly to face him.

His grin suggested he knew it. "Then answer the question so we can both stop talking."

A frustrating pressure flared between my legs. "Vero's having fun and she doesn't want to come back yet."

"So you're not going to tell me what room she's in?"

"Not a chance."

Nick hooked his hands around my thighs, hoisting me up and wrapping my legs around his waist. I leaned down to kiss him, gasping with surprise when his arms came out from under me and I fell backward onto the bed. He planted a knee between mine, his eyes going molten as he climbed over me. "Sure I can't convince you to tell me?"

"Totally sure." I arched into him, perfectly content to discontinue the conversation. "The kids are right across the hall," I panted. "And my mother could be back any minute."

His mouth moved down my chest, stretching the collar of my shirt. "Susan and Sam just left," he murmured, unfastening a button. "And the kids and Georgia just started a movie."

Which meant we had at least an hour.

I grabbed Nick's face and kissed him, my fingers raking up and knotting in his hair as a ferocious need took hold of me. He was right.

He would figure all of this out on his own—where Vero was, who was in that room with her—and once he did, everything we had would grind to a crashing halt. Frantic, I reached down for his belt, the bed creaking as I pulled him against me. If this was our last hour like this, I was determined to make it count.

We both started as something heavy smacked into the door connecting Steven's room to mine. Nick froze over me as the unmistakable sound of a football game blared through the wall, as if Steven had turned up the volume on his television to drown us out. I pushed Nick back by the chest, my own still heaving.

"Sort of kills the mood, huh?" He rolled onto his back and tucked me under his arm. I curled into his side as our ragged breathing slowed. He pressed his lips to my hair. "I'd invite you back to my room, but Charlie's taking a nap. I want him fresh when Garrett and I go to Pleasantville to look into the Grindley case this afternoon. I don't want any surprises while we're gone." His fingertips traced lazy patterns on my arm. I shivered and burrowed deeper into his side. "What's the matter?" he teased. "Don't want to spend the afternoon with Charlie?"

"Do I have another option?"

"You could come with me and Garrett. We're going to Grindley's house to meet with his wife. I was going to wait until Charlie woke up, but if you want to come, we can leave now and let Charlie sleep."

I lifted my head. This might be my only shot to learn exactly what the police knew about Ike's disappearance, or what, if anything, Ike's wife knew about us. And Vero and Cam would need at least a few hours to make heads or tails of whatever secrets were hiding in Louis's tablet anyway.

"I'll grab a quick shower." I untangled myself from Nick's arms and climbed off the bed, digging in my suitcase for my toiletries and a change of clothes. Nick sat up against the headboard, watching me with shameless interest as I retreated to the bathroom. I locked myself inside, avoiding my reflection in the mirror, wondering how much longer I could keep up this shell game.

CHAPTER 11

Nick held my hand the entire way to the parking garage, his body angled toward mine, always careful to stay a half step ahead of me. He darted cautious glances at every corner, behind every ramp and concrete support column. I fought a twinge of guilt as he guided me toward the passenger door of a familiar red Cadillac.

"This isn't your car," I said as he pressed the key fob and the doors unlocked with a chirp.

"It's Charlie's," he said. "It's a little more comfortable than my Impala." A wave of déjà vu washed over me as Nick held open the passenger door for me. I wasn't feeling particularly comfortable as I settled into the passenger seat, and I fidgeted as Nick got in and started the car. He angled the vents toward me and turned my seat heater on, but the air was already feeling a little too warm.

"Where's Agent Stokes? Isn't he coming with us?"

"He's meeting us at Grindley's house." He reached over the center console for my hand, periodically glancing at his mirrors as we drove the short distance to Pleasantville. He checked his rearview as we exited the expressway. Then again as we pulled into a run-down neighborhood of dated split-levels and 1960s Ramblers. He parked in front of a rusty chain-link fence surrounding a drab, gray single-story box with a ramshackle, shed-style garage tucked around the back. The chipped concrete walkway out front was overgrown with weeds, stopping just short of a spindly front porch. It reminded me a little of Cameron's grandmother's house.

A sleek, black SUV with tinted windows pulled in behind us and flashed its lights. "That's Garrett," Nick said, ducking low to study the yards on either side of us. A group of ragtag adolescent boys were gathered on a nearby corner, checking us out. "I was going to let you stay in the car, but the neighborhood's a little sketchy, and this car sticks out like a sore thumb. Come on," Nick said, slipping his badge into his jacket and opening his door. "I'm sure Mrs. Grindley won't mind if you wait inside her house."

My mouth went dry as Nick rounded the car and opened my door for me. Garrett waited beside the fence gate in crisp blue jeans and a navy peacoat. He might have ditched his FBI-emblazoned windbreaker, but he still looked like he'd stepped off the set of a TV police drama, and between the three of us, we were attracting some attention. A Rottweiler shot through the flap of a dog door on the side of the garage and charged the fence, snapping at us through the mesh. A curtain peeled back in the front window of the house. A casement cranked open, and the woman inside let out an ear-piercing whistle. The dog went silent and retreated to the backyard.

The woman appeared in the door and held it open with her knee. A cloud of strawberry-vanilla vape smoke spooled from the house, carried to us on the frosty wind. "Come on. She won't bite," the woman called out.

Garrett was cautious as he opened the latch on the gate, testing it a few inches before holding it open for me and Nick. Nick led the way up the sidewalk, one eye on the side of the house where the dog had disappeared and a hand pressed firmly against the small of my back. Garrett climbed the weatherworn steps to the porch and presented his ID to the woman. I risked a long look at her as she studied it. Her hair fell over her shoulders, brittle and brassy. Deep smoker's wrinkles around her mouth and on her hands made it hard to tell her age, but she was dated by the shape of her nails and the severe cut of her thick, rounded bangs. I guessed she was somewhere in her late forties.

"Trina Grindley? I'm Agent Garrett Stokes. We spoke on the phone. This is Detective Nicholas Anthony with the Fairfax County Police Department in Virginia. He's one of the local investigators assisting us with your husband's case. Thank you for agreeing to meet with us." Her eyes flicked to me as she took a drag off her vape. She glanced down at Garrett's ID, then at Nick's. Her gaze traveled back to mine and lingered, as if she were trying to place something about me.

"This is Ms. Donovan," Nick said as he returned his ID to his jacket. "She's riding along with me today. Would you mind if she waits inside while we talk? It's a little cold in the car."

Mrs. Grindley blew out a long, strawberry-vanilla exhale before opening the door the rest of the way and leading us inside. There wasn't far to go. The door opened into a disheveled living room boasting a disproportionately large flat-screen television on one wall and a glass trophy cabinet on the other. A threadbare sofa sagged in the space between them.

Garrett nudged aside a distractingly large chew toy, clearing a place for us to stand in the cramped space. The room smelled close and hot, like fruit smoke and dog food. The radiators clicked as the heat kicked on in the wake of the draft from outside.

Nick closed the door behind us as he took in Mrs. Grindley's home.

"Your lady friend can wait here," Trina said, gesturing to the couch. "I've got sodas in the kitchen if you want to talk in there."

"I'll only be a few minutes," Nick whispered in my ear as she led Garrett a few feet away to the kitchen. I looked around me for a clean place to sit, moving a stack of magazines and a handful of dog toys off the couch and swatting away the dog hair before gingerly taking a seat. Nick and Garrett pulled out two rickety chairs from her kitchen table and sat down.

I stiffened at a soft snuffling sound beside me as Trina opened her fridge. I turned to see the woman's Rottweiler creeping toward the couch, her nostrils wiggling. I froze as the dog gave my sneakers a curious sniff. She moved closer, the stub of her tail wagging faster. *Oh, god.* My shoes probably smelled like Marco's suite. Did this Rottweiler have a thing for tiny wiener dogs?

Her nose climbed my pant leg and I nudged her away. She pressed her snout against the top of my jeans. I crossed my legs and folded my arms over my crotch to deter her, but she only became more intent. "Go away," I whispered as she started to whine. I angled my body away from her, but she wasn't trying to get a whiff of my groin. I was pretty sure she was trying to cram her nose inside my pocket.

I pressed a hand to the denim, my fingers going still over the tiny bulge inside it.

Oh, no!

Ike's tooth.

I smiled wanly at Trina when she emerged from the fridge and glanced over at us. She tipped her head, watching me wriggle on the couch as her dog put her two massive paws on my lap, her stubby tail wagging faster as she attempted to burrow under my jacket.

"That's weird," Trina said. "She don't like most people. Aside from Ike, that is. She adores him." She held up a Coke can. I politely demurred. Or at least, as politely as one can with one hundred and fifty pounds of canine in your lap and a face full of slobber.

As soon as Trina turned away, I retrieved Ike's tooth from my pocket and tucked it inside my shoe. The dog sat back and sank to the carpet. Her chin rested on her paws at my feet, her ears perked and her face mopey as she stared wistfully at my sneakers.

Trina set the two sodas on the table and sat down across from Nick. She leaned back in her chair, eyeing the men warily as she took a leisurely drag off her vape. "Have they found him yet?"

"Not yet," Garrett said. "The investigators assigned to the case have a few leads, but Culpeper County PD is still treating this as a missing persons investigation."

"Then what are you two doing here?" She tipped her head at Nick. "He's Fairfax and you're FBI. You just said the case is being investigated by another county—"

"The county where your husband's car was found. Yes, ma'am," Garrett clarified.

"None of that explains what you two are doing in my house," she said sharply.

Garrett folded his hands on the table. "We're here because of those leads I mentioned. Detective Anthony and I are part of a joint task force investigating organized crime." Trina's posture tightened a fraction, but I was sure Nick noticed the shift. "We have reason to believe that the people who set your husband's car on fire have ties to the mob, and it would be helpful if you could tell us a little more about what kind of business your husband may have been conducting in Virginia."

She crossed her arms, pushing her chair back a few inches from the table with her foot. "I don't know nothing about none of that. I already told the police, Ike's boss is a private investor. Ike handles collections for him when people don't pay back their loans. Marco sent Ike to Virginia for a job, and that's all Ike told me."

"Is that all Ike does for Mr. Toscano?"

"Far as I know."

"Does Ike's collection work ever involve threats of violence?"

Trina's mouth hardened. "Some people don't like paying their debts, Detective. If they get a little roughed up over it, it's their own damn fault."

"Does Ike ever do that kind of work for anyone else?" Nick asked. "You know, rough people up for money?"

Trina narrowed her eyes at him. "What are you trying to say?"

"I'm just trying to get a better understanding of the nature of his work. It might help us narrow down a list of possible suspects in his disappearance if we knew the kinds of people your husband might have interacted with while he was in Virginia."

Trina sucked on her vape, studying Nick and Garrett through

her long exhale. "Sometimes Ike does a little repo work on the side. That's all."

"Are you sure your husband was in Virginia doing a job for Marco? That he wasn't hired by someone else?"

"He told me Marco sent him. Why?" she asked, darting looks between the men.

Garrett was first to answer. "When the investigator from Culpeper County spoke with Mr. Toscano on the phone, he denied any knowledge of your husband's trip to Virginia. He said he doesn't have any clients in that area and Ike must have been there on a personal matter."

"That lying son of a bitch," she whispered.

Nick's eyes lit, as if he sensed an opening. "Do you know the name of the client your husband was meeting the night he disappeared?"

"No." She gave an agitated shake of her head. "I called Marco last week when Ike stopped answering his phone. I asked him where my husband was and who he was meeting with. Marco told me it wasn't any of my goddamn concern and keep out of it. I called him again when the police found Ike's car. Told him if he has any idea who messed with Ike, he ought to tell the police, but Marco doesn't like anyone knowing his business. He got sick of me pestering him every day, so he stopped taking my calls altogether." Nick and Garrett exchanged a long look.

My cell phone vibrated and I dragged it from my pocket.

Vero: *Where are you?*
I typed out a reply. *In Ike Grindley's house.*
Vero: *Very funny.*

I discreetly held up my cell phone and snapped a picture of Nick, Garrett, and Trina at the kitchen table in the next room. The dog's nose had steamed up the lower half of the photo, but the resulting image was clear enough.

I tapped *Send*.

My phone vibrated with an incoming call.

I answered, holding the phone away from my ear as Vero shrieked into it, "What are you doing in that man's house?"

I shooed the dog from my legs as I carried the phone to the other side of the living room. "Nick suspects Feliks had something to do with Ike's disappearance," I whispered. "He's convinced Ike was in Virginia doing a side job for the mob and it went sour. He came to question Ike's wife about it."

"Uh-oh. What's she saying?"

"Only that she thought her husband was in Virginia doing a job for Marco, but she says Marco refused to tell her anything about it."

"You think she's covering for him?"

"I don't think so. She sounds too angry at him to want to cover for him."

"Why?"

"She says she called Marco repeatedly after Ike disappeared, demanding answers, and Marco stopped taking her calls."

Vero fell silent, as if she was suddenly thinking the same thing I was. *How angry was Trina?*

Could she have grown tired of waiting for Marco to call her back and tracked him down at his hotel? Could Louis have let her into Marco's suite while Marco was bathing? Could she have demanded to speak with Marco anyway? Could Louis have tried to appease her to get her to leave, confiding that they were holding a very valuable car as a bargaining chip for more information about what had happened to her husband and they would call her as soon as they knew more? Could she have lost her temper and murdered them both?

I flipped to my camera roll and squinted at the photo of Trina, Nick, and Garrett sitting around the table in Ike's kitchen. Through the small window above the kitchen sink, I could just make out the shed outside. It was large, containing a single bay door. It could just as easily function as a garage.

Ike had made it painfully clear to us that he was planning to eliminate us and take the Aston Martin. Not for Marco, but for himself. The only way he could have kept a prize like that from his boss was if he was certain he had a safe place to hide it.

I enlarged the image on the screen, zooming in on the shed. The paint was patchy with grime, the hardware on the bay door covered with rust. A shiny silver padlock secured one side. A massive dog door flanked the other.

There was no question the shed was secure.

The only question was, what was inside it?

The dog followed me, curiosity piqued, as I moved to the sliding glass door at the rear of the living room. I peeled back the heavy drape and flipped the lock as quietly as I could. Easing it open, I slipped out into the backyard. The dog whined as I closed the glass between us.

I ducked low, sneaking under the kitchen window, blinking against the cloud of strawberry-vanilla smoke that ghosted through the narrow gap where Trina had left it cracked.

"Does your husband have any friends or associates who might have connections to foreign business entities . . . ?" Nick's question faded as I darted to the shed. I rounded the corner and pressed my back against the side, careful to stay out of view as I pulled my phone out of my pocket.

"Finlay! Where are you?" Vero's voice was a frantic whisper as I held it to my ear.

"I'm fine," I whispered, checking the back of the structure for another way in. "There's a shed in Ike's yard. Some kind of garage."

"What's in it?"

"I don't know. It's padlocked shut." There were no windows. No other doors I could see as I peered around the back. Except for the dog door . . .

The vinyl flap wavered in the breeze. I knelt, pushing it open to get a look inside. The shed was pitch black, the dense air carrying the earthy reek of damp ground, stale kibble, and unwashed fur. Careful not to drop my phone, I got down on all fours and pushed my head through the flap. Narrowing my shoulders, I wedged my torso through it, my knees sinking into the wet grass outside. I turned on my phone light and held it aloft, blinking as I waited for my eyes to adjust. The beam glinted off a stainless-steel water bowl beside a dog bed in the corner. A snow shovel and a rake hung from nails on the wall beside me, and a bag of potting soil and some boxes marked XMAS and EASTER lined the opposite side. Oil stains and tire tracks marked the exposed dirt floor.

"There was definitely a car in here," I said, angling my light for a better look. I doubled back over a bright red suitcase. It didn't look like it had been stored in here. It wasn't stacked with the other boxes, covered in dog fur and dust. It was clean, standing on its wheels beside the door, as if it were waiting for someone to reach in and grab it. A luggage tag hung from the handle on its side, and a tiny silver travel lock had been snapped around the zippers. Had Trina stowed it in here so the police wouldn't spot it?

If so, where was she going? And, more important, why?

A dog flap swung open somewhere behind me, followed by the sound of heavy panting.

"Oh, no," I said as a cold nose tickled my ankle. My jacket caught on the plastic frame as I tried to wriggle my way backward through the opening. I stiffened when the dog grabbed my shoe in her mouth and pulled. "No, no! Stop that!" I hissed, shaking my foot.

Vero gasped. "What's wrong?"

The dog whined, her teeth tightening around the sole. An icy wind chilled me through my sock as my sneaker was ripped off my heel. "Ike's dog has my shoe."

My head smacked painfully against the frame as I thrust myself backward through it. I landed on my butt outside of the shed.

"No! No, no, no!" I whispered, scrabbling toward the dog as she abandoned my sneaker and dropped it onto the grass. Her throat worked around one quick swallow. I wedged the phone under my jaw, gingerly using both hands to pry open the dog's mouth, but it was empty. Her tongue hung loose as she panted, dripping drool on my knees. She watched me with perked ears as I whispered, "This is not good."

"What's not good?"

"I think the dog ate Ike's tooth!" I crawled in frantic circles, searching for it in the damp grass.

"Try giving him the Heimlich! Maybe he'll cough it up!"

"I can't give the Heimlich to a dog! I wouldn't begin to know how!"

"Hold on. I'll look it up on YouTube."

Nick's voice came faintly through the open window. "Has Ike ever mentioned the name Feliks Zhirov before?"

"Doesn't ring any bells," Trina said.

"What about the name Finlay Donovan?"

My phone dropped to the ground with a quiet thump. I went still, my shoe in my hand, cold dirt soaking through the knees of my jeans as I listened through the interminable pause that followed.

"Wait," Trina said, her chair scraping against the floor, "that one sounds familiar." My pulse skyrocketed as she stood and turned toward the sink. I grabbed my phone, muting Vero's tinny shouts with my thumb as I scurried under the open window and pressed back against the siding. Papers rustled above me, as if Trina were rummaging through the envelopes and magazines I'd seen stacked on her kitchen counter. "I know it's here somewhere." A zipper whined. Her purse? Was one of Louis's photos inside it? A note from Marco with my name and address? The tag number of my minivan along with Vero's outstanding balance?

"Here," she said triumphantly. "I knew I'd heard that name before!"

Something heavy thudded down.

Oh, god. What was it? An entire file? A dossier? I couldn't stand the suspense any longer. I rose up and peeked through the crack in the window. The three of them huddled over the table with matching bewildered expressions. My phone vibrated against the siding. Nick's eyes lifted at the sound, narrowing on mine through the window.

Garrett and Trina looked up to see what had captured his attention. Trina lifted a tattered paperback off the table. She opened the cover and held it aloft in front of her, studying the inside flap, her eyes ping-ponging between me and the book. My name stretched across the front in hot-pink script, framed by a hunky cover model's armpit. I cringed, praying for the ground to swallow me up as Garrett studied my headshot over Trina's shoulder. It was the first romantic suspense novel I'd ever published, before I'd started using a pen name.

The kitchen door swung open, banging into the siding beside me.

"I knew I recognized you!" Trina said, leaning out and pointing her vape at me as I tugged on my sneaker and brushed the dirt from my pants. She shook a finger at the dog and waved me inside. "I found your books at the thrift shop next door to the hair salon where I work. Got three of them for a dollar! Ike loves 'em. He don't actually read too well, but he likes when I read him the juicy parts out loud."

I smiled tightly at her choice of words. Considering what I remembered of Ike's final moments, I was pretty sure we weren't picturing the same juicy parts.

Nick raised an eyebrow as I stepped, red-faced, into the kitchen, his astute gaze clearly registering the tangled hair escaping my ponytail and the damp, filthy spots on the knees of my jeans. "We were just playing a little fetch," I said, answering the question on his face. The dog flounced down beside me and rested her muzzle on her paws. She looked woefully at my chewed-up sneaker. I just hoped she didn't get indigestion and puke up a gold tooth.

Garrett checked his watch as Trina handed me a ballpoint pen. "Would you mind signing this for Ike?" she asked, holding out her book. "Maybe you could write him a special message. You know, like, *To Ike, my biggest fan. Love, Finlay Donovan.* Or something like that."

Because *my flattest fan,* while accurate, would probably not be the wisest choice.

I scribbled out the message and signed my name, hoping my novel wouldn't wind up shelved in an evidence locker as I handed it back to her.

Nick passed her a card with his phone number on it. "We don't want to hold you up, Mrs. Grindley. We know you have to be at work soon. Can you tell us where we can find Ike's boss? We called the cell number for Mr. Toscano in the case file, but we can't seem to reach him. Does he have an office number we can try? Or an address?"

Her laugh was raspy. "Take your pick. Marco could be in any casino in Atlantic City. The only person who might know where to look is his nephew, Ricky. He used to schedule appointments for his uncle."

"Any idea where we can find Ricky?" Nick asked.

Trina shrugged. "Last I heard, he was parking cars at the Royal Flush."

CHAPTER 12

My heart was still pounding when we left Trina's house and got into Charlie's car. Nick's head fell back against his headrest. It rolled sideways, his face breaking into a grin. His pulse beat fast in the dip at the base of his throat, as if his heart had been racing a little, too. "She really had me going for a minute when I asked her if she recognized your name. I would have bet my life someone put a price on your head and Ike had taken the job."

My laugh felt brittle. "That would be a stretch."

Nick cocked an eyebrow. "I haven't ruled it out. Either Marco Toscano was lying about sending Ike to Virginia, or Ike was lying to his wife about who hired him to go. There's only one way to find out which." He started the engine and set the navigation on the fancy touch screen to take us back to the Royal Flush. Agent Stokes waved as we pulled away from the curb and passed his SUV.

Nick was quiet as he drove us back to the turnpike, listening to the monotone instructions of the turn-by-turn guidance coming through the speakers. I sent Vero a quick text, letting her know I had survived the ordeal and was on my way back to the hotel. The Atlantic City skyline was already visible in the distance. I'd have to keep Nick from talking to Ricky once we got there.

"Does that happen a lot?"

"What?" I asked, startled from my thoughts.

"People waving your books around and asking you for your autograph?"

I laughed. I could count on two fingers the number of times it had happened to me, and both times, I had been with Nick. "Only when I'm with you, apparently."

My cell phone vibrated in my lap. I peeked at the screen. *Incoming Call from Sylvia.* Nick stole a sideways glance at me as I let it roll to voice mail.

"It's just my agent. I can call her later," I explained.

He looked surprised. "Isn't she your boss?"

"I'm an independent contractor. I don't have a boss." Sylvia was more like an advisor. Or a gatekeeper. Definitely a menace.

"What if it's important?"

"She's probably just calling to complain about my book." And I had far more pressing things to worry about at the moment than my heroine's problematic love life.

I drummed my fingers on the car door as Sylvia tried again. Then again. Nerves fried, I picked it up. "It's not a good time, Syl. Can I call you back?"

"No." I held the phone away from my ear as she shouted through the speaker. "You're never going to believe this."

"You hated my revision."

"No, your revision was fine. Very hot actually. Your editor loved it. I'm telling you, Finlay. Killing off the lawyer was the right call. The tension between the assassin and the cop is palpable. And those new action scenes were real nail-biters."

"You're telling me."

"Like when the big baddy is chasing your heroine on foot through the city, and he gets squashed by a car. Totally didn't see that coming."

I rubbed my temple. "That makes two of us."

"And the sex! When she thinks the hot cop is going to arrest her, but instead he ravages her in the back seat of his car and does that thing with his tongue." She moaned and smacked her lips together. "Chef's kiss, Finlay. Your best work yet."

Nick smirked.

"Then what is it, Syl?"

"The early review copies of your latest book went out."

My stomach bottomed out. "When?"

"Last week, while you were away at your police thingy."

I sat up in my seat. "Seriously? Why didn't you tell me?"

"I would have if you'd bothered to return my calls." Nick threw me an *I told you so* look.

I angled away from him, tamping down my rising panic. Advance copies of my book were out in the world. People were reading it. Dozens of them. Maybe hundreds. "How many?" I asked.

"Three thousand."

I felt the blood drain from my face. This was the first book of my brand-new series, the one I'd based loosely on my involvement in Harris Mickler's murder. Vero kept insisting it was fine, that no one could possibly read my novel and make that leap. I'd convinced myself that no one would spot the truths hidden beneath the fiction when I'd cashed that advance check. After all, Feliks had already been arrested for the crime. The evidence against him had been overwhelming, but after everything that had happened since, publishing this book now seemed like a very bad idea. Feliks had escaped. He presumably was in possession of a body (or at least, parts of one) that had belonged to a man I'd had a hand in squishing. A single phone call to a tip line could turn the entire investigation against me. Nick was already suspicious that something was off about Harris Mickler's death. It wouldn't take him long to connect the dots he'd been too stubborn (and hopeful) to see clearly. Hope (and luck) could only get you so far.

I cleared the knot from my throat. "Is that it?"

"No, there's more. A Hollywood scout passed a copy of the book to a big-time producer who's hot to buy the rights. I just got an email from his people. They want to set up a call. What's your schedule over the next few days?"

Nick gave my knee an encouraging squeeze as words failed me. My schedule? Besides playing *Weekend at Bernie's* with two corpses while concealing their murders from the cops, hiding an irreverent teenager from people who wanted to kill him, and tracking down a stolen sports car so I could take down the leader of the Russian mob before he got to me first? "Like I said, Sylvia, it's not a great time. I'm dealing with some family stuff right now, and—"

The Cadillac swerved as Nick's attention shot to me. I pressed a finger to my lips to shush him as he said, "Are you kidding? This is a huge opportunity, Finn! You should take the call."

"Who is that?" Sylvia demanded. "Is that him? The hot cop your accountant told me about? The one who inspired the character in your book?"

I squeezed my eyes shut. I was going to murder Vero next. "No."

"I knew it. Put him on the phone."

"I'm not putting him on the phone!"

"Hello, Sylvia," Nick called out, grinning at my scandalized look.

"Good god," Sylvia said, "that man has a very sexy voice. I think my panties are wet, and at my age, that's really saying something. Put me on speaker."

"I'm not putting you on speaker."

"*In one-quarter mile, take the exit onto the Atlantic City Expressway.*" The navigation assistant droned on as I rushed to mute my phone.

Sylvia gasped. "Was that your car? Are you in Atlantic City? You are, aren't you? When can we meet? How about dinner? I can be there in an hour."

"I have plans."

"Great. You can bring your hot cop with you. The Brighton Cafe on Atlantic. I'll meet you there."

"No," I said as Nick called out, "We'll be there."

I glared across the car at him as Sylvia disconnected. "We'll be there?"

He nodded as he rolled through a yellow traffic light, not the least bit remorseful. "I'm not letting this mess with Zhirov ruin an opportunity for you. We're going to dinner with your agent."

"When did this become a *we* thing?"

He frowned. "It's not like that, Finn—"

"No, then what's it like? Just because we slept together one time . . . okay, three times, in *one night*," I reminded him in answer to his dubious look (though I'm not sure that detail was helping drive home my point), "that doesn't give you the right to make decisions for me."

"You have something better to do?"

"Yes! I was supposed to have dinner with *you*!"

"You can have dinner with me anytime. This is more important."

"That's exactly what I'm talking about."

I gripped the door as he hooked a sharp right and threw the Cadillac in park, his eyes dark with resolve as he twisted in his seat to face me. "You don't want me to come with you? Fine. But you're not turning your back on a shot at a TV deal just because you're afraid of what might happen if you get it. You deserve opportunities, Finlay. And you deserve to be with someone who cares about what those opportunities mean to you, who puts what you need first—in *and* out of bed. And you know what else you deserve? Someone who'll be honest with you, even if you don't want to hear it. Sometimes that means being with someone who's going to make you face what you're afraid of, because he's planning on standing right behind you, covering your back." He scrubbed a hand down his face, turning away from me as he lowered his voice. "If you don't want me there with you, then Charlie can take you. But you're not leaving the hotel alone." He shut off the ignition. I looked out my window, my palms going sweaty when I realized where we'd stopped. Ricky appeared through the tinted glass of the valet window of the Royal Flush.

"Stay here," Nick said, getting out of the car. "We'll finish this conversation when I get back."

I ducked in my seat as Ricky jogged to Nick's side of the car and held out his hand for the keys. Nick handed him a business card instead. Ricky's face sobered as he read it.

"Ricky? You're Ricky, right? I'm Detective Nicholas Anthony with the Fairfax County Police Department in Virginia. I'm investigating the disappearance of a man named Ignacious Grindley. He's from around here. You know him?" I listened through the closed window, piecing together what I could hear of their muffled conversation.

Ricky nodded. "Yeah, I know him. Ike's my cousin. You figure out what happened to him?"

Nick shook his head. "We're working a few leads. I was hoping to talk to your uncle, Marco Toscano, but I'm having a hard time reaching him. Ike's wife mentioned you work for him?"

"Used to," Ricky said.

"What kind of work did you do for your uncle?"

"Scheduling mostly. Errands sometimes."

"Ever do any jobs like Ike's?" Nick asked. Ricky shifted his weight, darting uncomfortable looks around him as if he was hoping another car might pull up and relieve him of having to answer that. "Hey, Ricky," Nick said, stealing back his attention. "I'm not looking to get anyone in trouble. I'm just trying to figure out what happened to your cousin. That's all."

Ricky hesitated. Shook his head. "Marco never trusted me with anything like that. He called me a shithead and said I couldn't do anything right."

"Is that why you don't work for him anymore?"

Ricky nodded, shame coloring his cheeks.

I watched Nick's gaze dip to the scuffed name badge on Ricky's uniform, cataloging every detail, from the wrinkles on Ricky's jacket to the frayed shoelaces peeking out from under the hems of his pants. Satisfied, he asked, "You know where I might find your uncle? I need to ask him a few questions about Ike's case."

I held my breath but Ricky only shrugged. "Marco moves around a lot. Could be anywhere."

"Any idea how I might get ahold of Marco's wife?"

"Giada?" Ricky's sudden burst of laughter broke the tension. "Giada and Marco haven't lived together since I was a kid. She got the house when they split. The only thing they have in common as far as I know is Kevin Bacon."

Nick's brow furrowed as I blanched. "The actor?"

"No, the dog. Uncle Marco gets Kevin when Giada's in Florida. Giada gets the dog when she's at her place in Venice Park."

"And she's in Florida now?"

"Beats me. Marco's my mom's brother," Ricky explained. "Giada's the other side of the family. Things got weird between everyone after Marco and Giada separated. If it hadn't been for their pre-nup, they would have divorced a long time ago. We mostly all keep to our respective sides of town. The Toscano side sticks close to Ducktown."

"Ducktown?"

"And Chelsea."

"Is that where Marco lives?" When Ricky didn't answer, Nick said, "All I've got is a cell number, and he's not picking up."

"He doesn't pick up for anybody," Ricky muttered. "He screens his calls."

"You know where I can find his house?"

Ricky spread his arms, gesturing to the city around them. "Why would a guy like Marco need a house? Any hotel on the boardwalk is home to Marco. A high roller like him? One who's brought in a lot of business for them over the years? He can get a free room any day of the week, eating free meals and drinking free booze at any one of these places. Why buy the cow when you can get the milk for free? It's just one more thing he'd have to split with Giada." Or give to her entirely, depending on their prenup.

Nick's gaze skated from Ricky to the towering hotels behind him.

"Good luck finding him," Ricky said, as if he were reading Nick's mind. "You gonna give me your keys? I got to get back to work."

Nick handed Ricky the keys to the Cadillac. I slipped out of the car as Ricky ducked into the driver's seat.

Nick stood for a moment, staring at the Cadillac's taillights as Ricky drove off. My cell phone vibrated with a text message from Vero.

Found something. Get your ass back here.

"Want me to take you to your meeting with Sylvia?" Nick asked, startling my attention from the screen.

I shook my head. If Nick was my escort, I wouldn't stand a chance of ditching him. "Charlie can drive me. He can wait in the car."

I left Nick standing on the curb and headed into the lobby. I typed a message to Vero as I walked:

I'll be there in an hour.

Nick followed a few steps behind me, remaining silent in the elevator, as if he sensed I needed some space. He didn't bother to ask to come in when I unlocked the door to my room and said a hasty goodbye. After all, it was his own fault I was in a hurry to meet with Sylvia.

I dug a fresh pair of jeans and my only decent sweater from my luggage. After a quick change of clothes, I swabbed some gloss on my lips and ran a brush through my hair. I was just coming out of the bathroom when I heard raised voices through the wall. I pressed an ear to Steven's door.

"Don't you think you're being a little unreasonable?" Steven asked.

"Your child defecated in the pool. I don't think it's unreasonable to say your family's no longer welcome to use it."

Delia's small voice interrupted the two men. "Daddy, are we in trouble? Maybe we should call Mommy."

"We don't need to call Mommy. Daddy has it all under control."

Steven did not sound like he had anything under control. Zach started crying. Delia turned the TV on too loudly to try to calm him. Steven raised his voice, shouting over it, making the hotel manager raise his too, escalating their argument. "Fine. If you're going to be a dick about it, we won't go back to the pool."

"Daddy, Mommy says that's not a nice word. We're not supposed to say that."

"Just a minute, Delia. Let the grown-ups talk."

"Sir, we still need to discuss the matter of the broken vase in the lobby."

"Look, my son was just trying to push the button for the elevator and he knocked over the vase. It was an accident."

"I'm sorry, but that's our policy. You signed an agreement to be responsible for damages when you paid for the room."

"You want to charge me four hundred dollars for that piece of crap?"

"We're not supposed to say that either, Daddy."

"Maybe the child is right and we should call their mother."

"We don't need to call their mother! I'm their damn father, and I'm standing right here!"

"Daddy—"

"I know, Delia!" Steven barked. "It's a bad word. I won't say it again."

"I can see where the children learned their poor manners," the manager said.

Delia's breath hitched on a sob.

"Look," Steven said with a forced calm as I opened the door and strode into the room behind him, "I don't know where my credit card is. I can't deal with this right—"

"I'll handle it," I said, yanking my wallet from my purse. I unfolded the stack of bills I'd confiscated from Vero in Marco's suite, counting out four hundred-dollar bills and thrusting them at the manager's chest. "Are we finished here? Or do I need to contact the owner of this establishment and let him know his manager is harassing families of small children and making them cry? And while we're on the subject of accidents," I said, seething as I backed him over the threshold and into the hall, "I should advise you that you're missing a STOP sign on the fourth level of the parking garage, your temperature regulator on your hot water is set high enough to scald a child, and a smoke detector is chirping in the stairwell. Would you like for me to come downstairs with you and file a report?"

The manager stared at me, wide-eyed, his hands frozen around the cash. "That . . . won't be necessary. I think this should cover it. I'll just be going."

I slammed the door.

The children ran at me and I scooped them into quick hugs. I wiped Delia's eyes and held Zach to my chest, placing his woobie in his arms as he sniffled and calmed.

"I could have handled it," Steven said.

I didn't waste my time arguing with him as I picked up clothes and food wrappers from the floor.

"Don't look at me like that! You can't just swoop in here and be the hero, throwing money around and pretending to fix everything. Not after leaving me alone with them all day." I laughed at the irony. "Do you have any idea what I had to deal with? Zach took a dump in the pool."

"Was he wearing his swim diaper?" I asked.

"What swim diaper? He has a swim diaper?"

I sighed as I changed the children hastily into their pajamas and nestled them against their pillows, drawing the comforter over them and tucking them in. I adjusted the volume on the TV to a soothing, low level before kissing them both good night.

I handed Steven the remote. "I have to go."

"Where?" His voice rose with panic as I returned to my room for my purse.

"To a dinner meeting with my agent," I said, slipping on my shoes. "I'll be back in a few hours."

"A few hours—?"

I pivoted toward him, dropping my voice to a whisper. "Pull your shit together, Steven. You're their father. It isn't all that hard."

He watched me, dumbstruck, as I grabbed my things and walked out the door.

CHAPTER 13

Thirty minutes later, Charlie was right behind me, his shoulder brushing mine as he reached around me to hold the restaurant door open, his easy smile twisting around his scar.

"Let's get this wrapped up quickly," he said. "You and I have a car to find." It was the same phony chivalrous gesture, the same charismatic smile he'd worn two days ago when he'd opened the door of his Cadillac to me, then proceeded to trap me and Vero inside it. He'd threatened us, taken all our money, and told us he'd been working for Feliks all along. I had that same feeling of being trapped as he politely nudged me into the restaurant and the door fell closed behind us.

Charlie stood close as I clocked the room. My gaze traveled furtively over the long, narrow dining area behind the hostess stand, over the cloth-lined candlelit tables, to the bright red EXIT sign above the entrance to a narrow corridor at the back, probably where the restrooms were located. A long, polished bar was situated close to the front of the restaurant, where brightly lit shelves displaying top-notch liquors could be seen through the windows facing the street. Charlie's Cadillac was parked at the nearest public lot a few blocks away. Without knowing it, Sylvia had managed to pick the perfect location.

"Do you have a reservation?" the hostess asked.

"I'm meeting someone." I pointed out Sylvia's table.

The hostess gathered two menus from her station. "Right this way," she said, gesturing for us to follow.

I dug in my heels as Charlie started after her. "Oh, we're not together. This man just has a problem with personal space." I pasted on a pitying smile. I could play the phony game, too.

Charlie reached for one of her menus. "I'll just take a seat at the bar." His eyes bored into mine as he claimed the stool closest to the end of it, offering him a clear view of Sylvia's table.

I shed my coat and took a seat across from my agent. She had dressed for the occasion. Her hair was big, her makeup was glam, and her low-cut cheetah-print dress was brimming over with . . . anticipation.

"I took the liberty of ordering you a drink," she said, pushing a glass of bubbly in front of me with her press-on nails. "Why is your police friend sitting at the bar? Why don't you ask him to join us?" She teased her curls, craning her neck to get a look at Charlie.

"That guy is not my friend. Nick couldn't make it," I explained as I slugged down my drink. "He asked someone else to drive me."

"Trouble in paradise, already?"

You could say that. "No, he's just busy working a case."

Sylvia leaned in, chin in hand. "Ooooh, sounds juicy! Like fodder for a book." *If she only knew.*

I gestured with my empty glass for our waitress to bring another. "Look, I don't have time to stay for dinner—"

"Appetizers then. Or maybe just dessert."

"Appetizers," I said, scanning the menu for something that could be brought to the table quickly. "I'll just have a salad. And maybe some fried meatballs." I wasn't completely immune to the mouthwatering smells wafting through the room.

I peeked over at Charlie as Sylvia studied her menu. He sipped his beer, pretending not to be keeping tabs on me as he glanced up casually from his phone.

"We need to talk about this TV deal," Sylvia said, slapping her menu closed. "I talked to the producer—"

"About that—"

"I like him, Finn. He's got big ideas."

"I don't think this is the right time to go out with this book—"

"He's got an exclusive with a major studio. He's thinking Margot Robbie for the lead."

"But I'm not—"

"She'd be perfect. And I'm picturing Oscar Isaac as the hot cop."

"But—"

"You're right," she said at my stupefied look, "we'll push for Ryan Gosling."

"Sylvia!" Her head snapped up, her false lashes frozen wide. "I don't want to pursue this deal." A few heads around us turned. I could feel Charlie's watchful gaze on me from across the room. I lowered my voice. "It's my book and my story. I need time to think about it."

Sylvia stared at me. After a long moment, she reached for her drink. "Fine. We'll wait."

"We will?" Sylvia had never bothered to listen to me before.

"This is normal. It'll pass."

"What will pass?"

"Impostor syndrome. Don't bother denying it," she said when I started to object. "You and I both know you're not Margot Robbie. I mean, Jesus, Finn, look at you. You've got a unicorn sticker in your hair, by the way. Regardless," she said dismissively as I fished one of Delia's tiny stickers from the strands, "the only thing standing in the way of a TV deal is you. You're afraid of it."

My cheeks burned. "I'm not afraid of it."

"You are," she insisted, pointing her champagne flute at me. "You're afraid of your own success, just like you're afraid of ordering dessert. Because you don't think you deserve it. But I'm telling you, Finlay, this book is good. This whole *series* is good. The plots may be a little far-fetched, but these characters are so *real*! It's like they just leap off the page! Someone was bound to want to buy it. This self-doubt will pass. It always does. And when it does, you'll be unstoppable. Then, we'll go back to this producer and get your TV show."

"Thanks," I said as she polished off her drink. "I feel bad you drove all this way to meet me. I'm sorry to disappoint you."

"The only thing I'm disappointed about is that I didn't get to meet your hot cop. He sounds too good to be true, Finlay. I'm thrilled for you, truly. The rest we'll figure out when you're feeling up to it."

He was too good to be true, which was precisely the problem.

Sylvia surprised me, taking my hand as I reached for a breadstick. "What else is eating you? And don't tell me you're fine. I've been your agent long enough to know you're never fine. Something is always wrong with you."

"Thanks," I deadpanned.

"And why does that guy at the bar keep staring at you? Who is he?"

"Charlie?" I glanced over as the bartender cleared Charlie's empty glass and set another in front of him. "He's one of Nick's friends, a retired detective. He's supposed to be keeping an eye on me."

Sylvia gasped. "Do you have a stalker? Is some crazy fan harassing you?"

"Not exactly," I said, biting into my breadstick. "Nick's in town investigating a case, and Charlie's running interference."

"Why? He doesn't want you getting in the way?"

"In a manner of speaking."

Sylvia leaned in. "What's involved in this case? Is it a murder?" Her eyes lit. I could practically see the dollar signs adding up inside them.

If there was any chance of escaping, it had to be now. I set down my bread and leaned toward her, my head bent close. "Possibly two." Sylvia sucked in a breath. "A man went missing," I continued. "There were signs of foul play—"

"How foul are we talking?"

"His car was set on fire but no body was found in it. And a key witness in the investigation seems to have disappeared. Nick's probably trying to find him right now. I wanted to go with him—I mean, what a perfect research opportunity, right? That's where we were going when you called me earlier. But when Nick heard you wanted to meet me about a TV deal, he said this dinner was too important to miss, so he asked Charlie to drive me."

"I had no idea," Sylvia breathed as she glanced toward the bar.

"It's fine. Charlie doesn't want me involved in the case anyway. He said it's far too dangerous for a civilian to be riding along. They could find a body. There could be dangerous people with guns. You know, hackers transporting secret files or thieves with stolen property! Even if I could manage to catch up with Nick, we'd probably have to go deep undercover. We might have to rent a room together, posing as a married couple. There would probably be only one bed. And sharing it would be *completely* out of the question. That sort of thing is strictly forbidden between cops and civilians during a stakeout." I left out the fact that it was forbidden for me to even be *on* a stakeout. "It's probably better that I'm here with you. *Anything* could happen if I was out there with a rogue cop, searching for bad guys in a seedy nightclub or a swanky hotel suite. There's no way Charlie would ever let me out of his sight long enough for me to find Nick and help him work the case."

Sweat bloomed on Sylvia's bosom. Her hand shot across the table and closed around mine, clammy and hot. "Maybe I can help," she said urgently. "I'm your agent, aren't I? My job is to clear your path of any obstacles to your success."

"You think it's possible to shake him?"

"Leave that part to me." She sat up tall and flagged down our server, requesting two salads be brought immediately to our table. When our server rushed to the kitchen, Sylvia reached under the table. "Take this," she said, pressing something against my knee.

"What is it?"

"My purse. Hang it on the back of your chair, over your coat. When our salads get here, leave the coat and purse and take the rear exit through the hallway behind you. Your friend at the bar will assume you've gone to the ladies' room and you're coming right back. It will take him a few minutes to realize you're gone. Don't worry, I'll cover for you. Now go find your man, and come back with a story. I want to hear all the details when you get home." She winked at me as our server returned and set a plate of salad in front of me.

"Thanks, Sylvia," I said, slipping her purse over the back of my chair. "You're the best."

Without looking at Charlie, I excused myself from the table and followed the signs for the restroom. When I was certain Charlie couldn't see me from the bar, I dashed through the narrow hallway and out the back door. Then I raced around the building and flagged down a taxi. A yellow cab screeched to the curb. I ducked inside and slammed the door.

"Where to?" the driver asked.

"The Villagio," I said, twisting in my seat to see Charlie fly through the front door of the restaurant, shaking his head. I could have sworn he laughed as he watched us drive away.

CHAPTER 14

My anxiety spiked as I knocked a third time on the door to Marco's suite, and I considered the very real possibility that Cam and Vero had murdered each other while I'd been gone. I raised my hand to knock again, then paused as footsteps trotted to the other side of the door. "I charged it to the room," Vero called through the door. "Just leave the tray outside."

"It's me. Open up and let me in."

The dead bolt flipped and the door swung open. "What took you so long? I was starting to worry."

I followed her into the suite, lurching to a stop as I reached the living room and spotted a pair of hotel slippers sticking up over the arm of the couch. Cam didn't look up from the telenovela on the TV. He was wrapped in a plush hotel bathrobe, his head propped high on a mountain of king-sized pillows. Marco's wiener dog rested on a cushion beside him, and a plate of hotcakes and syrup rested on Cam's lap.

He speared a breakfast sausage and held the fork out to the dog. Kevin glared at me as he gobbled up the link.

I felt my blood pressure rise as I looked around the room. Every surface was littered with empty, crumb-covered serving trays. A platter had been left on the floor, presumably for the dog, who was now strung out on the couch in some kind of sausage-induced coma. "What on earth were you two doing while I was gone?"

"Babysitting," Vero said, arms crossed, scowling at Cam from the opposite arm of the couch.

"Shhh," he said, turning up the volume on the remote. "La Reina just told that cartel dude to step off or she'll put a cap in his ass."

"Don't look at me," Vero said to me. "You're the one that brought him here."

I snatched the remote control from Cam's hand. Kevin growled, and Cam looked stricken as I turned the TV off. "You two were supposed to be working! While you were up here having a pajama party, two dead men have been decomposing in the bathroom, and if we don't figure out who killed them, there's no chance we'll find the car. *Or* Javi!" I reminded Vero.

"Relax, Mrs. D." Cam swung his slippers off the arm of the sofa and sat upright, wiping his syrupy chin on the collar of his robe. "We already know who murdered Mario and Luigi." He held his empty plate toward Vero. She got up to take it, grinding her teeth.

"What?" Vero said at my slack-jawed expression. "I lost a bet, okay?"

"She's just sore because I solved the mystery first."

"Wait," I said, looking between them. "You *know* who killed Marco and Louis? How? What did you find?"

"Check it out." Cam held Louis's tablet out to me. A document was open on the screen, containing a short list of names with dollar amounts and check marks beside them. One name jumped out from the others— VERONICA RUIZ (AKA RAMIREZ): $200K—one of only two names with no check mark beside it.

"What is this?" I asked, trying to make sense of what I was looking at.

"A list of people Louis was hired to spy on. The ones with checks beside their names already paid their debts to Marco. The only two that aren't checked are—"

"Vero and . . . *Pokey*?" I skimmed the dollar amount beside the second unchecked name. Apparently, Francis Slocumb—aka Pokey—was in debt to Marco for a whopping hundred grand. Not as much as Vero, but certainly enough to be a motive for murder.

"You think this Pokey person killed them?" I asked.

Cam leaned back and propped his feet on the coffee table. "Always follow the money, Mrs. D."

"That's *my* line," Vero snapped. She turned to me. "Remember that little black book Marco had in his pocket at the restaurant? It was a ledger. Cam and I searched every inch of this place and that book isn't anywhere in this suite. Whoever killed Marco must have taken it to cover their tracks."

"A ledger? Like the one we found in Steven's drawer? Why would a loan shark keep his records in a book? Why wouldn't he keep them on a computer, like Louis?"

"Because books can't be hacked," Cam said wryly.

"But they can be stolen," Vero pointed out. "And someone must have wanted this one pretty badly."

I had no idea what the names and numbers in Steven's book translated to, or the significance of them, but the thought of someone breaking into my ex-husband's house and strangling him for it was enough to send a chill up my spine. I shook it off.

"What about the car?" I asked. I didn't have the bandwidth to worry about Steven's secrets right now. Those would have to wait until after we'd found Javi.

Vero shook her head. "Nothing in either of their texts or emails suggests they moved the Aston someplace else. We know the car was here—the valet at Caesars told us that much. My guess is the keys were sitting out in plain sight, and Pokey took those, too."

"Okay, so where do we find this Pokey person?"

Cam shrugged. "Couldn't find much about him online. He's twenty-nine years old. No recent pics. No social media accounts. The guy's credit report was a mess though. A couple of collections, back taxes, dozens of late payments on his rent. As far as I can tell, dude got evicted from his apartment about a month ago. No new hits under his name with the local utility companies. Looks like he's lying low. The guy's pretty broke. He's probably couch surfing."

"Which would explain why he took the Aston," Vero said. "That car's worth a lot of money. He'll probably try to fence it."

"If we don't know where he lives, how are we going to find him?" I asked.

"We follow the money." Vero tossed Cam the remote and put on her shoes. "Don't open the door until we get back. Finlay and I are going to the casino."

CHAPTER 15

"How are we supposed to find Pokey in here?" I asked, narrowing my shoulders to squeeze between the crowds clogging the Royal Flush's casino. The place reeked of cigarettes, liquor, and cheap cologne, but Vero had figured it was a logical place to start. "I thought you said Pokey was broke. And even if he wasn't, we don't even know what he looks like."

"Don't need to," Vero said, rising on her toes to scan the room.

I followed her through a bank of slot machines. "Where are we going?" Marbles spun on roulette wheels on the periphery, and onlookers gathered to watch. Vero navigated smoothly through the crowd toward the table games beyond them, slowing her pace to study the dealers and the players. She picked a blackjack table and sat down, passing me a handful of chips as I claimed the empty seat beside her.

She arranged her own chips into neat piles and pushed one toward the dealer.

"What do I do?" I whispered. Aside from the occasional scratch-off ticket in the fast-food drive-through, I'd never actually gambled before. Vero tossed one of my chips onto the bet line.

"Just do what I do," she said in a low voice. Her eyes tracked the cards as the dealer doled them out. Vero slid another chip forward. "Hit me," she said, taking another card. She peeped at it, her face revealing nothing as she told the dealer she'd stay.

The dealer pivoted to me. "Hit me," I said.

Vero frowned. "What are you doing?"

"What? You told me to do what you do. That's what you did." She smacked me in the shoulder. "Ow!"

"You have seventeen. If you take another card, you'll probably bust."

"You peeked at my hand."

"I didn't peek at your hand. When would I have peeked at your hand? You never even looked at your cards."

"Well, you obviously saw them!"

"Are you accusing me of cheating?" Vero asked a little too loudly. The dealer glanced up at a ceiling-mounted camera.

"Lower your voice," I hissed at Vero. "You're making a scene."

The other players abandoned the table as Vero continued to argue.

"Don't look now," she whispered out of the corner of her mouth. "Pit boss is on his way."

"Who?"

An attractive man in a black-on-black suit appeared behind us.

"How are we doing, ladies?" he asked, resting a hand on each of our seat backs.

"We'd be doing a lot better if my friend here wasn't so obtuse," Vero said.

"I am not obtuse!"

"If you had actually bothered to watch the YouTube tutorials I sent you before we came, you might have *some* understanding of table etiquette." Vero pushed a twenty-dollar chip toward the dealer. "I'm sorry she scared away all of your players. We should probably go catch a show instead. I don't have the patience for this." Vero opened her purse wide and began scooping her chips into it, revealing a thick stack of twenty-dollar bills she had drawn from the ATM in the lobby.

The pit boss's eyes locked on the cash. He stopped her as she began to close her bag. "How about I give your friend a quick lesson instead? Then you both can stay and put those chips to good use." He walked around the table and relieved the dealer of her post, the two of them engaging in some odd ritual that seemed to mark the end of her shift.

"What's your name?" Vero asked him as he reloaded the shoe.

"Miles. And you are?"

"Call me Patricia," Vero answered. "And this is my friend Irina."

I waved politely at Miles as I kicked Vero under the table.

"Well, Irina, you look like a pretty smart lady to me. Shouldn't take me too long to show you the ropes."

"Looks can be deceiving," Vero muttered.

Miles spent the next few minutes explaining the rules of the game, giving me a quick primer in what Vero had referred to as table etiquette before dealing our first hand.

"So, Miles," Vero said as we played. "I've been looking for this guy I met here last time I was in town, but I lost his number. I'm pretty sure he's local. He goes by Pokey. Maybe you know him?"

Miles's smile quirked higher on one side. "Yeah, we all know Pokey. But he hasn't stepped foot in here for a while. Got himself a little upside down. Pretty sure he's been blackballed from every casino on the board-walk. Sure you met him here?"

Vero's face fell. If Pokey had been blackballed from every casino, that would make him much harder to find. "My memory of that night's a little foggy," she admitted. "Do you know where he works?"

Miles called out to the dealer at the next table. "Hey! Where's Slow Poke working these days?"

The other dealer smirked. "Last I heard, he was bussing tables at Chubby's."

Miles raised an eyebrow. "Chubby's sound familiar to you ladies?"

Vero snapped a finger. "Of course! Irina and I have been there loads of times."

Miles smiled to himself as he dealt out the last of the cards and cleared the table. Vero tossed him a tip as she hopped off her stool. "Come on, Irina. I've got a sudden craving for Chubby's."

I thanked Miles for the lesson, hurrying after Vero as she hustled back through the slot machines and into the lobby.

"There you are!" a woman called out. We both whirled at the sound of my mother's voice behind us. "Where on earth have you two been?"

Vero elbowed me in the side.

"Mom!" I sputtered. "What are you doing down here?"

"Looking for you! I wanted to hear all about your meeting with Sylvia. How did it go?"

"It was . . . surprisingly helpful," I said, glancing over her shoulder, hoping my sister or Sam hadn't followed her downstairs. "Where is everyone?"

"Steven's putting the kids to bed, and Georgia and Sam are watching a movie in their room. I didn't see any sense in bothering them," she said with a dismissive wave toward the elevators. An awkward silence fell as she narrowed her eyes at us. "Where were you two off to just now? And where's Charlie?" she asked, scanning the faces in the crowd.

I gestured loosely toward the street. "You just missed him."

Vero nodded a little too hard. "He said he was hungry. He's probably just going to get something to eat."

My mother held her belly. "I was just going to do the same. I'm starving."

"You should go upstairs and order room service. You shouldn't be out by yourself."

She dug in her heels as I nudged her toward the elevator. "No more room service. The food in this place is awful. I'm going out. The lady at the front desk said there's a decent Italian restaurant a few blocks from here. You two should come with me," she suggested brightly.

"I had dinner with Syl—"

"What a coincidence!" Vero interrupted. "Finlay and I were just talking about going out to eat. How about a diner?"

My mother beamed. "A diner sounds fun!"

"More fun than a bathtub full of monkeys!"

"This is not a good idea," I warned Vero through my teeth.

"This is a perfect idea," she said through a tight smile.

"Of course it is," my mother insisted, looping an arm through Vero's. "We won't be out long. Georgia and Sam won't even know we were gone, and the three of us haven't had any girl time since we got here. Besides, I want to hear all about this mysterious friend Vero's been spending so much time with. He must be quite a hunk!"

"You have no idea," I muttered as they strolled arm in arm through the lobby door.

"Come on, Susan," Vero said. "Let's go see what's cookin' at Chubby's."

CHAPTER 16

It was just after nine by the time Vero and my mother hailed a taxi and we all climbed in.

"Where to?" the cabbie asked.

"Chubby's," Vero answered.

"I could really go for a burger," my mother said as she buckled herself in. "Is the food there any good?"

The driver raised an eyebrow at his rearview mirror. "I never heard anyone complain about the menu."

"Perfect. Let's go." Vero slammed the door.

Five minutes later, the cabbie jerked to a stop beside a short, brick building. A hot pink OPEN sign flickered in the window, which had been darkened with black paint. Loud music played inside, and a boisterous crowd had formed in front of the place.

"The line looks pretty long," Vero said as we exited the taxi.

"The food must be very good here," my mother said, rising on her toes to search for the end of the line.

"Wait here," I said, passing my mother off to Vero. "I'll see how long the wait is for a table." I squeezed past a group of tipsy women in matching BRIDESMAID T-shirts and maneuvered to the front of the line.

"Hi," I said, tapping the hostess station to get the attention of the young woman behind it. "Can you tell me if Pokey's working tonight?"

She glanced up from her tablet, her thick false eyelashes fanning the air. "Slow Poke? Yeah, he's working."

"Great. How long is the wait for a table?"

"Does your party have reservations?"

"No, but it's only three of us."

"I have an opening at eleven." She turned away from me and called over the crowd, "Wagner party. Your tables are ready." A cheer arose from the group of drunken bridesmaids.

I checked my phone. Eleven was two hours from now. The entire FCPD would probably be looking for us by then. I offered the hostess a folded twenty I'd scraped from the bottom of my purse. "We'll just sit at the bar."

"No seating at the bar." She waved me away from the door, holding it open for the clash of women rushing toward it. She counted their heads as they stumbled inside, searching the line for more of them. She called out to one of the bridesmaids. "Where's the rest of your party? You're missing three people." The girl only shrugged, her answer swallowed by the thumping music inside.

I didn't have time for this. I retreated to find Vero and my mother.

"Come on," I said, plucking them out of the crowd. "Let's try around back. Maybe there's another way in."

We weaved through a crowd of noisy middle-aged women wearing "over the hill" party hats and carrying black balloons, then past a group of much older women as they disembarked from a nursing home bus and shuffled on canes and walkers to the end of the line. We rounded the side of the building, nearly tripping over two drunken bridesmaids in the alley. A young woman braced herself against the building between them, her bushy white veil blowing across their faces as they attempted to hold her hair back while she puked. One of the bridesmaids blew out a mouthful of tulle. In a fit of impatience, she plucked the veil from the bride's head and tossed it onto the ground.

I stepped around them and tried the back door of the restaurant, but it was locked.

My mother stopped to fuss over the girls. "Oh, you poor thing," she said, digging in her fanny pack for one of Delia's elastic hair bands and offering it to one of the bridesmaids. Vero ducked, picking up the abandoned veil as she took my mother's hand and led her quickly back to the front of the restaurant.

I ran to catch up as Vero pulled the veil over my mother's head. "What are you doing?"

"I have an idea."

"Maybe we should go someplace else," my mother said through the thick layers of tulle as Vero arranged them to cover her face.

She pointed my mother toward the front of the line and nudged her ahead of us. "Out of the way! Bride coming through!" Vero and I ducked behind her and followed. The hostess opened the door for us with an impatient huff, and the three of us slipped past her into a dimly lit antechamber.

Strobe lights flashed across the floors and house music shook the walls. A red velvet rope blocked access to the larger room beyond it.

I jolted to a stop, pulling Vero up short in front of a flickering neon sign.

CHUBBIES, it read in hot blue script.

"What's wrong?" my mother asked, stumbling into us. Brightly colored lights streaked across her veil as she tried and failed to bat it out of her eyes.

"It's *Chubbies*," I said to Vero. "Plural, with an *I-E*. Not singular, with a *Y*."

"I can see that," she said, her eyes wide with appreciation as a bare-bottomed server in leather chaps strode by. Men clad in little more than baby oil and G-strings carried trays of drinks and appetizers through the room, angling their hips toward tables of ogling women who tucked cash down the front of their scant thongs.

"I thought you said this was a diner!" I hissed in her ear.

"What's going on?" my mother asked, swatting back her veil.

A man in a tuxedo swooped toward us. "There you are!" he said, opening the velvet rope and ushering us through it. "Your party has been waiting for you. Right this way," he said, hurrying us past the barrier into a room of cheering women.

An announcer leaped onto the stage. The music faded as he tested the mic. "Our bride has finally arrived, everyone! Let's show her a *Chubbies* good time!" A few women let loose piercing whistles. The announcer's face sobered. He tipped his head, one hand cupped dramatically around his ear. "Oh, no! Do you hear that?" A siren whooped loudly over the speakers. "Some of you have been very bad girls, and you know what that means." The audience whooped, forcing him to raise his voice over the din. "That's right, ladies! The long arm of the law has arrived on the scene. Let's give it up for Officer Steele Johnson!"

The audience hollered and cheered as two men in fringed G-strings swooped in and took my mother by the elbows. Her hand slipped from mine as they whisked her toward the stage, carrying her up the short steps and setting her on the platform. Smoky mist poured from the floor, backlit by violet and fuchsia swirling lights as my mother stumbled this way and that, a sea of white gauze obscuring her face. Sirens whined as the curtain on the stage parted. A man stepped out wearing a skin-tight police uniform and mirrored shades. He tossed his sunglasses into the screaming crowd.

"Oh, no," I said as my mother threw back her veil. Vero clapped a hand over her mouth.

My mother's jaw dropped, her gaze glued to Steele Johnson's hips as he strode slowly toward her and tipped up her chin. The microphone beside his mouth projected his deep voice over the crowd. "I've got a BOLO here for a very special lady."

"You do?" my mother croaked as he pulled an arrest warrant slowly from his pants.

"Someone has been a very naughty bride." The audience went wild as he tossed the warrant into the crowd. "And baby, I am here to take . . . you . . . down."

The music began to pulse. Women screamed as Steele began swinging his hips. He locked a hand behind his neck, tensing his abs, his other arm extended in a choreographed dance move that reminded me of Mrs. Haggerty's lawn sprinkler.

"Oh, god." I covered my eyes as he unfastened his police belt and gyrated toward my mother. She gasped, her cheeks flushing hotter than the stage lights as bits of his police costume were plucked away and flung into the squealing pit of feral women below.

That's it. I was going to kill Vero in front of a room full of strippers. I searched out the nearest server and flagged him down.

"Excuse me," I said over the music, trying not to stare at his fringe. "This is all a very big misunderstanding. That's my mother up there." I cringed as I pointed at the stage. "See, we thought Chubby's was a diner . . . you know. Chubby, singular. With a *Y*. We had no idea it was referring to . . . Oh, wow," I said as Officer Johnson bent low at the waist, grabbing two fistfuls of fabric around his ankles and tearing his pants clean off his body. I gestured to the large sock ball I could only assume was stuffed inside the strained piece of fabric that remained intact. "We had no idea it was referring to that."

My mother stumbled backward, unable to tear her eyes from it. Steele caught her hand before she could trip backward off the stage.

"You're not here for the bachelorette party?" the server asked me.

"Would you believe we came here looking for hamburgers?"

His grin was neon white against a canvas of glittering, spray-tanned skin. "Hate to break it to you, but we're not really known for the food here."

"I gathered that." I ducked as Steele's police hat flew over our heads. Two women in the audience lunged for it, collapsing in a fit of drunken giggles on the floor. The server held up his tray, sidestepping to avoid them.

"I'm actually looking for someone who works here," I said over the music.

"Sorry. We're not allowed to do house calls, if that's what you're into—"

"No," I said quickly, "nothing like that. I just need to talk to him. His name is Francis Slocumb. Is he here?"

"Slow Poke? Yeah, he's here." He turned to search the room. "That's him," he said, pointing out a seminude cowboy in a wide-brimmed hat on the far side of the room.

Pokey leaned over an empty table, his tight bottom peeking out of a pair of leather chaps as he loaded empty beer bottles and shot glasses into a plastic bin.

I glanced back at the stage as Steele took my mother's hand and lowered her gently into a folding chair, his microphone catching her breathy *oh my* as his muscular thighs straddled her lap. The rest of her was obscured behind the broad expanse of his chest.

Seizing my moment, I pulled two fifties from my pocket and pressed them into the server's hand. "Can you do me a favor and keep my mother occupied until I get back? I'll only be a few minutes," I promised, dashing off before he could object.

I squinted against the strobe lights, searching for Vero. Our eyes caught. I pointed frantically at Pokey over the crowd, but she was already on the move toward him, weaving between tables, her path to our mark slowed by the grabby women standing in the aisles, waving dollar bills and shouting to get Steele Johnson's attention as he ripped the handcuffs from his belt.

He swung them over his head and let them fly into the audience. I dove for them as they sailed toward me, the breath rushing from my lungs as a large woman in a party hat tackled me sideways to the floor. The cuffs flew out of my hands and skittered away from me. She grabbed me by my shirt, pulling me back as I lunged for them. The crowd began to chant, begging for a catfight, a circle forming around us as we scrabbled for the cuffs.

"I really need those handcuffs!" I growled as her nails dug into me.

"I saw them first!" she shrieked, yanking a fistful of my hair.

I kicked her away. She grunted, both of us baring our teeth as I wrestled the cuffs from her hand. The crowd cheered as I shot to my feet, victorious.

Pokey glanced up at the commotion. His smile fell away as our eyes locked and Vero and I started toward him from opposite sides of the room. Tucking his tray under his arm, he started briskly toward a door marked EMPLOYEES ONLY.

"Somebody stop him!" Vero shouted. When no one moved to block his retreat, Vero stood on a chair and yelled, "Francis Slocumb, I'm having your baby!"

Every woman in the room turned to stare at Pokey.

His eyes went wide and he took off running. An elderly woman extended her cane as he sprinted past her table. He tripped, stumbling out of one of his cowboy boots. His bin of empty bottles went flying and his glistening skin squeaked against the parquet floor.

Vero jumped down from the chair. Aisles cleared for her as she picked her way toward him. Pokey scrambled to his feet, his hat falling back, the cord catching around his Adam's apple and his leather tassels flying as he bolted out the closest fire door.

A cheer went up from the audience as Vero and I dashed through the emergency exit after him.

"Which way did he go?" Vero asked, panting as she looked both ways down the alley.

"There!" I said, pointing at the flash of Pokey's bright white backside as he limped past a streetlamp at the end of the narrow passageway, hobbled by his single boot. We chased him between two buildings. The concrete sidewalk gave way to crumbling asphalt. Pokey swore, grabbing his bare foot and hopping in place as Vero plowed into him and tackled him to the ground. His breath burst out of his lungs as they both hit the gravel.

She unhooked his flimsy lasso from his belt, looping it around his ankles. I bent double at her side and fought to catch my breath.

"Are you Francis Slocumb?" she panted.

"I swear, I didn't get anyone pregnant!"

He yelped as she wrenched one of his arms behind his back. "I know that, you idiot! Just answer the question."

"I'm Francis," he said with a defiant lift of his chin. "Who the hell are you?"

A familiar spark lit in her eyes as I passed her Steele's handcuffs.

"I'm Detective Dolce," Vero said, assuming her fake cop voice as she snapped the cuffs around his wrists. "And this is my partner, Detective Gabbana."

Pokey's eyes narrowed. "Like the handbags? You seriously expect me to believe that?" He craned his neck to look at us. "If you two are cops, let me see some ID."

"You have the right to remain silent," Vero warned him, "but I would strongly advise against it."

"I don't have to tell you shit. Did Steele put you up to this?"

"Where were you last night between the hours of ten P.M. and midnight?"

He writhed against his cuffs. "I was here all night, working my shift!"

"So you didn't pay a visit to Marco Toscano's suite?" Pokey went still, his eyes wide as Vero continued. "Because somebody stole Marco's ledger last night, and your name was in it."

Sweat trailed down Pokey's temple, along with a few other parts of him that were hard not to notice, given his current position. "Why the hell would I steal Marco's ledger?"

"Probably because you were overdue for a hundred Gs and Marco was trying to collect."

"What . . . ? No!" he sputtered. "I mean, yeah, I owe the guy a lot of money. Sure. What do you think I'm doing working here? You think I like having my ass pinched by handsy old ladies? Hell no! But I didn't steal from the guy!"

She put her hands on her hips. "So you don't have his little black book? Or his car?"

"If I had Marco Toscano's car, I sure as hell wouldn't have taken the bus here tonight! I was at Chubbies last night, open to close. You can check my time sheet. It's hanging on the wall back at the club."

A metallic snap echoed behind us. A cool voice said, "I hope for your sake you're telling the truth about that."

All three of us stiffened at the cock of Charlie's magnum. Pokey's eyes squeezed shut and his voice cracked. "I swear to god, I didn't do anything wrong. I didn't take anyone's book, and I didn't steal anyone's car. Please don't arrest me."

Vero gaped at him. "You think *he's* a cop! Just because he's a guy?"

"Because he has a gun! And by the sound of it, it's a really fucking big one. So unless this guy tells me his name is Detective Versace, I'll err on the side of caution, thank you very much."

"Are you two finished playing detective?" Charlie asked.

"Are you finished being an asshole?" Vero sassed.

"Turn around." We both raised our hands and slowly turned around, until we were staring into the mouth of Charlie's revolver. "What's this business about Marco Toscano having the car?"

Vero and I glanced at each other. How much of the conversation had Charlie heard? And, more important, how had he known where to find us?

"Marco's people took the car from us," I said with a cautious glance at Pokey, afraid of saying too much. "Now Marco's disappeared, and we have no idea who has it. Whoever has the car most likely took Marco's ledger, too."

"I swear to god, it wasn't me," Pokey said, wrenching his neck to see over his shoulder. "I had nothing to do with any of this."

Charlie swung the revolver, aiming it at the back of Pokey's head. "Then I guess we won't be needing you anymore."

"Wait!" I cried. "We don't know that."

Charlie scowled at me, like he was torn between listening to reason and shooting Pokey just to spite me. "Fine. But unless you want Nick finding out what you two have been up to tonight, you're going to walk out of this alley right now and get in my fucking car. And neither one of you had better give me any trouble." Charlie gestured impatiently through the gap between the buildings. Hands above our heads, we started walking toward his Cadillac, leaving Pokey in the alley.

"How the hell did you find us anyway?" Vero asked as Charlie's shoes crunched softly behind us.

"You assume I can't just because I'm retired? You're not as cagey as you think," he mocked us, clucking his tongue. "I might be old, but it wasn't that hard."

"I hear they make medications for that."

"Keep moving," he said, jabbing his gun into her back.

I flinched at a loud crash. Vero and I whirled in time to see Charlie crumple, his gun clattering to the ground amid a spray of broken glass.

Pokey stood behind him, wielding a broken bottle of Jim Beam. Steele's handcuffs dangled from one of his wrists. He tossed the neck of the bottle aside, looking like he might be sick. "Tell me I didn't just brain a cop!"

Vero kicked Charlie's gun out of reach as Charlie groaned, struggling to come around. "You didn't," she assured him. "Technically, he's retired."

He stifled a cry and began pacing the alley, his bare, oily bottom shining like a target in the dark. "Oh, shit. *Oh shit oh shit oh shit,*" he chanted to himself as he worked the second cuff free.

"How'd you do that?" Vero asked as he thrust them at her.

"I'm covered in baby oil!" he snapped.

She considered that and wiped the cuffs on her shirt. She closed the metal loops until they made a full circle and opened again with a series of soft clicks. Charlie moaned as she rolled him onto his side and snapped the restraints around his wrists.

I frisked his pockets for his phone and keys. Vero retrieved his gun and tucked it into her jeans. "A little help here?" she asked, stooping to grab Charlie under his armpits.

Francis raised his hands. "I draw the line at abducting cops."

"I told you, he's retired."

"It's a very slippery slope."

She rolled her eyes as I bent to grab Charlie's feet, and the two of us loaded him into the trunk of his car. Vero dusted off her hands as I slammed the lid. She raised an eyebrow at the triangle of spandex framed by Pokey's chaps. "It's looking a little cold out here. You should probably go inside." Pokey blushed under the streetlamp. His eyes dipped to the .357 in Vero's pants, and he wisely chose to keep his own mouth shut.

"Can we all agree not to say anything to anyone about this?" I asked, hoping he wouldn't feel a need to report this to anyone. I really didn't want to have to wrestle him into the trunk, too.

He gestured to his lone boot. "You think I want to tell anyone?" He dusted alley grime from his fringe, wincing at the weeping road rash on his thighs. "I'm going home. After tonight, I'll probably get fired anyway."

"You could just quit," Vero pointed out. "Marco's book is gone. It's not like you need to worry about paying him back the money."

Pokey straightened his cowboy hat as he limped bare-assed to the corner. "You two don't know how shit works around here, do you?" he called over his shoulder. "That book is Marco's business, and Marco's business is valuable. That ledger won't just disappear because someone walked off with it. It'll turn up somewhere. Secrets always do."

For all our sakes, I hoped he wasn't right.

CHAPTER 17

"Where to now?" Vero asked, hands on her hips as she frowned at the Cadillac.

"We can't take Charlie's car back to the hotel."

"He's going to be pissed when he wakes up."

"Hopefully by the time he makes it out of this trunk, we'll have found Javi and the car and be on our way back to Virginia."

"What are you going to tell Nick?" she asked.

"As little as possible." I thumbed open Charlie's phone and found the long string of text messages the two of them had been exchanging all day. "All we have to do is respond when Nick checks in. If we keep our responses short and sweet, he probably won't suspect anything." Sure enough, Nick and Charlie had last messaged each other an hour ago.

Charlie: *How's the manhunt going?*
Nick had responded with a poop emoji. *How was Finn's meeting with her agent?*

Charlie had answered that with a series of surreptitious photos he'd taken at Chubbies. There was one of me passing cash to a scantily clad server. There was one of Vero, pointing and shouting, standing on a chair in an audience of cheering, thirsty women. There was even one of my mother, eyes wide and covered in glitter, with Steele Johnson sitting on her lap. Every photo looked perfectly incriminating and yet somehow altogether harmless, like we were actually having a good time. I squinted at the caption.

I'll let Finlay tell you all about her meeting later. The ladies wanted to do some manhunting of their own. Looks like we'll be out late. You owe me for this, partner.

Nick had replied with a laughing emoji. *I'll buy you a beer when I get back to the hotel.*

"That duplicitous bastard!" I said, tipping the screen toward Vero so she could see the photos Charlie had taken of us.

"At least now you won't have to lie to Nick about where you went. What else is on Charlie's phone?"

I sifted through his other calls and messages, then his email account, searching for any incriminating messages between Charlie and his mob contacts—anything to prove he'd been working for Feliks Zhirov.

Nothing. It was as if Charlie had compartmentalized his two identities entirely, and this phone bore no evidence at all of his other life. I opened his camera, not surprised to find he'd snapped a few pictures of Sylvia and me during dinner. It was as if he were building a case for himself, documenting evidence he'd done exactly what Nick had asked him to do tonight. I sighed, defeated. "There's nothing here."

"There has to be something," Vero said, taking the phone to look for herself before handing it back to me. "He's probably using fake names in his contact lists. You know, making dummy email accounts and using forwarded numbers to hide what he's up to from Nick. I bet if we gave that phone to Cam, he could find something in it."

"Maybe," I agreed. "But for now, we just need to keep Nick from suspecting anything." I crossed my arms over my sweater, wishing I had my coat. "We should go find my mother and take her back to the hotel."

"Then what?" Vero cocked an eyebrow. "Nick's expecting us to be out late, thanks to Charlie's texts."

"What do you have in mind?"

Vero thought about that. She stared at Charlie's trunk as she spun his key fob around her finger. "Remember what Pokey said, about Marco's book? That ledger is like the car," she explained. "It has value. Lots of people might want to buy a fancy car, but only one kind of person would be interested in a little black book listing all the names of people who took out markers from a loan shark, and that's another loan shark. And I'm willing to bet Marco Toscano wasn't the only loan shark in this town. In a city with this many casinos, there must be others."

"Meaning what?"

"Whoever stole that ledger knew it was valuable. And it was taken from the crime scene, so they'd probably want to get rid of it fast."

"Which means it might already be sold."

"All we have to do is find the person who bought it and figure out who sold it to them."

"And work backward to find Javi and the car." It sounded plausible in theory. "How do we find a loan shark?"

"We don't," Vero said, tossing Charlie's car keys into the dumpster behind us. "We let the loan shark find us."

CHAPTER 18

It was almost midnight when Vero finally materialized through the crowd. "Where have you been?" I asked. "You were gone so long, I was starting to worry." She'd left me sitting in front of an empty slot machine in the Villagio casino an hour ago, wearing a sequined jumpsuit and a curly black wig. I looked like a Cher impersonator. Over the course of the last hour, at least three elderly men had stopped to hit on me and another had asked me to hold his portable oxygen tank so he could light a cigarette. I'd almost rather have been stuck in a bathtub with Marco and Louis.

She fluffed her blond, feathered bangs and tugged at the strap on her acrylic heels. While I had escorted my tipsy mother to our hotel after we'd taken a cab home from Chubbies, Vero had gone shopping for wigs and clothes. The only place that had been open at that hour was an adult novelty store, and together we looked like two-thirds of a rerun of *Charlie's Angels*. I was just glad my mother hadn't insisted on tagging along.

"I had to stop to pick up some money," Vero said, adjusting her cleavage.

"Were you charging by the hour?"

She threw me a look as she unzipped her purse.

"This plan is completely ridiculous, Vero. I don't know how to gamble. There's no way this is going to work."

"You don't need to be good at it. I'll be right beside you the whole time. Let's get this over with so we can figure out who stole that ledger and find Javi." My heart stuttered as the massive grip of Charlie's gun protruded from her open purse. I reached to cover it, glancing frantically around us to make sure nobody else had noticed it.

She shoved my hand away. "Relax, Finn. This is Atlantic City. Half the people in this place are probably packing a weapon." She scooped a handful of chips from her bag. It was full of them, bulging at the seams. They were bolder and brighter than the ones we'd been playing with last night, and I gasped as I read the dollar value printed on them.

"These chips are worth five hundred dollars!" I lowered my voice as she shushed me. "Where did you get these?" There was far more money in chips in her purse than Steven had in his bank account.

"Louis's debit card. His PIN is the last four digits of his Social Security number. Cam figured it out."

"You got all of these off of Louis's card?"

She pulled a face. "Of course not. I won a few hands of poker for the rest."

"Vero!"

"We need a lot of money to lose a lot of money."

"You're lucky you came back with any money at all!"

"Luck had nothing to do with it," she said, jamming the last of the chips down the front of my jumpsuit when my pockets wouldn't hold any more. "Poker isn't the same as playing the lottery or slots, Finn. It's not just about chance. It's about reading people. The game isn't in the cards, it's up here," she said, tapping her temple. "Everyone has a tell. All you have to do is pay attention. You do it every day."

"I do not," I said, slapping her hand as she tucked another chip down my bra.

"Case in point," she said, zipping up her purse and leading us deeper into the casino, "how do you know when Zach's getting ready to bust out a BM?"

"He grabs the nearest doorframe and his face turns red."

"How about when Delia's coming down with a cold?"

"She cries for no reason and goes to bed without an argument."

"And when Steven's about to lie?"

"His left eyebrow twitches," I said without thinking.

"See? Even you could have won all this."

"I beg to differ," I said, adjusting the lumps in my bra.

"Poker's all about faking it, Finn. After eight years being married to Steven, you've got plenty of experience with that."

"Very funny."

"No? Then what about Nick?"

"I definitely didn't have to fake it with him."

A laugh burst out of her as she maneuvered through the crowd. "I wasn't talking about the sex. I was talking about everything else."

She wasn't wrong. The list of secrets I was keeping from Nick was getting longer every day. Soon, they'd be as impossible to hide as the chips inside my jumpsuit. "I don't know how much longer I can keep lying to him," I said, smoothing them down.

"The way I see it, you only have two choices: you can fold—and probably go to jail—or you can go all in and take a gamble on yourself. You want my advice? Stop worrying about the cards you've been dealt. As long as you don't give anything away, no one else can see your shitty cards but you. Fake it 'til you make it, Finn. Your odds of winning might be better than you think. Besides," she added, "if you tell your detective boyfriend everything, you're not going to prison alone, and I refuse to wear a polyester onesie. Though I admit, that one doesn't look half bad on you."

"Thanks," I mumbled.

"Don't mention it," she said, pausing to lean against a craps table.

"What now?"

She sighed as she stared longingly at the lumps in my top. "Put your chips on the bet line."

"How many?"

"All of them."

"All of them?" I shielded my pockets.

"If you want to look like a queen, you've got to gamble like one."

"What if we lose it all?"

"How else do you think we're going to get their attention? Hurry up. We're wasting time." Vero pried my hands away, reaching down the front of my jumpsuit and emptying the last of my chips onto the felt. The croupier raised an eyebrow as she pushed a set of dice toward us. Vero took them, her gaze flicking to the nearest security camera as she passed them to me. "Give them a blow."

"Why?"

"For luck."

"You said we were supposed to lose all our chips."

"Why do you think I asked *you* to blow on them?"

I glared at her as I blew into my hand and tossed the dice across the table.

The croupier called out a number and the other players clapped.

"What just happened?" I asked as chips were passed around the table. Vero's mouth fell open as the croupier plunked a thick stack of them in front of me. The players beside me offered congratulations as the dice were pushed toward me again.

Vero frowned. "Blow harder this time."

I blew hard on the dice and tossed them across the table. The croupier called out a number, and this time everybody cheered.

I whooped, unable to contain myself as more chips were piled in front of me. "That's good, right?"

"Yes . . . I mean, no!" Vero's eyes were wide as she stuffed a handful of my winnings into her pocket. "Maybe try a little less enthusiasm this time."

A hush fell over the table as I rolled again.

"Eleven!" The table erupted in victory shouts as the croupier doled out our winnings. A waitress set two free drinks between us as a crowd of onlookers formed. Vero's fingers grew clammy around mine. She stuffed another handful of chips into her pocket, leaving a teetering pile of them behind on the bet line. Her laugh was slightly manic. "One more time couldn't hurt, right?"

People huddled around us, the air coiled and hot as I took up the dice. I started to blow, sucking in a startled gasp as I spotted a familiar face through a gap in the crowd. Nick and Garrett stood twenty feet away, talking with the pit boss. "I think it's time to go," I whispered to Vero.

"Maybe just a few more rolls, to make sure we caught their attention."

I ducked, attempting to tug her down with me. "We don't want any more attention."

She followed the direction of my stare and crouched beside me. "Oh, no."

"What if they recognize us?"

Vero looked at our chips, torn. "Maybe they won't. You look pretty hot."

"Vero!"

"Fine, we'll go." She scooped up the dice and threw them a final time.

"Craps!" the croupier called out. The crowd groaned, our cover thinning as they quickly began to disperse. Nick and Garrett turned in our direction.

"Get down!" Vero grabbed my hand and pulled me under the table, crawling fast to the other side. The carpet smelled like urine and sweaty socks, and I gagged when a piece of chewing gum clung to the knee of my jumpsuit.

"Did they see us?"

"I don't think so," Vero said. We peeked through a field of pant legs and heels in time to see Nick and Garrett approaching. Their shoes paused inches in front of us. We listened, snatching bits and pieces of their conversation with the croupier through the surrounding chatter.

". . . looking for someone . . . hoping you can help us . . . any idea where I might find Marco Toscano?"

"Sorry, can't help you." The croupier called for everyone to place their bets. The detectives' shoes reluctantly turned away. Vero and I waited until they disappeared from sight before crawling out into the open. "That was close," she said, dusting off her knees. I dug frantically in my purse for a wet wipe, certain I'd contracted some casino-borne disease.

"Excuse me, miss?" I yelped as someone touched my shoulder.

"That didn't take long," Vero whispered in my ear. She smoothed down her wig and we both turned around.

A smarmy man in a suit jacket extended his hand to me. "I couldn't help but notice your luck ran out prematurely tonight. Such a shame. You were doing so well." A business card appeared between his index and middle fingers, as if he'd pulled it from his sleeve. "If you'd like to continue playing this weekend, Enzo Russo would be delighted to speak with you. He is a man of exceptional means, with a keen eye for talent and opportunity." The man inclined his chin toward a dome on the ceiling. "May I tell Mr. Russo you'll be in touch tomorrow, Miss . . . ?"

Vero nudged me.

I glanced up at the camera and smiled as I tucked the business card inside my bra. "Reina. *La* Reina. Tell Mr. Russo the pleasure will be all mine."

CHAPTER 19

My cell phone buzzed as Vero and I left the casino and took the stairwell to Marco's floor. I paused halfway up, frowning at my screen. I didn't recognize the number, only the 703 area code of the caller.

"Who is it?" Vero asked, holding on to the wall as she adjusted the straps of her heels.

"I don't know." I connected the call, answering cautiously. "Hello?"

"Finlay? It's Joey Balafonte. Got a minute?"

I could practically hear the toothpick clenched between his teeth. "I'm actually a little busy—"

"I'm worried about Cam. I've been looking for him everywhere. He hasn't returned any of my calls, and none of his buddies have heard from him either. He hasn't even checked in with his grandmother. That's not like him. I'm afraid he's gotten himself in over his head. Has he called you? Do you have any idea where he is?"

I hesitated, torn between honoring my promise to Cam and the terrible worry I recognized in Joey's voice. He might not be Cameron's father or legal guardian, but he did feel responsible for him. And there was no worse feeling than the fear of losing a child.

"You've heard from him, haven't you?" he asked, latching on to my pause, his fear turning to hope.

"Why would I have heard from Cam?"

"Because he trusts you. I saw it that night you caught us arguing behind the dorm at the police academy, the way you tried to protect him. Cam must have seen it, too. I swear, Finlay, I was only trying to help him." It came out desperate, pleading. "My brother would haunt me from the grave if I ever let anything happen to that kid." The phone went quiet, as if he were holding his breath. "Look," he finally said, resigning himself to my silence. "I know Cam's scared of getting in trouble for starting that fire, but if he's arrested for it, you tell him I will be with him for all of it. I won't let him go through it alone. I'll call in every favor I have and make sure they go easy on him. Just, please . . . if you know where he is, tell me so I can come pick him up."

I pressed my lips tight, resisting the urge to tell Joey what his nephew had done. That what Cam feared was so much bigger than the fire he'd set at the police academy. I couldn't keep Cam safe, because neither of us were. Joey owed me a favor after I'd saved his life, and he was far more qualified than I was to protect Cameron from the retaliation of the mob and the dirty cops who worked for them. But Cam had come to me because he had trusted me. More than his uncle. More than the cops. And that, more than anything, gave me the greatest pause. "I'll be sure to tell him if I hear from him," I promised.

Joey sighed. "You're both in over your heads, you know."

"So you keep telling me."

"Don't let him do anything stupid."

"He's a bright kid. I'm sure he'll make responsible—"

Joey disconnected.

". . . choices," I finished, hoping Cam wasn't the only one.

Vero started up the last flight of stairs ahead of me. "You made the right decision," she reassured me over the clack of her heels against the metal treads. "If you'd told Joey where to find Cam, you'd have to tell him why Cam was here. You'd have to tell him about the car and the thumb drive, and then you'd have to tell him what was on it. And since *our* names are probably on the spreadsheet on that drive, that would have been a highly inadvisable choice. You're right," she said, breathing hard as we reached the landing to the seventeenth floor. "Cam's smart. He won't do anything to draw unnecessary attention to himself."

She pushed open the fire door.

Music blared through the hallway, growing louder the closer we got to Marco's room, until the walls shook with it. Vero and I paused in front of the suite, ears tipped toward the laughter and loud voices bleeding through the door.

"That little shit," she muttered, swiping her key over the sensor.

Club music assaulted us as we pushed our way inside. Sweating, dancing bodies packed the foyer. Beer bottles and red plastic cups covered every inch of furniture that wasn't already occupied by empty chip bags or room service trays. We wriggled through the mass of people, searching for Cam. I caught sight of him through the crowd, reclining on the sofa like a prince with Kevin Bacon in his lap. His arms were slung over the shoulders of two women who looked decidedly like hookers.

His eyes went wide when he spotted us shouldering our way toward him. Vero snatched the remote control off the coffee table and turned off the music. My ears rang as the room went abruptly quiet and the crowd groaned in protest. I shoved my way down the hall toward the master suite. A lacy red bra hung from the doorknob, and I prayed as I turned it, relieved to find it locked.

"Party's over. Everybody out!" Vero shouted, grabbing glasses that belonged to the suite's kitchen out of people's hands and shooing the crowd out the door as I stormed back to the living room.

I pointed at Cam across the sea of red cups littering the coffee table. "You have so much explaining to do!"

"Me? You're the ones dressed like 1970s porn stars."

One of the call girls scratched Kevin Bacon's head as she sized us up. The other ran a set of obscenely long nails around Cam's ear. "You paid for two hours. You've still got fifteen minutes left. Your friends are welcome to join us."

Vero jerked her thumb hard toward the exit. The women unwound themselves from Cam and got to their feet, adjusting their skirts and garters on their way out. When the last of the partygoers was gone, Vero bolted the suite door shut, waving weed smoke from the air on her way back to the couch.

"What were you thinking?" I snapped at Cam.

"There are two corpses in the next room and you threw a party?!" Vero hurled a pillow at his head.

"Relax!" he said as he brought his arm up to dodge it. "No one saw them. I locked the bedroom door and told them Marco was shacking up in there with a lady friend."

"A lady friend?!" I cried. "Those were prostitutes, Cam! You said you were broke! How on earth did you pay for them?"

"I didn't. Marco did. And Sapphire and Rochelle are not *prostitutes*," he corrected me, "they're *escorts*. You know, like professionals and shit."

"And where did you find these *professionals*?" I asked. "On Tinder or LinkedIn?"

"Neither. I called room service and told them I was Marco's nephew. I said my uncle was throwing a party and our butler hooked me up. But don't worry, he comes with the room. And get this," he said, looking far too proud of himself, "they sent up a whole cart full of booze. They even brought one of those huge trays with cheese and grapes on it and shit. There were these monster shrimp," he said, demonstrating their size with his outstretched hands. "Delicious, by the way . . . highly recommend," he added with a chef's kiss. "They went pretty fast, but there might be some of those little weenies on toothpicks left in the kitchen if you're hungry."

"I'll show you a weenie on a toothpick." I held Vero back as she lunged for him.

It took everything in me not to murder him myself. "Someone could have complained about the noise and called the police. Did you even think about that?"

"Of course I did. You think I'm an idiot?" I refrained from answering that. "Why do you think I invited all those fucking people?" At our stupefied looks he said, "I asked the butler to find a couple of girls and send them up. I showed Sapphire and Rochelle the room service spread and told them to invite a few friends. When people started coming, I made sure everyone knew Marco was here, scoring with some high-roller chick in the bedroom, and he didn't want to be disturbed. You're welcome for taking care of your little police problem."

"What little police problem?"

He sighed over the burden of having to explain it to me. "What's the first thing the cops do when they find a crime scene? They tape it off, to keep boneheads like us from crapping all over the evidence. Well, guess what? Dozens of hookers, junkies, and scam artists just tromped all over this place, had sex in the coat closet, pissed in the potted plants, and puked in the sink. And they're all convinced Marco invited them here to do it. Tomorrow, every one of them will be telling all their friends how they partied with the infamous Marco Toscano. All we have to do is get rid of the bodies and *poof*," he said, wiggling his fingers, "as far as Atlantic City is concerned, Marco was alive and kicking it last night, which means you and your BFF over here no longer need an alibi when the cops figure out he's missing."

Vero and I gaped at him as he strutted into the kitchen and came back with two weenies. He offered one to Kevin Bacon and stuffed the other in his mouth.

"What about you?" he asked around his hot dog. "Did you find our guy?"

"Pokey didn't do it," I said, rubbing my eyes. "He was bussing tables at a restaurant called Chubbies last night."

Cam frowned. "Restaurant? Sounds more like a strip joint. That explains the outfits," he said, gesturing to our costumes. I shot Vero a look. "So what now?" Cam asked.

"Why don't you tell us," Vero said, "since you seem to think you have this whole thing figured out. How are we supposed to just magically disappear two dead bodies?"

A shrill ring echoed through the suite. We all turned to stare at the hotel phone on the credenza.

"Someone must have complained about the noise. What do we do?" Vero asked.

Cam reached for it. "It's probably just my man, the butler. I'll have him send up some more shrimp."

I smacked his hand away from the receiver. "No more shrimp!" He and the butler were already cozy enough, and the red light on the phone indicated the call was coming from the front desk. "Let it ring."

"If we don't answer, they might send someone to the room," Vero pointed out.

We all stared at the phone. Cam rolled his eyes and reached for it again. I grabbed the receiver and cleared my throat, affecting an accent. "Marco Toscano's room. His assistant speaking. May I help you?"

"I'm sorry to bother you. This is Elaine at the front desk. We're trying to reach a guest of Mr. Toscano. We've received a noise complaint . . ." I turned to glare at Cam. ". . . actually, more than one, from several rooms on the fifteenth floor. A rather loud banging noise seems to be coming from Mr. Delvecchio's room. We were hoping you could convey the message and ask him to look into it."

Mr. Delvecchio's room? Louis had a room? Two floors below us?

"Of course," I said, momentarily forgetting my accent. I cleared my throat again. "Mr. Delvecchio's here with me now. I'll ask him to handle it right away. I apologize for the disruption."

"Handle what?" Vero asked when I disconnected. "Are they sending someone up?"

"I don't think so. Where's Louis's wallet?"

Cam reached inside his pocket and tossed it to me. I threw him a chastising look as I thumbed through it, searching for anything that resembled a hotel key card. Finding nothing, I hurried to the bathroom, pausing to hold my breath before I opened the door. A scented candle burned on the vanity top, and a layer of shrinking ice cubes bobbed on the water's surface between layers of dissipating lilac-scented bath bubbles. A half-empty bottle of lavender and rosehip oil sat open on the tub's lip.

"Cameron!" I called out.

"I know, right?" he called back from the couch, sounding pleased with himself. "I had the butler send up a bunch of those bath bombs from the spa downstairs. Smells pretty good, huh?"

"It smells like a funeral home!" I angled my head away as I reached inside the pockets of Louis's jacket. My fingers closed around a water-logged paper envelope containing a plastic card. The handwritten room number had become impossible to read. Hopefully, the banging noise all of his neighbors had been complaining about would be loud enough to give away the location of his room. But that begged the question: What . . . or *who* . . . was doing the banging?

I made my way back to the ransacked kitchen, grabbed a box of trash bags, and handed them to Cam. "I want this entire mess cleaned up before we get back. And no more room service," I said sternly.

"Where are we going?" Vero asked, following me to the door.

"Hopefully to rescue Javi."

CHAPTER 20

Vero and I straightened our wigs as we slunk out of the suite, hoping to blend in with the other partygoers who had left only moments ago. We crammed into an overcrowded elevator and got off on the fifteenth floor. Room key in hand, we hurried down the corridor, pausing beside every door to listen.

"Hear that?" I asked, ears tipped toward a room near the end of the hall. A DO NOT DISTURB sign hung from the knob. A man's deep voice boomed through the walls. An argument. Then the rapid *tat, tat, tat* of gunfire.

"It's just a TV," Vero said, scurrying to the next door.

My mind raced back to the night Vero and I had bound Steven's wrists and ankles and duct-taped his mouth shut, locking him in a cheap motel room to hide him from a contract killer. I'd put ESPN on the TV as loud as it would go, hoping to cover up Steven's angry thrashing and muffled shouts. "Try the room key," I suggested.

Vero came back and swiped Louis's key card over the sensor. My heart skipped a beat as the light turned green.

Vero cracked the door.

The sound of shouting and gunfire grew louder. A lamp had been left on inside, illuminating a standard-sized room with two double beds, only one of which looked slept in. A single suitcase lay open across the other.

"Hello," I called over the noise, in case someone was inside. When no one answered, Vero shoved past me into the room. A cop drama blared on the flat-screen over the dresser. I reached for the remote on the night-stand and turned it off.

A dense silence filled the room. Vero rushed to the bathroom and turned on the light, swearing when she found it empty. "Javi's not here."

"Try not to leave any prints," I reminded her, handing her a wash-cloth from the bathroom to wipe down all the surfaces she'd touched. "Look for anything that might tell us where they took him."

I began picking through the spare contents of Louis's suitcase. The handful of outfits inside were all neatly arranged, folded into crisp bundles. I moved to the closet and found a heavy leather jacket, the same one Louis had been wearing in the security footage the night he'd taken the car.

I reached into the pockets, hoping I'd discover some clue inside, but all I found was a handful of crumpled sales receipts—gas stations, fast-food stops, convenience stores, hotels, highway tolls—re-creating a roadmap of Louis's trip here. Nothing to suggest he'd made any suspicious stops.

"Finn, look at this," Vero said, kneeling beside the vanity in the bathroom, studying the floor below the U-bend under the sink. The decor of the room was modern, the plumbing exposed, framed by sleek wooden shelves containing a hair dryer, bundles of toilet paper, and stacks of towels.

"What is it?"

Her face paled as she held up a broken zip tie. "Javi was here. He had to be." She shot to her feet, her high heels clicking frantically as she searched every inch of the bathroom, desperate for clues.

I checked the time on my phone. Only fifteen minutes had passed since the front desk had called to alert us to a noise complaint. "You think Javi got away?"

She swallowed, her voice strained by the obvious lump in her throat. "Or someone knew he was here and came back to move him." She maneuvered past me, back into Louis's room. She scanned every surface, her eyes doubling back on an empty notepad beside the landline phone on the desk. A ballpoint pen was uncapped beside it. Vero picked up the notepad and held it under the light. Then she hurried to the coffeepot and tore open a packet of decaf.

"What are you doing?" I asked as she ripped open the small disc of filter paper and shook the grounds into her hand. She dusted the tips of her fingers, carefully running them over the surface of the notepad, studying the indentations left in it from a previous page that had been torn away.

"It's a phone number."

Vero picked up the handset of the landline beside it.

"What are you doing?"

"I'm calling it."

"What if they recognize the number?" I reached for the receiver, but she was already dialing. She held the phone between us as the call connected.

"Where the hell have you been? I called you yesterday." The voice belonged to a man. He shouted over a persistent ear-piercing whine and a deafening clatter in the background. Vero put the phone closer to her ear, frowning as she listened. "Speak up. It's too fucking loud in here, I can't hear you," the man said when she didn't answer.

Vero erupted into a fit of deep coughs, masking her voice as she pitched it deeper. "Sorry. Got tied up."

Tied up? Seriously? I mouthed.

"What do you want me to say?" she whispered back.

"You know I'm on a tight schedule. I'm not running a charity here, Lou. Are you coming with the money or not?"

Vero covered the receiver with her palm, careful to give nothing away as she listened.

She disconnected, blinking at me through the fringe of her Farrah Fawcett wig. "I think I know where they took Javi. Whoever answered that phone was inside a garage."

"How do you know we called a garage?" I asked as Vero paced the short span of Louis's room.

She chewed on her thumbnail. "I don't."

"But you said—"

"I said the man who answered it was *in* a garage, and judging by the number of torches, compressors, and sandblasters I was hearing, that shop wasn't small." Which meant someone had planned to send the Aston to a garage for repairs, or they were sending it to a chop shop. Either scenario didn't bode well for Javi. Or for Cam's thumb drive.

"Okay, that's more information than we had before, right? We'll just find a list of all the garages in Atlantic City and check out each one until we find the Aston."

"Any place shady enough to work on a stolen car for a man like Marco probably isn't going to be listed with the Better Business Bureau, Finlay. These kinds of places do not want to be found. We can't just google it."

"Then how do we find it?" I asked, scratching an itch in my jumpsuit.

"By asking someone just as shady as Marco." She reached inside my bra strap and plucked out Enzo Russo's business card. "And I know just the guy."

CHAPTER 21

Vero and I tore the phone number from the notepad, wiped down Louis's room, and took the stairs back to the seventeenth floor. We pounded on Marco's door, rushing inside as soon as Cam opened it. He held Kevin Bacon in one hand and a slice of cold pizza in the other.

"I thought I told you to clean this place up."

"I did," Cam said, gesturing indignantly to the overflowing trash bags lying on the foyer floor. Red plastic cups spilled from their gaping mouths. Cam kicked one with the toe of his boot. A shower of empty liquor bottles cascaded to the floor. "I separated the recycling and everything."

Vero nudged open a bag, her nose wrinkling as she peered inside. "What's all this?" she asked, pinching a dirty sock before realizing what she was holding. She dropped it back into the bag with a grimace.

"A bunch of clothes people left behind when you told everybody to leave. A couple coats, shoes, some bras . . . I tossed a few pairs of underwear around the place." He tapped his temple with a conspiratorial wink. "You know, DNA and shit."

Vero rolled her eyes. She shoved the paper with the phone number at him and snatched his pizza. He nearly dropped Kevin Bacon as he scrambled to hold on to it. "What the hell is this?"

"I need you to find out who this number belongs to," she said, tearing off a huge bite. "And hurry it up, we don't have time to waste while you eat." I'd known Vero long enough to know the signs of stress eating. She shoveled in another mouthful as she lifted the lid of the pizza box on the serving cart, searching for another piece.

Cam set Kevin on the floor and unfolded the paper, frowning as he held it closer to his eyes to read the number in the coffee residue. "Cell phone users aren't just listed out there for anybody to find."

"I thought you were supposed to be some wunderkind hacker. So hack something." She picked up his laptop bag and thrust it at him.

"Hacking isn't just knowing how to use a freaking computer. It's about knowing what makes people tick. You know, tricking them into giving you the information you need to break in. I need to know something about who this guy is," he said, waving the piece of notebook paper at her.

"He's the guy who knows where your thumb drive is. Is that enough motivation for you?"

"The man who answered that phone works in some kind of garage," I offered. "He said he called Louis yesterday. See if you can find any records of calls or texts between Louis or Marco and that number. Maybe one of them has it stored in their contacts with a name."

Cam sucked a tooth, looking between me and Vero before carrying his laptop to the sofa and settling in.

The hotel phone in the suite rang again.

"I'll get it." Cam plucked it from the cradle before I could stop him. "Yeah," he answered casually, cramming the receiver under his jaw as he typed. His fingers froze over the keyboard. His eyes lifted to mine as he swung his legs off the coffee table and bolted to his feet. He thrust the phone at me. "It's for you," he said, slapping his laptop closed. He fumbled with his backpack zipper as he shoved his computer inside it and slung it over his shoulder.

Vero grabbed hold of it as he hurried past her, stopping him in his tracks as he bolted for the door. "Sit down," she said, eyeing him suspiciously. She took him by the shoulder and set him firmly on the couch.

I cleared my throat and put the phone to my ear. "This is Mr. Toscano's assistant."

"I'm so sorry," Elaine said in a hushed voice, "but a police officer is here, and he's asking for a room number—"

Vero's knuckles whitened around Cam's shoulder as she registered my face.

"But I've spoken with Mr. Delvecchio, and the noise complaint has been handled," I insisted. "There's no need for the police to get involved."

"The officer's not asking for Mr. Delvecchio's room. He's asking about Mr. Toscano's." My eyes skated over the room, then darted to the bathroom door. "I told them it's not our policy to give that information unless they have a warrant, but he flustered me. He's very charming," she blurted, the words coming faster as she fumbled over her apology, "and when he asked me which floors our VIP suites were located on, the FBI agent who was with him insisted that I wouldn't technically be breaking any rules to disclose that. So I told him we have VIP suites on the tenth, twelfth, and seventeenth floors."

We were on the seventeenth floor.

"Where are they now?" I asked, my heart leaping into a gallop.

"In the lobby, waiting for an elevator. I told them Mr. Toscano was entertaining company tonight, but they—"

I slammed down the phone. "Nick and Garrett are on their way up."

Cam stood up again. Vero pushed him back down, her face pale. "How much time do we have?" she asked.

"They don't have a warrant." My hands shook as I paced the living room. "The front desk didn't give them Marco's room number, only the floor numbers for the VIP suites. They'll have to go door to door. With any luck, they'll start on the tenth floor."

"If they don't have a warrant, we don't have to let them in," Cam said, wringing his hands. "We can put up the DO NOT DISTURB sign and bolt the fucking door shut."

I knew Nick well enough to know that would only make him more suspicious. The front desk had already let it slip that Marco was entertaining guests tonight. If no one answered, it would ping his cop radar. "He'll only come back. Or worse, stake out the room. We have to move the bodies."

"Where?" Vero cried. "We can't just sling them over our shoulders and carry them through the damn lobby!"

"No, but we can roll them up in bedsheets and drag them down two floors to Louis's room. Nick and Garrett aren't looking for Louis," I reminded her. "They probably don't even know he was involved." Vero glanced toward the bathroom, looking mildly horrified at the prospect of what I was suggesting. But we didn't have time for her to get comfortable with the idea. "We'll never find Javi if we're sitting in a jail cell."

"I'll get the gloves," she said.

"Cam, get your things," I said, snapping him to attention. "And bring Kevin Bacon with you. Take the stairs up one flight and get in an elevator. Push the buttons for every floor."

"Then what?"

"Keep going. Hit all the floors above ours. Stall the elevators as long as you can. Push all the emergency stop buttons if you have to. Just slow them down and make sure Nick doesn't spot you."

Cam grabbed Kevin Bacon and his backpack and ran from the suite like his jeans were on fire. If I had any other choice, I would have been right behind him.

Vero followed me to the bedroom. I flung the massive duvet off Marco's king-sized bed and dragged it to the bathroom, spreading it over the tile. "Help me lift him," I said, reaching around Marco's shoulders. Swallowing back my revulsion, I wedged my hands under each of his clammy armpits, drenching the front of my jumpsuit. "Grab his feet."

Vero plunged her hands into the water. "I really, really hate you right now."

"You're the one who got us into this."

"I voted to burn the place down. Why won't his legs move?"

"Rigor mortis." I grunted as we both heaved. "It sets in . . . between twelve . . . and thirty-six . . . hours postmortem. The muscles and soft tissue . . . become stiff."

"Apparently, not all of it." Vero squeezed her eyes shut as Marco's midsection rose from the water. "I'll never be able to unsee that."

We each braced a heel against the side of the tub, holding fast to his arms and feet as we leveraged his weight. I did the math in my head, welcoming the distraction from the squeak of Marco's wet skin against the porcelain. "His arms and head are pretty loose. The rigor mortis phase is almost over . . . After thirty-six hours . . . the next stage of decomposition starts."

"What happens during that one?" she asked as we dragged Marco's body over the lip. It landed on the comforter with a wet thump, and we both grimaced.

"You don't want to know," I said, wiping sweat from my brow. I pulled the plug in the bathtub and the last of the ice water swirled down the drain. I set the hot water running and tossed in a handful of bath bombs. Vero took the last of the lavender-scented rosehip oil and splashed it over Marco.

"You have something better you planned to do with it?" she asked at my disgusted look.

We hiked up our bell-bottoms, dropped to our knees, and started rolling the bedding around Marco, repeating the process with Louis using the queen-sized comforter from the second bedroom.

"What now?" Vero asked, breathing hard. That entire ordeal had taken less than ten minutes. I had no idea how much time we had left until Nick made it to our floor, but probably not long. I turned off the water. The bathroom smelled cloyingly sweet, blending with the marijuana stench that lingered in the wake of the party.

I stooped to grab the bundle of linens closest to the door. Vero knelt to grab the other. She leaned back with all her weight, dragging Marco through the suite behind me.

"Why do you get to carry Louis?" she said between labored breaths.

"You're younger," I grunted back.

I cracked the foyer door, poking out my head and peeking both ways before bracing the hinge open with a crushed beer can and dragging Louis over the threshold. The suite was located at the end of the hallway. Thankfully, the entrance to the stairwell wasn't far away. "Just a few more feet," I said, giving Louis another heave. Static sparked under Vero's duvet as she dragged it over the tightly looped carpeting, staggering in her high heels. I used my backside to fling open the fire door and towed Louis onto the landing, relieved when the carpet gave way to smooth tiles and the duvet glided easily.

We stood in the stairwell, wheezing, backs to the wall as we struggled to catch our breaths. A door smacked open somewhere below us. Footsteps plodded up the stairs. A man's voice echoed up the passageway. "What floors did she say those rooms were on?"

A familiar voice responded, "Ten, twelve, and seventeen."

I stiffened. *Nick!*

"Sure your leg is up for it?" Garrett asked.

"It's only five more flights. Elevator was taking too damn long anyway. Don't worry about me. I can make it."

Five more flights . . . He and Garrett had already finished searching the twelfth floor.

"What do we do?" Vero whispered.

I grabbed the corners of my duvet, my pulse hammering as I considered the stairs. There was no way we could get both bodies up a full flight before Nick and Garrett reached our floor. And dragging the bodies back over the carpet to the suite would take too long. We'd have to get to the fifteenth floor before Nick and Garrett made it that far.

"Come on," I whispered, dragging Louis to the edge of the steps. I held fast as gravity pulled him over the brink, letting the slick Egyptian cotton ease his fall down the metal treads. He bounced down the first flight with a series of muted thuds, punctuated by the echo of Nick's and Garrett's shoes.

My heels clicked too loudly as I descended the steps. I kicked off my stilettos, abandoning them in a corner of the stairwell. Vero did the same. I rounded the next landing barefoot, hissing at her to hurry up. She gave Marco a firm push with her bare foot. The sudden drop of his weight ripped the duvet from her hand. She gasped as Marco's body rolled down the stairs, the fabric unwinding around him, leaving a lavender-and-rose-hip-scented trail as he tumbled down the risers with a series of wet slaps. My heart lodged in my throat as he landed ass-side up on the landing beside me.

Nick and Garrett couldn't have been more than three floors below us.

"Slow down, Stokes. My leg's killing me. Give me a second to catch up," Nick said.

Vero scurried down the steps. We dropped to our knees, frantically working the duvet under Marco's belly to the steady, slow beat of Nick's and Garrett's soles plodding upward. I grabbed Marco's arms. Vero took his feet. They were slick with oil and hard to hold. With gritted teeth, we hauled him into the center of the duvet and threw the corners over him, towing him the rest of the way down to the fifteenth floor.

Flinging the fire door open as quietly as I could, I hauled Louis over the threshold into the empty hallway. I rushed back to help Vero with her messy bundle, dragging Marco out of the stairwell just as Nick and Garrett crested the last flight of stairs.

We pressed our backs against the door, but the latch wouldn't close. I glanced down at the bundle at our feet. Marco's bald scalp was peeking out of its wrappings.

Oh, god.

"His hair!" I hissed, searching for his toupee.

Vero gasped and pointed at the doorjamb. A nest of matted black strands was wedged in the hinge. Nick's shadow limped toward the narrow crack between the door and the frame. My heart stopped when he paused beside it, close enough for me to hear his labored breathing through the gap.

"Last flight," Garrett called over his shoulder. "You coming?"

"I'm coming," Nick said, eyes squeezed shut as he clutched the railing and massaged his thigh. He wiped his brow with his sleeve as he resumed his ascent. Vero and I listened, hands clasped, as his staggered footfalls faded up the stairs.

"Let's get out of here," she said, yanking the toupee free of the door. With the last of our strength—and maybe the last of our sanity—we towed the bodies to Louis's room and dragged them over the finish line.

CHAPTER 22

Vero and I situated the bodies in the bathtub in Louis's room. It was significantly smaller than the jetted luxury tub in Marco's suite, and I was grateful the rigor mortis phase had (mostly) passed, making it possible to squish them more easily into the narrow basin. Though that didn't leave much of a window before the next stage of decomposition was going to become a bigger problem. By my best estimates, we had less than thirty-six hours left to identify the killer and locate the car. Assuming said killer had no desire to turn himself in, that also meant we'd need to purge every trace of ourselves from this hotel and get the hell out of Atlantic City before the police found the men's remains.

I sent Cam a text, telling him he could relax his assault on the elevators, but to stay out of sight on the upper floors until he heard from me again.

I stripped the pillowcases off the bed and tossed a few to Vero.

"What are these for?" she asked.

"We need more ice. A lot of it. The closest machine is upstairs. While we're there, we can check and see if Nick and Garrett are gone."

We put up the DO NOT DISTURB sign and crept to the stairwell, listening to make sure it was empty before returning to the seventeenth floor. We peeked out into Marco's hall. We'd left the door braced open when we left the suite, and I prayed Cam was right, that the mess inside would paint a convincing illusion.

Voices carried from inside. A plastic bag rustled. The clank of empty bottles and a low whistle.

"Looks like someone threw one hell of a party." *Nick*.

"Smells like it, too," Garrett chimed in.

Vero and I ducked behind the stairwell door as a woman stormed out of the elevator and turned down the hall toward Marco's suite. "Where is he?" she called out in a shrill, angry voice, her thick New Jersey accent echoing through the corridor. Her silver bob bounced with her determined stride. She barged through the open door into the suite, her slingbacks clacking on the marble before jolting to a stop. "Who the hell are you two? And where's Kevin Bacon?"

"Kevin Bacon was here?" Garrett asked.

"Of course he was here," she said with an exasperated huff. "Out of my way. Marco!" she shouted. "Marco Giovanni Toscano, where the hell is my—" The woman's gasp was audible from the hall. "What on earth has been going on in here?" She called out for Kevin Bacon, doors opening and slamming inside as if she was searching every room for him.

"Are you Mrs. Toscano?" Nick asked as her heels clacked back into the foyer.

"Only because that cheap bastard refuses to give me a divorce. Who are you?"

"My name is Detective Nicholas Anthony, and this is—"

A hotel employee with a walkie-talkie clipped to his belt rushed down the hall to the suite. "Gentlemen," he said, breathless when he arrived, "unless you have Mr. Toscano's permission to be in here, I really must ask you all to— Oh." He paused abruptly in the doorway. "Mrs. Toscano, I apologize. I wasn't expecting you."

"Where is Kevin Bacon?" she demanded.

"I assume he's with *Mr.* Toscano."

"And where is *he*?"

"Is he not here?" the man asked, clearly confused.

"No, he is not!" she snapped. "When you see him, you tell him I'm going to kill him if there is one single hair out of place on Kevin Bacon's head."

The man pressed back against the wall, his toes narrowly avoiding her heels as she burst through the door. She stormed back toward the elevators, her cell phone already pressed to her ear.

A trash bag rustled in the silence that followed.

A throat cleared. "Sir, what are you doing?" The men's voices became faint as if they'd moved toward the living room. Vero and I snuck closer to listen. "You can't be in here. As you can see, Mr. Toscano is not on the premises. I'm going to have to ask you to leave."

"Were you aware the door to this suite was propped open?" Nick asked.

"Er . . . no. I was not aware of that, but that has no bearing on the fact that—"

"Are you the hotel manager?" Garrett asked.

"No, sir, I'm the butler assigned to our VIP suites. Who, may I ask, are you?"

"I'm Special Agent Garrett Stokes with the FBI."

"Oh, I see," the butler said, clearly taken aback. "I hope there isn't a problem?"

"Not at all. We just wanted a word with Mr. Toscano. Any idea where we can find him?"

"I . . . I really don't know. He was here all evening, entertaining guests. There was quite a crowd in attendance." The butler lowered his voice. "He did ask me to invite two lady friends to join him. Perhaps he left to escort them home before *Mrs.* Toscano arrived."

"Or someone told him we were coming, and he didn't want to be here when we showed up," Nick said quietly.

"Thank you for your time," Garrett said. Vero and I ducked back into the stairwell as Nick and Garrett exited the suite. "Want to take the stairs?" Garrett asked.

"Elevator," Nick said, limping the opposite way.

I peered through the crack, watching them go. The butler emerged, his nose wrinkled against the smell. He pulled the walkie-talkie from his waistband and plucked the crushed beer can from the hinge with a disgusted frown. "Have housekeeping send their best crew to suite 1702," he said in a low voice. "Mr. Toscano has stepped out, and I want the entire suite cleaned before he gets back."

CHAPTER 23

Vero and I filled the bathtub with ice, pulled the curtain around Marco and Louis, and closed the bathroom door.

"What now?" Vero cast a begrudged look over her shoulder at Cam. He reclined against the headboard, his stocking feet crossed at the ankles, his boots kicked haphazardly to the floor. His laptop rested on his thighs, and Kevin Bacon was curled under his arm.

"This room sucks," he grumbled.

"It's free," I pointed out. And no one was looking for it, which was arguably its best feature.

"It doesn't exactly inspire brilliance," he said, rubbing his heavy eyelids.

I switched off the lamp on his nightstand. "You can be brilliant in the morning."

"What about Javi?" Vero asked. "We can't just stop looking for him. He's been out there, alone, god knows where for more than two days. He could be hungry. Or cold. Or—"

"We're going to find him," I assured her. "Just not tonight." I brushed a blond lock of her wig back from her face and wiped away the start of a tear. "Javi's biggest threats are on ice in that bathtub, and we're not going to solve anything if we're too exhausted to think. We need rest," I said firmly as she started to protest. "Cam doesn't have any leads, and we have no idea where to start looking for this garage. We'll come up with a plan once we've all had some sleep."

"Fine, but I'm not sharing a bed with Teen Hugh Hefner or Kevin Bacon. I'll sleep on the floor," she said, taking a pillow from the closet and tossing it onto the carpet.

"You're coming with me. Nick's getting suspicious, and if you don't show your face at the Royal Flush soon, he'll probably send out a search party. We'll catch a few hours of sleep and sneak out again in the morning."

"With three cops watching our room?"

"We'll come up with something. Let's go." I turned her toward the door as Cam's laptop slid from his legs and he drifted off to sleep. I scribbled a note on the hotel pad, letting him know we'd be back in the morning, and to text us if he found the owner of the mysterious phone number on Louis's notepad or, better yet, the location of the garage. Then I set his laptop on the dresser, drew the blanket over his legs, and switched off the overhead light.

I checked to be sure the DO NOT DISTURB sign was hung securely on the knob, and Vero and I headed back to the Royal Flush.

"So how are we going to play this?" Vero asked as we got into the elevator at the Royal Flush and pushed the button for our floor.

We had changed out of our costumes in the first-floor bathroom, where we'd stashed a bag of our clothes and shoes earlier that night. I shook out my hair, wrinkling my nose at the faint smell of lavender on my hands. "It's after midnight. Everyone's probably in their rooms for the night. We'll just be really quiet and hope Sam's not on her laptop watching the security cameras."

The elevator opened to a cacophony of raised voices. Sam, Georgia, my mother, and Steven were gathered in the hall, each one shouting over the other. Vero lingered in the elevator, her finger poised over the button for the lobby.

I held the doors open, listening as my mother snapped at Steven. "The children know better. They would never have done that!"

I stormed out of the elevator, raising my voice over them all. "What on earth is going on? If you all don't keep your voices down, you're going to wake them up!" My mother whirled around. She clapped a trembling hand over her mouth.

Steven paled. "They're not with you?"

"Of course they're not with me. They're supposed to be with you." My stomach bottomed out as he closed his eyes and swore.

"They were asleep in the room," he said. "I went downstairs to get something to eat."

"You left them alone?" I cried.

"Your mom was right next door!"

My mother clutched her robe to her chest. "I didn't know Steven was gone. They must have woken up and left the room while I was asleep."

"How long ago?" I asked, my palms growing clammy.

Steven shook his head. "We don't know. I got back thirty minutes ago and they weren't in their bed. I assumed they'd woken up and gone to your mom's room. We didn't realize they were gone until just now."

Vero put a hand on my shoulder, but it was shaking as badly as I was.

"I'll check the security footage," Sam said, darting back into her room.

"I'll check Nick's room," Georgia said, jogging to his door.

"I'll check the vending machines," Vero said, tearing off in the other direction.

"I'll get dressed and help you find them," my mother said, leaving Steven and me alone in the hall.

My voice shook as I paced. "I can't believe you left our children alone in a hotel room!"

"I was looking for you! It was getting late and you hadn't come up to your room, and I was worried."

"You were worried, or you were checking up on me?" We locked eyes in a silent standoff, both of us shaken.

Georgia knocked loudly on Nick's door. He answered it, half-dressed, as if he'd been readying for bed. "What's going on?"

"Delia and Zach are missing," my sister said. "Are they with you?"

"No." There was a flurry of activity as Nick dragged on a T-shirt and joined Sam and Georgia in the hallway, pelting them with questions. "Okay, everybody calm down. They probably just left the room and wandered off." The air felt thin, like I couldn't get enough of it. I put an arm against the wall, holding myself up. He took me gently by the shoulders, forcing me to focus on his face. "Think, Finn. Where would they go?"

I shook my head, his features swimming through the burn of rising tears. "I don't know . . . Delia's been obsessed with the elevator since we got here."

"And Zach threw a tantrum yesterday when I wouldn't let him play the slot machines," Steven added, wringing his hands.

I pushed him out of my way to see Vero as she rushed back from the vending area. She shook her head as I stifled a cry.

Sam burst out of her room. "Got 'em! They got off the elevator on the casino level twenty minutes ago."

I choked back a sob and started toward the elevator. Nick grabbed my hand, anchoring me to his side. "We stay together."

"I'm coming with you," Vero said.

"I'm going, too," Steven insisted. "I just need to grab my shoes."

Nick turned to the rest of them. "Someone needs to stay up here in case the kids come back."

"I'll stay," my mother offered.

"Georgia will stay up here with you," Nick said. "The rest of us will split up. Sam, you're with Vero. Finlay's with me. Where's Charlie?"

Everyone looked to me. Last I'd seen Charlie, he was passed out in the trunk of his Cadillac behind Chubbies. I couldn't care less where Charlie was now. I just wanted to find my children.

"He said he was going out," Vero answered for me.

Nick turned to Georgia. "Call the front desk and have them notify hotel security. And get Charlie on the phone and tell him to get his ass back here." He took my hand, walking me briskly to the elevators. Sam, Vero, and Steven hurried after us, and we all packed inside the first open car. Nick pressed the button for the casino level, then jabbed the button to close the doors.

"When we get downstairs, Sam and Vero will take the left flank. Finlay and I will take the right. Steven will check the arcade. If you spot them, call out. If you're not within shouting distance, send a text." He took my face in his hands, as if he could feel my insides spinning. "They can't have gone far. We'll find them. I swear."

I nodded, fighting the urge to be sick as I considered how far two small children could run in the span of twenty minutes.

The elevator slowed its descent, and we all faced the doors, willing them to open. We were greeted by flashing lights and buzzers and bells, the tinny sound of coins spilling from machines. We bolted out of the elevators, shouldering past the crowds of people waiting to get inside. Sam and Vero split off to the left. Steven jogged toward the arcade. Nick towed me toward a waiting security guard as I rose up on my toes, scanning the casino, desperate for a glimpse of my children. My heart started to race. There were too many people in the aisles. Too many crowded tables and tall banks of slot machines. There could be twenty security guards looking for them, and we would never find them this way.

Vero's eyes met mine across the casino.

What would Zach do? she mouthed, pointing at the floor.

I looked down, following the tacky swirls in the burgundy-and-brown carpet. I glanced back at Vero, but she had already broken away from Sam and disappeared out of sight.

I slipped my hand from Nick's as he gathered a group of hotel staff, giving them descriptions of the children. I ducked under the nearest roulette table, crawling on all fours as I scanned the sea of boots and high heels and loafers around me. The crowd around the table parted and my breath caught.

Zach's woobie lay abandoned on the floor two tables away, pinned under the heel of a woman's shoe.

I scurried under the next table, closing in on Zach's woobie, calling his name. Nick called mine, his voice drowned out by the rattle of the marble against the wheel. A man yelped as I ducked between his legs. A woman gasped, her drink splashing the backs of my ankles as I crawled out the other side, gunning for the woobie, until only one table stood between me and my son's most prized possession.

A wall of ankles blocked my way. I crawled left, then right, seeking a clear path through them. A pair of scuffed loafers paused beside the blanket, six feet in front of me.

The man stooped, peering under the table, doing a double take when he spotted me. His clothes were covered in alley grime, and a patch of road rash darkened his cheekbone. Charlie sneered as he tucked the woobie under his arm. "Lose something?"

"If you touch either of my children, I will end you," I warned him. I fought to free myself from the legs around the table. By the time I sprang to my feet, breathing hard, Charlie was already gone.

Shit!

I stood on my toes. Spotted Vero through the crowd. I mouthed Charlie's name. Her eyes went wide as we both turned in circles, searching the casino for him.

Suddenly, she bolted, shoving an urgent path through the crowd. I spotted Charlie's head halfway between us. I started toward him, my heart thundering in my chest as he ducked and came up again.

Time stood still as he stood, holding my son in his arms.

I jolted to a stop as Charlie turned toward me, his other hand resting on my daughter's shoulder. Our eyes caught across the casino floor. He smiled, triumphant. A dangerous feeling swelled inside me, livid and reckless. An irrepressible need to tear the skin from his bones.

"Look who I found wandering around the casino, all alone," he drawled, his shit-eating grin twisted by his scar as he strolled toward me. The hard lines of his smile softened as Nick, Sam, and Vero broke through the crowd and rushed toward us.

Nick sagged with relief. Sam let out a nervous laugh as Charlie set the children down. They ran into my arms as I dropped to one knee, grabbing them by their fuzzy pajamas and holding them tightly, my skin numb with adrenaline.

Nick frowned at Charlie's clothes. "What happened to you?"

Charlie waved him off. "Just a little car trouble. Nothing I couldn't handle," he said smugly. "Seems like I got back just in time. These two hooligans were just about to sweet-talk some nice old lady into giving them a dollar for the arcade."

I tipped Delia's head back, inspecting every inch of her as Vero scooped Zach into her arms. "What are you two doing down here?"

Delia pointed at her brother, quick to share the blame. "Zach woke up, and then he woke *me* up. Daddy was gone and Nana was sleeping, and we were bored."

"Yeah," Zach said, mimicking his sister's pout. He babbled animatedly about how Daddy hadn't let him push the buttons in the elevator.

"You know better than to leave the room without a grown-up. You could have gotten lost. Or worse," I scolded them with a shudder. After the last thirty minutes, I didn't want to think about that.

"We were fine," Delia said. "Charlie found us. Right, Charlie?"

Charlie grinned at me, as if he were waiting for some public display of gratitude. Vero held Zach protectively to her side.

"Thanks for wrangling them," Nick said, slinging an arm over Charlie's shoulders. "And thanks for taking Finn to her meeting tonight."

"Wouldn't have missed it. We had quite an adventure. Wouldn't you say so, ladies?"

I gritted my teeth, my blood still boiling. Vero tucked her hair behind her ear with a stiff middle finger, making sure Charlie saw it. "It was full of surprises."

Charlie turned to Nick. "How about you? You find this guy you were looking for?"

Nick shook his head. "It was a bust. His nephew pointed us in the right direction. We found Toscano's hotel, but the guy's a ghost. I still have no idea how Grindley or his boss are connected to Zhirov."

Charlie clapped him on the back. "Maybe you can ask Feliks when you arrest him in Newark later." Nick looked at his watch, as if only now realizing it was well after midnight, already Sunday. Charlie scratched his chest. "I'm going to head up to the room and get some sleep. It's going to be a busy day, and I want to be fresh so I can keep a close eye on all my charges while you and Stokes are off hunting bad guys." He stared right at me when he said it, a warning in his eyes.

Nick excused himself to call Georgia and fill her in while Sam went to find Steven to tell him the children had been found.

I held tightly to Delia as Charlie stepped close, holding Zach's woobie hostage between us. "I believe you have something of mine," he growled. Zach whined for the blanket. I reached to take it, but Charlie gripped it tighter. I glanced at Nick. I would only look suspicious if Charlie and I got into an argument now. I reached into my pocket for Charlie's phone and dropped it into his hand, snatching the woobie from him.

Vero glared at him as he discreetly reached behind her and drew his Magnum from her pants. "See you two in the morning," he said, slipping it quietly into his coat. "Don't even think about leaving the hotel without me."

Vero pressed Zach to her chest as we watched him go.

Delia sagged against my hip, her eyelids growing heavy. "We should get the kids to bed," I said, stroking her hair as we walked.

"Finn, wait," Nick called out, running to catch up.

Vero reached for Delia. "Come on, Dee. You can tell me all about your casino adventure on the way to bed."

"I'll be right up," I told her as she shuffled the kids to the elevator where Sam and Steven were waiting.

Nick pulled me to him. My breath shuddered out of me as he held me against him, his lips warm against the top of my head. "You okay?"

I nodded into his chest. "Just tired."

He drew back, brushing my hair back with his thumb. "I want to apologize."

"For what?"

"For what I said this afternoon in the car. You were right. It wasn't my place to get involved in your business with Sylvia. I was trying to help, and I overstepped. I shouldn't have. This was supposed to be a quiet weekend away so you can unwind with Vero and your mom, and this whole thing with Feliks screwed that up. I shouldn't have made it more stressful by pushing you to meet with your agent." He dropped his hands, lacing his fingers with mine. "Garrett and I will be in Newark most of the day tomorrow, but I can ask Georgia to watch the kids, and Charlie can take you anywhere you want to go. There's a spa at that fancy hotel next door. The lady at the front desk was telling me they have one of these special package deals going on. You know, massages and facials and pedicures and stuff. If you want, I could book you, Vero, and your mom some appointments there tomorrow, to make up for messing up the rest of your weekend."

"You don't have to do that."

"Charlie wouldn't have to go," he insisted, ducking to catch my eyes. "I can ask Sam to go with you. She'd probably jump at the chance to get her nails done. It would be a girls' day out, just like you wanted." He seemed to be holding his breath as he waited for my answer.

Sam, he'd said. Not Charlie.

Spa packages could last for hours. Hours without Charlie looking over our shoulders.

I smiled up at Nick, a plan taking shape. "On second thought, I could really use a massage."

CHAPTER 24

"Rise and shine, girls! We're going to be late for our massages!" My mother threw open the thick curtains of our hotel room with a flourish, lifting her face toward the rising sun over the boardwalk and drawing a deep breath through her nose, as if she could actually smell the beach in our hotel room. I luxuriated in the bed, basking in the last few moments of my first real night of sleep in days. I curled into the small, warm corner of sheet Vero had left me. One of her legs sprawled across my side of our double bed, her backside pressed snugly against my hip.

A heavenly smell wafted through the room. I sat up slowly and sniffed. "Is that coffee?"

Vero lifted her pillow off her face. Her nostrils wiggled and she sat up fast, taking the last of my sheet with her. She blinked against the sunlight streaming through the window, her hair a nest of snarls.

Three large coffee cups were nested in a cardboard carrier on the dresser, our names written on the sides. A fourth cup had been filled to the brim with extra creamers, sugar packets, and stirrers.

"Nicholas brought them." My mother said his name with a reverence she usually reserved for her hairdresser, George Clooney, and her priest (and once for Steele Johnson as he'd hugged her goodbye). "Wasn't that thoughtful of him? And he brought breakfast for each of us. The children, too." She unrolled a paper bag, releasing tantalizing, buttery bakery smells. She held out a blueberry muffin. Vero dove for it, peeling back the pleated paper and moaning as her teeth sank into it. I reached for the lemon-poppy my mother offered me, chasing it with a long gulp of coffee. It had the perfect amount of sugar and cream, exactly the way I liked it. By the rapturous look on Vero's face, hers was perfect, too.

"I think I'm in love with your boyfriend," she said, licking her fingers.

"Where is he?" I asked my mother with a lingering twinge of guilt. I'd been so hard on him yesterday afternoon in the car, and after the trauma of losing the children in the casino, I'd been quick to say good night after he walked me back to my room.

"Garrett and Nicholas left a few minutes ago. He asked me to give you this." She handed me a folded piece of hotel stationery, careful to avoid eye contact with me. My name was printed on the front, and I gave her an admonishing look, certain she had read it. "What?" she asked, looking offended as I took it.

I turned my back to her as I unfolded it. Vero peeped over my shoulder as I read.

Hope you got some sleep. Garrett and I hit the road early to meet with the local PD in Newark. Didn't want to wake you. Hoping to have Zhirov in custody this afternoon and make it back in time to take you to a late dinner to celebrate. I'll text when I know more. Have fun at the spa with the girls. — Nick

"You two hurry up and get ready," my mother said, taking a muffin for herself. "Nicholas booked massages for each of us at ten. Georgia is watching the kids and Sam's coming with us. She'll be here in fifteen minutes to pick us up."

"What's Charlie doing?" I asked casually.

"He left right after Nick and Garrett. He said he had some errands to run." My mother dusted crumbs from her hands. "I'm going next door to get the children ready for the day. Your sister and Steven are taking them to the beach and the arcade." My mother carried another bag of pastries to the adjoining door and rapped loudly before opening it. The children cheered as she announced that Nick had brought them muffins for breakfast. She offered one to Steven. He rejected it with a bitter "no thanks."

Vero leaped up from the bed and closed the door between our rooms. "Let's find this loan shark so we can track down the damn Aston and rescue Javi." She dug in her bag for Enzo Russo's business card. I got dressed and used the bathroom while she made the call.

"Where are we meeting him?" I asked as I put on my sneakers.

"At his office."

"He has an office?"

"A few blocks from here, apparently."

A loud knock startled us both. I unlocked the door and Sam breezed in, fresh-faced and glowing, her dark hair pulled back in a fashionable twist. She looked like she'd stepped right off the Lululemon homepage, in a pair of bright pink leggings and a coordinated top that made our black yoga pants and hoodies look dull by comparison. "Hey, girls!" she sang, coffee in hand, waving her half-eaten chocolate croissant at us. "Who's ready for some pampering? Nick booked a four-hour package for each of us—massages, facials, pedicures, the works! He was either feeling really grateful or really guilty. Which was it?" she asked, wagging her perfectly plucked eyebrows. "Inquiring minds want to know."

"Definitely guilty," Vero chimed in.

"Ooooh, what'd he do?" Sam asked, sitting cross-legged on our bed.

"He was hovering, being overprotective, and getting up in Finlay's business."

"Because he cares," my mother said, coming back into the room. "I think it's very noble that he goes to such lengths to keep you and the children safe."

Sam nodded sagely. "Well, if it makes you feel better, Finlay, I promise not to bring any Big D energy to the spa." Vero raised an eyebrow at
the floral pattern on Sam's very fancy yoga pants. "Big Detective," she
clarified. "Today is all about us girls. By the time Nick gets back from
Newark, you'll feel like a brand-new woman."

I laughed at that as I zipped up my hoodie. Today, I'd settle for staying out of prison.

Sam, my mother, Vero, and I sat in recliners in the waiting area of the
Villagio's spa. Aromatherapy candles flickered on every surface. Soothing wind chimes and pan flutes piped through speakers, and a foun-
tain bubbled down a mosaic of polished stones on the wall. I tugged my
plush robe closed around my legs, concealing the yoga pants I'd hiked
over my knees underneath it. Vero and I had had no choice but to leave
our shoes in our lockers in the changing room, but at least we could grab
them quickly once we managed to sneak out.

A woman in scrubs peeled back the curtain. Another followed her
in, carrying a tray of mimosas, cheese, and fruit. "Good morning," she
said, handing us each a glass. "We're going to start our treatments today
with ninety-minute couples' massages and hot towel facials."

"Finlay and I can go together," my mother said. "A mother and
daughter massage sounds like fun!"

Sam didn't look so sure. "Maybe I should go with Finlay."

"You promised, no Big D energy," Vero reminded her. "You and Susan should spend some time together anyway. You can share embarrass-
ing stories about Georgia and plan the wedding behind her back."

Sam choked on her mimosa.

The attendants led us all down the hall, a parade of slippers and
robes, into two dimly lit rooms, each containing a set of massage tables.
Vero waved jauntily at my mother and Sam across the hall as the doors
closed. "Ta-ta! See you in a few hours."

Our attendant scrutinized her clipboard. She looked up and smiled,
her voice low and soothing. "You're in for a treat, ladies! The Johanssons

will be doing your massages today. They're twins, and they're absolutely amazing," she said, looking a bit starstruck. "I'll give you a few minutes to disrobe. When you're ready, lie facedown on the tables. Your masseuses will be with you momentarily." As soon as she was gone, Vero and I shook off our robes.

"How long should we wait before we sneak out of here?" she asked, checking the clock above the door.

"Just long enough for their massages to start." Once Sam and my mother were facedown on the table, we'd have ninety minutes before either of them noticed we were gone.

The door to our massage room swung open as Vero reached for the knob. A large woman in a white smock filled the doorframe, her hair tied back in what should have been a headache-inducing bun. Agnes—according to the name badge pinned to the front of her apron—stepped into the small room. Another woman followed, nearly identical in appearance and attire, only Ingrid wore her own bun slightly higher.

Ingrid frowned at my clothes. "There is no reason to be shy here," she said, turning me around and patting the top of the table. "In our line of work, we see all kinds of bodies."

A nervous laugh burst out of me. "I'm sure all of us would rather not see any more."

"Don't be silly." She lifted my feet out from under me and swung me onto the massage table, pushing my face into a headrest shaped like a donut. "We will start with clothes on. You will see, after a bit of lavender and rosehip oil, you will be ready to try without the clothes."

"No rosehip!" I lifted my head, but Ingrid pushed it back down.

Vero whispered sharply from the table beside me. "I've fantasized about being naked with Swedish twins, but this is not what I had in mind! What do we do?"

"We'll just tell them we have to go. I'm sure they'll understand if we . . ." Ingrid's hand slid under my sweatshirt and began kneading my lower back. "Oh," I said languidly as my body turned to Jell-O. "Maybe five more minutes wouldn't hurt."

"Finlay!" My head jolted out of the donut. "We need to get out of here."

"Right!" We both sat up, apologies pouring from our mouths as we climbed down from the tables.

Vero pulled a bankroll of cash from the waistband of her yoga pants as Agnes and Ingrid watched, their eyes growing wide.

"This is not necessary," Agnes insisted. "Your services were paid in full when the appointments were scheduled."

"Consider it a tip," Vero said, counting out a stack of hundred-dollar bills into her oil-slicked hand. "My friend and I have somewhere we really need to be, but this spa day means a lot to those two ladies across the hall, and we don't want to disappoint them. How much will it cost for you to pretend we're in here for the next ninety minutes, having a wonderful time?"

Agnes stared at the cash as if she were having a moral crisis.

"What if they ask where you are when it's time for your pedicures?" Ingrid asked.

Vero passed her a stack of bills to ease her guilt. "Just tell them we had one too many mimosas and we're sleeping them off."

The women stared open-mouthed at us as Vero and I snuck out of the room.

We tiptoed down the hall and hurried to the locker room. I pushed the door open and jolted to a stop.

A woman with a sleek silver bob stood in the changing area beside our lockers. She glanced up at us as she stepped into a pair of Louis Vuittons. Her nostrils flared and she paused, giving us an odd look. I stared back, unable to move as Marco's wife sniffed the air, a dark voice inside my head wondering if she could somehow smell the stench of her husband's corpse on our clothes.

I swallowed as she reached into her handbag, her fingers grazing the pearlescent handle of the smallest pistol I had ever seen. She pushed it aside, withdrawing a pair of designer sunglasses that probably cost more than my house. Not a single hair dared to fall out of place as she placed them on her head.

Her smile was impeccable, her lipstick perfectly applied. "Lavender and rosehip," she noted. "Good choice. You should really try their bath bombs while you're here. They're on special. Two for one." She draped her mink stole over her arm, her heels clacking to the beat of my racing heart as she strode out.

Vero and I collapsed against our lockers.

"That felt like an omen," Vero said. "How much you want to bet Charlie's out there waiting for us?"

"I'm counting on it," I said, holding up my cell phone as she grabbed her gym bag containing our wigs. Charlie's photo game was strong, but I could tell a story with my pictures, too. "Let's go."

Vero and I snuck out the emergency exit at the back of the spa, emerging into the bright sunlit boardwalk behind the hotel. We kept our pace brisk, darting glances behind us.

"See him yet?" I asked, checking the side streets.

"About fifty feet behind us and closing in fast."

I held up my phone, waiting until we were all captured in the frame. "Say cheese." Vero and I grinned and I took the shot. I held the phone between us as we walked, showing her the photo. Charlie's smug face was framed in the space between our heads, twenty feet behind us. I tucked my phone back into my pocket. "In ninety minutes, we'll text that photo to Sam. We'll tell her you were allergic to the massage oil, so we called Charlie to pick us up and we left the spa to get some air. That should buy us a few hours. Now all we have to do is figure out how to ditch him."

"I say we make a run for it. He's old and out of shape."

"He has a gun," I reminded her.

"He's not going to shoot us on the boardwalk in broad daylight. If he wanted to shoot us, he would have done it last night."

She had a point. With a sigh, I followed her as she slung the strap of her gym bag over her head, arranging it snugly across her body as she broke into a jog. I fell in step beside her, blending in with all the other recreational runners on the boardwalk, weaving through groups of tourists with cameras and dodging oncoming bicycles.

I risked a backward glance. Charlie was jogging, too.

"Have we lost him yet?" Vero asked.

"No, he's right behind us."

"Then we'll just have to run faster." The gym bag bounced against her back as she increased her speed, forcing me to keep up. I shot a quick look over my shoulder. Charlie had broken into a run, and he did not look happy about it.

A crowd had gathered to watch a group of street clowns in front of us. "'Scuse us! Coming through!" Vero shouted. Heads turned as we cut between the spectators and the collection bucket. Vero reached into the pocket of her sweatshirt and dropped a hundred-dollar bill into the bucket as we passed. She hitched a thumb over her shoulder as she ran, pointing at Charlie. "A little help?" she called out to the nearest clown.

The performer rose up on the toes of his floppy red shoes for a better look. His eyes went wide as Charlie barreled through the audience, knocking spectators out of his way. I watched over my shoulder as the clown took a giant step forward and shoved a shoe in Charlie's path. We turned at the sound of a collective gasp, then a round of applause, as Charlie went flying. The clown rushed to his side, offering to help him up as he tripped him again. The crowd burst with laughter as Charlie's face hit the boardwalk. He shoved the clown away, straining to keep us in his sights as he pulled himself upright.

"This way!" Vero said, grabbing my hand. We dodged behind a crowd of tourists and ducked into the nearest shop, hiding behind a display case full of carved dragons and crystals, peering over it through the window as Charlie started running, making a beeline right for us.

"In here!" a voice said from the back of the store. Vero and I hurried through a satin curtain into a dimly lit room. The woman inside whipped the curtain closed behind us, studying us as we bent over our knees, breathing hard. Her bloodred lipstick left a garish ring around the plastic holder of her cigarillo. She blew out a long band of smoke, raising a shaggy brow at us as she gestured for us to sit.

Vero dropped her gym bag on the floor. We sagged into the two high-backed velvet chairs across the table from the woman, too winded to speak. A crystal ball rested in the center of it, beside a deck of brightly painted cards. Sweet clouds of incense smoke wafted through the room. On second thought, I was pretty sure it wasn't patchouli.

The woman pointed a long black fingernail at a chalkboard sign. PSYCHIC READINGS $25. PALM. TAROT. CRYSTAL BALL. "You want a reading?" she asked, affecting an accent that sounded a lot like my agent doing an impression of Count Chocula.

"No thanks," I said, dabbing sweat from my face.

The woman tapped her forehead. "Too bad. The Eye of Romelda is very powerful."

Vero sniffed. "Something of Romelda's is very powerful. I think I'm getting a contact high."

She shrugged. "If you want to sample Romelda's herbs, that will be an extra twenty-five."

"No herbs," I said as Vero seemed to consider that. "We just need to catch our breath. Then we'll be out of your way."

Romelda gestured to the curtain as she took another drag. "Because you are in a hurry."

Vero looked unimpressed. "What gave it away, the running or the sweat?"

"Don't be rude," I whispered.

"Why not? She's a phony! Even her accent's fake. She's probably from Hoboken."

"Trenton," Romelda corrected her.

"See?" Vero said, as if this proved her point.

"Romelda doesn't have to use the Eye to recognize a woman running from her problems. However," she said, reaching for her tarot cards, "the answers to those problems are another matter."

"I'm not paying for that," Vero said, slapping a hand over Romelda's before she could turn the first card over.

Romelda sucked in a sharp breath as their fingers made contact. Her pupils flared wide. A chill swept over me as her fake accent slipped and her eyes became unfocused. "You're looking for a man," she said in a low voice. "I see him in a vision. He is handsome. With dark hair."

Vero yanked her hand away. "For twenty-five bucks, you could at least be original."

"He has a very toned backside."

Vero crossed her arms but didn't argue with that.

Romelda blinked and her accent snapped back in place. "He wears many stories on his skin. One of them is about you."

"His tattoo," I whispered to Vero.

"She's talking in riddles, Finlay. Quit giving her clues."

"Yes! Tattoos. And he's tall."

Vero shot to her feet, pointing at Romelda. "That's where you're wrong! Javi's only five foot nine and a half."

Romelda stood, her bangles clanking as she thrust her arms wide and glared up at Vero. "Everyone is tall compared to Romelda!" The woman couldn't have been more than four-eleven in her shoes.

I tugged the hem of Vero's sweatshirt until she plopped back down. "What else did you see?" I asked to smooth the air.

She turned to me. "Pizza."

Vero rolled her eyes.

"And a gun."

"Not since Charlie took it," Vero muttered.

"And I saw a car. With wings," Romelda said, squinting. "Like a bird. Or maybe it was a bat?"

Vero barked out a laugh. "A car with wings. That's a good one."

I jabbed Vero in the side. "The hood ornament," I whispered. Her face paled. There was a set of silver wings on the hood of the Aston.

"You will find the car," Romelda said, "but the key won't be in it."

I stiffened. That had to be a coincidence, right?

"And your unwelcome friend with the scar on his face is coming into the shop right now."

Vero gasped. "How'd you know that?"

The woman pointed her cigarillo at the closed-circuit TV mounted in the corner behind our heads just as Charlie entered the store. He snapped hangers aside on their racks, searching inside the T-shirt displays and peering behind the counters.

I grabbed our gym bag. "Do you have another way out of here?"

Romelda held out a palm. Vero frowned as she slapped a wad of bills into it. The woman signaled for us to follow her through another curtain behind her. It opened into a storage room littered with boxes of junk. She led us to an exit hidden at the rear. "You," she said, stopping me at the door, "you will find what you seek, but you must take a leap of faith to acquire it. And you," she said to Vero, "you will find what *you* desire in someone close to you. He holds painful secrets inside him, in festering, broken pieces. Be patient. It's only a matter of time before he reveals what he's been keeping from you."

Vero blinked at the psychic as she held the door open for us.

"Come on," I said, nudging Vero through it. "You heard the woman. We're going to find him."

CHAPTER 25

Vero and I took the elevator to the thirty-fourth floor of a condominium building that reminded me of a tacky department store dressing room. Every wall was mirrored, every surface was veneered, and every carpet looked like it could have been ripped from the aisles of a 1980s movie theater.

"What's the plan?" I asked, checking my wig in the mirrored walls. We had changed clothes in the alley behind Romelda's shop. My jumpsuit still reeked like a bath bomb, but at least it had dried.

Vero tugged on her wig and smoothed it down.

"We'll wait until we're inside Russo's office, and then we'll jump him."

"And then what?"

"We'll search the place for Marco's ledger and make Russo tell us how he got it."

The elevator doors opened into a vestibule with a small sitting area. A man in a three-piece suit stood sentry beside a door. His jacket strained around his broad chest, and a disconcertingly large bulge protruded near his belt.

"There's a security guard," I whispered out of the side of my mouth.

"Let me handle this," Vero whispered back. She fluffed her blond locks as she strutted slowly out of the elevator, the gym bag slung casually over her shoulder. The security guard stood in her path as she reached to knock.

"Name?"

Vero tossed her hair, staring down her nose at him. "Tell Mr. Russo *La Reina* is here."

The security guard checked his phone, his eyes bouncing between us and an image on his screen, probably one captured by the camera in the casino last night. "Turn around and face the wall," he said, returning his phone to his pocket. I put my hands on the wall as he conducted a very thorough frisk.

He gestured for Vero to assume the position.

She narrowed her eyes at him. "If you cop a feel, I will make you regret it."

He considered that a moment before doing a hurried pat down and confiscating her gym bag. Unzipping it, he examined the contents. He raised an eyebrow, withdrawing a leather whip in one hand and a ball gag in the other.

"Seriously?" I whispered.

"It was either that or a glow-in-the-dark dildo," she whispered back. "Which would you have picked?"

The guard shook his head at a pair of pink fuzzy handcuffs before returning the items to her bag. He handed it back to her and pushed a buzzer on the wall.

A moment later, the door swung open. The middle-aged man framed inside it wore a bright red Speedo, a shower towel around his neck, a pornstache over his mouth, and an expansive terrain of manscaping that could have warranted its own HGTV show. I stared at his flip-flops, too repulsed to speak.

"You're Enzo?" Vero asked with an expression of mildly checked disgust.

"In the flesh."

"So it would seem. We're happy to wait out here while you get dressed," I suggested.

"No need," he assured us in a thick New Jersey accent. "It's just a body, right. Two beautiful women like you have probably seen plenty of 'em before."

"You have no idea," Vero muttered.

I shoved an elbow in Vero's ribs. "It's just that we didn't expect to see quite so much of yours."

He scratched his chest. "What can I say? I'm feeling generous." He consulted a calendar on his phone. "Which one of you is *La Reina*?"

"She is," Vero and I said in unison, each of us pointing at the other.

"I thought you were supposed to be taking charge," Vero whispered.

"You're the one who brought the handcuffs!" I whispered back.

The guard leaned over and said something in Enzo's ear.

Enzo glanced at Vero's gym bag with a lascivious grin. "Right this way, ladies." He held the door open wide, his flip-flops smacking against his heels as he showed us inside, leaving his security guard in the hall.

My jaw dropped as we followed Enzo into a brightly lit penthouse. Natural light poured through two stories of floor-to-ceiling windows, the sun high and bright above miles of boardwalk, the enormous balcony offering a striking view of the crashing surf below. Gripping the ends of the towel around his neck, he threw his arms out wide, showcasing more real estate than either of us needed or wanted to see. "What do you think? Pretty sweet digs, huh, ladies? There's a sauna upstairs, if you don't mind a little sweat."

"Thanks, but I think we'll pass," I said before Vero could utter a retort.

"Can I get you something to drink? Perrier? A martini? Maybe some Dom?" There were some sights even alcohol couldn't improve. Enzo, bent over the open door of his mini fridge, was one of them.

Vero looked at me like I was a traitor when I said, "Perrier would be fine."

"This is your office?" Vero asked, discreetly unzipping her gym bag as I scanned the room for Marco's little black book. There was no office furniture or conference table in the room. Just a dated leather sectional, a bar, a glass-top coffee table, and a flat-screen TV.

"Just moved in," Enzo called over his shoulder. "I'm thinking about selling my place in the Marina District now that I'm expanding my business south."

South. Into Marco Toscano's backyard. That couldn't be a coincidence.

Vero hid the leather whip behind her back as Enzo turned around and passed me a Perrier. He removed his towel and slung it over the bar, plucking a satin cheetah-print robe from a nearby coatrack and shrugging it on as he carried his drink to the sectional. He flung the sash wide, assuming an impressive manspread as he sat down. "Better?"

"Much," I agreed around a grimace.

He set down his drink and shucked his flip-flops, splaying his arms across the back of the couch. "I'm nothing if not profession—"

Vero pounced, looping her whip around his neck and drawing the ends tight. She straddled his legs, using her own to pin his hands to the front of his thighs. "Quick! Get the handcuffs!" she called back to me.

"Right!" I searched frantically for the restraints, blowing black curls out of my eyes as my wig slid sideways down my forehead. "Got 'em!" I crouched between Enzo's knees and wedged the cuffs under Vero's groin. Pink down clung to the hair on his thighs as I groped blindly for his wrists. He didn't seem to be putting up much of a fight.

His eyes were wide with awe, his mouth parted with wonder. "I'm so turned on right now. I love a woman who isn't afraid to get down to business. If you want, I'll call you *La Reina* while I let you spank my—"

Vero shoved the ball gag in his mouth. "Listen, buddy. You're going to keep your mouth shut and do exactly as we tell you." He nodded eagerly, the whip flopping loose around his neck.

A pair of high heels clicked into the room. Vero and I looked up sharply as a woman with a severe silver bob entered from the kitchen. An apron was tied around the front of her silk blouse. She dropped a plate of cookies onto the coffee table with a revolted look at Enzo, sending up a cloud of sugar dust. She started to leave, then paused to sniff the air.

"Why do you smell like lavender and rosehip?" she asked, coming closer, until her face was only inches from Vero's and mine. Almost as close as it had been in the locker room an hour ago. Giada raised her voice. "*Che due coglioni,* Enzo! Have you been using my massage oil for your creepy little sex party? I just bought it this morning!"

Enzo mumbled unintelligibly around the gag.

She made a disgusted sound. "Hurry up and finish whatever nonsense this is so we can go find Kevin Bacon. You promised you'd help me look for him."

Vero and I gawked at her through the fringe of our tousled wigs as she stormed off.

Enzo spit out his gag. "Thank you, Gigi!" he called after her. She flipped him the bird as she retreated to the kitchen.

I fell back on my hands as Vero scrambled off Enzo's lap.

Gigi, he'd called her. No . . . *G.G.* Like the initials in Marco's phone. The person who had been texting with Marco on Friday night must have been Giada Toscano.

But what was Marco's wife doing in Enzo Russo's penthouse?

"Don't mind my sister," Enzo said. "Her dog is missing, and she bakes when she's stressed. You'd think the damn dog was her kid, the way she fusses over him." He held up his wrists and wagged his eyebrows at the fuzzy handcuffs around them. "Now, where were we?"

Vero and I exchanged a look.

Enzo sighed. "She killed the mood, didn't she?" He slumped against the couch, his skin squeaking against the leather cushions. "Do you mind?" He inclined his head toward the cookies. Vero stuffed one in his mouth. "Delicious," he said as he began to chew. A spray of crumbs and powdered sugar dusted the carpet of dark hair on his chest. He jutted his chin toward his drink. I held the heavy glass to his lips as he slurped down a long sip.

He wiped his mouth on his wrist and sucked cookie dough from his teeth. "I guess we might as well skip the pleasantries and get to the less interesting reason for your visit. I understand you ladies had a stroke of bad luck at the craps table last night." He clucked his tongue. "That's a real shame. Your poker game was pretty impressive. Hated to see you lose it all on one roll like that. Take it from me," he said, shaking a finger at us, "no good ever came out of laying everything on the table and rolling the dice. You gotta play smart." He tapped his temple. "You look smart. Are you smart?" he asked me.

"Jesus, take the wheel," Vero muttered.

"Because if you are, I'm prepared to make a deal." Enzo got up, the long ties of his robe dragging along the floor as he crossed the room to a life-sized acrylic painting of Madonna (*like* a virgin, not the actual one) and swung it away from the wall, exposing a hidden safe. He used his nose to punch in the code and nudged open the door with his cuffed wrists, revealing stacks of bills bound in tight rubber bands.

He grabbed a thick brick of cash, dropping it onto the coffee table in front of us.

Vero reached for the money. "I like him better already."

I slapped her hand away. "What's that?" I asked Enzo.

"Play money. That's why you're here, isn't it? Normally, I don't let anyone walk out of here with this kind of cash for less than twenty percent interest, but I like you, so I'm willing to take fifteen. All I need from you is a little collateral," he explained as he reached for a cookie. "You know, houses, boats, jewelry, cars . . ."

"Cars?" Vero asked.

"Whatever you've got. Just has to be worth enough to cover your losses." At my frown, Enzo held up his hands. "Standard practice. Any private investor in this city will ask for the same." My eyes slid to Vero, wondering what she had promised as collateral when she'd cut her deal with Marco for two hundred thousand.

"Not all of them," she said defensively, as if she'd been reading my thoughts. "I've *heard* that *some* private investors in this town don't require any collateral. They just charge *stupid* amounts of interest instead, which is how *some*one," she emphasized, clearly directing her comment to me, "might *happen* to end up owing a lot more than she originally thought she was borrowing."

Enzo laughed. He collapsed backward onto the couch, propping a foot on the coffee table. "If you're talking about Marco Toscano, his business has been falling apart for months. He's spent more money chasing deadbeat clients than his interest-only schemes were ever bringing in. It's a very high-risk model, if you ask me." Enzo shook his head. "If Toscano had any money left to lend, the pit bosses in his own hotels wouldn't be feeding his prospects to me. He should have let me buy him off the boardwalk when I made him the offer."

Vero raised an eyebrow as our eyes caught. When had Enzo made this offer to Marco? Had it been as recently as Friday night? And what might have transpired when Marco refused?

"I have a car," I offered cautiously, "but it has a few . . . title issues. They might make it difficult to legally sign it over to you. That is, unless you know someone who might be willing to help me with that."

"Say no more," Enzo said. "I know exactly what you mean. I see this sort of thing all the time. Women looking to fence their ex-husbands' Caddies. Twentysomethings cashing in on their great-granddads' Buicks, hoping their parents won't find out about it." He shrugged. "Don't worry. If you've got a car, I got a guy who can sell it. He'll do whatever you need—disappear a VIN, paint it, scrap it for parts, put it on one of those container ships and dump it across the pond . . . whatever it takes."

"So this man has a garage?" I asked delicately.

"Where is it?" Vero asked a little too eagerly.

Enzo jutted his chin at a notepad on the coffee table and recited a street address from memory. Vero scribbled furiously and tore the address from the pad, stuffing it inside her bra.

"Ask for Hector," Enzo said. "Tell him I sent you. He'll hold the car at his shop for a few days. You pay me back on time, he gives you back your car."

"What happens if I'm late?" I asked.

"He sells it. I let him keep a slice of the profit, and everybody's happy. It's a win-win." He laughed. "Unless you lose. Then it's just a win for me. But don't worry," he said, the leather squeaking under him as he got up and reached for his money. "I've got a good feeling about you two. I'll hold on to this for you until I hear from Hector." Vero craned her neck, peering over his shoulder as he returned the cash to the safe. "See, if I was Marco, I'd probably just let you take the money. But then you'd lose it all in the casino and I'd have to send a guy to find you and break a few of your bones. That's no way to do business. It makes me sad. This way, we can all still be friends," he said jovially. "And maybe next time, you'll bring your bikinis and try the sauna."

"It'll be a cold day in hell when we—"

"—pass up an offer like that!" I finished for Vero. "If you'll excuse us, we should be getting to Hector's. Thank you for your time." Vero stole a cookie off the plate as I grabbed her gym bag and dragged her out of the condo.

"I will never be able to unsee that," she said when we were safely in the elevator. "Did you hear that, Finn? Hector's garage sounds like a chop shop."

"It also sounds like Enzo and Marco were in the middle of some kind of turf war. You think Enzo could have killed him for his business?"

"It doesn't sound like Marco had much of a business worth stealing."

"No, but Enzo could have been doing his sister a favor. Giada hated Marco. And they were technically still married when he was murdered, so she'd likely inherit his assets. Enzo also admitted to doing business with this garage. The pieces all fit."

"Not all of them. Louis was the one who contacted the garage about the car, not Enzo."

"But we don't know who actually delivered it."

Vero thought about that as the elevator slowed. "If Enzo was the murderer, why didn't he take Kevin Bacon and give the dog back to his sister? Why leave him locked in a bathroom for the police to find? And why wasn't Marco's ledger in Enzo's safe?"

There were far too many questions we didn't have answers to. But we were one step closer to finding Javi and the car. "Let's go visit Hector's garage and see what we can find."

CHAPTER 26

Vero and I got out of a taxi a few blocks away from the address Enzo had given us. We hunched against the cold, an icy wind slicing through our sweatshirts and our wigs blowing over our eyes. I turned every few feet to look over my shoulder. This was not a street I was comfortable exploring in broad daylight, and as the afternoon sun started dipping closer toward the horizon, I was beginning to question the logic in our plan, or if we even had one.

"We'll check it out from a distance," I reminded Vero as her pace quickened.

She squinted at each poorly marked structure we passed, searching for the building numbers. "One oh seven," she read as we hurried past a darkened pawnshop with bars on its window, then a smoke shop with a neon marijuana plant beside the door.

"We're not going to confront anyone."

"One oh nine."

"We're going to hang back and look for signs of Javi or the car."

Vero's sneakers ground to a halt in front of a lopsided awning. She turned back the way we'd come, counting storefronts. "This is it," she said, pointing at an unmarked door. The paint was chipped and faded but the lockset was new, the window beside it boarded up, not a sliver of light visible through it. A chain-link fence barred access to the narrow gravel driveway running between this building and the next one. I squinted between them, trying to see what lay beyond the NO TRESPASSING sign.

"Hear that?" Vero asked, tipping an ear toward the fence. A droning hum was drowned out by a sudden high-pitched whine, then the clatter of metal against metal. "That's a garage."

"No, that's a fence," I said as she slung the gym bag over her shoulder and grabbed the mesh, shoving her foot in one of the holes. "And whoever's down there obviously doesn't want any visitors."

"So?"

"So what if they have a dog? Or a gun?"

I wasn't sure which of those two possibilities made her pause. "What do you suggest we do, then? Knock on the damn door?"

When I didn't answer, she started climbing. Before I could get another word out, she'd landed like a cat on the other side, her sneakers splashing quietly into a puddle.

"Come on," she said, straightening her wig.

"This is a bad idea." Against my better judgment, I stuck a toe through the chain link and hoisted myself up. The metal was nerve-numbingly cold, and my breath fogged out in thick puffs when I finally reached the top. I straddled it, clinging to both sides as the metal wobbled under me, glad we'd had the forethought to change back into our yoga pants and sneakers before we'd come.

"This isn't nearly as high as that dormitory window we climbed out of at the academy last week."

"We fell out of it, Vero."

She grabbed my foot with a firm tug. With a yelp, I tumbled off the top of the gate and slid down the fence, landing on my butt in the wet gravel. "See? That wasn't so hard," she said, pulling me to my feet. I glared at her as I wiped the dirt from my bruised backside and followed her down the alley.

The whine of power tools grew louder, punctuated by the backbeat of a stereo. Light flickered through a window above us. Vero arched on her toes to peek inside. "I'm not tall enough. Give me a boost." She pushed me down by the top of my head and wrapped a leg around my neck, straddling my shoulders until she was perched on top of them, her feet tucked under my arms. She leaned forward, arms outstretched, nearly toppling me forward. "Higher. Now get closer to the window."

"Stop kicking me! I'm not a horse!"

We stumbled forward like clowns in a three-ring circus. Using the wall for balance, Vero placed her feet on top of my shoulders, my legs wobbling as she stood for a better look. She wedged her fingers underneath the rotting wooden sill above me. I blinked, dirt and rust peppering my face as she forced the window open a few inches. The hiss of acetylene torches filled the alley.

"What do you see?" I asked, holding tightly to her feet.

"It's definitely a chop shop. They've got five or six cars down there."

"Any sign of Javi?"

"No. But there's a room in the back that looks like it might be an office. The door's shut and the blinds are closed." She hopped down and dusted off her hands. "Where are you going?" she asked as I started back toward the gate. "We can't knock on the front door and ask for a tour of the place. We don't have a car. We'll look too suspicious."

I clambered back over the fence, eager to be out of the alley. It reminded me too much of the one we'd been dumped in front of our first night here. If it hadn't been for the mouthwatering smells of Italian food wafting from that creepy cellar door, I never would have let my guard down and followed Vero inside.

I paused, considering that. How the promise of food could chip away at defenses. How a bag of Cheerios could lure a toddler into compliance, or a platter of cocktail shrimp could distract a room full of people from noticing anything else . . .

"How many people did you see in the chop shop?" I asked.

"At least six." A spark lit in her eyes. "Why? Are we going to kick the door in and take them by surprise, like the heroine in your book?"

"No. We're going to feed them."

Vero paced the sidewalk a block away from the chop shop, gnawing on a fingernail as we waited for the pizza delivery driver. A rusted Ford Focus screeched to the curb beside us, and a scraggly-looking teenager in a Domino's uniform got out. Balancing a mountain of cardboard boxes on one hand, he held his other out for a tip.

"How much for the hat?" I asked, gesturing to the logo-emblazoned cap on his head.

He frowned at me like he thought I was kidding. "Fifty bucks?"

"Deal. I'll buy your shirt, too," I said, passing him a hundred.

He stripped off his shirt and handed me his uniform, grinning as he got back in his car and drove off in his undershirt. Vero sniffed the T-shirt and grimaced as she put it on. The hat was dark with pizza grease and didn't smell much better. I tugged it on over my wig as we started toward the chop shop. The sun had begun melting into a puddle of dull colors behind us. It was nearly dinnertime. With any luck, Hector's crew would be hungry.

"Pizza delivery!" I shouted as I knocked, hoping someone would hear me over the roar of tools inside.

The door yanked open, jerking to a stop at the end of a metal chain. A shaggy eyebrow wrinkled on the other side. "Get lost. We didn't order any pizza."

I held up the receipt. "Are you sure? I've got an order here for Hector." The man glared at it through the narrow gap, frowning at Louis's name. Vero opened the lid on the top box, revealing a pepperoni with extra cheese.

The door slammed shut and the chain slid free.

The man who opened the door was huge, wearing grease-stained coveralls and gauges in his ears. His long, dark biker-beard was streaked with copper. He pointed a tattooed finger toward the door behind him. "Leave the food on the folding tables and get out."

He followed us as we carried the pizzas through the dim front room of a dilapidated, abandoned storefront into the bright fluorescent lights of the makeshift garage behind it. The air smelled like paint fumes and exhaust. Men bent over open engines and work boots protruded from under cars on lifts. Music blared. Tools clanked and torches hissed, showering the room with sparks. No one seemed to notice as we set the boxes down.

Vero stared at a bright blue tarp in the corner of the shop. A pair of expensive-looking rims peeked out from underneath it.

The Aston.

Her eyes leaped to the closed office door.

I cleared my throat and shouted, "Who wants free pizza?"

Heads craned out from under open hoods. Vero and I backed away from the table as a surge of mechanics rushed toward it. Two more men came out of the office behind us, rifles slung over their shoulders as they pushed past us for a slice. Even the burly man who'd opened the door for us crammed in to claim one before they were gone. Someone turned the music up. The men stuffed their mouths, laughing and talking as they huddled around the table, none of them bothering to notice as Vero and I backed into the abandoned office and locked ourselves inside.

She sucked in a sharp breath.

Javi was slumped in a chair across from a cheap, industrial-looking desk. Receipts and files littered its surface, hand tools acting as paperweights, holding stacks of errant papers down. A makeshift blindfold had been tied around his eyes and a strip of duct tape covered his mouth. A wide band of it circled his arms and chest, lashing him to the seat back.

Vero whispered his name.

Javi's head snapped up, the duct tape stifling his protests as Vero rushed to his side. I hurried to the desk, looking for something to cut the tape with. I tossed Vero a box cutter and jerked open a drawer, searching for the key to the Aston Martin.

A handgun slid toward me. My skin prickled with goosebumps as I recalled Romelda's vision. There would be pizza, she'd said. *And a gun* . . .

I checked the safety and stuffed the pistol in the back of my yoga pants.

Vero pulled the blindfold from Javi's eyes. There was dried blood in his hair and a deep bruise darkened one cheekbone. He frowned at her wig, then down at her pizza delivery uniform as she dropped to her knees to cut the tape from his ankles. He tried to speak through it, his eyes growing wide as she grabbed a corner of it and started to pull.

He bit back a scream as she ripped the adhesive from his face, taking several days of dark stubble with it.

"Are you crazy, Veronica? The guy who runs this place will be back here any minute! What the fuck are you doing here? And why do you smell like Axe and pepperoni?"

"We're rescuing you!" she snapped, sawing through the tape on his wrists.

"Where's here?"

"New Jersey."

"That explains the hair." The tape snapped free. He shook out his fingers and shot to his feet. "How did you know where to find me?"

"The security footage at Ramón's garage. We saw the men who kidnapped you, and we traced them here."

"Those guys are carjackers, V! If they find you here, they'll kill you. And if *they* don't, your cousin will when he finds out you came here to look for me!"

"A simple thank-you would have sufficed." They were nose to nose, jaws set and faces close, the tension palpable between them.

"I found it!" Neither one of them looked up as I waved the key to the Aston.

A voice boomed through the garage. "Why don't I hear any tools? I've got four cars out back that need to be stripped and out the door by midnight! Which one of you assholes ordered pizza?"

Javi positioned himself between Vero and the door. "It's Hector. We need to get out of here."

I pointed out a metal grate high on the wall. "What about the vent?"

Javi moved the chair, climbing up to study it. "The screws are all stripped." He reached above his head and gave one of the ceiling tiles a push. It lifted off its frame and he shoved it aside, revealing a maze of ductwork and wires. "Come on," he said, using the desk to boost himself higher. Vero climbed up after him as he disappeared into the ceiling.

"Will it hold our weight?" I called up as loudly as I dared. "Be very careful how you answer that," I warned Vero before she could utter a reply.

"There are steel crossbeams every fifteen feet or so," Javi called down. He reached for my hand. "Stay on the beams. You'll be fine." With a grunt, he hauled me up into the ceiling with them and nested the ceiling tile back in its frame, covering our tracks.

Vero turned on her phone light, and I suddenly felt sick. We were standing side by side on a beam no wider than my feet, no less than fifteen feet above a concrete floor, with nothing below us but a sea of ceiling tiles made of foam. I clutched Vero's hand as Javi maneuvered carefully around us to take the lead. He lost his balance and overcorrected, pinwheeling to right himself. Vero whispered something that sounded like a prayer. The walls swam, and I dropped down on all fours, my breathing shallow as I gripped the edges of the dusty metal.

"See those pipes?" Javi said in a strained voice. He pointed at some dripping copper lines on the far wall. "They probably lead to a bathroom. We can climb down and wait inside it until the coast is clear."

Vero nodded. Steadying her breathing, she put one foot in front of the other, her arms stretched out beside her. "Easy," she said, a laugh trembling out of her. "Like dodging Legos in the playroom."

This was nothing like stepping on a Lego. If we stepped on a Lego, we weren't going to die. Rusty grit and cold metal cut through the knees of my jeans as I inched after her. Water dripped somewhere close. "Are we almost there?" I asked, disoriented by the sudden shift of her phone light.

"There's a vertical beam about five feet ahead of us," Vero said. "You're going to have to stand up."

"Why?"

"It's the only way around it."

I glanced up to see Javi gripping both sides of the square column. He sucked in a sharp breath as he threw one leg around it, then the other, teetering as he spread his arms wide again to regain his balance. I felt like I was watching a low-budget episode of *Squid Game* as Vero followed, taking his hand and letting him swing her to the other side of the column.

Her phone slipped from her fingers. She lunged to catch it. I gasped as her foot left the beam. Javi grabbed her hand as she fell, muscles straining in his forearm as he struggled to keep hold of her. One of her shoes punched through the foam tile below her, sending it crashing to the floor of the room underneath us.

A shout echoed from the garage. The music stopped. Power tools wound down as if they'd all suddenly been shut off. A booming voice carried through the ceiling tiles. "He's not in the office! Find him!"

Javi hauled Vero up beside him, sending a shower of foam dust and bits of tile to the floor.

"Up there!" someone shouted.

I curled in on myself, hands over my ears as bullets rained through the ceiling, pinging into the ductwork, dust motes swirling through the rays of light that sliced the air around me.

"I'm getting *so* tired of being shot at!" A ceiling tile collapsed to my left. A flashlight beam cut through the resulting hole.

Someone shouted, "It's that pizza delivery chick! I can't get a clean shot from here. I'm going up!"

Javi reached around the column, urging me to take his hand. "Come on, Finlay! We have to move!"

I pushed myself to my feet, feeling much higher than I had a moment ago, when I couldn't see the floor.

"Don't look down," he warned me.

But I already had. I gripped the column, unable to tear my gaze from the gaping hole below me. The blue tarp beneath it was covered in tile dust.

The tarp . . .

The Aston Martin was directly under me.

. . . you will find what you seek, but you must take a leap of faith . . .

"Take my hand, Finlay! They're coming!" Javi shouted.

I was fifteen feet up. The car's roof had to be at least four feet high. *Oh, god.* Was I seriously listening to the advice of a boardwalk psychic with a phony accent?

A flashlight beam cut across my back, casting shadows over the walls. The steel beam shook beneath me. I glanced back as several armed men poured through the ceiling above the office and shuffled toward me, inch by inch over the crossbeams, using their rifles for balance.

"Only one way out of here, sweetheart," one of them called out to me.

Considering my present situation, I was fairly certain he and Romelda were right.

I yelped as bullets ricocheted off the column. Shoving the car key down the front of my sweatshirt, I lay down across the beam, pivoting sideways and dropping my legs over the side.

"Finlay! What are you doing?" Vero cried.

"Get to the bathroom! I'll meet you there!"

The men started shooting again. Javi shouted for Vero to keep moving, steering her toward the copper pipes.

I held fast to the beam, bits of broken tile showering the tarp as I lowered myself through the hole in the ceiling until I was dangling by the tips of my fingers, my feet hanging over the car.

I shut my eyes and let go, falling the last few feet and landing on my ass on the hood. The key fob bounced out of my sweatshirt and clattered to the floor. There was a shout from the garage as someone spotted me.

The men above me fired through the ceiling. Mechanics scattered to avoid the bullets circling the car. I tried sliding sideways off the hood, reenacting an action sequence I'd written in a book once, which had seemed far more graceful when my heroine had done it. My backside stuck stubbornly to the tarp, and I scooted the rest of the way to the edge and fell over the side, landing on the concrete as bullets gouged the floor. I scooped up the key and dove under the shelter of the tarp, prying open the driver's side door and locking myself inside the car.

The interior lights came on, illuminating the cabin in a soft glow. The dashboard was intact, the upholstery perfect. There wasn't a single bullet hole in the Aston Martin beyond the ones it had when it had arrived here, as if Hector's men were too afraid to shoot it.

The gunfire paused as they shouted orders at one another. I reached behind the passenger seat, my fingers seeking out the small bullet hole in the headrest. I wedged a shaking finger deep into the crevice. No thumb drive.

I opened the glove box. Searched the center console and the storage compartments. No sign of Cam's thumb drive.

I jumped as the tarp was ripped away from the windshield. Armed men surrounded the vehicle, guns drawn.

A man in a pair of crisp, clean chinos and a collared shirt stood beside my window, hands on his hips beside his empty holster. "Get out of the car!" he demanded. I assumed this was Hector. He was the only man in the room not covered in grease. He was also the only one not pointing a gun at me, probably because his pistol was in the back of my pants.

My palms were slick with sweat, every instinct telling me to comply. But these men did not want to shoot this car, I reminded myself. And as long as Hector's guys were all here, watching me, it would buy Vero and Javi time to get out.

I shook my head and pushed the button for the ignition. The car purred to life. I gunned it once before putting it in gear, my foot firm on the brake as I looked around me for a way out of the garage.

Hector smirked, as if this amused him. His men started to laugh. Hector knocked on my window and gestured for me to lower it.

Curious, I cracked it.

He rested an elbow against the top of the car and leaned close to the gap, speaking over the growl of the engine. "I don't know who sent you," he said in a chilling, measured voice, "but unless you're planning to pay Louis for the car, plus the thirty grand he owes *me* for babysitting it, you ain't takin' it. So why don't you be a good little girl and get out of the car before I tell these guys to make you?" He smiled, looking pleased with himself as I reached for the gearshift.

I smiled back as I threw the car in reverse.

Shouts broke out behind me as I hit the gas. The car shot backward, the wall behind me filling my rearview mirror as I slammed on the brakes and screeched to a stop.

The men dove for cover as I shifted back into first and stomped on the gas. I cranked the wheel hard, the way Charlie had shown me during our driving class at the police academy, when he'd taught Mrs. Haggerty and me how to do donuts in an old run-down patrol car.

Rubber smoke filled the air, the smell of it thick as the Aston's tail spun around, taking out tool carts and compressors and two gunmen with it. I let the wheel slide through my fingers as Javi and Vero came flying out of the bathroom. I jerked the car to a stop beside them. Javi dove in, dragging Vero onto his lap. I shifted into reverse as he slammed the door shut.

I made a rushed and clumsy three-point turn, narrowly avoiding a few mechanics as I cut the wheel toward the single bay door at the back of the garage.

Javi braced against the dashboard as I hit the gas. He wrapped an arm around Vero's waist. "Finlay? What are you doing? The door!" He tensed as I accelerated toward the only exit. I prayed I was right, that these men would rather let us escape than watch us total a three-hundred-thousand-dollar sports car.

They scrambled, one of them rushing to slap a button on the wall. The bay door started to rise. I cringed, closing one eye when the underside of it raked over the car's roof, and with an earsplitting screech, we tore out of the garage. The automatic headlights came on, cutting through the dusky sky, glaring against the hoods and windshields of the cars waiting to be stripped and sold in the vacant lot behind the building. I cut the wheel, kicking up gravel as we careened through the alley, back toward the street.

"The gate!" Javi gripped Vero as we raced toward it. I pulled Hector's pistol from the back of my yoga pants and handed it to Vero.

Her window hummed open. The chain-link fence shimmered in our headlights. Behind us, men flooded out of the garage, ducking into cars, their engines gunning one by one. Javi held Vero by the seat of her pants as she leaned out of her window and fired three shots into a hazardous waste barrel as we flew past it. I watched in my rearview mirror as a stream of dark liquid spewed from the barrel and spread across the alley.

"It didn't work!" she cried, ducking back inside the car. "In your books, they always expl—"

An explosion rocked the car. I wasn't sure if it was the gate crashing in around us as we mowed through it or the wall of flames behind us, consuming the chop shop.

I didn't care.

We'd found Javi and we'd survived.

That was all that mattered as the Aston's wheels caught the road and we peeled away from Hector's garage.

CHAPTER 27

I navigated the Aston Martin down a series of narrow side streets, waiting until we were a safe distance from the fire before parking between two derelict warehouses. I killed the engine, my hands still shaking as we all got out. Javi paced the alley, breathing hard. His hair had come loose from the band at his nape, the dark strands falling haphazardly over the bruises on his cheek.

He caught Vero by the arm, his eyes frantic as they skimmed over her. He peeled off her wig and cupped her face in his hands, turning her chin this way and that to catch the narrow blade of light from the streetlight before pulling her to him. "You shouldn't have come here," he said into her hair. "You could have been hurt."

She backed out of his arms and threw a punch at his shoulder. "I just saved your life!"

He reeled. "Don't you get it? There's nothing left of me to save! You ruined me the first time you kissed me, Veronica! You completely destroyed me for anyone but you, and I've been living in a fucking purgatory since you left!"

"Since *I* left. You were the one who disappeared!" Her voice cracked on that last sharp word.

"I'll wait in the car," I said quietly.

"You'll stay right here!" Vero snapped in an unquestionable mom-voice. "Anything Javi has to say to me, he can say to my family." She caught him firmly by the cheek and forced him to look at her. "I waited for you," she said, her voice trembling. "I waited all night to pack my bags for college because you said you were coming to help me. At six in the morning, I packed them myself." Her eyes glistened with pent-up tears, and my heart broke for her. "Ramón and my mother had to drag me into the car when it was time for us to leave, because I was still so certain you were coming. Because you *promised* me you would. You *swore* it, Javi! So why didn't you show up?"

He swallowed hard and closed his eyes, as if the words were fighting to stay inside. "Because your cousin asked me not to." Vero's hand fell from his face. "Don't be mad," he said, desperate to placate her. "Ramón was only trying to protect you."

"Protect me? He *knew* how I felt about you!"

"He and your mom only wanted what was best for you."

"My mom was in on it, too?" she cried.

"It wasn't their fault."

"Of course it was their fault! Who else's fault would it be—?"

"I got arrested, Vero!"

She took a stunned step back. I covered my mouth, trying to melt into the background as they stared at each other, wide-eyed and shaking.

"It was stupid," he said through a thick throat. "I was on my way to your mom's place to help you pack, but I couldn't do it. I was so damn proud of you! And at the same time I was so angry at you for leaving us. For leaving *me*," he said, clutching his chest. "The three of us had been together every day since we were kids, and then suddenly we weren't kids anymore, and that summer everything changed, and I'd fallen so fucking hard for you. I was scared you would go off to college and meet someone else—some rich, smart trust fund kid who actually deserved you!" He winced and shook his head. "I took the long way to your house that night because I couldn't stand the thought of watching you pack. I didn't want to see you put those pictures of us in your suitcase. Or worse, leave them at your mom's house, locked away in some drawer you'd never open again. I walked right past your street and ended up in a bar, thinking the whole thing would be easier to stomach if I just couldn't *feel* anything. By the time I got up the nerve to leave the place, I was shit-faced drunk. Some asshole in a BMW was double-parked out front. Not just over the line," he said, sweeping his arms wide, "but straddling the last two spaces in the whole damn lot just so no one would park too close and scratch his precious fucking car!" Javi dragged a hand down his face as if the memory still haunted him. "I don't know what I was thinking. I *wasn't* thinking, I just snapped. I took a rock to his driver's side window. I wasn't going to steal it, V, I swear. But some-one saw me and called the cops and told them I was trying to boost it." His shoulders sagged with the weight of his confession. "The morning you left for college, I was in jail, Vero. That's why I didn't come to say goodbye."

The edge on her voice softened. "Why didn't you call me?"

"They only gave me one phone call."

Vero's dark eyes seethed as she realized who Javi had chosen that night.

"Don't be mad at Ramón," Javi pleaded. "He was right not to bail me out. You were too young to know what you wanted, and I needed time to get my shit together. It was better this way."

"Better to let me think you abandoned me?" she cried, shoving his chest. "That it was just a stupid summer fling and you didn't care about me?"

"What would you have done if I called you? Used your scholarship money to bail me out? Ditched class so you could come with me to my arraignment? You think I wanted that for you? You think I wanted you to skip sorority parties and football games for the next nine months so you could drive me to my court-ordered community service gigs, pick-ing up trash on the side of the highway and serving lunch at the old folks' home? I did care, Vero! I cared about you too damn much! That's why I told Ramón to leave me in that cell. Your mom was right. You worked too hard to waste your shot on someone like me. You were better off not knowing."

She jabbed a finger at the air between them. "Since when do *you* get to be the one to decide what's good for me? You're no better than my mother and Ramón!"

He winced as if she'd landed another blow. "Why is it so wrong that I wanted to protect you?"

"Because you're an idiot, Javi! I never wanted your protection! I just wanted to love you!" She shoved him again. He caught her fist and held it between them, knuckles white.

"Say that again." His voice was rough, like it had been dragged over hot coals.

"You're an idiot," she said stubbornly.

"Not that part."

"I don't know what you're talking about—"

He pulled her to him. Her eyes closed as he caught her mouth with his. Slowly, she un-balled her fists. Neither one of them bothered to come up for air as he looped an arm around her waist, the tenderness and intensity of their kiss making me feel like I should turn away. I told myself it was the smoke in the air that was making my eyes water.

Sirens wailed a few blocks away. I cleared my throat. "We should probably get out of here before the police start looking for us."

Javi looked up, still a little dazed as two police cars and a fire truck roared past the end of the alley. "Trust me," he said, "no one in that chop shop stuck around long enough to say a word to the cops about any of this. If we leave now, we can get the car back to Ramón's before sunrise."

Vero and I exchanged a look.

I spoke first, sparing her the lie. "Vero and I can't leave town yet. My kids and my mother are back in the hotel waiting for us, and you're in no condition to drive home." Javi looked exhausted. For that matter, so did we. And with a bullet hole in the back window and another in the trunk, the Aston was far too conspicuous to risk driving very far. "We should find a safe place to hide it for the night."

"Where's your hotel?" he asked.

"Some dump on the boardwalk called the Royal Flush," Vero answered.

"Good. The crappier the hotel, the less likely anyone will come looking for the car there. We'll cover it and leave it in the parking garage until Ramón can get here with his tow truck tomorrow. Give me your phone."

Vero put a protective hand over her pocket. "You're not calling my cousin."

"You have a better idea?"

"What are we supposed to tell him?"

He stepped close, his expression tender. "Maybe we should all start telling each other the truth for once." He brushed her lower lip with his thumb, and I was pretty sure she would melt into a puddle as he pressed a last soft kiss to it.

"You're going to owe me for the next four years for this," she warned him.

"You can beat me up over it tomorrow," he said, waving the phone he'd just picked from her pocket. "For now, I just want a hot shower and some sleep." He held up a hand for the car keys. I tossed them over.

An irrepressible smile stretched across Vero's face as she watched him get in and shut the door. "We did it, Finn. We found everything we were looking for, exactly like Romelda said we would." She started toward the car, frowning as I held her back. Vero had indeed found what she'd desired in someone close to her, someone who was letting his secrets fester in broken pieces inside him. And he *had* revealed the truth, just like Romelda had predicted. But we hadn't found everything we were looking for. Not yet.

"Cam's thumb drive isn't in the Aston," I said. "Someone must have found it."

"I doubt any of those guys at the chop shop will be lining up to give it to the police. We have Javi and the car. We're two for three. I call that a win. Let's go."

"The spreadsheet Cam stole isn't the only thing on the thumb drive,"

I blurted. I had no choice but to break my promise to Cam. Too much was at stake. He had seen too much, and once Charlie's hunt for the car was over, his search for Cam was sure to begin. Our only hope was to find that thumb drive, make sure there was nothing on it that would incriminate Vero and me, then turn the whole thing over to the police. Joey would have all the proof he needed that Charlie was a criminal, and Nick would have no choice but to believe him. They could put Cam under witness protection, arrest every dirty cop in the department (including Feliks's shady lawyer, Kat), and shut down Feliks's entire operation. With nothing to come back to, he could live out the rest of his years avoiding extradition in Brazil, far away from me and my family.

I took off my wig and looked Vero in the eyes. "The key to Feliks's cryptocurrency is on it. I don't know how it works exactly, but apparently that key is the only way to access the money."

"How much money?"

"Fourteen million dollars."

Vero's eyebrows shot up. "Come again?"

I nodded.

"You couldn't have opened with that yesterday?"

"It didn't seem as important as the evidence Cam stole."

Vero threw up her hands. "*This* is why you need an accountant!"

"People who have *money* need accountants. And right now, we don't have any."

"You think Hector took it?"

I shook my head. "If he'd found a key to fourteen million in the car, why would he have been so hung up on getting thirty thousand dollars for storing it for—"

"Louis," we said at the same time.

Suddenly, I was seeing a new angle in the story. Louis could have found the thumb drive *before* he'd had the car delivered to Hector's garage. All that time, we'd been searching for clues about where Louis had taken Javi. We hadn't been looking for the flash drive when we'd searched his hotel room, we'd been looking for the car.

Vero rushed to the Aston like her ass was on fire. "Come on, Finn. We've got fourteen mil in crypto to find."

As Javi drove us back to the Royal Flush, Vero came clean with him about her debt to Marco and the subsequent theft of the Aston Martin. She left out the gruesome discovery we'd made in Marco's suite. She also conveniently omitted Ike's death from the story, the fact the car was now wanted by the Russian mob, and exactly what information the missing thumb drive contained. Considering how angry Javi looked after hearing the few watered-down facts we *had* elected to share with him, Vero's choice not to divulge more than necessary seemed wise.

Javi did a double take as we got close to our hotel, craning his neck to read a glowing marquee as we passed the entrance to the Villagio. The car behind us honked their horn as Javi braked hard, making an impossibly tight U-turn.

Vero grabbed the back of his seat. "Where are you going? That's not our hotel!"

"I know that logo," he said, pointing at the Villagio's marquee. "That's the same logo that was on the soap in the bathroom where those assholes were keeping me. That must be the hotel where those two guys are staying."

"What exactly are you planning to do?" I asked as he swerved into the Villagio's parking garage.

"I'm going to find those jerks and get your thumb drive back so we can all go home." He revved the engine, urging the Aston faster up the ramp to a dark, vacant corner of an upper deck. He swerved into an empty space behind a column, obscuring the car from view. "Let's see how tough these guys are without the zip ties."

We scrambled out of the car after him.

"Wait!" I said, chasing his long strides to the lobby. "I promise, these guys are not tough, Javi! Vero and I can definitely handle them. Why don't you let us take you back to the Royal Flush and get you a room?"

He stormed into the hotel, ignoring the stares of the other hotel guests as he shouldered his way into a packed elevator before it could close.

"We don't even know what room they're in," Vero reminded him as we all crammed inside.

"I know exactly what room they're in. I saw it on the placard as they dragged me out." The other passengers darted uncomfortable looks at his bloodied clothes and his bruised face, inching away from him as he punched the button for the fifteenth floor.

I returned their stares with a tight smile as I whispered in Vero's ear, "*Do* something."

When the doors opened, Vero and I scurried after Javi. He followed the room numbers to Louis's locked door, glaring at the DO NOT DIS-TURB sign on the knob. "Give me the key," he said to Vero in a low voice.

She feigned ignorance. "The key?"

"The master key you said you took from housekeeping. The one you said you used to get into Marco's suite."

She blinked at him, yelping in protest as Javi jammed his hand into her pocket to retrieve it. He reached into her waistband for the gun and pressed the pistol's grip into her hand. "We'll go in on the count of three. You block his exit. I'll beat him until he talks."

"This should be interesting," I muttered.

"Maybe we should reconsider this plan," Vero suggested.

On the count of three, Javi rushed into the room. I waited for the cacophony of a barking dog and a pissed-off teenager protesting the interruption of his telenovela, but the room was silent. The TV was off, and Cam's computer bag was nowhere in sight. For that matter, neither was Kevin Bacon.

Light bled through the gap under the bathroom door. The exhaust fan whirred quietly on the other side, combating the faintly pungent smell that had begun creeping from the tub. Javi sniffed, pulling a face.

Vero put a hand to her temple as he reached for the doorknob. "Before you go in there, Javi, there's something I should probably—"

"Bathroom break's over, asshole!" Javi threw the bathroom door open. Vero and I stood back, knuckles to our teeth as Javi went still. Marco and Louis sat in a shallow puddle of melted ice. Louis's tie hung loose around his neck and rosehip oil glistened on Marco's belly. His skin had turned a pasty shade of blue around his haphazardly placed toupee, and Louis's gray lips were parted as if in surprise.

Javi turned slowly to face us.

Vero crossed her arms over her chest. "Don't look at me like that. Those guys were dead when we got here."

"There's a very reasonable explanation for this," I said calmly. "We just don't know exactly what it is yet."

Javi tore out of the bathroom.

"Come on," he said, towing Vero toward the door.

"Javi, wait—"

"Do not say one more word, V. You're not confessing to anything." He paced to the nightstand beside the bed. "I'm getting you out of here. Help me look for my phone. Those assholes probably took it. Maybe it's still here." He jerked open the drawer, then flung the comforter off the unmade bed. We all paused, staring at the distended belly of the sickly-looking wiener dog nestled in the rumpled sheets. Kevin lifted his head, too miserable to growl at us.

Vero turned to me as he whined and rested his muzzle on his paws. "Where's Cam?"

"Who's Cam?" Javi asked.

"I don't know," I said. "I assumed he was walking Kevin Bacon."

Javi frowned. "This day could not possibly get any weirder."

"Think it was the sausages?" Vero asked as Javi resumed his search.

"Maybe. But he seemed fine when we left them here."

"You don't think . . ." Vero paled.

"*No!*" I gasped. Was it even possible? We both turned to stare at Kevin's swollen belly.

". . . *you will find what you desire in someone close to you* . . ." she whispered.

"He holds painful secrets inside him . . ."

". . . in festering, broken pieces. Oh, shit."

"No! Absolutely no shit!" I insisted. "That drive has to be here somewhere." I ransacked drawers and closets. Vero searched the bathroom. She knelt to check under the bed, stifling a cry as she pulled a tiny, mangled piece of plastic out from under it. She held it out to me, mortified. It looked suspiciously like the cover of a chewed-up thumb drive.

"He couldn't have eaten the drive!" I argued. "It has metal in it!"

"Ike's dog ate his tooth!"

Kevin whined again. We both turned to stare at him.

"What do we do?" Vero whispered while Javi rummaged in Louis's luggage, looking for his cell phone. "We can't leave Kevin Bacon here. For all we know, his next dump is worth fourteen million dollars."

"We'll take him with us. I'll text Cam and tell him we took Kevin for a walk."

"My phone's not here," Javi called over his shoulder. He swore, whipping his hand back as Vero shut the suitcase on his fingers.

"Will you please quit touching everything! You're leaving fingerprints all over the place."

"Good," he said. "Better mine than yours."

"What's that supposed to mean?"

"I'm screwed anyway. My DNA's all over this place," he said, searching the gap behind the dresser. "I was zip-tied in that bathroom for two days, which means I had a very good reason to kill those assholes. I'll just tell the cops they kidnapped me. I'll say I got myself free, and I had no choice but to defend myself. No one ever has to know you were here. We need to get you out of here before someone comes looking for these guys. Then you and Finlay are going back to Virginia, and I'm going to turn myself in to the cops."

"You're going to *what*?!" Vero shrieked.

"If I confess to killing these guys, the investigation ends and no one will come looking for *you*," he told her. "I'll plead guilty in exchange for a lesser charge. I can prove these guys kidnapped me. You said it yourself. There's a video of the whole thing on Ramón's computer."

Vero bit her lip. "Not anymore," she said in a small voice. "I deleted the video."

"Jesus, Vero, why!"

"Because the Aston Martin was in it, and I promised Ramón no one would know that car was ever at his garage!"

"How the hell am I supposed to claim self-defense if I can't prove those two guys hit me on the head and stuffed me in the trunk of a car?"

"Wait," I murmured, a fleeting thought racing through my mind, too fast to make any sense of it. The details were a blur as I struggled to catch and hold on to it. "That's it," I said louder. "There were two drivers." But neither of them was listening to me. They were both too busy arguing with each other. I raised my voice. "No one is claiming self-defense!"

The room fell silent.

I refused to let any one of us take credit for a crime we hadn't committed. No more hiding bodies. No more running from our problems. We were going to find the person who murdered Marco and Louis and get a full confession out of them. That was the plan.

"There were two men in that video," I said. "There were two cars with two getaway drivers, one in the Aston and one in the Audi. Louis would have been driving his own car, but we have no idea who was driving the other. Whoever it was probably had access to Marco's suite." I turned to Javi. "Tell me everything you remember. Did you see either of the drivers' faces?"

He shook his head. "I woke up blindfolded in the trunk. Their voices echoed when they opened it. I'm pretty sure we came in through the parking garage."

"What else did you hear?"

Javi sat on the edge of the bed, thinking. "One of them—the guy in the Audi—he sounded older, like he was in charge. He kept talking down to the one in the Aston, calling him a fuckup, or a dumbass, or a shithead or something. *Slow down, shithead, you're gonna get pulled over.*" Javi snapped his fingers. "Shithead. That's what the guy kept calling him."

"How could you have heard that if you were in the trunk?"

"The guy's phone was connected to the car's speakers and the volume was turned up. I heard the whole thing. The one in the Audi kept calling him, getting on his case for driving too fast. The guy driving the Aston told him off. Said he had to be back in time for work."

"The car," Vero said, locking eyes with Javi.

"The car would remember his phone." Javi and Vero both bolted for the door.

I scooped up Kevin Bacon and followed them into the hall and down the stairs, none of us pausing for breath until we reached the parking garage. Vero unlocked the Aston Martin and dropped into the driver's seat, pulling up the Bluetooth history on the dashboard display. Only one entry came up—a local phone number. I read over her shoulder as she checked the number against the contacts in Marco's phone.

The number matched one entry—*S.H.*

We scrolled back through Marco's recent calls and texts, scrutinizing the messages he had exchanged with the Aston's driver. *S.H.* had called Marco the night we'd first arrived at the Royal Flush, at approximately the same time we'd snuck down to the lobby, searching for a particular valet who had the power to request a meeting with a loan shark. It was the same person Marco had texted back almost immediately. Marco had texted *S.H.* again, later that night, right after we'd left the restaurant, saying he had something that needed to be moved, presumably the car.

I thought back to our first encounter with the young valet. Remembered his conversation with Nick, when Nick had questioned him about his relationship with Marco.

What kind of work did you do for your uncle?

Scheduling mostly. Errands sometimes . . . He called me a shithead and said I couldn't do anything right.

S.H. wasn't a set of initials. It was an abbreviation for a nickname. A moniker. Like *B.B.* for *Boss Bitch*. Or *G.G.* for *Giada*. It was a code that only the user of the phone might know.

"*Shit Head*," I whispered as I connected the dots.

The phone number in the Aston belonged to Ricky.

CHAPTER 28

I tried Cam's cell number a third time from the parking garage. Still no answer. I sent him a quick, vague text, discreetly letting him know we were taking Kevin Bacon with us and not to return to Marco's hotel. After appropriating a laundry cart and cleaning supplies, we'd wrapped Marco and Louis in hotel comforters, packed up their luggage, and used the giant cart to move their bodies to the garage. Then Javi, Vero, and I had loaded the men into the trunk of Louis's Audi, put their luggage in the back seat, and locked all the evidence securely in the car. The temperature in the garage was well below thirty degrees. With any luck, the bodies would freeze overnight.

Once the bodies had been moved, Javi had called Ramón, explaining only that someone had stolen the Aston Martin from the shed in the salvage yard behind his garage, and that he and Vero had tracked down the thieves to Atlantic City. He'd given Ramón the address of the Villagio and asked him to come first thing in the morning with his flatbed to tow the Aston home. If worse came to worst and we couldn't force a confession out of Ricky, the truck was large enough to tow the Audi, too, and we all silently agreed that we would cross that bridge if and when we came to it. The last thing I wanted was to involve one more person Vero cared about in this mess, and I certainly had no desire to bury two more bodies on Steven's farm.

That said, we were running out of options.

We covered the Aston Martin with several king-sized bedsheets, wiped down every surface of Louis's room for prints, mopped and vacuumed the floors, left generous tips for the housekeeping crew, and used the remote checkout feature to let the front desk know both Marco and Louis had vacated the hotel.

Once we were safely out of the Villagio, I texted Cam again, fighting the niggling worry that something was wrong when he didn't respond.

Javi slung an arm over Vero's shoulder as we walked slowly back to our hotel. I followed, holding Kevin's leash, a poop bag at the ready in case the thumb drive decided to make a sudden appearance. Javi had cleaned himself in Louis's room, washing his hair and face in the sink and trading his sweat-soured clothes for a pair of chinos and a button-down shirt he'd found in Louis's luggage. He looked dapper under the boardwalk lights, his damp hair falling loose around his face, concealing his bruises as he leaned in, speaking close to Vero's ear. Whatever he said made her burst out laughing. I couldn't remember the last time I'd seen her smile so brightly, and I dropped back a few more feet, offering them some privacy.

Kevin paused to pee on a signpost. As I waited for him to finish, I checked the calls and text messages I'd missed over the last few hours.

Mom: *Sorry we missed you at the spa. Our massages must have run longer than we thought. Do you and Vero have plans for dinner? Maybe all of us girls can go out. My treat.*

Sam: *You two have some explaining to do.*

Steven: *The kids won't sleep. When are you coming back?*

Nick: *Newark was a bust. Lead was a dud. Leaving now. Back in a few hours.*

* * *

Nick's message had come ninety minutes ago. That didn't leave us much time.

I tugged gently on Kevin's leash, letting the cord go slack as I spotted a flyer stapled to the signpost where he'd just been peeing.

There was a photo of a dachshund on it.

REWARD: LOST DOG, APPROXIMATELY 28 LBS., ANSWERS TO
KEVIN BACON. IF FOUND, PLEASE CALL.

Giada Toscano's name and phone number were printed at the bottom.

I checked around me to make sure no one was looking as I ripped the flyer from the signpost, picked up Kevin, and hurried to catch up to Vero and Javi as they entered the Royal Flush. Tucking the dog under my arm, I followed them through the casino to the lobby, then to the valet station out front. Ricky was nowhere in sight.

Vero tried calling his number, but it rang straight to voice mail. Javi and I eavesdropped from behind a column as she approached the valet on duty and asked him where Ricky was. According to the valet, Ricky had disappeared during the middle of his last shift, and he wasn't scheduled to be back until Wednesday. We listened as Vero attempted to sweet-talk the young man into telling her where Ricky lived. When that didn't work, she tried bribery.

The valet pocketed the twenty that Vero offered him. "Be here at nine tomorrow morning," he said in a low voice. "It's Ricky's day off, but he'll be here."

"Why? What happens at nine?" Vero asked.

"Paychecks get cut. Trust me, he'll show up."

A car horn honked in the valet lane, and the young man trotted off to grab the keys from the driver.

"Guess we're stuck until then," Vero said. She wrapped an arm around Javi's waist as we emerged from behind the column. "I'm going to the front desk to get Javi a room. Then I'm taking him to the bar for something to eat. Want to join us for a drink? You should come, too," she said, patting Kevin on the head. "A little greasy bar food might be just what the doctor ordered. Maybe it'll help move things along."

The promise of greasy bar food and a drink was sorely tempting, but anyone in this hotel could be six degrees of separation from Kevin Bacon, which meant I should probably keep our four-legged celebrity out of sight. "You two go on without me. I'll take Kevin upstairs and check on Steven and the kids."

"Suit yourself," Vero said, towing Javi to the front desk.

I held Kevin securely under my arm as I cracked open the door to my hotel room. I prayed my mother was already asleep. That I could crawl into my bed and sleep for the next eight hours and explain why there was a constipated wiener dog in our room in the morning.

Kevin's ears perked up and he sniffed through the gap. A lamp was on inside. My mother's bed was neatly made, and her fanny pack and shoes were gone. I set Kevin down, frowning as I checked my phone. It was nearly eleven. It wasn't like my mother to stay out so late.

I cocked my head, my ear tipped toward Steven's room, wondering why I was still hearing a television and my children bickering on the other side of the wall. The kids should have been asleep hours ago. I knocked softly on Steven's door.

He opened it, looking disheveled in a rumpled T-shirt and sweatpants. There were bags under his eyes, and his hair stood on end. The children cheered as they scrambled to greet me.

"Why aren't they sleeping? Is everything okay?" I gave them each a quick kiss as I peered around the room. It looked like a tornado had run through it. Clothes were strewn over every piece of furniture. Toys and crayons littered the floor.

Steven rubbed his bloodshot eyes. "Their schedules are all messed up. They napped too late, and I can't get them down."

"Daddy, look!" Delia said, scooping up Kevin and holding him out in front of her. The dog blinked at us, his legs pinwheeling as he wriggled to get down. Zach held out a french fry, giggling as Kevin gobbled it up.

"Hey!" Steven scolded him. "Don't give him those. They're not good for him. You'll make him sick."

"It's fine," I assured him. Maybe Vero was right and some greasy food would actually help.

Delia set Kevin down, chasing after him as he waddled toward a table covered in fast-food wrappers and oily crumpled napkins. He rose on his hind legs, sniffing the remains of a Happy Meal.

"What's with the dog?" Steven asked.

So much for having eight hours to dream up a story. "I found him on the boardwalk. It was cold, and I didn't have the heart to leave him out there alone." Delia wrapped the dog snugly in her brother's woobie while Zach played with Kevin's floppy ears. Kevin didn't seem to mind as Delia snuck him another french fry. "I'll take him to the shelter in the morning. Have you seen my mom?"

Steven scratched his chest, fighting back a yawn. "She left a few hours ago. Said she was going to the casino."

"The casino? Are you sure?" My mother was not the gambling type. She didn't take risks. Not even in the kitchen. Susan McDonnell followed her recipe cards to the letter. Unless she was angry. Or upset. That's when she tossed the measuring cups aside and things got a little extra salty. "I should find her and make sure she's okay," I said, reaching for the dog. Delia cried and held on. Zach let out an ear-piercing wail, slapping my hand away as I tried to pry Kevin out of his sister's arms.

"Stop!" Steven shouted, startling us all. Even Kevin turned to stare. Steven pulled me aside. "Look," he said, pinching the bridge of his nose, "this is the first time they've been happy all night. I'm one tantrum away from a migraine, and if you take that dog now, they're both going to lose it." He took a slow, steadying breath. "Leave the dog here while you check on your mom."

I glanced back at the children as they started giggling again. "I don't think that's such a good idea. The dog should probably come with me."

"Why? You think I can't handle him?"

"No," I said in a placating tone. "It's just that he ate something he shouldn't have, and I need to keep an eye on him until he passes it."

Steven blanched at the roll of poop bags I held up. "Must have been important. What'd the dog eat? A piece of jewelry or something?"

"Something like that." He winced, and I dropped my voice to a whisper. "Look, I'd rather nobody know about this, and you know how Delia is. She can't keep a secret—"

"Give me the damn bags," he huffed, "before I change my mind."

Surprised, I handed him the roll. "I'll be back as soon as I can. If he poops while I'm gone, just leave it in the bag. I'll deal with it later." I kissed each of the kids good night and left to find my mother.

CHAPTER 29

I stood in the middle of the crowded casino, searching for my mom. Given her low tolerance for risk, the slot machines seemed like a logical place to start. I walked through several aisles of blinking, beeping stations, pausing when I caught a glimpse of my mother's teal sneakers sticking out from the last row. I checked for signs of my sister or Sam, but my mother seemed to be alone.

I raised my voice over the noise. "Mom?" Her head snapped up, her hand flying to her chest. "I thought you weren't supposed to be out of your room without a police escort."

She made a dismissive sound, turning back to her game, pressing the button to place a bet. The screen spun through a series of images, one after another, each new spin slowly eating away at her balance. "Samara saw me leave my room and offered to come. I told her I'm a grown woman and perfectly capable of taking care of myself."

"So she just let you wander off to the casino on your own?"

"Of course not. She's trying very hard to impress your sister."

"Then where is she?"

"In the ladies' room. Where's Charles?"

I gestured vaguely around me. "I'm sure he's here somewhere."

She fed another twenty into her machine when her credits ran out. "You should stay here and keep me company until he gets back. Nick is a very competent detective. If he says we have nothing to worry about, I believe him, but there's no harm in being cautious."

"I was actually just going upstairs to get some sleep. You should come with me."

"I'm not finished with my game," she said stubbornly.

I contemplated excuses to leave, wondering if I could make it to the elevator before Sam returned from the bathroom, but I couldn't shake the feeling that something was wrong as I watched her press that button over and over again. "What are you doing, Ma? You should hold on to your money. Buy something nice for yourself or take yourself out for lunch tomorrow."

"I'm tired of taking myself out."

I rested a hand over the button when she tried to increase her bet to ten cents. "You're not a gambler."

"There's a first time for everything," she said, nudging my hand away. "There's nothing wrong with taking risks. Look at you! You took a risk leaving Steven, and look how well that turned out." I studied her face as she slapped the button again, spending her credits with a numb, hollow-eyed expression that reminded me too much of the people who wandered the sidewalks here in the early hours of the morning, hands deep in their pockets as if they were clinging to whatever unspent hope still remained inside them. "You give and give, year after year," she said. I wasn't sure if she was talking to me or to herself. "Before you know it, you've put years of your life into something, and then you wake up one morning and look in the mirror and you've got gray hair and wrinkles, and you've spent your best years pouring yourself into someone who doesn't give back. You were smart leaving Steven when you did. You were better off cutting your losses and moving on while you're still young enough to find someone who appreciates you."

I sat at the empty slot machine beside her and put a hand on her shoulder, feeling the shudder in the breath she was trying to calm. "Mom, what's going on? Is something wrong between you and Dad?" My parents had argued plenty over the years, but it had always just been part of their dynamic—the way they set boundaries with each other and expressed their frustrations, the same way Steven and I had. That thought made me a little sick to my stomach.

"Nothing is wrong. Nothing is *ever* wrong. In his mind, everything is perfect. And why shouldn't it be? He wants something for dinner, I make it. He wants to spend the weekend doing something, we do it. He wants to go somewhere, we go where he wants to go. He has a kidney stone, I sit in the hospital with him and listen to him moan and groan about it. But who listens to me?" she asked, smacking the button without pausing. "I thought if I left, it might fix something. That he might worry about where I was or what I was doing and beg me to come home. Heaven forbid he might miss me and realize how nice it is to have someone there with you, asking how your day was. It's been three days since I left, and he hasn't called once."

"Wait," I said, shaking my head, trying to rewind the conversation. "You didn't tell Dad where you were going?"

"I told him I was leaving."

"With me, right? You told him you were going away with Vero and me. Just for a few days."

She sniffed. "Not exactly." I pressed my hands to my eyes, having second thoughts about skipping that drink at the bar. "Don't you dare feel sorry for him, Finlay. His clothes were all washed and put away before I left. There were leftovers in the refrigerator and a meat loaf in the freezer. That's more than anyone's ever done for me. If he doesn't like it, he can cook for himself. I don't care anymore."

"Yes, you do," I said. She bit down on her quivering lip. "You can't stay here forever, Ma. What do you plan to do when it's time for all of us to go home?"

"I'll go to your house and live with you and the children."

"Mom—"

"You lived with me for eighteen years."

"What about Georgia?"

"She doesn't have a guest room."

"Vero's living in mine."

"I'll sleep in your office," she said, reaching into her fanny pack for another twenty-dollar bill.

"What are you doing?" I asked as she fed it to the machine.

"I'm starting over."

"You've lost forty dollars in this one already."

"Which is why I have to keep playing it. That woman to my left has been eyeing it for the last half hour. If I leave now, she'll take my seat and she'll probably win."

"I don't think that's how this works."

"Of course that's how this works. That's how life works. Your father has probably forgotten all about me. He's probably signed up for one of those online dating sites and found a younger woman who's willing to put up with him. That's probably why he hasn't called."

I heaved a sigh. I had not seen finding a marriage counselor for my parents on my New Year/New Me bingo card. For that matter, I had not anticipated finding a dead loan shark in a bathtub either. "Come on," I said, ignoring her protests as I pressed the button to cash out her credits. I sent a quick text to Sam, took my mother's hand, and led her out of the casino.

"Where are we going?" she asked.

"We're going for a drink."

Eighties music blasted from the hotel bar, but the Sunday-night crowd was sparse compared to the throngs of drunken club-hoppers we'd seen bursting from the place when Vero and I had returned last night. Only a handful of tables were occupied. A young woman in a white minidress and cheap chiffon veil sat at the bar, sipping a beer with a man in an even cheaper-looking tux. An Elvis impersonator sat alone at the opposite end, swaying a little as he tried to coax the bartender into giving him another round.

I settled my mother into a stool in the middle, ordering a glass of Chardonnay for her and a vodka tonic for myself.

On second thought, what the hell.

I called out to the waiter to change my order. My mother beamed as the bartender set two straws in the giant frozen fishbowl of margarita he placed between us, along with two shots of tequila for each of us.

I held a shot glass out to her. "What are we drinking to?"

"To us," she said, her eyes watering as we each knocked one back.

She turned in her seat. "Congratulations," she said wistfully to the newlyweds. "You two make a lovely couple."

"Thank you!" the woman said, holding out her left hand to show off the small diamond perched on her finger. "We're not married yet. Our appointment at the chapel isn't until midnight."

"How romantic! You're eloping then?" My mother hid her wince behind a smile. "Isn't that a little impulsive?"

The woman gazed lovingly at her partner. "We've actually been planning it for a while."

He reached into his breast pocket and unfolded a certificate, showing it off to my mother. "We applied for the marriage license weeks ago."

"Oh, well, I suppose that's okay then," she said. "Since you've probably already been to premarital counseling."

The bride shook her head, confused.

"Mom," I said in a low voice, "that's really none of our busin—"

"You know," my mother pressed, "when the priest asks why you want to marry one another and if you've had premarital relations. And of course, they always ask if you've ever lied or cheated." The man cleared his throat as my mother sucked down her second shot. "You've probably already discussed the things that really irk you about each other, all those little pet peeves that get under your skin."

The man signaled to the bartender, looking a bit ill as he asked for another drink, too.

"Mom—"

"Like maybe he insists on watching football for hours on end every Sunday. Or maybe he falls asleep in front of the TV every time you suggest watching a movie together, or he turns the thermostat down an extra two degrees to save money on the electric bill, even after you tell him you're freezing—"

"And maybe *we* should take our drinks someplace else. Excuse us," I said to the bride and groom. I carried my second shot in one hand and took my mother's elbow in the other, practically dragging her from her stool as she continued to lecture the poor couple on the importance of compromise and mutual respect. She scooped her fishbowl off the bar, cradling the massive drink in both hands as I nudged her toward an open table several feet away.

I peeked back at the couple as my mother and I took our seats. The bride had taken off her veil and they were arguing quietly. "Was that really necessary? Maybe you should spend less time worrying about everyone else's relationships and spend more time trying to fix your own."

"Is it so wrong that I want to make sure that nice, young couple is ready? You and Steven didn't go to premarital counseling, and look what happened to you."

"You know what, never mind," I said, throwing back my second shot.

Sam appeared behind us and ogled our drink. "Looks like I got here just in time. Nice of you to join us," she said, cocking a suspicious eyebrow at me as I sucked on a lime wedge.

I passed her the fishbowl, hoping she might not press me for information about my mysterious exit from the spa earlier.

"I'll get us another," my mother said, steadying herself as she slid off her stool.

Sam studied me as she sipped. "I suppose you're not going to tell me where you and Vero disappeared to," she said over the music. "And since I don't want to be on the receiving end of Nick's wrath if he were to find out I lost track of you today, I'm not going to say a word to him about it."

"Say a word about what?" Vero asked as she and Javi appeared beside our table. Sam turned on her stool to greet them. Javi's arm was draped over Vero's shoulder. Sam's eyebrow lifted as she sized up Javi.

"Javi, this is Detective Sam Becker," Vero said, putting a delicate emphasis on Sam's title. Javi stiffened. "Sam, this is Javi." I was sure Vero had left his introduction intentionally short. The less Sam knew about Javi, the harder it would be for her or my sister to do a background check if either of them got curious about who Vero was spending her time with.

"I was just telling Finlay that Susan and I had a lovely time at the spa this afternoon. I can see now you had a very compelling reason to leave." She gave Vero a sly wink as she extended a hand to Javi. "You must be Vero's elusive friend we've been hearing so much about."

Louis's jacket was slung over Javi's shoulder, the sleeves of his white dress shirt rolled up his forearms, revealing the dark canvas of tattoos underneath. His long hair fell rakishly over one eye as he reached to shake Sam's hand, the pink and purple strobe lights masking the bruise on his cheek.

"Nice to meet you," he said, quick to recover. "I'm going to the bar. Can I get anybody a drink?"

"I'll go with you," Vero said, leading the way.

"Javi's an old friend of Vero's," I explained when the silence between Sam and me became awkward. "Vero wanted to spend as much time with him as she could while we were in town. She didn't think Nick would let her go, given everything—"

"Say no more," Sam said, mooching a sip of my drink. "Your secret is safe with me. That explains why Charlie was so vague about where you all had gone when I texted him this afternoon. It was sweet of him to cover for you. Where is he, by the way? I haven't heard from him since."

I shrugged. "I have no idea where he went. I'm sure he isn't far."

Sam waved at someone behind me. I turned, half expecting to see Charlie, but it was only Georgia, pushing through the thin crowd to our table. Sam reached up and dropped a kiss on my sister's cheek, making her blush brighter than the magenta lights over the dance floor. "Where's Mom?" she asked.

I pointed to the bar, where our mother was deep in conversation with Javi. He tipped his head back and laughed at something she said. Whatever it was seemed to scandalize Vero, and he reached an arm around her hip as she burrowed her face in his shoulder. His thumb casually stroked the place on her lower back where her leggings concealed the letter *J* that I knew was tattooed there—the one that matched the *V* on Javi's chest. My mother passed them each a shot glass. She pointed out our table and gestured for the bartender to bring more.

"Who's that with Vero?" Georgia asked, donning her cop face.

"That's Vero's friend Javi," Sam answered. "And no, we're not giving him the third degree. I'm sure your mother has already handled that, and he obviously has her seal of approval." Georgia watched our mother with an open-mouthed stare as she took Javi by the hand and led him to the dance floor.

Sam dragged Georgia down into our mother's empty stool. I pushed the margarita toward my sister.

"Javi and Vero have known each other since they were kids," I assured her. "He's very nice and she's crazy about him, so don't go all angsty cop on him."

A server arrived balancing a tray of margaritas, along with several shot glasses. She offloaded them onto our table and we began passing them around.

"Mom looks like she's having a good time," I mused.

"How much has she had to drink?" Georgia asked.

"Not enough for you to get worked up about," Sam said, passing her a shot.

"Did you know Mom and Dad were having problems?" I asked.

Georgia shrugged. "No, but I figured. Not counting the night Delia was born and the day Steven left you, I can't remember the last time she left Dad alone overnight." She winced as she tasted her drink.

"You saw Dad before you left. Did he say anything?"

"Only that Mom was upset with him and he had no idea why. You know how he is. He said she'd get over it and be back in a few hours."

"That was three days ago."

"Which means the meat loaf she left him has probably thawed. He'll be fine." Georgia gave me a playful shove. "Quit worrying. They've been together for forty years, Finn. A couple of days apart isn't going to kill them. It might even do them some good. You know, distance makes the heart grow fonder and all that stuff. It worked for you. You and Vero were barely gone before Nick had Sam and me packing our bags into the back of Garrett's Suburban so we could come looking for you." My mind stuck stubbornly on that image, though I couldn't place why.

"Now that the goose chase for Feliks is over, we can probably all head home tomorrow."

"You think Vero will be ready to say goodbye to her boyfriend by then?" Sam teased.

"Javi lives in Virginia," I said cautiously. "He caught a ride up here a few days ago. We have room to squeeze one more person in my mom's SUV. We can give him a lift home."

Sam frowned. "That sounds a little cramped. Maybe you and Nick can ride back together with Charlie."

My lips were feeling a little too loose from the tequila, and I was cautious of the direction the conversation was veering. I had no idea where Charlie had gone after we'd ditched him on the boardwalk that afternoon, and I certainly had no intention of ever getting in a car with him again. I stood up, pleasantly light on my feet. "I should go save Javi before Mom starts planning another wedding." Sam laughed, giving my sister an affectionate squeeze as I excused myself from the table. I meandered across the dance floor and tapped my mother's arm to cut in. A sheen of perspiration gleamed on her brow, the color high in her cheeks as she passed Javi off to me.

"Doing okay?" I asked, looping my arms around his neck and letting him lead.

"I'm fine," he said, staring over my shoulder. I glanced back to where Vero was dancing to "Super Freak" with my mother, and Javi fought back a grin. "Your mom's pretty great. She reminds me of Norma."

"I've never met her," I said, feeling a stab of guilt that I hadn't ever even spoken to Vero's mom. Apparently, she lived just across the bridge in Maryland, a short drive away, but Vero had kept her family at arm's length, reluctant to involve them in her legal troubles. The few times I'd suggested we invite her mother to visit, Vero had been quick to shut me down.

"Norma's feisty," he said, fondness twinkling in his eyes as he watched Vero dance. "She's strong-willed. Not afraid to call it like she sees it. She's a lot like Vero."

"That must be why my mother likes you."

Javi laughed. "That would be one thing she and Norma *don't* have in common."

I touched his cheek, redirecting his gaze. "Vero's a grown woman, Javi. She knows what she wants, and she can make her own choices."

"Yeah, well, we don't always want things that are good for us."

"Maybe not," I agreed, "but that doesn't mean we want them any less."

His attention shifted to the entrance of the bar. "Speaking of which, some guy just walked in. I'm guessing he's your boyfriend since he's looking at me like he'd like to hit me and throw me in the trunk of his car for dancing with you. Should I be concerned for my life?"

I turned to see Nick casually reading the room as he made his way to Sam and Georgia's table. Our eyes caught, something softening in them as Sam leaned in, probably explaining to him that this was Vero's mysterious boyfriend and not some stranger I'd just met in the bar. I patted Javi's chest. "I think you're safe."

Vero swooped in, thrusting an arm between us. "Your boyfriend's back. Time for you to do some damage control. I'll keep an eye on this one," she said, nudging me aside with her hip.

I thanked Javi for the dance and found Nick sitting alone, resting his elbows on the bar. I slid onto the empty stool beside him. The bartender wiped the counter in front of us, moving aside the wedding certificate and cheap gauzy veil that the betrothed couple must have abandoned during their fight. When he was finished, Nick ordered a whisky, neat.

"Long day?" I asked.

A weary smile spread over his face as he took me in. "You could say that."

"No luck in Newark?"

He shook his head. "Zhirov wasn't on the flight. Was never supposed to be on the flight. Seems like someone was having a little fun at the expense of the FCPD."

I hated that I knew that someone was Cam, but mostly, I hated that I couldn't confess that to Nick. "I'm sorry."

He glanced up, offering a quiet "thanks" as the bartender slid a glass toward him.

"What now?" I asked.

He took a sip, contemplating that. "You were right. I needed some distance from all this."

"Did I say that?"

He shook his head. "You didn't have to. Zhirov's still in Brazil, I've gotten nowhere with Grindley's case, and I'm way outside my jurisdiction here. It feels like I'm chasing my tail, and, if I'm being honest, the only reason I even came to New Jersey is because I was worried about you." He turned toward me, taking the collar of my sweatshirt gently in his hands and resting his forehead on mine. "Tell me you're coming home with me tomorrow. Because I'm exhausted, and I could really use some sleep."

He smelled like warm skin and rye and faintly of his aftershave, even this late at night, though his jaw was dark with stubble. I wanted to tell him yes, that I would go home with him tomorrow, but more than that, I wanted to take the advice I had just given to Javi. To trust Nick and me to be adults who knew what we wanted. To make our own choices even if they weren't good for us. There was nothing more I could do to solve our problems tonight. Javi was safe. My mother was happy. My children were probably asleep with their father. For now, that was all that mattered. I rested a hand on Nick's. "Do you want to get out of here?"

He pulled back to look me in the eyes. Whatever he saw inside them made him finish his drink in one deep slug and ask the bartender for the check.

CHAPTER 30

We stumbled over the threshold into Nick's room, bumping into walls and fumbling over each other's clothes, buzzing on liquor and adrenaline.

"What about Charlie?" I asked, craning my head to make sure he wasn't waiting in the room. A single lamp had been left on, on the nightstand between the beds. Both of them were made, corners tucked, not a crease on either of the gaudy red-and-gold comforters.

"Haven't heard from him since this afternoon," Nick said against my neck as he dragged down my zipper.

"What if he comes back?"

Nick's grin was deliciously wicked as he swung the dead bolt in place, locking Charlie and the rest of the world out. "Better?" he asked, unfastening the last two buttons of his shirt and shucking it onto the bed.

"Much," I agreed, reaching for his belt.

He backed me to the mattress, then onto it, peeling off my sweatshirt and dragging my tank top over my head. He hooked his thumbs into the sides of my yoga pants, his lips kissing a path toward my navel, as he slowly inched them down. "I've been meaning to ask you about that book Sylvia was talking about," he murmured against my skin. "The one where the hot cop ravages the heroine in the back seat of his car."

"What about it?" I panted.

His lips traced the waistband of my panties. "What exactly did he do with his tongue?" he asked, his breath hot against the narrowing strip of cotton.

I was pretty sure my head would explode if he didn't take the damn things off. "It's a long book," I said, arching to meet the teasing kiss he planted there.

"I have a long attention span."

"Do you want the CliffsNotes version?"

He laughed. The low rumble of it nearly sent me over the edge as he spoke through the thin fabric. "Not a chance."

"But if I tell you the whole story, it might spoil it for you. And it's only a rough draft."

"Do the cop and the assassin end up naked together?"

"At least three times."

He grinned up at me as he relieved me of the last of my clothes. "I like it already. Don't leave anything out."

Tequila is cruel in the morning. I recoiled from the sun glaring through the window and burrowed into the crook of Nick's arm. His bare skin was warm, one long leg snug under the comforter between mine. A lazy smile spread over his face. He stroked my arm, his voice deep and rough with sleep. "I could get used to this."

I could, too, but it felt too much like tempting fate to say it out loud. "It's getting late. I should get dressed."

"I disagree."

"I thought you wanted to get home."

"Can't leave until Charlie gets back." He checked his watch. "He really must have tied one on last night. Hope he's not too hungover. Garrett's sticking around here to wrap up a few interviews, which means Charlie's going to have to drive us back." He rolled onto his side and snaked an arm around me. "Until he decides to come banging on that door, I'm staying right here," he said, nuzzling my neck.

I snuck a peek at the alarm clock on his nightstand. It was only eight o'clock. I still had an hour until Ricky was due to arrive to pick up his paycheck, and I had no burning desire to face the day that lay ahead of me yet. I relaxed back into the pillow, spent from last night. After I'd spoiled three of the more memorable scenes in the book for Nick, he had proceeded to spoil me for any other man. And while I felt a little guilty about the parts of the story I'd left out, I didn't necessarily have any regrets.

"I can't believe I wasted an entire day chasing my tail around Newark when I could have been in bed with you, all because some jerk decided it would be fun to call in a bogus lead just to mess with . . ." He paused, the bed going cold as he threw off the blankets and bolted out of it.

"I'm an idiot," he said, grabbing his pants off the floor. "I can't believe I didn't think of it before."

"Think of what?" I asked, pulling the comforter back over me as I sat up.

"Who likes to mess with the FCPD more than anyone?" Nick asked, zipping up his pants. "Feliks. That's who. What if he called in that tip himself, to make sure the cops and the FBI were in Newark all day?"

"Why would he do that? It doesn't make any sense."

"It does if he was planning to arrive somewhere else." He dragged his shirt on, leaving the buttons unfastened as he dialed his phone. A faint ringtone started in the adjoining room.

Sam's sleep-addled voice called out through the wall. "Seriously?"

Nick pounded on her door. "Sam," he said when she finally picked up, "I need you to find me a list of every private charter that flew into Atlantic City International Airport from Brazil yesterday. I want a passenger manifest for every one of them. Cross-reference it against all of Feliks Zhirov's known aliases. Has anyone heard from Charlie? . . . Have Georgia track him down and tell him to get his ass back here. And get dressed. I'll be over in a minute."

I held the sheet around me as I scrambled to my feet. "I thought you said we were going home. That you were out of your jurisdiction—"

"If someone inside Feliks's operation called in that bogus lead, it would explain everything," he said, the words rushing out. "We know the Russian mob was involved in Ike's disappearance, and his boss is acting cagey. Ike's wife hasn't been returning any of our calls since we left her place, and when I called her salon yesterday on the way home from the airport, her boss said she never showed up for work. What if Feliks had something to do with all that? What if he's here, chasing down loose ends? What if he flew in right under our noses while Garrett and I were in Newark looking for him? Maybe that's why no one's been able to reach Marco, because Feliks got to him first." He grabbed his shoes and planted a kiss on my head. "Lock the door behind me. I'll be back in a few minutes."

I didn't even have time to formulate a response before he tore out of the room.

I stood there in his bedsheet, staring at the floor.

If Nick suspected Marco was dead and that Feliks was behind it, it was only a matter of hours before he and the FBI would be all over the Villagio, searching for answers. Vero and I needed to find Ricky and get his confession before anyone found those bodies. Which meant I needed to get dressed and out of this room before Charlie made it back.

I searched frantically for my clothes, dropping to my knees to hunt for a missing sock under the bed. Nick's muffled voice drifted through the wall, along with Sam's and Georgia's, their room sounding more and more like a remote command center as the minutes wore on. I searched behind the bed for my shoes, finding one of them behind a suitcase in the corner of the room.

I paused, kneeling on all fours as I stared at it.

At the familiar faint smear of pink nail polish on the handle. At the residue on the bright red shell, matching the telltale shape of a *Blue's Clues* sticker that had only recently been removed. Something only I—or Vero—would have recognized.

This was *our* luggage, a suitcase I had let her borrow for our trip to the police academy. The same one Charlie had taken from us when we'd left the training campus four days ago—the one with Feliks's money in it.

I lifted the lid. A handful of his pants and shirts were neatly stacked inside, a few still bearing price tags. I dug around under them, but there was no sign of Vero's clothing. It was as if he'd dumped all of her personal belongings and repacked it with clothes he'd purchased for himself. As if he hadn't had time to deliver the suitcase of mob money to its intended recipient. Or had simply chosen not to.

I unzipped the top compartment. My breath caught as stacks of bound cash spilled out, revealing a slender black book inside. Marco's ledger.

All this time, Charlie had had the ledger.

But how? We had secured Marco's suite our first night here, as soon as we'd found the bodies.

Unless we weren't the first ones to break in . . .

I rewound through the fog of tequila to the conversation I'd had last night with Sam and Georgia in the bar.

You and Vero were barely gone before Nick had Sam and me packing our bags into the back of Garrett's Suburban so we could come looking for you.

Garrett had driven them here.

Not Charlie.

Nick said Charlie had *offered to come.* He never said Charlie had brought them here.

Nick and the others hadn't arrived until the morning after Marco was murdered. But Charlie could have arrived anytime after we had. Maybe even *right* after we had. Early enough to have followed us to dinner with Marco, then followed him back to the Villagio.

A new story began taking shape in my head. One in which Ricky wasn't the killer at all.

There was a knock on the door between the adjoining rooms. "Finn? It's me," Nick called through it.

"Hold on! I'm getting dressed!" I tore a single page out of Marco's black book—the one containing Vero's name and how much she'd owed Marco—and tucked it into my shirt. When Nick eventually found it—and I was certain he would—at least Vero's history with Marco wouldn't be spelled out in it.

I returned the rest of the ledger to the suitcase. My hands shook as I stuffed the cash back into its compartment and zipped it up. I did a quick scan of the room, checking to make sure everything was how it had been before turning the dead bolt.

"We got him," Nick said, a triumphant fire in his eyes as he blew into the room and held out his phone. The grainy image on the screen was taken at a high angle, as if from a ceiling-mounted security camera, but I would know that profile anywhere. The razor-sharp cheeks and regal posture. The slicked-back hair and icy frown.

My mouth went dry. "Feliks is here?"

"He landed in Atlantic City right after we left for Newark." Nick grabbed his badge and his wallet off the dresser. "Garrett's picking me up in a few minutes. We're meeting with the local PD to track Zhirov's movements since he landed. I'm hoping he got sloppy and we can figure out where he is." He dragged on his coat. "Charlie's not answering his phone, and no one's heard from him since yesterday afternoon. Sam said you were the last one to see him. Did he mention where he was going when he dropped you off last night?"

I shook my head. Charlie was probably still out looking for the thumb drive.

My stomach dipped as I stole a glance at my phone. Cam still hadn't responded to any of my text messages. I hadn't seen or heard from him since we'd left him asleep in Louis's room. And for that matter, where had Ricky gone when he'd mysteriously disappeared from his last shift at work?

Nick reached for his coat. "Sam and Georgia are staying here to keep an eye on things. Don't let the kids out of your sight. I want all of you to stay in your rooms until I get back. Or better yet, stay right here." He leaned in to drop a quick kiss on my lips, and then he was gone.

CHAPTER 31

As soon as Nick was gone, I hurried down the hall to Javi's room and banged on the door. Someone groaned inside.

"Go away!" Vero said, her voice muffled as if she was speaking into a pillow.

"It's Finlay! Open up!"

Footsteps shuffled closer. The dead bolt unlatched. Vero opened the door wearing the shirt Javi had been wearing last night and very little else. Her hair was tangled around a cheap white veil that hung crooked on her head. It looked like the same one I'd seen lying on the bar last night when Nick and I had left.

"What time is it?" she mumbled, wincing as she pressed a hand to her forehead. A hideous neon-green spider ring clung to her fourth finger, the same kind we'd seen in the plastic eggs being dispensed from the quarter machines in all the boardwalk arcades.

"Eight thirty. Get dressed," I said, stepping around her into the room and switching on the light.

She blinked several times, smears of mascara around her eyes stretching wide. "Oh, shit. Ricky!" She ran back to the bed, searching for her clothes in the mounds of tousled blankets. She grabbed a corner of the comforter and yanked it aside, both of us freezing in place as Javi bolted upright. He raised an arm against the glare, wearing nothing but Louis's argyle socks, two sleeves of tattoos, and a purple bat ring on his fourth finger.

"Jesus, V!" He yanked the sheet over his waist. Vero and I stared at the purple bat, then down at the spider on her hand. She reached up, touching the veil in her hair.

"Oh, god!" She grabbed a folded piece of paper off the nightstand. Her mouth fell open as she read it.

Javi took it from her, frowning at the wedding certificate the bride and groom had left on the bar last night. "Mr. and Mrs. Todd Liebowitz?"

Vero put her hands on her head. "Tell me we didn't get married."

Javi paled. "I think we got married."

"I knew I shouldn't have had that sixth shot of tequila!"

"What are you doing?" Javi asked as she tugged fiercely at the plastic spider on her finger.

"It's fine. Everything's fine. We'll just get an annulment." She whirled to me. "We can do that, right?"

"I don't think you need an annulment, Vero. Your name isn't even on the—"

Javi threw off the sheet and launched out of the bed. I covered my eyes, convinced several parts of him were now burned into my memory as he followed her to the bathroom. "What if I don't want an annulment?"

"Then I'll hire a divorce lawyer. And for the record, if we ever *do* get married again, I am not walking down the aisle to ZZ Top, and we're not doing it in some cheesy hotel chapel with a discount Dolly Parton drag queen for a witness and a stoned justice of the—" Vero gasped. I peeked between my fingers as she jabbed a finger at the enflamed, raw tattoo on Javi's chest, making him wince. "What the hell is that? Did you . . . Did we . . . ? Oh, god!" she cried, shoving him aside and turning her backside toward the mirror as she lifted up her shirt. The *J* tattooed high on her rump had been joined by the remaining letters of Javi's name. "No. No, no, no!" she said, storming back into the room for her clothes.

I shut my eyes and handed Javi his pants as he chased after her, waiting for the whine of his zipper before opening them again.

"What are you doing?" he asked as she tried once more to rip the spider from her hand.

"We're not married. You heard Finlay. Our names aren't on that certificate. It's not real."

"Well, it's real to me! I made a promise to you before, and I broke it. I'm not doing that again. I meant what I said in that *cheesy hotel chapel,* and I'm going to honor that promise until death do us part!"

"That can be arranged!"

"Will you two stop!" I shouted. They both turned to scowl at me, hands on their hips. "I know who murdered Marco and Louis! It wasn't Ricky. It was Charlie. And if we don't find him soon, Ricky and Cam might be next."

"So let me get this straight," Vero said as she hurried to get dressed. "You think Charlie showed up at the Villagio after Marco and Louis got back from their meeting with us?"

"It all makes perfect sense," I said, handing her her shoes. "Charlie could easily have impersonated a police officer to get access to Marco's suite." I could see the entire scene play out in my mind. "When the killer arrived at the suite, Marco was in the bathtub. Louis must have been the one who answered the door."

Vero nodded, catching on. "Charlie probably flashed a badge and pushed his way inside that bathroom, demanding to talk to Marco. But there's no way Marco would have told Charlie the location of the car," Vero said. "Marco would have told Charlie to get the hell out."

"No." I shook my head, seeing the scene a little differently. "Marco was vulnerable. He was still in the bathtub. Louis probably confronted

Charlie. That's probably how Louis hit his head on the marble vanity top—Charlie must have pushed him," I reasoned. "Then Charlie strangled Marco to keep him quiet."

"It all tracks," Vero said thoughtfully. "Charlie probably assumed the keys to the Aston were somewhere in Marco's suite, but by then, Ricky must have already taken the car to the chop shop. So Charlie took Marco's black book and Louis's phone, determined to find the car on his own."

Charlie must have seen Louis's phone sitting out in plain sight and assumed it belonged to Marco. Meanwhile, Marco's own phone had been left undiscovered, hidden under his boxer shorts on the bathroom counter.

Vero frowned. "But if Charlie killed them, why didn't he call Kat and have Feliks's cleanup crew cover the whole thing up?"

"Probably because he didn't want Kat to know." I thought back to the suitcase in Charlie's room, still bursting with the cash Feliks had sent him to take from us. Charlie hadn't bothered to deliver it on his way here. And he obviously hadn't been communicating with Kat. If she had been able to reach him, she wouldn't have bothered calling me.

Charlie must have seen that stolen thumb drive as more of an opportunity than a threat. With fourteen million dollars in his pocket, he could go anywhere. All he had to do was be the first person to find it. "He probably assumed he'd get his hands on the thumb drive and make it out of town before anyone else was the wiser, but he couldn't find the car. And then we stumbled into the crime scene and tainted all the evidence."

"Making you two the perfect patsies," Javi said. He popped two ibuprofen and chased it with a palmful of water from the tap.

"Well, that's just great," Vero said. "How are we supposed to get a murder confession out of Charlie if no one can find him?"

"Charlie hasn't left town," I suspected aloud. "Charlie only wants one thing, and right now, Kevin Bacon has it."

* * *

Vero, Javi, and I crept past Georgia and Sam's room and knocked on
Steven's door. He opened it, still wearing his pajamas. The children sat
on one of the beds, watching cartoons with Kevin Bacon. They barely
glanced up as we pushed our way inside.

"Who the hell is that?" Steven glared around me at Javi, who had yet
to put on a shirt.

"I'm Vero's husband," Javi answered. "Who the hell are you?"

Delia's head snapped up. She leaped out of bed, gasping at the bright
green spider on Vero's finger. "Vero, you got married?"

"No!" Vero said as Javi said, "Yes!"

"Zach, did you hear that?" Delia shouted. "They're going to have
babies!"

My mother burst through the open adjoining door. "Who's having
babies?"

"Vero is!" Delia said, jumping up and down. "She got married, and
Daddy said that's when babies happen!" Delia grabbed Javi's hand and
dragged him toward my mother, pointing at the swollen new tattoo on
Javi's chest. "And look! That's Vero's name!"

My mother's bloodshot eyes ping-ponged between their plastic rings
and the veil tangled in Vero's hair. I wasn't sure if the tinge of green in
her complexion was the result of a hangover or of deep dismay.

She walked to the closet and put on her coat.

"Where are you going?" I asked.

"There's a Catholic church a few blocks away."

"Mass was yesterday."

"And confession is today."

"A tequila hangover isn't penance enough?" I asked. She ignored
that, patting her pockets for her rosary. I found it on her nightstand
and handed it over. "You shouldn't leave the hotel by yourself, Mom."

"I'm not. You're coming with me."

"I have nothing to confess."

She looked disappointed. "You didn't spend the night with Nicholas?"

I lowered my voice, turning away from Steven and the kids. "I'm not asking anyone's forgiveness for that."

My mother's huff was heavy with judgment. "Fine, I'll ask Georgia to take me. And you," she said, pointing around me at Javi. He looked up at her, a deer caught in her headlights. "You're coming to my house for dinner next Thursday with your wife. Be prepared. I'll have questions for both of you." She clicked her fanny pack around her waist and walked out.

I watched through the peephole as my mother crossed the hall to my sister's room. Sam was probably still busy making phone calls for Nick. If Vero and I could slip out on the heels of my sister and mother, we might make it out of the hotel without being noticed.

Steven pulled me back from the door and dragged me into the bathroom. He dangled a plastic snack bag in front of me. A tiny thumb drive was stuck to the bottom of it.

"What the hell is this?" he asked me in a low voice.

I snatched the bag and stuffed it in my pocket. "You didn't have to go digging around for it. I told you I would deal with it."

"You *told* me it was important."

"No, I told you it was . . . Wait." I tipped my head, recalling the hurried conversation we'd had last night. "You asked me if the dog had swallowed a piece of jewelry."

"What did you expect me to think?" he whispered. "You were being all weird and secretive about it, and you said you didn't want Delia to know!"

"So you thought you had a right to go digging around, because you thought Nick had given me a present?"

"I was doing it for you, Finn! You hardly even know him!"

"Because heaven forbid another man buys me anything nice!"

His cheeks flushed, and he turned away from me.

A humorless laugh boiled out as I put the pieces together. "You were afraid he'd proposed?" I asked in a low voice. Steven didn't bother to answer. He didn't have to. I was certain I was right. It had been fine for him to get engaged to Theresa right after he'd left me—to move in with her and have our children sleeping in her house—but it wasn't okay for me to have a relationship with anybody else?

Javi knocked softly on the doorframe. "Ramón's on his way," he said. "I'm gonna go get dressed."

"Great idea," Steven grumbled.

Javi gave him a cold once-over before turning to Vero. "Come find me when you and Finlay are ready to go."

"Wait, you're leaving? Again?" Steven asked, blocking my way out of the bathroom. "You can't keep dumping the kids on me, Finlay."

"Why not? You're their father."

"So I'm just supposed to stay here with them," he spat, "while you're out doing god knows what with Vero and sleeping over in your boyfriend's room? I should just be expected to handle everything because you've decided you have more important things to . . . ?"

I crossed my arms and raised an eyebrow, daring him to finish that thought. Isn't that what he had been expecting of me for years? That he could walk out on our family when it suited him? That he could spend lazy Saturdays in bed with his fiancée in her town house down the street, or go out drinking with his buddies after work instead of picking up the kids? That the children would be my responsibility until a visit with them was convenient for him?

So why was I the one being made to feel guilty about it?

I didn't feel guilty for asking him to do his part. I just felt foolish for waiting this long to put my foot down. And my children weren't the only ones who needed me right now. "You were the one who asked for this, Steven. I never asked you to come." I walked past him into his room and gave each of the kids a hug. "Vero and I are going out for a while," I explained. "We have something very important to do. And when we get back, we're all going home."

"Home to our house?" Delia asked.

"Yes, home to our house." No more hiding the children at Steven's and my mother's. No more running from Feliks and Charlie. Whatever happened next, we would face it head-on. "Stay in this room," I told Steven, breaking out my mom-voice. "Do not let the children out of your sight."

"Where are you going?" he called after me as I gathered up the dog.

"Out," I said without looking back. Mommy was going to chase down some bad guys.

CHAPTER 32

"They call this a business center?" Vero grimaced as we entered the small room with a smoked-glass door off the lobby. There was a single outdated desktop inside connected to a cheap printer, a keyboard, and a mouse. The Wi-Fi password was handwritten on an index card and taped to the peeling tabletop. I set Kevin Bacon on the floor, keeping him on a short leash as he sniffed a stain on the carpet. I handed Vero the plastic bag containing the thumb drive.

"Just be grateful there aren't any cameras."

She made a gagging face as she gingerly used a Kleenex to plug Cam's thumb drive into the computer. After a bit of clicking, she swore under her breath. "The file's encrypted."

"Can you open it?"

"Not without a password. I'm guessing the only people who know it are Cam, Feliks, and possibly Kat."

Which meant we had no idea what information was contained on the spreadsheet Cam stole—or who it might incriminate.

Cam needed this file to cut a deal with the police, but turning the drive over to Nick would be a dangerous move. Not only because of what Nick might find on it, but because once Charlie knew the police had the file, he'd have no reason to spare Cam's life. Charlie desperately wanted what was on that thumb drive.

And he wasn't the only one.

Feliks was terrified of losing it, scared enough to hop on a plane and risk being caught here. And I knew better than anyone that desperation made people do foolish things. It had made a woman as smart as Vero put all her chips on the line for a dice roll. It had made a jealous man like Steven face down a highway of speeding cars, for the slim chance he'd win my admiration.

But greed?

Greed made people turn on each other. Steal from each other, like siblings fighting over a toy. And fear of losing a prize to someone else might make them do far worse.

Giving the thumb drive to Nick would mean risking my entire future. On the other hand, if I used it to barter with Charlie, he would walk away from the table with everything he wanted. The police would never know the horrible things he'd done, and Vero and I would still be left with two dead men and a mountain of incriminating evidence pointing to us. No matter how you cut it, the deck was stacked against us.

But what if I could change the odds?

I'd been thinking about this as a game of chance. But what if I could turn it into a game of strategy? Vero was right, I knew how to pretend. I made up stories for a *living*. I already felt like the world's biggest impostor, but maybe that's what made me good at my job.

Fake it 'til you make it, Finn.

I tucked Cam's original thumb drive back into the plastic bag. "Stay here," I said, putting Kevin's leash in Vero's hand. I hurried out of the room to the convenience center in the lobby. Passing over the candy and soda dispensers (and one selling an impressive variety of flavored lubricants and condoms), I shoved a twenty-dollar bill into the last machine. It contained a selection of chargers, disposable headphones, and a few overpriced burner phones, and *eureka*! I pushed a button. A cheap thumb drive fell to the dispenser with a muffled thump, and I tore it from its packaging as I hurried back to the business center.

Vero was hunched over herself in front of the computer, tugging at the spider on her finger. She jumped, dropping Kevin's leash when I tapped her on the shoulder.

I handed her the flash drive. "Can you make a dummy file on this? An encrypted one that looks identical to Cam's?"

She looked skeptical as she took it. "Sure. But why?"

"We're going to cut a deal," I said.

"With Charlie?"

"With everyone."

Vero, Kevin, and I hid behind a column in the lobby, avoiding the security camera mounted behind the front desk. Vero and I had agreed that our plan would work better if Javi wasn't involved. And if Lady Luck was not on our side, at least we wouldn't take anyone else down with us. We'd left her newly minted husband upstairs in his room, where he was probably still waiting for us. By the time he realized we weren't coming back, we'd be on our way to Ricky's house.

"What now?" Vero asked.

"We find Ricky's home address."

"There's no way that woman at the front desk is going to let me commandeer her computer."

"We don't need a computer," I said, dropping Kevin into Vero's arms. "Ricky's address is probably printed on his pay stub. All we have to do is get a look at it. Stay here," I said, straightening my wig before stepping around the column. I approached the desk, smiling sweetly.

"Hi," I said, affecting an accent that sounded disturbingly like my agent's. "My cousin, Ricky, works here. He's out sick, and he asked me to pick up his paycheck for him."

"Sure, what's his last name?"

I stumbled. Only his first name had been printed on his name badge. "Ricky . . . the valet?"

"Oh, no! He's sick? That must be why he left early the other day. We were all a little freaked out, honestly. It's not like Ricky to blow off work. He must be feeling pretty terrible."

I peeked over the counter, hoping for a glimpse of his pay stub. "Nothing a big, fat check won't fix."

She sifted through a stack of envelopes under the counter and slid one toward me. Ricky's full name and home address were visible through the window.

"Thank you!" I said, committing it to memory. "On second thought, I have an appointment at the spa next door. Maybe you should hold on to this and I can come back after my massage to pick it up."

"Sure thing," she said, tucking it under her station.

Vero stepped out from behind the column and followed me out the front door.

"You really think this will work?" she asked as I hailed a cab.

"It has to." I wasn't here to play craps with Charlie. I was holding some pretty powerful cards, and I was willing to bet I knew what all the other players in this game would do.

I was betting Feliks had flown here because he didn't trust Charlie with the files on that thumb drive.

And I was betting that distrust was justified.

I was also betting that Charlie and Feliks weren't the only ones willing to gamble for those files. Behind most powerful men, there was often a woman maneuvering on the outskirts of their game, watching for tells, biding her time until she found just the right opening to play the cards up her sleeve and claim her own seat at the table.

Cam said only two other people in Feliks's inner circle had access to the wallet containing his crypto, and I was betting Feliks's attorney was one of them.

I opened my contacts to *B.B.* and dialed Kat's number.

"Ms. Donovan," she answered. "This is quite a surprise." There was an unusually ragged edge to her voice, as if the stress of all this was beginning to wear on her.

"Well, buckle in, because you're about to get another one. I have something that belongs to your boss."

"You found the car?"

"I found the key." The line went silent. "Charlie has Cam. I have the flash drive. I think you and I can help each other."

Kat's pause was palpable. "Who else knows you have it?"

I grinned, certain I'd played the right card. "For now, just you and me."

Vero and I scoped out Ricky's house from a distance. The aged bungalow was only a few blocks west of the hotel, but it felt like miles from the gaudy trappings of the boardwalk. Charlie's red Cadillac looked grossly out of place here, parked haphazardly between the overflowing trash cans along Ricky's street. There was no sign of Feliks yet, but I didn't imagine we had long to wait before he'd show up.

I set Kevin Bacon down behind Charlie's Cadillac and snapped a picture of him with a burner phone I'd purchased from the vending machine in the lobby. I zoomed in, making sure the make, model, and license plate were clearly visible in the photo. In the background, I'd managed to capture the faded house number on Ricky's front porch. I unfolded the LOST DOG flyer I'd found on the boardwalk and entered Giada Toscano's cell number into my phone. I started typing.

I saw the man who stole your dog. Be careful. He has a gun.

I attached the photo to the message and hit *Send*.

Giada's reply was immediate. *Who is this?*

I held the burner over a trash can, ready to dump it, then paused.

Cam, I texted back.

I wiped my prints from the phone before getting rid of it. "Come on," I said, scooping Kevin under my arm. "Let's get a closer look."

Vero and I crept down the narrow gap between Ricky's house and his neighbor's. We crouched below a window, scratching Kevin Bacon behind the ears to quiet his whines as we listened. Loud voices carried from inside, and I rose up just high enough to peek in.

The house was sparsely furnished, the interior as drab as the dull aluminum siding and peeling shutters outside. Ricky and Cam sat on the floor of the kitchen, their backs to the shabby cabinet doors. They were zip-tied at the ankles, their hands behind their backs. Cam's nose was bleeding down the front of his coat, and Ricky's head wobbled, as if he were fighting to hold it up.

Charlie walked into view. "Let's try this one more time. Where's the car?" The barrel of his Magnum tapped an agitated rhythm against his thigh.

"I already told you everything I know," Ricky said through a thick throat. "I took it to Hector's garage on Friday night. That's the last time I saw it. I already gave you the address. Go see for yourself."

"I went to that garage, and my car wasn't there! So unless you want to spend another night bleeding on this floor, you're going to tell me where to find Hector!"

"I don't know!"

Vero and I jumped as Charlie took Ricky by the hair, yanking his head up. "Where would he take the car? Who would he sell it to?"

Ricky's chest hitched, his sobs so deep they were nearly silent as he slowly shook his head. His eyes were swollen shut, one cheek badly misshapen. I took out my phone, turned on my video camera, and started recording.

"Leave him alone," Cam cried. "He doesn't know anything."

"And I told you to keep your fucking mouth shut. The only reason you're still alive is because I need you to get me into that goddamn file!"

I stopped the video and texted it to Nick, Sam, and Georgia. I also texted a copy to Cam's Uncle Joey. By now, they should have all received a separate text from an anonymous whistleblower within Feliks's inner circle. That message would have contained a spreadsheet—the same

one Cam had copied from Feliks's servers and taken for leverage—a list
of every person who'd ever done a job for Feliks Zhirov, including evidence of wire transfers they'd received from the Russian mob. I was
assured this spreadsheet included countless payments to Charlie.

By now, someone on Nick's team would have opened that attach-
ment and alerted the others. They would have seen Charlie's crimes
spelled out in black-and-white. And if Nick still held stubbornly to
the idea that his best friend was innocent, this video would erase any
doubts.

Once they saw it, it wouldn't take them long to find us.

I just hoped it wasn't before Feliks did.

Charlie pressed his gun to Ricky's head. "I'll ask you one last time.
Where did they take the car?" Ricky's eyes rolled back as he passed out.

"Cut it out!" Cam shouted as Ricky slumped to the floor.

Charlie struck Cam hard across the face. I stood and banged a fist
against the window, consumed with white-hot rage.

Charlie whirled. I held up the dummy drive. Cam blinked up at me,
a warning in the frantic shake of his head. He had no way of knowing
the real drive was in my shoe.

"I'm coming in," I said through the glass.

Charlie made a sweeping gesture toward the back door with his gun.

"That's a promising start to negotiations," Vero whispered.

"We're not negotiating," I said. The time for diplomacy had passed.
I was done letting myself be pushed around by people like Charlie and
Feliks Zhirov. I returned the dummy drive to the pocket of my hoodie
as we started toward the back of the house.

Charlie met us at the door. His eyes skated to the neighboring
windows and alleyways before he opened it. Kevin growled low in his
throat. "Leave the dog outside."

"Not a chance," I said firmly. "You know as well as I do, he'll only
start barking, and I don't think either of us wants that much attention."
I was guessing he and Kevin were already acquainted.

"Fine, but keep him quiet." Charlie frisked me and Vero for weapons
before letting all three of us inside.

I held Kevin to my chest, positioning myself between Charlie and the boys while Vero knelt to check Ricky's pulse.

"What are you doing, Mrs. D?" Cam asked in a panicky voice.

"Hand it over," Charlie demanded. He reached for me when I didn't comply. Kevin Bacon's lips peeled back with a menacing growl and Charlie changed his mind.

"First, we discuss terms," I said.

"I'm the one holding the gun."

"And I have the keys to the car." I gave him a quick glimpse of the Aston's key fob before stuffing it back into my right pocket with the dummy drive. "Don't you want to know where I found it?" This move was a gamble. The Aston had never been important to Charlie. But this whole hunt for the car had been one big game to him, and I had won by finding it first. I was betting on his pride.

Charlie licked the scarred corner of his lip, as if he were fighting the urge to ask. "Where?"

"Exactly where Ricky told you it would be. In Hector's garage."

"Bullshit. I went to that garage. There wasn't anything left of it."

Vero stood beside me and clasped my right hand, a show of solidarity. "Who do you think burned it down?"

Charlie choked out a surprised laugh. He wagged a finger at us. "I thought I warned you two about setting fires."

"We confessed our crimes. Now, it's your turn," I said. "What happened to Marco and Louis?"

Charlie's laughter calmed. "That was some mess, huh? Nice of you to save me the trouble of scrubbing the place down. That's why you're here, isn't it? You're in over your head and you want to make a deal? Probably want me to clean it all up for you before Nick finds the bodies?" He took a moment to consider that. "Give me the thumb drive, and I might be willing to work something out."

"The boys go free first," I insisted. "And you promise not to harm them."

Charlie shook his head. "You know I can't do that. Cam's got one more job to do for me before I cut him loose."

"What about Ricky?"

He shrugged. "Like I said, you hand over the drive and let me deal with the mess."

I didn't like his implication, that these young men were expendable, something to be swept under the rug. I held my ground, one hand pressed protectively to the right pocket of my hoodie, making sure Charlie noticed. I nodded toward the front window as a black SUV with tinted windows rolled up behind Charlie's Cadillac.

Feliks Zhirov had finally arrived.

My poker face was flawless when I asked, "Were you expecting company?"

Charlie swore, his voice suddenly urgent. "Put the dog on the floor and your hands in the air. Both of you." I set Kevin carefully on the peeling linoleum. He scurried to Cam, tail thumping as he crawled into Cam's lap and licked his wounds.

Vero and I slowly put up our hands. Charlie kept both eyes on the front window as he reached inside my right pocket for the key fob and the thumb drive and stuffed them into his coat. He took a carefully measured step back, giving himself a clean line of sight through the living room to the front door. He stared at it, knuckles white, a sheen of perspiration beginning to glisten on his brow. His jaw tensed as someone knocked.

This was it, the final reveal. I had played the ace up my sleeve, and it was up to Charlie to fold or double down.

Cam pulled his knees in tight, making himself small, curling himself protectively around Kevin Bacon as Feliks knocked again.

"Fuck!" Charlie muttered. He lowered his weapon and went to unlock the front door.

Feliks stepped inside, his commanding presence shifting the balance of power in the house. He straightened his cuffs, his crisply tailored suit cutting a slow, silent path through the living room as he assessed the situation. He strode confidently to the kitchen, his cold, dark eyes making a smooth pass over each of us.

Charlie glanced anxiously at Feliks's driver, who stood sentry by the door. The man was built like a Russian tank, dressed all in black, his pistol openly displayed on his hip and his eyes trained on Charlie.

Feliks paused in front of me, his features as sharp as I remembered. I swallowed, my throat suddenly dry.

"Ms. Donovan," he said in a low voice. I flinched as he picked a piece of lint fuzz from my shoulder. "I admit to being surprised to see you. Ekatarina tells me I have you to thank for recovering my stolen property."

I cast a meaningful look at Charlie. "It seems your associate would prefer to take the credit."

"Would he?" Feliks turned. He slid his hands into his pockets, the lapels of his suit coat spreading just enough around them to reveal the butt of the gun holstered at his side. "A fascinating development, considering my *associate* has been avoiding me for several days. Have you not received my messages, Charles?"

Charlie's scar twisted around a tight smile. "I've been a little busy."

"It seems you have." Feliks held out a hand. "My files, if you please."

Charlie held Feliks's stare. His index finger twitched against the gun he gripped at his side.

"My money's on Charlie," Vero said in an exaggerated low voice.

"Are you sure?" I whispered loud enough to be heard. "Because Charlie's kind of outnumbered."

"True, but there are fourteen million bucks at stake here, Finn, and he really, *really* wants that money."

"Shut up!" Charlie growled.

I ignored him. "This is Feliks Zhirov we're talking about, Vero."

"True. But Charlie clearly came here with a plan. If *I* was him, I'd be thinking about how to get rid of the muscle by the door. That would even the odds, and then he'd definitely have the advantage because of all his police training and whatnot. He could take the key to Feliks's crypto, destroy the evidence on the flash drive, and take credit for single-handedly taking out one of the FBI's most wanted—"

"I said shut up!" Charlie shouted. "I can't think!"

Feliks took a step closer to him. "I fail to understand what there is to think about. I asked for the files."

I leaned toward Vero. "That's a pretty compelling argument."

"I think Charlie's going to cave," Vero agreed. "He's been taking orders from the Russian mob for so long, he's probably forgotten how to—"

Charlie moved fast, firing two quick rounds across the room into Feliks's bodyguard. The man crumpled by the door.

Charlie turned the gun on Feliks. Feliks's hand didn't make it to his holster before the nose of Charlie's Magnum was pressed against his boss's forehead.

Feliks went still. He raised his hands very slowly. Everyone in the house seemed to be holding their breath. Kevin Bacon whimpered.

"She wasn't wrong," Charlie said through his teeth. "I *was* getting pretty tired of taking orders from you." Vero and I jumped as he pulled the trigger. Feliks fell to the floor, his eyes wide and sightless below the small hole that remained.

Vero gripped my hand. "That was definitely not in the script," she said quietly.

Charlie wiped the sweat from his lip. His shocked laugh was joyless as he lowered his weapon. He stooped to pick up Feliks's gun, holstering his own. "Sounds to me like you had it all figured out, Finlay. That's what they pay you for, right? To write a good story?" He shook his head as he watched the slick red halo of blood spread over the floor. "I wasn't planning to kill anyone," he admitted. "Hell, all I wanted was the flash drive and a one-way ticket out of the country. But I think I like your version of the story better." He released the magazine of Feliks's gun, checking the rounds. "You're right," he said, snapping it back in place. "It's so much better this way. Now I get everything—the money, the respect. I can already see the headlines . . . *Retired Detective Neutralizes FCPD's Biggest Threat.*" His arm made a slow sweep of the air, as if he were reading the headline off a marquee.

"You seem pretty proud of yourself for someone who was shitting his pants a few minutes ago," Vero said.

"Why shouldn't I be? I just accomplished what the FBI and the FCPD have all been wishing they could do for years. Feliks Zhirov is no longer a menace to the community. He won't be a drain on the department anymore. That, at least, will be a small comfort to Nick when I tell him I didn't get here in time to save the rest of you." Charlie pointed Feliks's gun at us. We backed into the wall. Nowhere to run. I held my breath, listening for the sound of sirens in the distance, but all I heard was Cam hyperventilating and Kevin Bacon whining.

"What should I tell Nick?" Charlie asked me. "You're the author. How should the story go? Should I be kind and tell him that you were a reluctant accomplice, that Zhirov threatened you into murdering Toscano? That you came here to meet Feliks to ask for his help, because you were scared you wouldn't be able to clean up the mess on your own?

"Or should I put my old partner out of his misery quickly, like ripping off a Band-Aid? Maybe I'll tell him you and Zhirov were tight. That you worked for the mob. That Feliks trusted you. Hell, maybe I'll even tell him you and Zhirov were sleeping together and that you murdered Toscano and his friend because Feliks asked you to. You'd be everything Nick despises—a liar, a criminal, a cheat. At least then I won't have to listen to him crying into his beer about you. He'll resent you so much, he won't have the stomach to mourn you." Charlie raised an eyebrow, like he was waiting for my opinion. But there was a piece of the story he hadn't considered. A character he'd overlooked. Someone who had meaningful stakes in all this. And I was betting she was ready to hear my version of the story—the real one.

"Nick deserves to hear the truth," I said, raising my voice. "I didn't kill Marco Toscano or his friend. You did, Charlie. You broke into his suite and murdered them in cold blood. You can tell the police any story you want, but in the end, it's all lies. They're not going to believe you." I resisted the urge to glance past him at the back door.

"The evidence will back me up," Charlie said, chambering a round. "There are seven bullets left in Feliks's gun and only four of you. Five if you include that goddamn dog. Hell, maybe I'll even shoot myself, just to make it look good. What makes a better story—a graze in the leg or a slug in the foot?"

A gun cocked behind him. "How about I save you the trouble of deciding?"

Charlie didn't have time to turn around before Giada Toscano pulled her trigger.

She stood in the open back door to the kitchen, her tiny pearl-handled pistol still smoking as she returned it to her pink Prada purse. A very wise detective once told me you could tell a lot about a person by the size of their gun and the way they chose to carry it. Giada Toscano was someone I hoped I'd never have to cross.

The scream of a siren drew her attention to the front window. Police cars swarmed the street, blue lights swirling. Nick rushed out of the passenger side of Garrett's Suburban, a tactical vest strapped over his clothes, his weapon drawn as he hurtled up the porch steps.

Giada spit on Charlie, cursing him in Italian. Kevin Bacon scrambled off Cam's lap, his tail wagging wildly as he rushed into her arms. She whispered to him in a soothing voice when the front door burst open and slammed into the wall. The rest of us put our hands in the air as Nick stormed in, Garrett, Georgia, and Sam fanning out behind him as they all entered the house, guns drawn. Nick paused as he spotted Feliks's body. Then Charlie's. Then me.

His voice was tight, body tense when he called out, "Everyone okay?"

"We are *not* okay!" Giada snapped, pointing a finger at Charlie. "That man murdered my husband and threatened to shoot my dog!"

"We're fine," I said, clarifying, "but there are two young men in here who need medical attention." Georgia and Sam moved quickly to the kitchen.

Giada did a double take, her head tipping curiously as she studied Vero and me. "You two look familiar. Do I know you?"

"*Not in the script*," Vero sang under her breath.

"I . . . think we may have met at the spa?" I suggested.

Giada smiled. "Right! The bath bombs. *Love* them!" She tucked

Kevin Bacon securely under her arm, waving off the uniformed officer who'd been sent inside to take her into custody. "No need for handcuffs. I'll come without a fuss. My husband's murder, I could have forgiven. He was a pain in my ass anyway," she admitted. "But no one—and I mean *no one*—threatens Kevin Bacon and lives to tell about it."

"What kind of asshole would threaten Kevin Bacon?" one of the officers murmured on the porch.

Garrett knelt beside Charlie, checking for a pulse. He shook his head at Nick. Nick nodded, his expression torn between anger and grief as Garrett reached into Charlie's coat, withdrawing the useless dummy drive and the key to Louis's Audi—the same key Charlie had taken from my right pocket.

The key to the Aston was currently safe in Vero's left one. It hadn't been an easy sleight of hand to switch the fobs as we'd clasped hands during our little show of solidarity. Charlie had just been too distracted by Feliks's arrival to notice that he'd taken the wrong one.

Joey rushed into the house. He blew past Nick, into the kitchen, calling Cameron's name. He pulled a utility knife from his pocket and started cutting his nephew free. "You okay?" he asked, tipping Cam's head back to inspect his bloody nose. Cam nodded, wiping it gingerly on his sleeve.

"Vero! Vero!" Javi surged up the front porch steps.

"Hey, you can't go in there!" one of the officers shouted.

"The hell I can't! My wife is in there!" Javi called Vero's name as a wall of officers tried to stop him.

"It's okay," Nick called out to them. "Just watch your step and don't touch anything." That's all Javi needed to hear. He shoved his way past the cops and skidded to a stop in the entry, blanching when he saw the bodies strewn across the floor.

Vero rolled her eyes. "You and I are going to have to have a serious talk about this whole *my wife* business when we get home." He stepped over the bodies and threw his arms around her.

They broke off their embrace as Nick crossed the room and took me by the shoulders. I searched his face, praying my gamble on Kat hadn't been a mistake. That she'd honored her word to scrub my name and Vero's from the spreadsheet before she'd sent it to him. Vero looked worried, too.

With a rush of breath, Nick drew me against him, held me tightly, and whispered into my hair, "It's over, Finn. It's over."

CHAPTER 33

Vero and I stood on the sidewalk an hour later, trying to stay out of the way of the various investigators who had all arrived to examine the mess in Ricky's house. Ricky had awoken after the incident with no memory of anything after he'd passed out, and had long since been whisked away by the EMTs. Cam, on the other hand, had stubbornly refused to go.

He stood a few feet away, waiting for his uncle. I pulled him aside while Joey was tied up talking with Garrett and the local police.

"I told you to stay out of sight," I whispered. "Why did you leave the hotel room?" I used a wet wipe from my purse to wipe the blood from his face. He winced when I hit a sore spot, but he didn't ask me to stop.

"I went looking for the thumb drive." Cam glanced around us to make sure no one had overheard. "The morning after you left me and Kevin in Louis's room, I woke up hungry. I was thinking about calling and ordering some food, and then it hit me. The butler at the Villagio was always so careful about not letting people up to Marco's room, and when I'd called down to order room service the first time, he'd gotten all suspicious and asked who was placing the order. I didn't want to give him a name, so I'd just said I was Marco's nephew. I worried he'd start drilling me, asking me for all kinds of ID, but he seemed cool with it. He just let me order whatever the hell I wanted like it was no big deal. Which got me thinking . . . Marco must have actually had a real nephew who'd been to the suite before. So I went online and did some digging. Turns out Marco had a nephew, Ricky, who lives here in Atlantic City. I pull up the guy's social media. We're close in age, similar build, similar height. It's all starting to make sense. Then I see where he works, and it clicks. The guy drives *cars* for a living."

"So you went to find him." I wasn't sure if I was more impressed by his deductive reasoning or disappointed that he'd done something so foolhardy.

"I figured Kevin would be okay alone in the hotel room for a couple hours while I went to the Royal Flush to check this guy out. Except Charlie was already there. He had Ricky pinned against the side of his Caddy with his huge fucking Magnum pointed at the guy's head, and that's when Charlie spotted me. He made us get in his car, and we ended up here. The only reason he didn't kill us is because neither of us knew where the car was. Where'd you find the thumb drive?" Cam asked.

"I didn't." I hated lying to him, but it didn't seem safe to tell him the truth. The less he knew, the better off he'd be. "It wasn't in the car."

Reckless hope lit in his eyes. "Wait . . . that drive you handed over to Charlie was a fake?" His breathy laugh at my nod was slightly hysterical. "So the real one's still out there?"

I shook my head. "Vero and I have reason to believe the thumb drive was . . . dumped by someone close to Marco." I cringed at my own choice of words, but at least they felt closer to the truth.

Cam's face fell. It must have seemed like an incomprehensible loss to a seventeen-year-old kid whose grandmother was barely scraping by. But the key to that money had never been his to lose. "The only thing that's important is that you're okay," I reminded him.

"Tell that to my grandma when they arrest me for setting that fire at the training academy. That spreadsheet I took is gone . . . I've got nothing to go to the cops with. They'll probably throw the book at me."

I lifted his chin. "Leave the cops to me." He nodded, not bothering to argue as I made a final pass with the wet wipe over his cheek. "Will you need a ride home? We have room in my mom's SUV for one more." Vero had slipped Javi the key to the Aston, and he'd taken an Uber back to the hotel to meet Ramón. With any luck, they'd all be on the road to his salvage yard in Virginia before the investigation was done here.

"No thanks," Cam said. "I'll catch a ride with my uncle."

I made a *zip it* gesture as Joey wrapped up his conversation with the local police and headed in our direction. He put his hand on Cam's shoulder. "You ready to get to the hospital?"

"I don't need to go. Ms. D already took care of me."

Joey shook his head. "You ride in the ambulance or I take you. That was the deal."

"Whatever," Cam said with a sigh. He took me by surprise, stooping to give me an awkward hug, reluctant to let go when I squeezed him back, as if maybe he'd needed that hug for a long time.

"Thanks for looking out for him," Joey said. "I owe you one." I cocked an eyebrow at him as he extended a hand. "Fine. Maybe more than one," he conceded. He leaned close to my ear as we shook on that. "When Nick asks what you and Vero were doing here—and he will ask—tell him I called his room this morning looking for him and you picked up the phone. Tell him I left a message that Cam was in trouble. You knew Nick was busy looking for Feliks, so you decided to come here on your own, thinking you could help. Sound about right?"

I nodded, touched by Joey's willingness to cover for me. "Nick's still inside, if you want to tell him yourself."

Joey winced as he glanced back at the house. "I don't get the impression he's ready to mend fences with me just yet. It'll probably be better coming from you." Joey nudged Cam toward his car. "Let's get you home."

"Cam?" They turned to find an officer in uniform jogging toward them, the same local cop who'd escorted Giada out. Cam looked uneasy as the officer handed him a folded slip of paper. "The lady in the car asked me to give this to you." The officer hitched a thumb at the patrol car behind him. Giada's face was visible through the rear window. She sat up tall, her chin high. Somehow, she managed to look regal, even in custody.

Cam hesitated as he unfolded the paper. He looked confused as he studied the handwritten check. "This is ten grand. I don't even know that woman. Why's she giving me this?"

The officer shrugged. "She says it's a reward. Something about saving Kevin Bacon?"

"But I didn't—" Cam shut his mouth at the small shake of my head. He waved uncertainly at Giada in the back of the patrol car. Kevin Bacon sat in her lap, his front paws on the window, his tail wagging. Cam stared after them, looking like he'd lost his best friend as the officer returned to his car and drove them away.

Joey slung an arm around Cam's shoulder. "Nice work, kid."

"It ain't like it's fourteen million or nothing."

Joey looked confused, the reference lost on him. "No, but it'll pay for a year of college."

Cam laughed. "Maybe when you went to school." He put his arm around his uncle. "Come on, old man. I'll buy you a Happy Meal on the way home." Joey cracked a smile and shoved him toward his car. "You think we could stop at the Humane Society, too?" Cam asked as they walked. "I've been thinking about getting a dog."

Vero shook her head as she watched them go. "I think we should be entitled to some of that reward money, considering we saved his life."

"We didn't save him for money," I reminded her.

"We never killed anyone for money either, but the money sure was nice."

I shushed her as Nick came out of the house. Squinting against the low afternoon sun, he met Garrett at the sidewalk and signaled for Vero and me to join them. "I just got off the phone with the manager at the Villagio," Nick was saying as we walked up. "He said one of Marco Toscano's guests purchased a parking garage pass for a blue Audi sedan last week. It's possible it's still there. Maybe you can track it down and see if that Audi key you found on Charlie is a match. On your way there, would you mind taking Finlay and Vero back to the Flush?"

Garrett clapped him gently on the shoulder. "No problem."

"Hold up," Sam called out from the front porch. "Georgia and I will catch a ride back with you." I lingered behind with Nick as Vero, Georgia, and Sam followed Garrett to his SUV.

"You should go," Nick told me. "I've got some things to wrap up here. I'll come find you as soon as I'm done." He bent to kiss me, but it felt distant. Detached. Like part of him was still inside Ricky's house.

"Are you going to be okay?" I asked, painfully aware that he'd just lost his best friend. Not when Charlie had taken his last breath, but the moment Nick opened that spreadsheet on his phone and had seen Charlie's name on it.

The man he thought he'd known had ceased to exist a long time ago, but I didn't imagine the discovery of that had done much to temper the loss.

"I will be," he said, touching his forehead to mine. "I just need a little time to sort some things out."

The ride back to the Royal Flush was a quiet one. Vero sat up front, gazing thoughtfully out her window, her left thumb absently rubbing the green spider on her finger that had stubbornly refused to come off. Or so she claimed.

Sam and I sat in the back seat with Georgia sandwiched between us. Georgia called our mother, letting her know we were all safe and on our way back to the hotel. She glossed over any mention of Charlie. I didn't imagine she, Sam, or Nick were ready for that conversation just yet. To them, this must have all seemed to happen so fast. They'd woken this morning thinking Charlie was a friend. One of them. They hadn't had much time to adjust to this new reality.

"You all didn't need to stay for the rest of the investigation?" I asked as delicately as I dared. I still had a loose end to tie up, and I had been counting on all four of our police escorts being busy for the next few hours.

"It's not our investigation," Georgia said. "We were only here in town to make sure you and Vero were safe. It's in the hands of the local police and the FBI now."

"What about Nick?"

Sam's smile was melancholy. "He'll come back when he's ready. It's been a crazy few weeks. I think we'll all be happy to get home." She put an arm around Georgia and pressed a sloppy kiss to my sister's cheek to lighten the mood. "I, for one, plan to go back to our room, take a long, hot bath while I marathon some cheesy rom-coms, and sweet-talk your sister into buying me some greasy boardwalk food."

My sister smiled a little, too. Georgia had never been one for *feelings* or displays of affection. She'd spent most of her life strapped up tight in an emotional tactical vest, but Sam seemed to have a way of loosening the Velcro. My sister needed that, someone to be naked with—in more ways than one. I was glad they'd found each other. And as my sister rested her head quietly on Sam's shoulder, I was grateful they'd have each other's company tonight to soften today's blow.

Traffic slowed to a crawl as we neared the hotel. Police cars lined the street with their lights on, and drivers braked to rubberneck as police blocked the entrance to the Villagio's parking garage. Vero glanced back at me, clearly worried about the same thing I was. Had Javi and Ramón managed to make it out of the garage with the Aston Martin before the police had cordoned it off?

Garrett dropped us all off in front of the Royal Flush. We thanked him for the ride, waving as he drove off, watching his blue lights swirl toward the Villagio.

Georgia and Sam walked arm in arm into the hotel. Vero texted Javi as soon as they were out of sight. "Where are you? Where are you? Where are you?" she whispered as she waited for him to respond.

"Right here." We both jumped as Javi came out from behind the column he was leaning on, gingerly prodding the bridge of his nose.

Vero gasped at his two black eyes. "Oh, god! What happened?"

He looked away. "Ramón . . ."

She clapped a hand over her mouth.

"Where is he? Is he okay?" Had he been caught moving the car? Arrested? I felt sick at the thought.

"Ramón's fine," Javi said. "He made it out with the Aston about ten minutes before the cops swarmed the place."

I sagged with relief. Vero frowned at his swollen nose. He winced as she fussed over it. "What are you still doing here? You were supposed to go with him."

"I told him to leave without me because I wanted to wait for my wife."

"You told him that?" Vero cried. "Why!"

"Because it's true! And *I*, for one, am not ashamed of it. Ramón, however, didn't feel the same way. I told him we're cousins-in-law, and that's when he hit me."

Vero's hands balled into fists. "Where is he? I have a few things to say to Ramón myself."

Javi plucked her phone away from her before she could dial her cousin's number. "He's halfway to the interstate by now. You can give him hell tomorrow." He put an arm around her as we walked into the hotel. "So I've been thinking," he said as the three of us got in an elevator, "we never had a chance to properly celebrate our nuptials."

Vero shoved him backward out of the elevator car and pushed a button. She waved goodbye to him as the doors slid shut.

The elevator was blissfully quiet as it started its ascent. Vero leaned back against the mirrored wall, thoughtful as she spun the spider ring on her finger. Apparently, it wasn't so stuck there after all.

"How long are you planning to keep him in purgatory?" I asked.

She shrugged. "I haven't decided. A little sweat won't kill him. You have to admit," she said, holding her ring up to the light, "it was a pretty exciting girls' weekend."

I laughed. "I think we could both do with a little less excitement in our lives."

"Maybe you're right. Next time, let's keep it just the two of us."

* * *

Vero got off the elevator on our floor. "Sure you don't want me to come with you?" she asked.

"Go put your husband out of his misery. I'll handle this on my own." Vero rolled her eyes at me as the doors slid closed between us.

I rode the elevator to the top floor, then took the stairs to the roof. It was nearly dusk, the first vibrant smears of color appearing over the city skyline to the west, the crash of waves against the sand a rhythmic whisper from the beach below.

Ekatarina Rybakov stood at the roof's edge, her dark hair blowing in the wind. I didn't bother to quiet the latch as the door fell closed behind me. She turned, smiled, her hands relaxed in the pockets of her trench coat, her stiletto heels rough against the concrete as she strode toward me, chin high.

"You came," she said.

"I said I would."

"I assume you brought the key."

"I assume you honored your promise."

There were echoes of Feliks in the way she held herself, the sharpness of her features. The same unwavering confidence, the dare in her dark eyes. But there was something else, too. Something I hadn't seen in them before. Admiration. Respect.

She nodded, a thoughtful dip of her chin. "The spreadsheet I sent to the FCPD contained no record of you or your friends."

"And Cam?" I asked.

"As far as the FCPD is aware, Charlie was responsible for the incident at the training academy. A payment was wired to his account on the morning of the fire. I made sure the notes were clear—Charlie orchestrated the inferno at Feliks's behest and was paid for services rendered. Cameron, as well as you and your childcare worker, are free of any further obligation to the organization. Or to me," she added. "And as for the small matter of Ignacious Grindley, his remains have been handled. They will not be found. You have my word." She held out her palm, awaiting the key to her throne.

I placed the thumb drive in it, turning over the key to Feliks's fourteen million dollars, which we had agreed to on the phone earlier that afternoon. I had presented her with an opportunity: Inform Feliks I had found the thumb drive, give him my location, send an anonymous tip to the police, and let the chips fall where they may. If Charlie decided to give in to Feliks, or if my scattershot plan were to fail, Kat would be no worse off.

But if my plan succeeded, this woman—the powerhouse attorney Feliks had entrusted with the inner workings of his entire operation—would inherit Feliks's estate. All she had to do was place a bet.

"It's encrypted," I said.

"I know." She smiled, her small wink catching me by surprise as she tucked the thumb drive away. "It was a pleasure doing business with you," she said, strolling toward the door, the sun setting like a shimmering tiara behind her. Her gait was regal, the unburdened pace of a woman with no one to answer to and everywhere to go. She paused, appraising me over her shoulder. "Perhaps you would consider—"

I held up my hand, declining whatever proposition this newly crowned queen was about to offer me.

I was done with the mob. I was done with my life of crime.

I was content to go home with Vero and my children and write about someone else's adventures for a while.

CHAPTER 34

"Hurry up and pick up your toys," I urged the kids. "We have a long drive ahead of us." I packed the last of Delia's and Zach's clothes into their luggage while Steven navigated to the remote checkout screen on the television. The sooner we made it out of the state of New Jersey, the better.

Vero leaned through the open door of our adjoining room. "Javi's all checked out of his room. We're ready to roll when you are." She turned to my mom, who was busy folding her clothes into a neat pile beside my suitcase. "Thanks for offering to let him ride home with us."

"Did you think I was going to let your husband take an Uber?"

"I'm never going to live this down, am I?"

"Probably not," I said.

There was a heavy rap on Steven's door. When he opened it, the hotel manager stood in the hall, frowning over a tablet.

"Excuse the interruption. As much as we are truly ready to see you and your children go, we have a problem with your method of payment for the room."

"What kind of problem?" Steven asked.

"We attempted to charge the credit card you provided, but it seems there are insufficient funds on the account."

"The problem isn't the card," Steven said curtly. "It's probably your machine. That's a platinum business card. There's more than enough room on it to cover an entire floor in this dump."

The manager turned his tablet toward us. "Not after we ran all the other room charges you authorized to it."

Steven paled as he read the balance. He turned around slowly as Vero crept back to our adjoining room. His eyes burned a hole in her back. "That conniving little—"

"This should cover it," I said, reaching for my purse. I counted off a stack of hundreds from a roll of cash and held them out to the manager. Both men gaped at me.

"Where'd you get that?" Steven asked.

"Got lucky playing craps."

The manager sniffed, his nose wrinkling as he poked it farther into the room. "May I also remind you, the Royal Flush has a strict no pets rule. The cleaning fee is two hundred and fifty dollars if a pet is found on the property. You signed a disclosure during check-in, acknowledging our policies. I'm afraid you'll have to—"

I slapped three more bills into his hand and slammed the door in his face. I'd cleaned up far worse over the last seventy-two hours. In a few minutes, we'd be out of this dump and put Atlantic City in our rearview mirror.

There was another knock, on our door this time. Vero opened it. Georgia walked right past her, holding her phone out for our mom. "It's Dad," she said. "He wants to talk to you."

Mom lifted her chin. "Tell him I have nothing to say."

Georgia put the phone to her ear. "Mom says she has nothing to say." She listened, then said, "Dad says he wants you to come home. He says the meatloaf you left for him is gone and the bed is cold without you."

"I can't decide if that's obnoxious or romantic," Vero whispered.

My mother snapped a shirt off a hanger. "Tell him if he's cold, he can turn the thermostat up a degree."

"He says he already did."

"He probably expects me to cook him dinner, too," Mom said, loud enough to be heard through the phone.

"He says he'd rather take you out. He says he can get a table for tomorrow night at that fancy French place you like. And tickets to that new George Clooney movie if you want to go."

Our mother's scowl softened. "Tell him I'll think about it."

"Mom says she'll think about it."

"And remind him to take his medications. The blue one, too," she added bashfully. I smirked as coffee shot out of Vero's nose.

Color flooded my mother's cheeks as Georgia relayed the message. "Mom says take your pills. She'll be home in six hours."

Mom snapped the suitcase shut and put on her coat. "Come on, everyone. It's time to go home."

It was well after midnight when my mother's SUV pulled in to my driveway. The children had been asleep for the last few hours of the trip, and it took some careful maneuvering for Vero, Javi, and me to climb out of the third row without waking them up.

I pried Zach from his car seat, his blanket smooshed between his cheek and my chest. The fraying, sticky fabric still smelled like the floor of the casino, but I hadn't had the heart (or the energy) to hide it from my son when he'd cried for it in the car. What had started the trip as a phony, unconvincing substitute was now a torn, stained, and battle-worn woobie, beloved and made all the more real because of its imperfections.

I handed Zach off to Vero and she carried him inside. Javi took my suitcase and followed her.

I came around the car and tapped on my mother's window. She started with a yelp, laughing at herself as she rolled the window down.

"Too much caffeine," she said, handing me her empty coffee cup. It had been a long day, and she still had to take Steven and Javi home. Javi had suggested he'd rather spend the night at my house with Vero, but when he'd caught my mother's judgy glare in her rearview mirror, he'd begrudgingly agreed to let her give him a ride to Ramón's.

"Are you going to be okay to drive?"

"I'll be great."

A speck of glitter shimmered in her hair, a souvenir from her lap dance with Steele Johnson. We both laughed as I caught it between two fingers, letting the wind carry it away.

She captured my face as I leaned into the window to kiss her cheek. "I had a lot of fun with you girls this weekend. Sometimes I regret not holding on tighter to the friendships I had when I was young," she said wistfully. "Your father and I met when we were barely teenagers. He became my whole world, and that's wonderful. He's a good man, and I thank god for him every day. But when I see you with Vero— the way you girls look out for each other and the way you make each other laugh—I'm jealous of what you two have. Thank you for letting me come along and be a part of that for a while."

"There's always room for you on my couch," I teased.

"I think I'll stick with my own bed. Besides, your father's probably up waiting for me," she said eagerly. I tried not to think about how long those blue pills might last.

"Will you and Dad be okay?"

She patted my hand. "We'll be fine. You go on and get the children to bed."

I waved goodbye as she rolled up her window. Then I grabbed the children's Rollaboards out of the back as Steven hoisted Delia gently out of her booster seat.

"She's getting so big," he said quietly as we walked side by side to the front stoop. "She's growing up so fast. She has so many questions. Like all that stuff about where babies come from . . . I didn't know what to tell her."

"She's a bright kid. She's not going to believe stork tales forever. I think it's okay to tell her the truth."

He blanched. "All of it?"

"Not *all* of it. Not yet, anyway. But I don't think we have to lie to her. It's fine to omit a lot of the details for now, but I think we should answer her questions as directly as we can."

He paused on the porch step, turning to face me. "She wanted to know if you and Nick were going to have kids. I didn't know what to tell her." It came out like a question. Delia clearly wasn't the only one who wanted to know the answer.

"I think it's okay to tell her that when two people really care for each other, anything is possible." A deep worry line cut into his brow. "I also think it's fine to tell her that having babies is a big responsibility. It's perfectly fine to choose not to, and it's perfectly fine to wait."

"Finn," he said gently as he seemed to gather his thoughts, "about what you said in the hotel earlier, about me not pulling my weight . . . You were right, about all of it. When I made the decision to move out, it wasn't fair of me to let everything fall back on you. I should have stepped up. I should have been around more for you and the kids. I'm sorry," he said, genuinely contrite.

I nodded. There wasn't really anything more to say. I didn't owe him a thank-you. I didn't owe him a "that's okay." But I could give him the benefit of the doubt and hope he'd learned something from his weekend away with us. And yet, there was still a lingering question that had been gnawing at me all weekend.

"Before I ask you to take the kids to your place next weekend, is there anything I should know? Anything you've never told me that you want to get off your chest?" I hadn't been able to get that ledger I'd found in his nightstand out of my head. Or what Pokey had said, about how the secrets inside a ledger don't disappear just because the ledger does. Maybe Steven's book was nothing more than a simple accounting of business-related receipts, but it hadn't felt that way. It had felt more personal, the way it had so clearly been kept in his back pocket, stored close to where he slept, as if it rarely strayed far from him. And after *EasyClean*'s inferences—that Steven had secrets he'd been hiding—I couldn't shake the feeling that those secrets were somehow connected to whatever was in that ledger.

"Nothing you or the kids have reason to worry about," he promised. "What about you?" he asked curiously. "If we're going to be sharing all the responsibility fifty-fifty, shouldn't I be asking you the same?"

"All my skeletons have been laid to rest," I confessed, hoping it was true.

"Okay," he said, pressing a soft kiss to Delia's head before passing her to me. "I'll pick the kids up on Friday." We shared a quick embrace, his smile melancholic as he returned to my mother's car.

Javi came out of the house, his shirt a bit more rumpled and his hair more disheveled than I had remembered them being before he'd gone inside. His grin was wide as he climbed into the back seat of my mom's SUV and pulled the door shut.

I waved them all goodbye as she backed out of my driveway, wondering how much of her weekend she would share with my father when she finally got home. If she would confess to having gone to a strip club or how much money she'd lost playing slots. Or that she'd skipped Sunday mass for a day at the spa. Would any of it matter, the inconsequential lies and omissions? Or would Dad just be happy she was home, safe and sound?

I finished putting Delia to bed and locked the house for the night. Vero came downstairs, already wearing her pajamas. She padded into the kitchen, the telltale crackle giving her away as she tore open a package of Oreos. She carried the whole bag under her arm to the living room, along with a heaping glass of wine in each hand, settling in beside me where I'd collapsed on the couch.

She passed me a glass. Then she stared up at the ceiling and stuffed a cookie in her mouth, the green plastic spider still perched on her finger. I wondered if she was thinking about Javi. If she had thought about taking off her ring since she'd gotten home, or if she was content to keep it on.

I took a long sip of my wine. The thought of Vero getting married— of her packing her things and moving out of my home—left a hollow feeling in my chest. I knew in my heart it was only a matter of time before she left. She had a bright future ahead of her, assuming we could both stay out of trouble, and eventually she'd want to start a family of her own. I wanted those things for her, too. Just maybe not yet.

She rested her head on my shoulder as she nibbled on her cookie. "It's good to be home, Finn."

I smiled as I stole a cookie for myself. "It's definitely good to be home."

EPILOGUE

My room was overly bright when I woke the next morning. I curled deeper into the blankets, listening to the children fighting over a toy in the playroom and Vero bickering with Javi on her phone. My room smelled faintly of the hamper of towels I hadn't had time to wash before we'd left for the police academy and the diaper pail in my bathroom that Zach had christened right after we'd returned home.

I relished all of it.

It had been nearly ten days since I had slept in my own bed, and there had been more than a few times when I'd been certain I never would again, making an otherwise normal Tuesday morning feel decadent and luxurious in spite of it all.

I rolled over and checked the time on my phone, shocked to discover it was almost noon. Three notifications were stacked on my home screen. A missed call from Nick; a text message from Cam, telling me he'd made it home; and an incoming call from Sylvia that I contemplated letting roll to voice mail. With a sigh, I picked it up.

"Hey, Sylvia."

"Where the hell have you been? I've been trying to reach you for two days. Did you find the hot cop after you left the restaurant?"

I smiled at the memory of our evening at Chubbies. "Several, actually."

"Tell me you got to shadow the investigation."

"You could say that."

"I want to hear everything. What did you do?" Sylvia sounded breathless as I considered what to tell her.

"Well . . . first, we chased down a suspect wanted for questioning in a strip club."

She gasped. "Then what?"

"Then we disarmed a violent assailant in an alley, cuffed him, and threw him in the back of a police car."

"My hair's standing on end, Finlay! I haven't had this many goose bumps since Barbra Streisand last performed at Madison Square Garden. What else?"

"Let's see . . . we broke up a party that got out of hand, secured a crime scene, searched for two lost minors, infiltrated a sleazy sex lair, freed a hostage, recovered a stolen car, engaged two armed villains in a dangerous standoff, and rescued a puppy."

"You left out the sex."

"And we had sex."

"Fantastic! I want to hear all about the sex and the puppy next time we talk. Speaking of which, I hope you're ready to discuss that TV deal. The producer keeps calling, and I can't keep him waiting forever. I have to tell him something, Finlay."

"Tell him . . ." I paused, thinking over all that was at stake—the possible risks and rewards. About the odds I had overcome just to get this far. "Tell him I'm ready to make a deal."

Sylvia smacked her desk, triumphant. "Great! I'll set up a meeting. You get back to your office and get those fingers back to work. You've had enough time off, and we have bestsellers to write." I laughed as she disconnected.

Vero's voice rose from the kitchen. "No, *Todd,* we are not going to Vegas! Not until I get flowers and candy and a ring that doesn't glow in the dark! I deserve to be wooed. And stop calling me Mrs. Liebowitz!"

I pulled the blankets over my face, stealing a final moment of peace before facing the day.

There was a soft knock on my door. I lifted the blankets from my head, expecting to see Delia's face as the door opened a crack.

Nick peeked cautiously inside. "Can I come in?"

I sat up, sliding over to make room for him. "Not that I'm not happy to see you, but what are you doing here? I thought you weren't coming back until tonight?"

He sat beside me, leaning back against the headboard and lacing his fingers with mine. "Garrett offered to stick around and wrap up the loose ends. He had to stay in New Jersey for a few more days to work a new lead on the Grindley case anyway."

"A new lead?"

"We sent someone to Ike's house to check on his wife. No one's seen or heard from her since we talked to her a few days ago. We worried that maybe Charlie or Feliks got to her, so Garrett sent one of his guys to poke around. He didn't find Trina, but he did find a gold tooth in the backyard. We think it might belong to Ike."

"Wow." I choked back a nervous laugh. "Do they have any idea how it got there?"

"That's the interesting part. We don't know," Nick said. "It looks like Trina skipped town. Maybe she just got spooked, or maybe she knew more about what happened to Ike than she was letting on. Either way, it looks like the focus of the investigation is moving closer to home, and Garrett didn't need me to stay. The Toscano investigation is moving pretty quickly."

"Oh?"

"It's all pretty cut-and-dried. Cam and Giada both heard Charlie confess to killing Marco and his associate. Ricky told us the same when he finally came around."

"Did he say anything else? About why Charlie was there?"

"Nothing more than what Cam already told us. Charlie had just returned to the Royal Flush when he spotted Cam leaving the hotel. According to both boys, Ricky was at work and got caught in the wrong place at the wrong time."

I knew that wasn't the full story. But it didn't surprise me that Ricky had made no mention of the Aston Martin to the police.

"All the evidence points to Charlie," Nick said. "And the attendant working the front desk at the Villagio said she remembered a man claiming to be a police officer asking for Marco's room number on Friday night. She positively ID'd Charlie from a photo. It should be an open-and-shut case. There's just one thing Garrett and I can't figure out." He looked up at me, his face troubled. "The ME's report is all pending an autopsy, but—unofficially—the estimated time of death is the only thing that doesn't fit the rest of the picture. Based on what she saw of the remains we found in the Audi, she thinks the murder could have occurred as early as Friday night, around the time Charlie would have been in Marco's suite. But the butler there said Marco hosted a party on Saturday. Garrett interviewed two escorts who were paid to attend, and they both said they remembered Marco being there that night."

"Maybe the ME was wrong. You did say it was just an estimate, right?"

"True, but here's the strangest part. The escorts who remembered seeing Marco couldn't describe him when Garrett pushed. They remembered meeting his nephew, but Ricky swears he wasn't there. His boss confirmed he was working at the Royal Flush that night."

"Sounds like a real mystery."

He nodded, his eyes never leaving mine. "Yeah, it does."

"Do you think the autopsy results will . . . change anything? As far as the investigation, I mean."

"Probably not," he said confidently. "We have three witnesses to Charlie's confession. He was found in possession of the keys to the vehicle where the bodies were discovered, and some of their personal items were found in his suitcase. When I searched his luggage, I found a quarter of a million in cash in it, probably an advance from Zhirov for silencing Ike's boss. But I found something else in it, too." He let go of my hand, retrieving a single stale Cheerio from his pocket. He held it between us, watching my face.

"That's strange." I held his gaze. Saw the doubt in it, even as he refused to acknowledge all the tiny new stains and imperfections on my conscience, though I was certain they must be obvious. Maybe because it was easier to see the woman he needed me to be. The woman he wanted. It was all I could do not to get on my knees and confess everything to him. "What happens next?"

"I don't know," he said quietly. "I'm stepping back from the case. I think I'm too close to the people involved." His eyes searched mine for an uncomfortably long moment. When I didn't speak, he set the Cheerio on the bed between us.

"I should probably go," he said, clearing his throat. He looked torn as he bent to kiss me. More so as I pulled him closer and our kiss deepened. He closed his eyes, letting me coax him back down with me into the tangled sheets of the messy bed I slept in.

It was over. Marco and Louis were gone. Charlie and Feliks were gone. But Javi and Cam were safe and alive. Vero and I were in the clear, and her debts had been resolved—at least the ones in New Jersey, anyway. Everything we had done had been to protect ourselves and the people we cared about. None of that would change if I were to confess to Nick now. And as he settled into the bed beside me, I didn't think either of us wanted me to.

"I've been thinking a lot . . ." he murmured against my lips.

"About us?"

"About Joey, actually."

"That's . . . not where I expected this conversation to go while your hand's up my shirt."

He laughed, pushing up on his elbow and brushing my hair behind my ear. "I've been thinking about how I've had some great partners over the years—people I trusted, that I cared about—and they were both keeping pretty huge secrets from me. I guess I'm trying to reconcile that."

"Can you?"

"I don't know. I keep coming back to Joey. He kept things from all of us to protect us, because that was the only way to root out the danger that threatened the department. That took a lot of guts. He made a lot of sacrifices to do it. And I think maybe I was a little tough on him."

"What do you plan to do about it?"

He traced a finger over my lower lip. "I asked him to meet me later for dinner."

"Should I be concerned?" I teased. "You still haven't taken *me* out to dinner."

"Figured I'd come here after."

"I wouldn't say no to a little dessert."

His grin stretched against mine, his arm looping around me, and I was pretty sure all thoughts of Joey—or any other partners he might have been thinking about—were far from his mind as I reached to unbutton his shirt.

We pulled apart at the rising wail of police sirens down the block. We turned toward the sound, listening as they roared closer, several sets of tires screeching to a stop. Nick hurried to the window and drew back the blind.

I bolted out of bed. "What is it? What's happening?" I asked, rising up on my toes to see over his shoulder as several police cars rolled to a stop along the curb across the street from my house.

"I don't know," he said as the officers got out of their cars. "Stay here."

"Nick, wait!" I grabbed my clothes off the floor and pulled them on, too late to catch him as he rushed out of the house. I found Vero and the children standing in front of the kitchen window, watching the scene outside. Nick jogged across my lawn to the street where four police cars had converged in front of my driveway.

This was it. The end of the game. The ME must have concluded that something wasn't right, or Garrett had found some damning piece of evidence we'd left behind. Something big enough to trump Charlie's confession and convince the detectives someone else had been involved.

I held Delia to me. Vero picked up Zach and clutched him to her chest. Both of us held our breath, waiting for Nick to turn around. For the police to swarm the house. For the dice to land and the universe to take everything we had put on the line since we'd made the ill-fated decision to bury Harris Mickler.

Nick didn't turn around. He watched, hands on his hips, as the officers strode up the sidewalk to Mrs. Haggerty's house. All the neighbors had begun to gather in their yards, whispering behind cupped hands, as two officers knocked on Mrs. Haggerty's door and escorted her from her home into the back of a police cruiser.

I ran out of my house, breathless when I reached Nick's side.

"What's happening?" I asked him. "Why are they taking Mrs. Haggerty?"

"Someone found a body buried in her backyard."

ACKNOWLEDGMENTS

My heart grows three sizes with the publication of each new Finlay Donovan book. Not because these characters are so fun to write (they are), and not because my readers are so fun to engage with (the best), but because of the team of extraordinary, talented people who create these stories with me.

For my agent, Steph Rostan, who is nothing at all like Sylvia, more than I deserve, and everything I never knew I needed in a champion. Thank you for adopting Finlay (and me) with such warmth and enthusiasm. I hope every lunch from here on out is on me.

For Catherine Richards, my incredible editor. Thank you for breathing life into me and this book when we needed it most. For your fierce support, your endless brilliance, and your willingness to stand behind my countless wild ideas. I'm so grateful for your collaboration and your partnership.

For Allison Ziegler, where do I begin? Your creativity and savvy astound me every day! Thank you for bringing so much life, fun, and passion to all you do.

For Sarah Melnyk, my fearless tour guide and indomitable publicist!

Thank you for keeping Finlay and me glowing in the limelight, and for making our 2023 tour such an unforgettable success. Here's to many more!

And thank you to the entire Minotaur Books/St. Martin's Press team, including Jennifer Enderlin, Andrew Martin, Kelley Ragland, Paul Hochman, Anne Marie Tallberg, Amber Cortes, Claire Beyette, Nettie Finn, Kelly Stone, David Rotstein, Janna Dokos, John Morrone, and Ben Allen. I'm so grateful for every person who has had a hand in making this series soar.

For the entire team at LGR Literary. A million thanks to Courtney Paganelli, Melissa Rowland, Miek Coccia, Michael Nardullo, and Cristela Henriquez for all you do in support of me and my books. And for all of our coagents and publishers, far and wide, for helping us grow the Finlay Donovan fandom.

For my oldest and dearest writing friends, Megan Miranda and Ashley Elston. Thank you for being there every step of the way. I will never forget that phone call (and the photo of the three of us you both tried to take). Your support and laughter mean the world to me. Here's to another ten retreats and another ten years.

And for the writers who supported me through this brutally challenging book while I battled my own impostor syndrome alongside Finlay. Thank you, Hannah Morrissey and Kara Thomas, for those enormously helpful Zooms.

For Flannery and Chelsea at Bluebird Books in Crozet, Virginia. Thank you for your friendship, your community, and your boundless energy. I'm so lucky to have landed in your path.

These acknowledgments would not be complete without a special shout-out to my very favorite Atlantic City restaurant. Chef Vola's didn't appear in the book, but it did provide some fun inspiration. While the restaurant has grown from the obscure cellar entrance I remember years ago, the food and hospitality remain exceptional, with ricotta pies that could stop your heart and the best crab cakes this Maryland-raised author has ever tasted. Chef's kiss.

A very special thank-you to my family—Tony, Connor, and Nick—always but especially this year. You've endured so much with me—every canceled vacation, every pressing deadline, every grumpy, sluggish morning after an all-nighter, and every out-of-town event—with love, encouragement, and understanding. I wouldn't be where I am without you. I love you more than words can express.

And to my readers in every region of the world—to all the bookstagrammers, the bloggers, the podcasters, the reviewers, the book clubs, the librarians, and the booksellers who have read and recommended my books—I am so grateful for each and every one of you.

1. In this book, Finlay is dealing with impostor syndrome. Her agent, Sylvia, suggests this is normal for writers, and that her self-doubts will pass, but not all of Finlay's insecurities are rooted in doubts over her identity as an author. In what other ways is Finlay feeling like an impostor and why?

2. Throughout the story, we see instances of women helping women. Even in the strip club and in Romelda's shop, women are lending each other a hand. How many examples can you find throughout the story? In what ways does each instance reinforce this theme in the book?

Discussion Questions

3. At the climax of the novel, Finlay orchestrates a series of events that rely on the involvement of two powerful women, both of whom she fears, and she isn't sure she can trust them. Were you surprised by the women Finlay enlists to help her? Why do you think these women, including Finlay, make the choices they do? How much of a gamble is this on Finlay's part—do you think she expected them to agree to help her?

4. In the beginning of the story, Finlay rejects Vero's suggestion that they resort to violence to rescue Javi. Instead, Finlay insists that she and Vero solve their problems using their words by talk and negotiation. At what point do we see Finlay's position shift? In what ways does Finlay take action and use her words to solve her problems?

5. Romelda, the psychic, made several predictions before Finlay and Vero left her shop. Do you think Romelda could truly see the future, or do you believe Finlay and Vero interpreted their fortunes based on coincidences as they happened?

MINOTAUR BOOKS

6. When Vero and Javi finally reunite, he confesses his reasons for walking away from their relationship years ago—that he was ashamed of a mistake he'd made and he feared he wasn't worthy of her. Which other characters in the story have made similar choices to conceal mistakes from their loved ones? Do you agree with their choices? Why?

7. While in Atlantic City, Finlay learns that her mother and father are having marital issues. Do you think the trip was good for Susan? What fears, regrets, or desires did you see Susan projecting onto her own children's relationships?

8. Steven has an eye-opening experience caring for the children in Atlantic City. What do you think he learns during the trip? What is your opinion of his revelations about partnership and co-parenting?

9. Nick presents Finlay with a piece of evidence he found in Charlie's suitcase, suggesting he knows she was somehow involved. Yet he doesn't accuse Finlay. Instead, he tells her about the realization he's had about Charlie and Joey, two other partners who lied to him, both for very different reasons. What was Nick implying by sharing these thoughts with Finlay? If he suspects she might be hiding something, why does he choose to look the other way?

10. At the end of the novel, Finlay reflects on her affection for Vero and the fear that one day Vero will inevitably decide to move out and start a family of her own. How has their relationship grown and changed over the course of the series? How do you predict it will change in the future, as the children grow older and both Finlay and Vero each develop romantic partnerships of their own?

Turn the page for a sneak peek at
the new novel by
ELLE COSIMANO

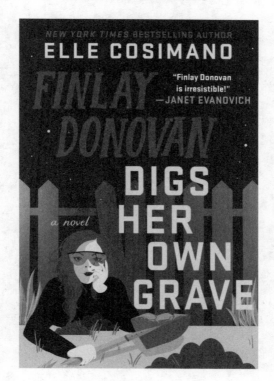

Available Early 2025

PROLOGUE

The stern-faced woman stared down her nose at me, her solid black smock dress and crisp white collar framed by the regal arms of her leather chair. The fingers of her left hand closed around a fancy Montblanc pen. Her right fist rested on my open file like a gavel, each letter of my last name printed sideways on the tab. "Do you have anything to say, Ms. Donovan?" Her narrowed eyes pinned me to my seat, reading me like a rap sheet across her wide mahogany desk.

He had it coming was probably not the answer she was looking for. "This entire situation has been blown out of proportion," I said as she took notes with harsh strokes of her pen. It was impossible to come off like a badass while I was down here and she was up there.

"The evidence speaks for itself."

"What evidence?" I inched higher in my chair, trying to read her terse scribbles from my disadvantaged position.

"We have two witnesses to the assault."

"Assault?" I held up a finger (not the one I wanted to raise), cutting her off. If she was going to conduct a trial and lay down a sentence, I'd be damned if I'd let her do it without putting on a defense. "That's a very serious accusation to level at a person."

"The victim suffered injuries that required treatment by a physician."

"It was only a few stitches!"

"And two bruised ribs," she added without looking up.

"I already said I'd be willing to cover his medical costs."

"You can't just buy your way out of this, Ms. Donovan. You said it yourself, assault is a serious violation. If I were to let this go with a warning, I'd be setting a dangerous precedent."

"But this wasn't an assault! It was self-defense," I insisted, fighting the urge to demonstrate the difference. "Whatever the outcome, Cooper provoked it. The situation clearly called for a response, and he got one. Unwanted touching is *also* an assault," I pointed out.

Her eyes lifted from the file, meeting mine over the rims of her glasses. "*That* would be blowing the situation out of proportion."

I put my hands on my hips. Or rather I would have, if the arms of my chair had allowed me to. "If you were in the same shoes, what would you have done?"

"I would have reported it to someone with the authority to handle the situation."

"Handle it how? With another slap on the wrist? He's a repeat offender!"

"Violence is never the answer, Ms. Donovan. Please sit down." She pointed a sharp finger at the small wooden chair I'd been relegated to.

I glanced down at myself, surprised to find I was indeed standing up.

I folded myself back into my seat.

The woman took off her glasses. She set them on her desk with an aggrieved sigh. Her weary lids made slow blinks, as if she hoped I might disappear between them. "Rules are rules, Ms. Donovan, and it's my job to enforce them. I've spoken with Cooper's mother about his behavior on the playground, and she has assured me the hair pulling will not continue."

I glanced sideways at Delia. Her head hung between her hunched shoulders, the short, downy ends of her blond pigtails still noticeably uneven after she'd tried to cut her own hair a few short months ago, mussed where Cooper had, according to Delia, repeatedly grabbed them. Her hands were tucked shamefully under her thighs, her tiny legs dangling from the edge of the chair she'd been perched on while she'd waited for me to pick her up after the principal had called me.

"Fine," I said, ready to put the entire ordeal behind us. "I'll have a similar talk with Delia about her behavior when we get home."

Mrs. Carmichael, the preschool principal, gave a stern nod. "I expect you will. Cooper's mother has filed a formal complaint. Given the extent of her son's injuries, she's expecting the school to take a hard stance. I'm going to have to ask you to keep Delia home for the next two weeks."

I leapt up again, the child-size chair clinging stubbornly to my hips. "You're suspending her!"

"Would you rather she be expelled?"

We both turned as her office door flew open behind me. My children's nanny burst in, her lungs heaving as if she'd run the full five miles from my house to get here. Her hair was wild where it had come loose from her long ponytail, and her cheeks were red with exertion. She clutched my naked two-year-old son to her side, his dimpled butt hanging over her arm. "Thank god," she said when she spotted Delia sitting penitently beside me.

The principal scowled at Vero. "Who are you?"

"This is Veronica Ruiz, my nanny," I explained.

"I came as soon as I got the message," Vero said, ignoring the principal's disapproving look. "Is Delia okay? I was in the bathroom with Zach when the school called. All they said is that someone was hurt." She rushed to Delia's side and sank down on her haunches until she was eye level with both of us, checking my daughter for injuries.

"Delia's fine," I said, taking Zach from her and resting him in my lap. The pint-size seat didn't leave room for his pudgy legs, so I turned him around and propped him on my knees. He beamed at the principal. She grimaced as every part of him wiggled in his relentless effort to get down. I set him on the floor to keep him from pitching a fit. He stood obediently beside my chair, momentarily content, beaming at the principal as he tugged on his tiny penis.

Vero threw her arms around Delia and picked her up, prodding every inch of her, just to be sure she wasn't injured. "What happened?"

"Cooper was pulling Delia's hair on the playground. She asked him to stop, and he didn't, so she defended herself." I threw a pointed look at her principal. The school might be holding Delia responsible, but I knew exactly where the blame for this fell and it wasn't on my daughter.

Vero glowed with pride. "That's my girl!" She held up a hand for a high five. I pulled it down before Delia could slap it. She might be the victim of a miscarriage of justice, but we didn't need to invite any more punishment.

I covered my eyes, swearing quietly as my ex-husband's voice boomed in the lobby. "Delia! Where's my daughter? Is she back there? Back off, lady," Steven shouted. "If my daughter's in there, I'm going in and you can't stop me!" He rushed past the front desk and through the open office door, blue eyes blazing and mud flaking from his work boots.

"Great," Vero muttered. "What the H-E-double pumpers is he doing here?"

"What's a double pumper?" Delia asked.

"Never mind," I said.

"We'll discuss it when we get home," Vero added helpfully.

"What's going on?" Steven asked, as breathless and red-faced as Vero had been when she'd burst in. "Why'd the school call my office? And why is Zach naked?"

"Potty training," I said. Steven looked confused. "Vero saw some boot camp on the internet that's supposed to guarantee success in three days. You take off their clothes and keep them close to the toilet."

"Is it working?"

We all turned as Zach began peeing on the carpet. The principal gasped. I gritted my teeth.

"Guess that answers that," Steven said.

Vero flashed a middle finger at him behind Delia's back.

The principal stared sternly at all of us over the rims of her glasses. "Need I remind you that you are in a school? We are models for young minds here. I'll ask you both to show some decorum!"

Steven frowned at his mud-spattered flannel and the dirt-caked toes of his work boots.

Vero tossed a fresh diaper over the puddle on the floor and used the toe of her shoe to blot up the wet spot.

The principal closed her eyes, lips pressed between her teeth as if it was all she could do to hold back a retort. She reached inside her desk drawer for a bottle of ibuprofen and shook two tablets into the palm of her hand as Steven helped me out of my pint-sized chair and pulled me aside. "I was walking lots with a developer when the school called," he said in a low voice. "I got here as soon as I got the message. They said they needed someone to come down to the school right away. What's going on? Is Delia okay?"

Steven's forehead crumpled as I explained. "A boy named Cooper has been harassing Delia on the playground. She gave him six stitches and a couple of bruised ribs."

Zach giggled when Steven's eyebrows shot up.

"And then I kicked him in the tentacles," Delia said, "just like Vero showed me."

Steven's chest swelled like a Little League coach whose star player just took home a trophy. He offered Vero a tentative salute. She answered it with an almost conciliatory nod as she tossed the wet diaper in the trash can. My god, were they actually agreeing on something?

"What?" they asked in unison as I looked back and forth between them.

"Delia's been suspended from school," I said sharply.

Steven extorted the equivalent of a double pumper, and Vero covered Delia's ears.

Mrs. Carmichael nearly gouged out her own eye in her hurry to put her glasses back on. She signed her name to the bottom of a disciplinary action report and pushed it across the desk toward me. "I see now where Delia has learned to model this kind of behavior. I'll ask Cooper's mother to send you a copy of the medical bills. You can collect Delia's belongings from the front desk before you leave."

Delia's lower lip began to wobble. I picked up Zach and settled him on my hip, then took my daughter's hand and helped her down from her seat. Steven snatched the report off the principal's desk, crumpled it up, and tossed it in the trash. Vero gave the principal a heavy dose of side-eye as I led our entourage out the door.

There was no way this day could get any worse, but I knew how to make it tolerable. "Come on, everyone," I said. "We're going out for ice cream."

ABOUT THE AUTHOR

Holly Virginia Photography

Elle Cosimano is a *New York Times* and *USA Today* best-selling author, an International Thriller Writers Award winner, and an Edgar Award nominee. Elle's debut novel for adults, *Finlay Donovan Is Killing It,* kicked off a witty, fast-paced contemporary mystery series, which was a *People* magazine pick and was named one of New York Public Library's Best Books of 2021. The third book in the series, *Finlay Donovan Jumps the Gun,* was an instant *New York Times* bestseller. In addition to writing novels for teens and adults, her essays have appeared in *HuffPost* and *Time.* Cosimano lives with her husband and two sons in Virginia.

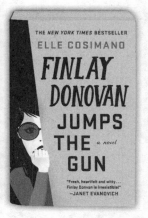
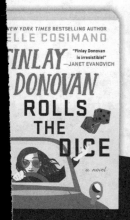
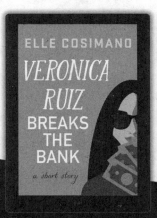

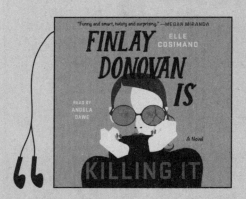